DEAN ING
SINGLE COMBAT

A JIM BÆN PRESENTATION:

A TOM DOHERTY ASSOCIATES BOOK

A TOR Book

Published by:

Tom Doherty Associates, Inc.
8-10 West 36th Street
New York, New York 10018

First TOR printing, November 1983
Second TOR printing

ISBN: 812-54-100-6
CAN. ED. 812-54-101-4

Cover art by Howard Chaykin

Interior Illustrations by Howard Chaykin

Printed in the United States of America

Distributed by:

Pinnacle Books
1430 Broadway
New York, New York 10018

DOUBLE-CROSS!

"Quantrill, get away," shouted the pilot. "We've got a problem with the bird!"

Quantrill trotted after the taller man, saw past him to the flight line. Five minutes before, there'd been several people currying their birds. Now the place was deserted. At the periphery of his vision was a charcoal-black mass, skating ten meters over the deck, and now Miles Grenier was running like a deer. The hurtling mass was a sprint chopper, arcing in between the two men. *Isolate your hit,* said a well-remembered voice in his memory.

As the chopper hovered he could see Howell in the cockpit, grinning, knowing he could slam a six-ton hammer into his victim. His high overhand toss seemed a ridiculous empty gesture until Howell, with a spurt of pure horror, saw the glitter of small objects in the sun.

The handful of broken concrete half-fell, was half sucked into the circular shroud. Hammer a few dents into a sprint chopper's shroud, especially near those prop tips, and its efficiency will plummet. Blow a dozen jagged holes in it while the props eat hardware, and you will see a coleopter go bonkers.

Quantril had that pleasure.

SINGLE COMBAT

For Howard and Marty;
because integrity is
thicker than blood.

PART 1:
SEARCH & RESCUE

CHAPTER 1

The reverend Ora McCarty faced the wall in the most sacrosanct office of International Entertainment and Electronics and watched a holo image of himself sing an old inspirational: 'Rocky Mountain High'. It had aired—or so McCarty believed—during his Sunday morning program. From the corner of his eye McCarty could see the expression on the face of IEE Chairman Boren Mills. It was, in Ora McCarty's jargon, nervous-makin'.

The holovised McCarty strummed a last chord on a sequined guitar, held the last note, then winked from existence as Mills keyed his hand-terminal. "Hey, you cut off my finish," McCarty said affably.

"Call me a music-lover," Boren Mills replied in soft derision. "But don't tell me you didn't know that song is on the prohibited list."

McCarty turned to face the smaller Mills. "Aw, that's for Mormons! That song don't tempt people to take drugs, no matter what they think in Salt Lake—"

"Do I have to remind you who subsidizes your gentile services?" Boren Mills snapped, his bright dark eyes flashing under heavy brows. "If the church is liberal enough to support a mildly heretical preacher, the least you can do is exercise judgment with your material."

"Censor myself, you mean," McCarty grumbled. "Seems to me, you LDS folks—"

3

"Correction! I'm a Congregationalist, Ora. Never, *ever*, link me with the Latter-Day Saints."

"Well, . . ." McCarty's half-smile suggested that he was buying a polite fiction, ". . . *those* LDS folks are happy with my mission just so long as it's mainly country-western entertainment that don't take issue with anything they want said."

"Entertainment is my middle name," said Mills with deliberate symbolism. IEE's middle name *was* 'entertainment', and whatever board members twice his age might prefer, thirtyish Boren Mills *was* IEE.

"Entertainment's what I gave my holo audience," McCarty nodded.

"Not with 'Rocky Mountain High,'" Mills rejoined, the receding vee of his widow's peak moving side-to-side in negation. "Your monitor has his orders. Since my last name is 'Electronics', what your holo audience got was 'In The Fourth Year of Zion'."

"The hell they did."

"The hell they didn't," Mills replied easily.

"I don't even know that piece," McCarty insisted, then formed a silent 'oh' of sudden enlightenment. Ora McCarty was still essentially a twentieth-century man in 2002 AD, coping with the technology of war-ravaged, Streamlined America. At times that coping was slow, and sullen. "You faked me."

"Regenerated you," Mills shrugged the implied correction. "Don't worry; thanks to us you never looked better or sounded half so good. Want to see what you really sang?" The Mills hand, small and exquisitely manicured, held the wireless terminal, thumb poised.

McCarty shook his head quickly, both hands up in dismay. "Now that's an abomination, Mr. Mills. And what's worse it makes me break a sweat to see a me that isn't me." To stress his rejection, McCarty turned his back on the holo wall and faced rooftops of Ogden, Utah outside the smoke-tinted glass panel. The giddy height of the IEE tower yielded a unique view; no other commercial structure in Ogden was permitted such an imposing skyward reach. McCarty supposed it had something to do with the microwave translators built into the temple-like spire. Even in architecture, IEE suggested its sympathy with the reigning Church of Jesus Christ of the Latter-day Saints. Now that a Mormon administration directed the rebuilding of an America whittled down by ravages of the SinoInd War, McCarty could condone such corporate cozening as good conservative business practice. He let his eyes roam past the city to salt flats shimmering in late spring heat, to the tepid Great Salt Lake beyond, so impossibly blue in the sun as to seem artificial.

As artificial, for instance, as his rendition of a song he'd never sung, or as his effectiveness as a man of God, when image-generating modules could replace him right down to the wrinkles in his shirt. Squinting against a glint of sunlight from the too-blue lake: "I wonder when they'll start fakin' the news," McCarty said.

"Oh,—I suppose someone will try it sooner or later," said Mills, but McCarty did not notice the subtle twitch that passed for a smile. "You can't imagine how much it cost FBN to regenerate your little ditty." It was, of course, very cheap. "If it happens again, you'll pay the tab. Try to curb your paranoid fantasies, Ora; as long as we maintain control of FBN Holovision, we won't often squander big money regenerating events."

Not once did Mills lie outright; as usual, his lies were chiefly implicit.

Reluctantly, McCarty faced Mills. "I guess the world isn't as simple as I'd like," he sighed, fashioning a shrug that ingratiated him to audiences;

awkward, gangling, suggestive of a reticent mind in the big rawboned body. "I appreciate your takin' your own time on this, Mr. Mills. A lot of men wouldn't bother."

"A lot of men don't succeed," Mills replied evenly, with a light touch at McCarty's elbow, steering him to the door. Boren Mills was one of those compact models that did not seem diminished when standing among taller men. With a forefinger he indicated the needlepoint legend framed behind his rosewood desk: SURPRISE IS A DIRTY WORD. "See that your programming people check your scripts from now on. We can do without any more surprises on the Ora McCarty Devotional Hour."

"That goes without saying," McCarty murmured.

"Nothing goes without saying," Mills replied. "That's the essence of written contracts. Read the prohibited list, Ora."

Damn the man, thought McCarty, and tried to respond lightly as he stood in the doorway: "You've made me a believer, Mr. Mills. If I lost network support by stickin' a burr under the LDS's saddle blanket, I'd wind up so far out in the sticks you couldn't find me with a Search & Rescue team."

"Nicely put," Mills grinned, and terminated the interview. Mills was still chuckling to himself as he returned to his desk, knowing that McCarty could not fully appreciate his own jest. If the federally-funded Search & Rescue ever *did* seek the reverend Ora McCarty, McCarty would not survive that search.

CHAPTER 2

Ted Quantrill was not yet twenty-one, Marbrye Sanger was twenty-four; and their entwined communion was as old as humankind. Their Search & Rescue uniforms lay near, boot-tips aligned with unconscious military precision. Had the lovers stood erect there would not have been a centimeter's difference in their heights, for the long taper of her questing fingers was repeated in the span of her arms, the extraordinary length of her legs. Yet many men would have been reluctant, viewing her naked splendor, to seek her embrace. Those long limbs revealed the muscles of an athlete, the physical equal of the youth who shared her delight. Only in the upper body could his sinew overmatch hers.

Presently she smiled for him, her eyes heavy-lidded through an errant lock of chestnut hair, and arched against him as she felt his thrusts quicken. At his faint moan she pressed a forefinger against his open mouth, now grinning, teasing him, then reaching down with her other hand to milk his masculinity. At the same moment she made her eyes wide, her mouth a tiny 'o' of innocence, brows elevated as if to ask, 'who, me'?

Gritting his teeth, laughing softly through the pulses of his own climax, he nodded back a silent, 'yes you'.

You, you and I, we together. They lay, mouths

7

open to silence their breathing, her roan-flecked eyes interlocked with the startling green of his own.

Then he rolled slightly to one side, brought his right hand up, said in sign-talk: *"I died. You?"*

She would not lie to him about the little things. Signing in the bastard dialect they had learned while still in Army Intelligence: *"No. Doesn't matter. Love to watch you."*

It was the only use either of them dared make of the heart-touch gesture, *love*. Each of them—mistakenly—assumed the other would recoil from overt words of tenderness.

"I'm only a sex object," he signed in mock dejection.

"A killing object. You died, remember?" Then she thought of something else; bit her lower lip.

"Problem," he signed. Not a question, but his eyes probed.

She nodded. Carefully, she placed a strong hand against his breast, rolled to one side, breathed in the conifer-spiced evening air of northern Wyoming highlands. Signing: *"My last hit. They always promised we'd never get a mission against someone we know."*

"So?"

"I knew her—second-hand."

There was really nothing he could do about it but: *"Sorry,"* he signed.

Momentarily then she wanted him to feel the full impact, and spelled it out for him. *"Dr. Catherine Palma."*

Quantrill froze. He had known the woman well, a stolid, fiftyish medic who'd risked lingering death in the fight against Chinese plague during the war. Palma, a mother-figure for him before his enlistment at age fifteen. He'd mentioned Palma to Sanger on many occasions, always silently by necessity. The late Palma? In a soundless agony he balled his fists, rolled onto his back, eyes closed.

Sanger placed her hand on his breast as if to smoothe away the tendons that stood out, fanning inward and up from pectorals to throat. Then she coughed, a demand for attention.

When he opened his eyes again she was smiling, almost in apology. "*I suspect she was on guard,*" said the lithe fingers. "*Rebel medic now; couldn't find her.*" About the big things, she *had* to lie.

"*Bitch. Could've told me an easier way.*"

"*Sorry; honestly,*" she signed in shame.

Suddenly suspicious, he squinted as his hands said, "*Really couldn't find her? Or wouldn't?*"

"*Think I want to die? Tried my best,*" she lied again.

His exhalation lasted at least five seconds. "*I believe you.*"

Now she was up on one elbow, frantic with the notion that he might *not* believe her. They were both professionals; it was his duty to report suspicions, even such a one as this. Perhaps she could phrase it in a way to compel belief. "*Listen hotsy; better believe me. If you ever deliberately funk a mission, make sure you tell me first.*"

"*Why?*"

"*Because I want you to get it from friendly fire,*" said graceful hands that could kill him as easily as caress him.

CHAPTER 3

Search & Rescue was both highly publicized and saturated in secrecy. Boren Mills was one of a dozen outside S & R ranks who knew its double purpose. At war's end in 1998 America's great Mormon president, Yale Collier, had envisioned a regular cadre of young civilians who would operate directly under executive orders, and who would be superbly trained to rescue citizens in mortal trouble. Freeway overpasses, weakened years before by nuclear blasts, still occasionally collapsed without warning—as did buildings, dams, and underground structures. Along the eastern border of Streamlined America, hotspots of paranthrax sometimes appeared, usually borne by some illegal immigrant from the Confederation East of the Mississippi River. Along the vaguely-defined southern border region called Wild Country, ranchers from Texas to the San Joaquin valley appealed for help against a variety of deadly problems.

To the North, Canada now controlled what had once been most of the northern U. S. until the keratophagic staph plague scare during the great war; and along that border, the problems were less obvious.

Collier had become infused with a dream that Streamlined America, under the Mormon stewardship of his administration and those groomed to follow, would be rebuilt into the true Zion. But

Yale Collier had been infused with cancer, too. He lived long enough to see his Search & Rescue teams become a symbol of young American altruism and audacity, and he entrusted the development of S & R to his successor, Blanton Young. Collier was spared any suspicion that Young might have his own ideas about the uses to which a small cadre of daredevils might be put.

Shortly after the death of Yale Collier in 1999, President Young exercised some executive options. Search & Rescue's three hundred regulars already had Loring Aircraft's sleekest new close-support sprint choppers, with the shrouded fans swiveling on stubby wingtips to provide both helicopter modes and level flight in excess of six hundred kph—and the hell with fuel consumption.

They already got the best training: paramedic skills, alpine and desert survival courses, flood and mine disaster seminars. Their equipment was already the latest, including dress and mission uniforms familiar to millions who saw holovised rescues to the greater glory of Blanton Young and his Federalist party.

What S & R did not initially have,—what the sainted Collier had not *wanted* it to have, as an arm reporting only to the Chief Executive—was a covert military charter. Blanton Young wasted no time in swelling the S & R ranks with another select group which had been attached to Army Intelligence during the war. The group had been known to its members as T Section; T, as in 'terminate'.

Survivors of T Section were almost all wary youthful specimens to whom the quick covert kill was paramount, and these few became S & R's rovers. Regulars gave each other nicknames. Rovers did not answer to nicknames, scorning even the small luxury of feeling damned together. Quantrill was only Quantrill; Sanger only Sanger.

Blanton Young did not regard himself as a heretic. He took great pains to show that one could remain on the church's Council of Apostles while serving as the nation's chief executive. America was recovering; and as always during a reconstruction period, the government relaxed its restrictions on business and industry. And individual freedoms? That was something else again.

An industrial spy, a union organizer, or an anti-Mormon activist was more likely to disappear than to face public trial. The President viewed his S & R cadre as a nicely-balanced tool. Regular missions, eighty per cent of the total, searched out the vulnerable and rescued individuals. The rover missions searched out dissidents and rescued the status quo. So far, Young's hit team was barely a rumor even among grumbling Catholics and members of masonic orders. Certainly the regular S & R members would not broach the secret because they did not share it. Just as certainly the assassins would not divulge it; each of them still carried small mastoid-implant transceivers, 'critics', with self-destruct charges that could drive a gram of debris into the brain with the same results as an explosive bullet.

The critic had been a wartime innovation and, working with Naval Intelligence, Boren Mills was as quick as Young to see the potential peacetime uses of this tiny, deadly audio monitor buried behind the ears of agents thoroughly trained in single combat. If government and business found common cause, they could also share common remedies. When both could fly the banners of a popular religious movement, a certain amount of excess could be made palatable to the public.

This was not to say that most Mormons, guided

by their Council of Apostles, sought a repressive society. In a genuine ecumenical spirit, LDS tithes helped defray the costs of some protestant sects and promoted open forums for debate. The church had even donated campaign contributions to some fence-straddling legislators of the Independent party, though Indys were similar to Democrats of the prewar era, many of them openly critical of this growing connection between the state and the church of the LDS.

It was not the fault of devout Mormons if open debate helped pinpoint certain rabble-rousers who might, if they proved both troublesome and refractory, simply disappear while crossing the path of an S & R rover.

CHAPTER 4

Quantrill felt the sprint chopper lurch in treacherous downdrafts behind Cloud Peak, wrestled his backpac into place without disconnecting his seat harness. "Sorry 'bout that," said the voice of Miles Grenier in his headset. "These ugly birds are too sensitive with a light load."

Like all regular S & R pilots, Grenier disparaged the beauty of his sprint chopper and his expertise in flying it, as a good Mormon curb against excessive pride. Grenier did not ask why he'd been ordered to leave the alpine survival exercises near Sheridan, Wyoming to drop this lone S & R rover into broken country to the South.

For an S & R regular, the primary virtues were skill, unquestioning obedience, a good nature, and good looks—in that order. Rovers were a phylum apart. The rovers trained first with one team, then another. They seldom talked about their 'surveillance' sorties and were clearly not LDS in outlook. For a rover, good looks were secondary and good nature just about nonexistent. Rovers had been known to rage against a mission, to swill illegal hard liquor, even to grow combative. The one thing a rover almost never did was to encourage close friendship with regulars or, so far as Grenier knew, anybody else.

Of course some rovers seemed to relax among themselves, thought Grenier. Quantrill, the youngest rover of them all, definitely seemed to unwind in the company of that gorgeous creature, Marbrye Sanger, during paradrop practice into rotting snow in the Bighorn National Forest.

Sanger, one of the half-dozen female rovers, could have had all the friends she wanted merely by a toss of those chestnut curls or a flirt of the long strong legs. Instead, she spent much of her time as companion to the silent, muscular Quantrill. Grenier thought them an unlikely pair: Sanger in her mid-twenties, elegant even in her mottled coverall, vivacious on a team problem but otherwise aloof. Ted Quantrill, and scarcely out of his teens, a sturdy churl of Sanger's height with chilled creme de menthe eyes and a talent for doing nothing until the last possible second. When Quantrill moved, you knew he'd been thinking about the problem; the little son of perdition might make a botch of it the first time, but it was the fastest botch anybody could ask for. The second time—with a rappel, recovery winch, whatever—he was usually perfect. And quicker still. Grenier decided that Quantrill had already had his second time with Sanger, and

SPRINT CHOPPER
SUMMARY SHEETS

SUMMARY DATA

DESIGNATION: SPRINT CHOPPER **CENCOM REVISION:** 16 Jan 2002

DEPLOYMENT: USMC/USCG/S&R

SPECIFICATIONS:

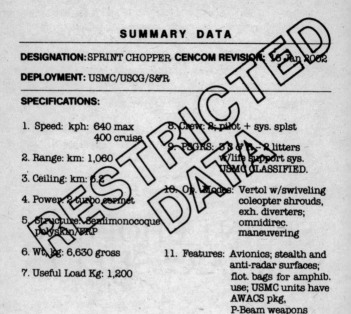

1. Speed: kph: 640 max
400 cruise

2. Range: km: 1,060

3. Ceiling: km: 5.3

4. Power: 2 turbo garnet

5. Structure: Semimonocoque polyskin/FRP

6. Wt, kg: 6,630 gross

7. Useful Load Kg: 1,200

8. Crew: 2; pilot + sys. splst

9. PSGRS: 3 S & R - 2 litters
w/life support sys.
USMC CLASSIFIED.

10. Op. Modes: Vertol w/swiveling
coleopter shrouds,
exh. diverters;
omnidirec.
maneuvering

11. Features: Avionics; stealth and
anti-radar surfaces;
flot. bags for amphib.
use; USMC units have
AWACS pkg,
P-Beam weapons

12. MFG: Loring Acft

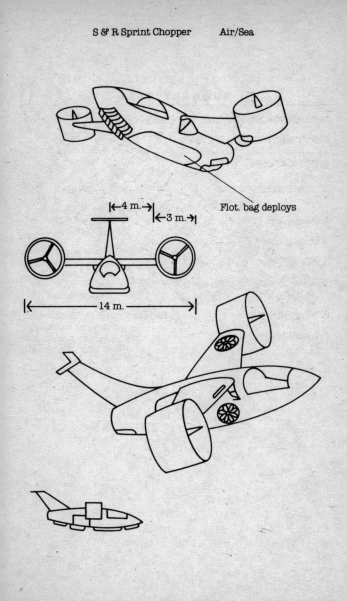

Flot. bag deploys

|←4 m.→|
|←3 m.→|
|← 14 m. →|

cheerfully damned him for getting there first. But then, Sanger was a rover, too . . .

Another lurch. Grenier let the autoleveller have its head, watching the coleopter shrouds at the wingtips jitter as they sought to obey the gyros. "Still with me, Quantrill?"

"If you really crave my lunch, bub, I'll come forward and flop it over your shoulder," was the reply, with a Carolina drawl in it.

"We're nearly out of it," Grenier promised. "That's Powder River Pass just below. I'll swing past Hazelton Peak and throttle back at the DZ. If it'd been up to me, we'd have come over the top." It was as near as Miles Grenier would come to complaining about a flight plot.

"You pays your money and you takes Hobson's choice," Quantrill said. "Maybe CenCom knows what he's doing; quien sabe?" in the S & R chain of command, the synthesized male voice of the central computer surrogated the President himself; could countermand an S & R instructor or even the Executive Administrator, Lon Salter. S & R regulars did not even joke about CenCom's omniscience, and felt discomfort when a rover did it.

Miles Grenier could not know that rovers obeyed a second, vaguely female, voice they called Control. To Control, rovers showed a more rock-bound obedience than a regular ever could; a surly obedience residing in a bit of chemical explosive that Control alone could detonate within the rover's skull. If Control was listening, whatthehell: she knew how complete was the rover's subordination.

CHAPTER 5

The sprint chopper, its dull radar-absorbent black surface set off with distinctive yellow S & R sunflower emblems, throttled back behind a grassy knoll and maintained a three-hundred meter altitude as a bulky object fell from its belly hatch. Quantrill, his descent controlled by a handheld frictioner on the thin cable, grimaced as the harness connectors pulled against the epaulets of his mission coverall. Now he was no longer falling, but hurtling over uneven ground twenty meters above high grass with God knew what footing beneath. "Once around the park, Grenier," he said into his helmet.

The 'once' was a joke; it took several tight circles for Quantrill's mass, pulling a tight curve into the cable, to stabilize over a precise point on the ground. Many years earlier the trick had been discovered by a missionary whose small aircraft, with a bucket winched on a rope, could maintain a circular bank with the bucket nearly motionless at the center. The missionary had supplied friends in a South American jungle clearing too small for a landing. A sprint chopper could land and take off vertically, of course; but any casual eye could see that landing and might draw sensible conclusions.

Quantrill's drop from the hatch to treetop height had taken only seconds. Several tight spirals by Grenier brought them near enough to a stale position that Quantrill could ease off the cable tensioner and hit the quick-release when his feet neared the rank grass that invaded from nearby prairies. A landing would have taken a little more time. From experience, S & R instructors knew that most casual witnesses at a drop zone only recalled seeing a sprint chopper banking in tight circles for a few moments before it accelerated away from the DZ with the droning whirr peculiar to shrouded props.

Quantrill was not concerned with *casual* witnesses. He dropped into knee-high grass, rolled, lay prone. "I'm down and green, Grenier," he muttered into his helmet mike in their 'green for go, red for no-go' jargon. "Hit it."

Grenier hit it. The cable's whine dopplered away behind the little craft which spurted off at full boost; and nothing but a rocket accelerated faster than a light polymer aircraft pulled by big props.

Quantrill lay quietly for a time, using his helmet sensors to test for the sounds of other humans. But the afternoon sun was hot, and the dry up-country breeze did not venture below the grass tops, and he heard nothing of interest. Quantrill quickly doffed his helmet, pressed its detent, let the visor and occipital segment slide into their nested positions. He stowed it, a greatly diminished volume no greater than a medium slice of watermelon rind, in the curve of his backpac that cupped near his left armpit. His right armpit was already occupied by a seven mm. chiller carrying explosive slugs in its magazine.

The nice things about a chiller were numerous. While it had only a small suppressor instead of a bulky silencer, it did not say BLAM! It said cough•cough•cough, and would say it twenty-four times, as quickly and delicately as a tubercular butterfly. Its gas deflectors kept recoil almost at a null category, so that you could aim it and keep it aimed. It was small enough, with few enough projections, for a breakaway holster. And thanks to the cold-gas plenum in each cartridge, there was exactly enough endothermic blowdown to match the ferocious heat release of the powder charge that consumed the cartridge case.

It was the so-called caseless cartridge, with no telltale spent rounds nor even a muzzle flash from the dual-propellant system, that made this sidearm practical. The exhaust gases were not literally chill; the chiller's name sprang from its lethal efficiency. A chiller's only limitation, went a rover joke, was that it couldn't hide the body.

Somewhere upwind was a reef of sage; below the twice-broken bridge of his nose, nostrils flared briefly in welcome. The sky was hard and laser-bright, with fluffball clouds herding obedient shadows beneath them—what the old hands called 'solly sombry' in bastardized Spanish. It would have been a good day for lazing, and Quantrill always felt a dangerous rush of kinship when he saw someone pause to savor the gifts old Earth lavished.

But it was a good day for killing, too. Now out of Grenier's sight, he dialed his coverall chameleon stud, watched incuriously as the mottled fabric became grassy green, the sunflower patch fading quickly. Outwardly now, Quantrill was anonymous. He checked his microwave compass, tuned by an orbiting SARSAT, and shuffled into a dogtrot toward high ground a klick southward. From there, he might spot the North Fork of the Powder, where his quarry had camped for some of the languid hatchery trout stocked there. As he always did, Quantrill found some hook of justification on which to hang his deadly purpose; any man who preyed on tame hatchery trout, he told himself, needed a bit of killing.

CHILLER
SUMMARY SHEETS

SUMMARY DATA

DESIGNATION: CHILLER   **CENCOM REVISION:** 31 Oct. 1998

DEPLOYMENT: Covert Federal agencies only

SPECIFICATIONS:

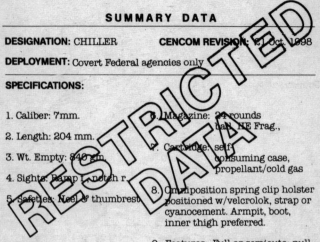

1. Caliber: 7mm.

2. Length: 204 mm.

3. Wt. Empty: 840 gm.

4. Sights: Ramp l, notch r.

5. Safeties: Heel & thumbrest

6. Magazine: 24 rounds
   ball, HE Frag.,

7. Cartridge: self-
   consuming case,
   propellant/cold gas

8. Omniposition spring clip holster
   positioned w/velcrolok, strap or
   cyanocement. Armpit, boot,
   inner thigh preferred.

9. Features: Full or semiauto; null
   recoil; noise suppressor;
   thumbprint ID on
   hammer (trigger
   reverse pinions finger
   of uncoded user);
   rounds are flashless.

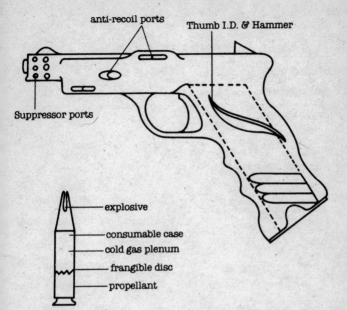

anti-recoil ports

Thumb I.D. & Hammer

Suppressor ports

explosive

consumable case

cold gas plenum

frangible disc

propellant

Side hammer in thumbrest contains print recognition plate.
Muffled; not truly silenced. Antirecoil practical because exhaust
is cool. The chiller's effectiveness comes from the round
w/consumable case that adds to propellant; so gas plenum takes up
more than half of case length. No ejector needed. Long rounds
angled in clip.
If print recog. program set, trigger-pull by anyone unrecognized
punctures only cold-gas plenum which forces trigger _forward_ to
lock finger with enough force to break it -- & hold it. Round doesn't
fire since hollow needle punctures plenum & drains gas into
trigger piston. S & R people have been known to test strangers by
making Chiller 'available'.

Quantrill did not care that Ralph Gilson, paunchy and fortyish, had waxed fatter smuggling unscrambler modules through his holovision dealership; was selling them for the express purpose of bringing Mexican—hence sometimes Catholic—holocasts to Americans. For that matter, Quantrill would not have cared if Gilson's crime had been spitting on a sidewalk or bagging a President.

A rover's day-to-day survival required strict compartmenting of one's concerns. Empathy, altruism, patriotism; all were casualties of the job. Quantrill's secret fear—shared by other rovers, though none admitted it—lay in those moments when pity or tenderness threatened to soften the tempered cutting edge of his killing skills.

So Ted Quantrill did not think about his previous night with Marbrye Sanger while he rested, scanning the North Fork that sparkled below his vantage point. He could not allow vagrant memories of his parents and sister, long dead; of little Sandy Grange, tracked and presumably eaten by an enormous feral Russian boar in the Texas Wild Country; of smiling Bernie Grey, cargomaster of the delta dirigible *Norway*, blown to fragments by a SinoInd fighter-bomber. It was safe to remember the dead, but not to mourn them. Memories of the dead could hone his appetite for revenge. He'd even returned to Wild Country early in 1998 to destroy the legendary boar, Ba'al, but hadn't cut its trail in a month of dogged search near Sonora, Texas. Ralph Gilson's trail was a simpler matter.

Quantrill spotted the wisp of smoke from smouldering campfire two klicks upstream. Gilson had a guide who might be with his client or lounging in camp, and Quantrill wanted Gilson alone. The young rover kept well above the stream, moving slowly, studying streambanks for sight of his quarry while he worked his way toward the campsite.

Once he spooked a brace of pronghorn; cursed as they bounded on sinew catapults to safer open country, because a pronghorn could give you away by keeping you in sight. When a pronghorn moves warily off, the predator is generally within three hundred meters. Quantrill gave them extra room, moved in sight of the camp, lay prone and studied the setup.

The two-man tent, twenty meters from the water, was too opaque to show movement within, but the place seemed deserted. A stainless coffeepot steamed among coals, leaning slightly, and this gave Quantrill an idea. The distance was a hundred meters; he took the chiller from its nest, removed the magazine of explosive rounds, replaced it with a spare magazine loaded with high-penetration jacketed ball ammo. It would sing faintly, but could be mistaken for a deerfly.

Quantrill jacked a round in, steadied the chiller with both hands while prone, elevated the rampsight. He had no need to steady his nerves; his rare mastery of adrenal response had been one of the Army's reasons for handing him a hunter's role in the first place.

The chiller grunted once. A hundred meters away, a puff of ash moved lazily from the firepit; otherwise, nothing. Quantrill waited a moment, considering the movement of the ash, and tried a hand's span of windage. Another round: charred wood jumped under the coffeepot, which toppled over, hidden momentarily in its huffing cloud of steam and ash.

"Ahh, shit," emerged from the tent, followed by a lean bronze-faced man wearing skullcap and jeans, naked to the waist. Quantrill changed magazines by rote, watching the guide snatch at the coffeepot.

The man said nothing more, did not gesture to

the tent, but stolidly inspected the pot before beginning to clean and refill it. The man betrayed no irritation, no sign that might subtly suggest the presence of another person. Quantrill reseated his sidearm. He had decided that his quarry must have fished downstream, a tenderfoot ploy since it was easier to return downstream than upstream after a tiring afternoon in the sun.

Finally the guide squatted to replenish his fire, his back to Quantrill who began to slither backward, still intent on watching the campsite, until he passed behind a lichen-spotted boulder that jutted from the grass.

"Fella," a gruff voice said from behind him, "you better have a good explan—", as Quantrill whirled onto his back.

Among a million humans, the gene pool may provide a few specimens with responses so blindingly fast they do not even dip near the norm. Ted Quantrill's synaptic speed and the output of his adrenal medulla made him one in a hundred million. Army Intelligence medics had tested Quantrill from hell to breakfast in 1996, found him one of those rarities posited by the early stress researcher, Lazarus. The admixture of adrenaline and noradrenaline that coursed through Quantrill's body during stressful moments did not provoke tremors, confusion, or panic; and so his response could be both fast and unerring.

Ted Quantrill's systemic response was as smooth and purposeful as a rattler's strike—and according to psychomotor tests, slightly faster. A recruiter, one Rafael Sabado, had recognized Quantrill's natural gifts while training the young recruit in unarmed combat; had then passed him on to T Section for the training in single combat which, eventually, coerced Quantrill into S & R. In the Twentieth cent. such men had been racing drivers, circus aerialists, stunt men. In the Nineteenth, they had been gunslingers. Now in the Twenty-first cent. it was gunsel time again.

Quantrill recognized the stubble-faced angler and flicked the chiller from his armpit. Gilson's challenge had taken almost three seconds. In less than that time, Quantrill judged that they were hidden from the campsite, made positive recognition, and squeezed the chiller's buttplate to jack a round into place.

The chiller coughed its apology, the HE slug's tiny azide charge muffled inside Gilson's ribcage. The man was holding three trout in his left hand, a wrist-thick hunk of brushwood threateningly in his right. He grimaced, shoved backward by the impact, mouth open as if to shout. Then he fell forward, still gripping weapon and fish.

Quantrill did not linger to study the effects of his shot; an HE's muffled 'pop' at ten-meter range was a lethal statement. He rolled to the boulder's edge instead, peering through grass toward the camp. The guide had turned; stood up slowly, scanned downstream, then swept his gaze past Quantrill's boulder and on upstream.

Quantrill pursed his mouth in irritation. Only once had he found it necessary to bag a guilty bystander, rover parlance for anyone who *knew* he had witnessed homicide by an S & R rover. Beyond the punishment meted out by Control for that gaffe, Quantrill's own brutalized, manipulated sense of fair play had punished him more. He willed the damn' guide to decide he'd heard nothing of importance, to squat again at the firepit—and finally, with a single shake of his head, the man did so.

Quantrill reseated his chiller, wriggled backward several paces, then began the feverish process of enclosing a fattish adult male in a polymer bodybag.

The bag was dull green outside, dull tan inside, and he chose the green face outward as camouflage. From a half-klick, he might be spotted as a man toting something heavy—perhaps a butchered-out antelope. He zipped the bag shut, perspiring now, risking a quick scan that rewarded him with the sight of the guide who was heading downstream in search of his missing client.

For a two-hundred-meter span downstream, Quantrill judged, the guide's path would bring him in sight of the bodybag—if he knew where to look. Quantrill hauled the bag toward the boulder, cursing his heelmarks. He felt justified in his caution when, before disappearing downstream, the guide stood atop a treetrunk which the annual spring runoff had abandoned.

The man seemed to stare directly at Quantrill for a moment, but even in the high clean air of Wyoming it is impossible to distinguish a squinting green eye and a patch of medium-blond hair from three hundred meters. Unless they moved.

The rover knew better than that. If his own incompetence led to a second death then and only then, in Quantrill's beleaguered value system, was the rover guilty of manslaughter. He had argued it out with Sanger, twice upon times, using their old T-Section short-hand sign talk. This manual conversation avoided any monitoring by Control through their mastoid critics. Control, and their cadre of hard-bitten instructors, came down hard on rovers who were disposed to argue ethics. The survival ethic, they said, had been proven paramount in a billion years of evolution—and S & R wanted acceptance, not argument.

Waiting for the guide to disappear, Quantrill looked about him for Gilson's flyrod, presumably dropped in the grass. Then he gave it up. If he couldn't find the thing, neither would a search party. He burrowed under the bag, came to one knee, then lurched off with ninety kilos of dead weight in a fireman's carry. He did not slow his pace until, sweat-sodden and breathless in the thin air, he had lugged his quarry nearly a kilometer from the stream.

Quantrill could have told Control of his progress then and there, via his critic and the relay stations at Mayoworth or Hazelton Peak. Some rovers seemed pathetically eager to keep Control advised of every step, like anxious children placating a stern, unknowable parent. Quantrill had found Control too free with pointless instructions and rarely initiated contact until his mission was complete. If he had any faith in the corporate state he served, it was faith that he would not be expended so long as his usefulness exceeded the rover average. His faith was not misplaced.

For all his physical gifts, Quantrill was not particularly quick in adjusting to the thin air of northern Wyoming. Control's human and electronic modules had juggled many variables; decided that S & R's youngest rover boasted a better success rate in rough country than anyone but the S & R instructors, Seth Howell and Marty Cross; and arranged for Quantrill to spend five days in a wilderness-area seminar before this 'surveillance' mission. The S & R regulars, almost all of staunch Mormon stock, were an altruistic friendly lot; but they'd been taught to let rovers rove without asking for details. Quantrill had left the seminar, and with luck might return to it, without a ripple in their routines.

At length, the rover felt rested enough to resume his carry and chose the route with the most cover, avoiding the few animal paths he struck. The main thing was to get well beyond the radius of any reasonable search by Gilson's guide, as quickly as possible. The guide probably would not succeed in bringing in a search party until after midnight—an S & R team of regulars, like as not—and no one knew better how to avoid a search pattern than a trained searcher. Long before that, the bodybag and its contents would be under a meter of earth, the bag's pheromones repellent to carrion-eaters. Quantrill put another klick behind him before awaiting dusk under a ledge, and learned then what had been poking into his shoulder. Gilson had been a meticulous man: his flyrod, in five short sections, lay ranked in tubular pockets along his trouser leg.

"One day," Quantrill said to the bodybag, "I'll be able to afford a packrod like this." He was not even remotely tempted to steal the rod while studying Gilson's wallet with gloved fingers. Expensive equipment was often marked with tiny dipoles, and getting caught with a missing man's toys was an error too stupid for serious consideration. Gilson had lived and died in a political clime that favored the already-favored, and equated price with value. Gilson's property was better protected than his life.

Quantrill lost another liter of perspiration before dark. The cold light of his chemlamp yielded less IR signature than his body did and, if the guide's 'mayday' came to officialdom, Control would know it immediately. Haste to be away on his own, not fear of discovery, prompted Quantrill's speed with his collapsible trenching tool.

Sometime after eleven P.M., Quantrill's critic intruded. "This is Control, Q." Who else? Well, stray tightband messages had been known to piggyback a beam upstream of a scrambler circuit.

"Rover Control, rover Control," Quantrill responded. In an IFF module near White House Deseret, his freq. pattern passed muster. His key phrase, its syncopation, and the voiceprint said that the rover Quantrill was on-line.

"Your program is running. Is it green?"

"Like Giuseppe Verdi."

Pause. It was dangerous to pique Control with dessicant humor but you sometimes provoked a suggestion of mirth if a human operator and not a pure machine intelligence happened to be on-line.

"Your program is running. Is it green?" No change of inflection but higher gain and slightly slower delivery. Exactly what a machine tries first to cure a communication problem.

"Green," he said. "Message delivered, disposition per orders." *Gilson dead; buried*.

"Can you go on the carpet, Q?" *Are you situated where you can be picked up by air?*

"I can in ten minutes," he said, uncoded. "I'm a klick North of the DZ."

Pause. "North? Say again, Q."

Quantrill sighed. When would Control intuit that rovers had to misdirect S & R pilots as well? "North. They'll find me walking South," he said as if to a simpleton.

"Affirm," said Control. "If you can cut your surveillance short, Q, a team of regulars can pick you up en route to an MP mission your area."

Quantrill chuckled. The missing person, of course, would be Ralph Gilson. He was not so pleased when Control added that he would be expected to aid in that search. For a brief instant he wondered what Control would do if he simply led the innocent regulars to the burial site and dug up the bodybag—would do exactly, that is. The general gist he knew well enough. It would serve Control right for scheduling him to work all night at an exercise in futility—but would serve Quantrill ill. Fatally.

Control coded out, leaving Quantrill at peace.

He'd remembered to reset his coverall's chameleon stud, but rechecked anyway, splitting his concentration between his equipment and a big buck—mulie, to judge by the big ears—that had moved downwind of him, sampling the rover's scent. The image intensifier on his helmet visor made hikes in darkness a cinch, but better still it let Quantrill study a night world peopled by creatures as wary as any he had stalked in government service. A curious vixen with her two fox kits came so near they might have been tame, but only a fool would think them so. They merely assumed the visored man was blind, and Quantrill let them. He liked to study other predators, too.

Free natural predator and captive synthesized predator studied each other a long while, until a familiar voice spoke in his helmet commset. He replied: "You again, Grenier?" The foxes, startled, vanished into scrub.

"CenCom said we could haul you in. Sorry." Grenier's apology sounded real. "Got an MP South of you; fishing, probably turned an ankle. Mind giving us some help?"

"It'll take me a little time to deflate my sack," Quantrill lied. He hadn't taken the gas-insulated mummybag from stowage.

"Give us a rough fix from our original DZ. I'll be there in about, ah, fourteen minutes."

"I'm about a klick, true heading three-forty degrees or so, from the DZ and I'll have my beacon on, bearing one-sixty to the DZ. If you can miss me, Grenier, you gotta be trying."

The strength of Grenier's signal was already gaining. "OK if I set her down? I'd rather not use floodlights; we'll need our night vision in a half-hour."

"Quicker if you just hover and snatch me by cable. Ground winds aren't bad enough to bounce me off the hatch, and I won't have to eat as much dust if you stand off twenty meters."

"It's your hide." Cable retrieval was tricky in darkness, even with image intensifiers. Quantrill had suggested a quick pickup that made him slightly more vulnerable. His motive was the training exercise, but Grenier misread it as a friendly gesture. "You're good folks, Quantrill," he murmured.

"Ram it." Quantrill's reaction was instant, unheated. It brushed away the hand of friendship in pure reflex action. It made his life bearable by constraining his worries within his own skin.

Too many of Quantrill's friends had died. The Sanger connection was—well, a potential problem. Though their shared embraces never extended to spoken pledges, too often their bodies spoke tenderly. He told himself that Marbrye Sanger would be repelled by spoken tenderness. Besides, Sanger claimed other partners on occasion—and Quantrill pretended to. Sanger was a rover, and a damned good one. She could take care of herself.

In thinking Sanger direct and uncomplicated, he underestimated her. He chose not to consider that she might long for an open outpouring of his love, even while knowing it might destroy them both.

Presently, striding through fragrant grasses on his promised heading, Quantrill heard a familiar soft drone in his helmet sensors and, almost at the same moment, "Gotcha," from Grenier in his commset. Moments later he was snapping carabiners, exhaling slowly through his nose to keep swirling grass chaff out of his personal pipes. A sneezing fit was a common hazard when you ran beneath a sprint chopper. The snatch was clean; Grenier did not accelerate until Quantrill had been winched entirely within the fuselage and the belly hatch indicator winked out.

The rover found a litter awaiting him; all three couches were occupied by a team of regulars, all lighthearted, all disgustingly fresh for the night's work. Quantrill snapped on his harness and tried for a few minutes of sleep. Sanger was not among the crew, but he had not really expected that pleasure.

CHAPTER 6

Ralph Gilson's disappearance might best be blamed on midlife crisis, that recurrent panic provoked by bald spots, occasional impotence with a wife who is munching celery in bed, and the fear that one's mistress can honestly ask, 'Ralph *who*?' two weeks after he dies.

In Gilson's case there was no mistress and no bald spot—though his wife chewed gum at the *damned*est times. In 1997, Ralph Gilson had been S/Sgt. Robin Gilbert, one of a hundred thousand troops who had survived the Bering Shoot and refused to stop retreating in Alaska.

For the first time in his life Gilbert had rebelled; had put Army training to its ultimate test, making his way back through Canada to California by shank's mare and cadged rides. But he found Mexican citizens occupying most of the California coast, and rumors that they carried Chinese plague. Gilbert did not want to be a citizen of Alta Mexico; he did not even care much to be Robin Gilbert, deserter.

So he became Ralph Gilson, modestly successful jobber of holovision equipment in Ft. Collins, Colorado. With so many records destroyed during the nuke strikes and the shrinkage of national boundaries, it was an easy matter to generate a new identity so long as you stuck to it. After three years came the onset of internal crisis; and for the second time—it would be his last—Gilbert/Gilson rebelled.

Gilson was a twice-a-year Methodist who believed the holo warnings about the threat New Israel would become, when the Israeli Ellfive orbital colonies were complete. He was not too sanguine about Catholics, either; it was Mexican Catholics who occupied the ruins ringing the dead sites of L. A. and San Francisco. But above all, he began to mistrust a government that made it gradually more difficult for jews and Catholics to share meetings or media exposure.

First came the tax on holo unscramblers, which 'coincidentally' were needed now for all but the major media networks. Gilson owned a little stock and knew how, for example, the Federal Broadcasting Network skipped to the tune of IEE, which pirouetted for Blanton Young's Federalist party and the LDS church. Gilson was not too surprised when the second turn of the screw prohibited unscramblers.

Montana stations were now—temporarily, both governments maintained—Canadian. Tucson stations hewed to regulations of Alta Mexico. In the Wild Country of South Texas and most of New Mexico, stations did as they pleased since neither Streamlined America nor distended Mexico had much success ruling those sun-crazed gunslingers in Wild Country. In this time of reconstruction, the new Southwest was becoming much like the old West of an earlier reconstruction. President Young sought to save the American people from radio and holocasts that might interfere with his peculiar vision of a new, and uniformly Mormon, Zion. Since most LDS and gentile voters might not understand how necessary those measures were, the President elected to mask them in committee recommendations. Of course, a few seditious sons of perdition smuggled unscramblers in from Wild Country. More serious measures would have to be taken; more summary justice.

Gilson could hardly miss the rumors shared by his illegal contacts. In Idaho Falls, now near the Canadian border, 'justice' had caught up with a thirty-third-degree Mason whose lodge formed a nucleus of dissent. In the deep-water port of Eureka not far from Alta Mexico, a bloated body had washed ashore, its dentition matching that of a good Mormon who had felt a calling to reorganize a longshoreman's union. The bishop of the New Denver Diocese had perished, with other prominent Catholics, in the cellar collapse of a Colorado monastery—and rumor insisted that the collapse was preceded by an explosion.

Ralph Gilson had nothing against Mormons—well, nothing much, anyway—in general. A hell of a lot of them had bought his unscramblers, and a few were willing to joke about the unsaintliness of the 'Lion of Zion', Blanton Young, whom one liberal Mormon had dubbed the Lyin' of Zion. But support for Young at the polls was the final punchline, and his reconstruction policies were steadily clotting the individual have-nots into groups of rebels.

Ralph Gilson's rebellion had put self-esteem into his step, and cash into his pocket. And eventually, an S & R rover on his ass. Gilson was the fifth smuggler to receive Quantrill's attention. He was the only one, however, to have unloaded over a quarter of a million illegal unscramblers by making the price attractively low.

CHAPTER 7

Gilson's contraband had run from Matamoros to Piedras Negras in Mexico, to Junction and Big Spring in Texas, to New Denver. Bits of it tended to flake off en route, like blocks of salt from a camel caravan, tribute to whichever bandits wore the badges during passage. Edwards County, Texas, a weathered piece of South Texas Wild Country, boasted twenty-four hundred people and twice that many limestone caverns honeycombing the heights of Edwards Plateau. Corrugated like Dakota badlands, covered with shrubs, it was an ideal setting for shipment and storage of contraband by the barnload. Gilson never new the debt he accumulated from folks in Edwards County. Anybody with a holo there could afford an unscrambler.

Seventeen-year-old Sandra Grange lived in broken oak-and-cedar land East of Rocksprings, the Edwards County seat, and swapped a three-kilo string of dried peppers for her unscrambler. In the current barter system, two kilos would have been fairer; but barter is more personal than money, and it was understood that Sandy Grange must always pay a bit more. The way that young woman spoiled her mute child, the women whispered, was a crime; and to come down from Sutton County insisting the spindly sprat was her sister! No big sister treated young'uns so well. The comely corn-silk-haired Sandy, they concluded, was simply too proud to tell the truth; claimed she was only seventeen but was probably twenty if she was the mother of silent, big-eyed, five-year-old Childe.

Had there been no Childe, Sandy's age would still have been suspect. She showed great patience but scant interest to the young ranchers around Rocksprings, clearly bored by their efforts to court her. She coveted dictionaries, earned a few twenty-peso pieces and household tools correcting notices and ads for a printer in town, and accepted the town's mild disapproval without complaint. Sandy Grange had known much worse during the war.

On the night of Ralph Gilson's disappearance, Sandy treated herself to an hour of holovision, wheeling her Lectroped into the snug soddy, the kind locals called 'two rooms and a path'. The two-wheeler's storage batteries yielded steadier power than her creaky fabric-bladed windmill, and furnished a reading lamp too.

The Ciudad Acuña station came in clear. Her voice soft-husky with affection, she called at the door: "Come on in, Childe, and watch holo with me." Childe, with the most unlikely playmate on Edwards Plateau, had ridden piggyback quite enough for one day.

After a moment the plank door swung open and Childe, slender where Sandy had once been plump, bounded into the half-submerged soddy. Childe was a houseful of kid, a dancing delight radiating affection for those few she trusted. "Want your lap," she piped, and swarmed up to sit on Sandy's legs, sidesaddle. In infancy, Childe had lived the life of an Apache; blistering heat, freezing 'blue northers', malnutrition, and hostile strangers comprising her enemies. She remembered no mother but Sandy, and no other human companion. Childe knew the value of silence in the presence of danger, and by now she was thought mute by all but Sandy and one other. The sisters made a symbiotic pair: Sandy the sturdy thoughtful leader, Childe the spindly little scout who knew the languages of Wild Country better than most adult trappers.

Earlier, Childe had taken Sandy's hand to lead her into dusk-shadowed garden furrows, to show her sister why they must not drive away the coyote that skulked near the garden. Sandy could not afford a fence and placed rabbit snares among the young crops—but there were far more rabbits than snares.

"Coyote's the best trap," Childe had insisted, pronouncing it 'ky-oat' in Sandy's own Wild Country lingo. She proved her contention with the tracks left by rabbit and coyote.

Now, half-watching the ancient cartoons on Mexico's XEPN holovision, Sandy directed her thoughts from the hapless animated coyote on holo to the shrewd mangy specimen which, she admitted, did patrol her garden. Were the rabbits innocent through their ignorance of guilt? Was ignorance of the law, in fact, the very truest defense? Well, —not when the coyote's justice was like the government's. Sandy had been too young to remember the more liberal prewar form of justice. She knew that she preferred Wild Country and the barter system over the kind of regulation imposed to the North. Any system that would take Childe away to a Mormon orphanage was one Sandy intended to avoid—and so Sandy Grange's personal combat against Streamlined America had begun as flight; South from the few tentacles of officialdom, from her home in Sutton County. Too many acquaintances there would have helped take Childe away 'for her own good', and those Sandy trusted had all been taken by the war. Their father, dead of radiation sickness; their mother, shotgunned by bandits; Sandy's friend, Ted Quantrill, perhaps dead on some Asian battlefield.

On balance, Sandy preferred to live on her land, bought with contraband she had found. Increasingly she lived with books: *The Way Things Work; Five Acres and Independence; Baby and Child Care*; Twain and Doyle, Traven and Dostoyevsky; and of course the poetry, Benton and Reiss, Neruda, Durrell, and the bits she wrote in her daily journal. Language, she decided, could be a luxury that paid for itself.

Presently, Sandy placed the sleeping Childe on their bed, unplugged the holo, took her journal from the high shelf of valuables and sat crosslegged with the Lectroped's lamp to illumine the pages. Sandy's journal was no longer the product of indifferent grammar multiplied by creative spelling. Her books, her teachers, tutored her daily. Not that isolation and spare time for books could entirely explain Sandy's astonishing grasp of language; it may have been a genetic gift.

Between her twelfth and fourteenth birthdays Sandy knew a verbal blossoming, a becoming, that she could not explain. To call it a sea change would be to ravage a metaphor; for Sandy had never seen a body of salt water larger than a pot of soup. All right, then: demonstrably a South Texas *land* change; a broken prairie change. A Wild Country change.

Sandy's journal, 16 May '02

Replanted tomatoes from coldframes. Popcorn & peppers flourishing. Childe is wiser than I in ecology, for however sad his harmonies, that coyote is my garden sentry!

Thoughts on holo: it furnishes more lies than

laughter. Surely no announcer can love language, the way they all butcher it. I hear so many castoff holo phrases when in town. No wonder I sorrow for the users. It must show in my face, and I cannot afford to be haughty. N.B.: ck. 'haughty' vs. 'haut'. French? Latin?

Childe's expertise in tracking brought me a queasy moment at dusk. Why? I have seen enough violence to harden me—or have I?

Childe reads animal signatures, crossing, doubling
    back;
A fable of flight from cruel attack.
Ebony droplets end one track—
For, in moonlight, blood is black.

CHAPTER 8

The holo image of Eve Simpson, once a buxom child star and now IEE's director of media research, was familiar to millions; a sultry-voiced pneumatic package and, by remote means, frequent FBN interviewer of important people. Few, including those interviewed, would have recognized the hundred kilos of Eve's real flesh which had swollen with her clout.

The public Eve, interviews and all, was an electronically-managed image. The private Eve was bloated, brilliant, willful, and in some ways unmanageable.

Boren Mills had lusted first for her famous body,

enjoyed it less as he wallowed in it more, and had finally turned toward still younger, less pillowy embraces. But by that time Mills knew the inner Eve, her mind incisive as a microtome, as voracious for media techniques as she was for sex. Mills's intellectual arrogance was tempered by the knowledge that Eve Simpson's subtleties rivalled his own. By now each knew the others uses. And abuses.

"You're going too far," Even snapped, thumbing the fax sheet Mills had carried to her condominium-sized office.

"Don't tell me the system can't handle a message uniquely tailored to each household," Mills wagged a finger in warning. "I've channeled too much money into your media research and read too many progress reports." It was such hot stuff that Mills had insisted on the electronic programs being stored in a government-controlled underground vault. There, it would not be pilferable by some industrial spy.

But Eve snorted, setting off ripples in the flesh at her throat. She had the trick of switching from the nasally sensuous to imperious tones without pause. "Not the electronics, goddammit, I'm talking about viewer reaction. Boren, you're asking for a level of message control that assumes viewers will *never* compare videotapes, *never* start a brush-fire under some Indy congressman once they have proof you're tailoring messages to each holo set."

Mills reflected on the lifetime appointments of media commissioners and waved the objection away. "Not that the Indys could do anything about it," he said.

"Legally? No, your risks aren't legal; they're charismatic." In media research, 'charisma' no longer referred strictly to people. Any message that approached overwhelming credibility was said to be charismatic. Eve was working on it. "As long as John Q. talks to his neighbor, you'll get some coalition of fruitcakes who'll call FBN's credibility on the carpet. Even if you cleaned up your act afterward, it'd be bye-bye charisma—and bye-bye to some network ad accounts for FBN. Is that what you want?"

Mills, sitting on an arm of Eve's ample couch, sighed and retrieved the fax sheet. "So the problem is still word-of-mouth," he mused. "Which means we work harder to alienate the bastards from one another."

"Divide and conquer," Eve chuckled. "Welcome to media theory. Nice to know my chief exec is still capable of an intuitive leap."

Sharply: "Don't patronize me, Eve. Papa spank."

"What would ums do," she cooed, sapphire insets winking in her fingernails as she reached out to knead the calf of his leg; "tie me down like old times? A wittle domestic westwaint for baby?"

He shifted his leg away. "How about lifting your pass to the synthesizer lab? Would that be enough restraint for you?"

A shrug; the sausagelike fingers flirted in the air. "Go ahead, bugfucker, then you'd need someone else to deal maintenance doses to your bloody Chinese slaveys."

"Someone easier to deal with than you are, my dear," said Mills, and let his threat lapse. "By the way: Young's protocol people expect us to put in an appearance when he presents those S & R citations in Santa Fe. Formal, of course."

"A politician after my own heart," she murmured, "parading his hit teams as saviours and reaping public applause for it."

"I don't know if the rover bunch will be there," he said, well aware that a man licensed to kill embodied raw potency to Eve Simpson.

"You know how I hate public display," she said, and Mills knew it was self-display she meant. "Will we be screened?"

"Not from the Prez, but they'll split-screen the dais to make the Secret Service happy. Nobody will see you—us—except Young and a few others like, oh, Lon Salter. You can ogle the beefcake all you like," he said wryly.

"It's not window-shopping I like; it's trying things on."

"Don't put yourself in a bind with Young over it, Eve. The President has some strict ethics about drugging his people."

Delighted laughter, as though Mills had sprung a salacious joke. "Shyster ethics: if you might get punished for it, it's unethical." Long ago, Mills had learned Eve's method of bedding a man who did not fancy tussling with cellulite. She merely laced his food with lobotol, a controlled substance developed to aid hypnotists in making the most intractable patient highly suggestible. While fuddled in this fashion, a man would believe whatever Eve told him, e.g., that she was the most desirable sexual provender he could possibly imagine. And he would further believe that he had hungered all his life to test the adage that whatever one can imagine, one can do.

Mills had discovered Eve's ploy two years previously, after waking one morning with a swirling recollection of boffing his blousy ex-bimbo in ways he had never before contemplated. Those memories did not please him much; the exhausted Mills had the distinct impression that he'd spent the night with a dirty joke. His cold rage on learning her deception had left Eve frightened and astonished; she'd thought the whole business would amuse him. She had never repeated her mistake on Mills but still found lobotol her chief procurer for the one-nighters she chose like a young Messalina.

Deliberately abrading a troubled spot: "Anyhow, I don't keep my slaves endlessly hooked on heavy shit—like *some* folks we know," she arched one brow, squinted the other eye.

Icily: "If there were any other way to pursue the most awesome breathrough in recorded history, *believe* me,—I'd do it."

"Without giving anything away to John Q. or our glorious government, you mean."

Mills, now standing, showed every sign of truncating their old debate. "Eve, if you can keep your great wanton ass out of trouble at the top—and if I can get the San Rafael Desert lab to come through for us—you and I will *be* the glorious government, for all practical purposes. I know you're laying poor strung-out Chabrier every time you visit the lab; considering the stuff he pollutes his system with, I don't think your lobotol could do him any additional harm. Be circumspect; that's all."

"I don't need lobotol with Chabrier," she said, feeling that her charm had been questioned.

"Thai hash, then," Mills sighed; "whatever. I must get back upstairs; thanks for the warning on individually tailored messages, I'm sure you're right."

Her languid purr followed him to the door. "With enough lobotol in a metro water supply you wouldn't need tailored messages, luv."

"Now you're being absurd, Eve. Only half the population would be tuned to FBN and besides, a steady diet of judgment suppressants would put Mexicans in New Denver inside a month."

"But I can see you've given it a lot of thought," she said, and her cruel cupid lips mimed a juicy kiss of parting.

Mills strode to the executive lift, exasperated.

She hadn't even said whether she'd go to Santa Fe. But Mills knew her cravings; she'd be there, all right. He made a mental note to check the remote monitors at the desert lab by way of his private access code. Eve Simpson was the only soul running loose, besides himself, who knew just how Marengo Chabrier's lab was run—and for what purpose.

CHAPTER 9

Cloistered in Utah's San Rafael desert region was Mills's most secure research facility, where need-to-know was as strictly monitored as on any proving ground in the world. There, Mills had carefully assembled a group of the technological elite whose drug requirements made them tractable. From Marengo Chabrier, the French program administrator, to the illegal aliens, all lived out their days behind particle-beam fences within a trackless waste. Their one goal: to find some way to scale up the mass synthesizer which China had developed during the war.

All but a few Chinese researchers had been liquidated by their own leaders, and only Boren Mills had a working model of the device. He had killed to get it. No larger than an overnight bag, the synthesizer had powered the reaction engine of a tiny Sino submarine, also providing oxygen and simple nutrients for the hibernating crew.

Now, twenty-seven months into his scale-up

program, Mills rejoiced and writhed. Chabrier, physicist-turned-administrator and a druggie of broad scope, boasted that the little Chinese synthesizer could now produce small amounts of organic dyes, pheromones, heavy alcohols, and other complex chemicals using plain air as conversion input mass. But an inherent limitation existed in the size of the gadget's toroidal output chamber. The Chinese had already built the thing with its maximum output, and neither Chabrier nor subtler asiatic minds in the lab could even posit, let alone demonstrate, a rig that could do any better.

Within a few weeks, the lab would try out the new prototype which could produce an incredible range of substances, so precisely metered that it could issue a shot of bourbon or a root beer complete with effervescence. Mills was no fool; his lab personnel, Chabrier very much included, wore implant monitors that kept Mills informed of their drug abuses. He could not prevent them from manufacturing booze or Fentanyl, but he would know if any one of them absorbed any of it at other than scheduled times. And that would mean cold turkey withdrawal in a padded cell for Chabrier as well as the abuser. So far, Chabrier's vigilance was flawless.

Still more disturbing, Mills found it easier to fund the lab's exotic needs from his own pocket than to continue siphoning money from projects known to IEE board members. Those expenses were mounting, but Mills did not dare permit use of the synthesizer for cash crops; gold, pharmaceuticals, plutonium. Not yet; not until Mills had absolute control of a synthesizer that could produce its goods in staggering quantity.

To make a million copies of the Chinese model would be to court disaster. Eventually its secrets would become known to others outside his grasp and, once every citizen had access to a synthesizer, government-by-scarcity would be a thing of the past. No wonder the Chinese had purged their technocrats; in the nether corners of his mind, Mills had scheduled something similar for his own lab people—but only after they'd done their work.

Mills, who loathed procrastination, had decided to put off his decision for another year. If by that time it still seemed impossible to design a factory-sized synthesizer, he *might* order a factory full of the small ones. But: should he try to coerce his captives into building wholly automated repair equipment for the inevitable maintenance?

If 'yes', they might prove laggards, even sabotage their own work. To underestimate them would be a disaster; they surely knew their utility would end when a million synthesizers were self-maintaining.

If 'no', then Marengo Chabrier and nine other brilliant trip-freaks would be the maintenance crew, the most expensive mechanics on earth and worth it—and they would know it! The plutonium scenario, for example: what if they produced enough of it, despite the best monitors Mills could employ, to build a—well, call it a negotiating device? It could be scarifying. Hell, it was *already* scary! With a factory full of small synthesizers, his goosepimple factor would be raised to the nth power. It was almost enough to make Mills ask for government control.

Hypothesis[1]: A special security force would help.
Hypothesis[2]: A special security force would multiply his security problems. Quis custodiet?

Boren Mills's basic problem was easily stated: he had a cornucopia by the tail.

CHAPTER 10

A half-century earlier, the Santa Fe Opera complex had been modern, a layered amalgam of steel and adobe on concrete, thrusting up from fragrant serrated hills at the city's edge. Noah Laker, the S & R regular who'd piloted Quantrill and four others into the huge parking lot, stood with him at parade rest stance near the nose of their sprint chopper.

"Quaint," muttered Laker, one of the few regulars who saw nothing unGodly about talking in ranks. "But that open roof is a crime against thermal efficiency. Saints! Just look at all that wasted concrete swooping around. Ever see such a thing?"

"Nope," Quantrill lied, lips barely moving. He had seen it often from the highway when T Section was based in Santa Fe during the war. "But who needs efficiency in Santa Fe?"

"Wha-a?" Minnetta Adams, one of the few female regulars, would not turn her head but eyed Quantrill sidelong. Adams was the kind of ecology nut who'd pick a dandelion salad outside a banquet hall; good-natured but serious in her beliefs.

"Come on, Adams; these people have sunlight to burn. Isn't that sweat you're lickin' off your mustache?"

The comely Adams had no mustache though she was the equal of most men in strength. "I'll get you for that," she murmured chortling.

"Bury me in that compost pile she calls her mummybag," he said, loud enough for the others to hear. Another calumny, for Adams kept her gear spotless. Several snickers rewarded him; any entertainment was welcome when three hundred young people stood sweltering in dress blacks for review.

"Quantrill, are you supposed to be in formation?" It was Control speaking into his mastoid. He guessed from the voice cadence that a human monitor was on-line.

"Um-hm," he hummed his admission softly. You never knew when the damned thing was monitoring you. Whatthehell.

"Is the President reviewing your assembly at this moment?"

Again he agreed. The President strolled a hundred meters away, taller by half a head than S & R's Lon Salter who strode in his shadow like a king's equerry. Young merely glanced at the teams in their formal dress. A score of rovers filled out the ranks, for four teams of regulars had stayed away on alert duty.

"You're a disgrace," said Control as if she could not care less. "Shut up and report yourself to Howell after your formation is dismissed." Pause. "Do you affirm?"

"Uhf-*furhhm*," Quantrill coughed aloud. It might have been just a cough. It would also probably irritate Control—but if Control demanded acknowledgement, you gave it. Somehow. What*ever* Control demanded—you gave.

"This is what we get for giving you a freebie entertainment," Control snarled, all too human for a change, and coded out.

Yep, that's what you got, Quantrill reflected. He hadn't asked for a two-hour cruise bouncing across the Rockies so he could stand on display with three hundred other tin soldiers in heat-absorbent black, waiting for a hulking politician to glance his way under a broiling afternoon sun. The flare-leg black formal synthosuedes had been designed to keep creases in, not to keep heat out. The black vee-necked blouse could have been cool but for its high stiff open collar, and the goddam canary-yellow side-tied neckerchief kept the dry breeze from his throat. Okay, so they looked smart as prodigies with the yellow sunflower S & R patch and suede low-quarters, and the belt medikit with sunflower and caduceus. All that pizazz was for the public and for the President who, increasingly for Quantrill, was no more and no less than the controller of Control; his ultimate oppressor.

He turned his mind to more pleasant employment. Somewhere in the front rank was Sanger, among a scatter of other women chosen for the on-camera impact they made. Perhaps, after the awards banquet, they'd find a way to duck out. They could stroll away from the Opera House to sit silently and watch the moon turn the brush-dotted hills to alien country, to smell the night-flower fragrances unique to late spring on a high, dry New Mexico evening.

Most likely, he thought, they'd be burping from the barbecued prime rib which, his flattened nose told him, was already steaming somewhere in the bowels of the place. His belly growled its readiness. In another hour he'd be savoring it, relaxing, glad that he did not have to parade up to a dais and accept a bit of ribbon before holo cameras.

From one-way glass in the Opera complex over-look, Eve Simpson gazed unseen on the Presidential inspection. She grasped the swivel of a magnifier, pulled the scope into position without moving from her motorized lounge chair, and let her mouth water. Eve was not thinking about cooked beef; she was enjoying the human stuff on the hoof which stood in its stalwart innocence, facing her unaware from a distance of three hundred meters. The magnifier made it seem like only ten.

The big one on the front row would be delightful, those long legs and slender hips stripped bare by lobotol and lust. Or—there, the lank towhead on the end, with the bulge at the crotch of his synthosuedes, the honest farmboy face gleaming with perspiration, the slender delicate nose straight and clean under his blue ingenue eyes.

They were all so photogenic Eve could not—suddenly did not want to—choose. *Let kismet choose*, she thought, *and surprise me*. She would go light on the barbecue, heavy on the man. In an hour she would be with S & R's top dog, the glum Salter, who managed to seem a harried bookkeeper while he kept secrets that could topple an administration.

Should she ask Salter specifically for one of his war dogs, a rover? Anytime an interviewer singled rovers out, Salter's pale eyes fairly jumped in their sockets. She would make her eyes huge, innocuous, and propose a brief private interview with a rover for FBN. Salter could hardly refuse under the circumstances—the whole evening was a media event.

The interview would be in Eve's suite at the De Vargas, naturally. She entertained no illusions about the impression her flesh made; she would ask Salter to choose someone, ah, typical of the S & R rover and to send him alone to her hotel in the city.

Eve giggled at the sweet tickle between her thighs, pushed the magnifier away, wrinkled her button nose at the scent of barbecue. Yes, she'd feed delicately on that.

It would be another matter when they sent the meat to her raw.

CHAPTER 11

Boren Mills stood in the reception room amid the hubbub of young voices, the clink of glasses, the exhalations of food and fruit juices, loathing the unstructuredness of it all. The banquet and the award citations, he admitted, had been well-staged and orderly. It was all this chaotic socializing afterward that gave him offense. Idly he sipped his execrable carrot cocktail and, over the rim of his glass, studied the throng for the layers of order he knew were woven through the gathering.

He spotted one of the heroes of the moment, resplendent in dress blacks, his citation ribbon a white satin slash against his breast. Mills murmured something appropriate, shook the youth's hand, touched glasses and moved on.

The President, as usual, stood stockaded within a crowd that was one-third celebrity-seekers and two-thirds Secret Service. Of course it was easy to spot Young's men among the uniformed S & R members, their dark blue suits almost festive against the yellow-accented black of the Search & Rescue people.

Mills began to smile. Order was on hand, you merely needed to know how to spot it. The foci were Young, surrounded by his praetorians; the regulars with the virginal white ribbons, accepting kudos from envious peers; and Salter, talking earnestly to a pair in dress blacks who were twice as old as most regulars—hence had to be S & R supervision.

He'd seen Eve, flirtatious and charming as a vampire whale, gently badgering Lon Salter over the salad course, but he hadn't seen her since the awards ceremony. Who knew what the self-indulgent slut was up to? She was as hard to figure as a Chinese speedfreak. Well, it probably had nothing to do with Mills's own troubles. He sidled to the refreshment table for a change of poisons—*celery* juice, for God's sake! Young's Mormons would kill him with nutrition—and moved toward Salter as if by Brownian motion.

Salter was saying to the craggy one, "—And she knows what rovers do, for better or worse; but all the same I'll feel better if you choose a rover who doesn't like to ham it up. Don't give the assignment to Ethridge, for example."

"Ethridge isn't a ham," said the smaller one. "Grandstander, maybe; ham, no."

"But you get the idea. The more laconic, the better—ah, Mr. Mills; salud," Salter finished, raising his glass with a manful attempt at good cheer.

"Health it is," Mills agreed, eyeing his own glass as though undecided whether good health were worth such sacrifice. The men laughed, taking their cue from Salter.

"Boren Mills, let me introduce two of my right arms; Seth Howell," he indicated the long-legged topheavy man with unruly brows, "and Jose Martí Cross," he went on, nodding at a man of Mills's own slight build. "Marty, Seth: Mr. Mills of IEE."

Mills had intended more polite conversation, but found this Mutt and Jeff team intriguing. Both were training supervisors—chiefly, Salter explained, of the rovers. To Mills it was obvious that the President hadn't told Salter just how much Mills knew about the S & R operations. Obvious: but true? In some ways, Salter was an opposite number to Mills; they both performed crucial operations for the Lyin' of Zion. They even did favors for each other—but at Young's direction.

Mills turned his attention to the supervisors. Most men preened for Mills, hoping to be remembered. These two seemed to care so little, they might have been members of some other species; Howell a middle-aging grizzly, Cross a graying weasel. To tempt them, Mills tossed out a small bait: "I'm always looking for good security men."

Howell, his wispy tenor suggesting an old larynx injury, his hard eyes amused: "Folks're always mistaking us for the fallen-arch brigade," he said easily.

Mills missed the connection for one beat, equated fallen arches with flat feet, and smiled. Seth Howell might look and sound like a brawler, thought Mills, but like a gosh-and-grits politician he could sandbag you. Or maybe break you like twigs in those huge paws.

Cross, his faint sibilants and high cheekbones tagging him as part Amerind: "Our kids are more like anthro field men—and women, Mr. Mills. Remember those hobo jungle fires two years back? Our rovers saved S & R lots of grief by a little field work."

Mills nodded. He knew rovers would have cover stories and wondered how much scrutiny they could stand. "Tell me about it."

"Army-issue canned heat," Howell husked. "Poor buggers thought it was gel alcohol and tried to process it to drink. But GI stuff makes good incindiary bombs these days." His eyes refocused on someone just behind Mills. "Yes, Quantrill?"

"When you have a minute," said a very young man with a faint southern accent.

Mills turned, smiled, and held that smile while a vague memory of violent death thudded at his

diaphragm. He'd seen this youth somewhere before in dangerous circumstances, but couldn't place
him.

Ted Quantrill's green gaze flickered in recognition, then returned to Howell's face. "Reporting
for extra duty," he said, using their term for disci-
plinary action.

Cross grinned, big wide-spaced teeth shining in
his small dark face. "Let me guess, Quantrill: you
spiked your fruit juice."

Quantrill did not smile, but his tone was sadly
whimsical. "Talking in ranks during inspection,"
he said.

"I'd sooner believe it of the Sphinx," Howell
joked, then pursed his mouth in thought. "Marty,
seems to me that Quantrill has just volunteered
for Salter's little tete-a-tete."

"If he's all through talking," Cross said with a
grunting laugh.

Mills felt the conversation sifting around him,
knew he was not supposed to understand it—and
besides, the sturdy Quantrill made him uneasy. "If
you gentlemen will excuse me," Mills said, lifted
his glass again, and moved off to mull it over.

From a distance, Mills studied the muscular
young rover. Somewhere he had met Quantrill face
to face. And the kid knew it. Eventually, watching
Quantrill's stoic acceptance of some duty as Cross
explained it, Mills shrugged away the problem and
slid into the vortex around Blanton Young.

Quantrill took it impassively. He was damned if
he would tell Marty Cross and Seth Howell just
how much he loathed interviews. It would only
give them another key to the small punishments
they could use against him. Then he excused himself and made a point of stopping several times,
swapping greetings with regulars, on his way to
Marbrye Sanger.

She leaned against a partition of decorative 'dobe, which told Quantrill she'd laced her fruit juice with some local lightning. You drew penalties for slouching in dress blacks. "I've already seen the old village," she was saying to one of the new regulars who hadn't yet given up on her.

"No harm in offering," he said equably, nodding as Quantrill moved near. "If you don't mind my saying so, you could use the fresh air. What's in that drink, anyway," he went on. It was half curiosity, half rebuke.

"Manna from hell," she grinned, smacking her lips.

"Most regulars don't believe in hell," Quantrill said.

"Show me a rover who doesn't," Sanger challenged, slurring it a bit as she turned toward Quantrill. "Hello, compadre."

In the private lexicon of Quantrill and Sanger, *compadre* served for *chum, lover, alter ego*. Quantrill had kept the word as tribute to a friend in the business, Rafael Sabado; long since gone, long since avenged.

Quantrill glanced at her drink, shrugged to the other man as if to say, 'what can you do? She's a rover.' "He's right about the fresh air," he said to Sanger. "Let's get about five minutes' worth of it."

"Five minutes? Don't do me any big favors," she said, nodding to the disappointed regular as she strolled with Quantrill toward an exit. "And where the hell have you been?"

"Drawing extra duty," he grumped. "That's why I've got only a few minutes. Gotta catch a monorail to the Alameda in town so I can give a goddamned interview." They passed outside, negotiating steps toward a scatter of trees near the parking area. Sanger stumbled once, caught his arm for support, spilled some of her drink. "You ought to dump that, compadre," he said gently.

She cast it onto the ground. "Sure. My source has more." Her hands mimed a sign: Ethridge.

"I thought so. I wish he'd drawn my duty tonight."

"Maybe he will," she said, dripping saccharine sexuality.

"Unfuck you," Quantrill parried. "I was thinking about the docudrama that was made when they were forming S & R. One of our people met Eve Simpson then; said she was fat as a pig, no matter how she looked on holo." It had been the ex-Iowa State gymnast, Kent Ethridge, who'd made that discovery. Ethridge was still a rover but had suffered too many disillusionments. Now he spent most of his leaves spaced out on pills and booze.

"Rumor says Simpson's a washed-out druggie; that they use a double for her interviews," Sanger mused, then jerked around. "Is *that* who's going to, quote, interview you tonight? Doesn't sound like extra duty to me, compadre. Sounds like fun and games."

"Reciting cover stories for a cooing sow? Some fun. Some games," he muttered, and drew a polymer poncho form his medikit. "Here; let's just sit and cool off for a minute."

In the pale glow from distant fluorescents, Sanger's honey-tinted skin took on a deathly greenish cast. It reminded him that life was brief, and that they had little of it to call their own. And Control could always be listening. Their shoulders touching, he rested his forearms on his knees, stared out across the dark line of hills under a billion stars.

He felt her hand slide into his lap, provocative, familiar; but shook his head. "What's the point," he said. "I don't have the time."

"Or the urge," she said.

He took her hand, placed his fingers in her palm, began a slow laborious manual conversation learned through moonless nights to deny Control their communion. *"I could just forget the interview."*

She signed back: *"And find yourself packing chutes or overhauling choppers for a month at Dugway?"*

"Done it before," he replied. *"Can almost fly damn' things myself, been on so many test hops."*

"You'd hate me every minute of it."

"Not hate," his fingers insisted.

She willed him to say more; *not* to say more; avoided this booby-trapped psychic territory by signing, *"If only Quinn had made it."*

"We don't know he didn't; only what Pelletier said," he signned.

"We know you have to go," she said aloud, rising, offering her strong hands to pull him up. They took little risk in allowing Control to suspect momentary sexual alliances, but there were some things as verboten as genuine love affairs. One of those things was talk about Desmond Quinn, who'd refused to accept the Army's word that a mastoid critic could not be removed. Quinn had disappeared at the war's end rather than continue his assassin's work in the new guise as S & R rover.

Max Pelletier, Quinn's closest ally, had backtracked Quinn months later. Apparently Quinn had found a Mexican surgeon willing to try removing the critic; a surgeon who had lost two fingers when the critic detonated during the operation, with poor determined Des Quinn the only fatality. Or so Pelletier had said.

"See you when I see you," said Quantrill as they parted near the monorail terminal. "Take it easy. I mean *easy*," he repeated, miming a sip from a nonexistent glass.

"Don't chide your elders, sonny," she said in

false gaity, giving him a fanny-pat toward the approaching transit module. "And take a good deep breath before you submerge in all that blubber."

Quantrill squeezed his eyes shut, wrinkled his nose at this deliberate gross-out from Sanger's lovely lips. Taking the steps to the platform three at a time, he called, "You've turned words into a martial art; you know that?"

"Don't let it put you on the mat," she called back, made cheerful by their brief moment together, hands on hips, her head thrown back to let the chestnut hair fall free.

He fought down a nearly overwhelming impulse to return to her side, but imagined that Sanger would have considered it weakness.

CHAPTER 12

Eve Simpson, alone in her suite, cancelled her outgoing video before answering the phone. What she saw incoming pleased her immensely. "Ted Quantrill, ma'am; Search & Rescue." You couldn't tell a lot from a room video but he looked like a hunky morsel. Unconsciously she moistened her lips with her tongue.

"Of course," she said; cordial, not too cordial. "Come right up. I'll leave the door unlocked, Mr. Quantrill, I'm—doing a few things," she ended vaguely, and punched off.

Chiefly she was doing one thing: sloshing lobotol in the bottoms of the crystal goblets she had brought, except for the one she would use herself. Faceted crystal didn't reveal trace coatings as a clear glass might.

When the young rover arrived with a diffident tap on the door, Eve was carefully arranged on a couch amid pillows and a satin coverlet. She saw his bemused glance at her camouflage and did not give a damn. She was used to it. "I'm a little dizzy after all that rich food, Mr. Quantrill," she temporized. "Forgive me for taking my ease this way."

"Oh. You were at the awards banquet?"

"I was there," she agreed, her eyes approving their scan of this splendidly uniformed creature, then abruptly shifting ground. She waved a languid hand toward the inert holocam rig nearby. "I hope these things don't make you nervous."

His headshake was too quick. "We get used to 'em."

"Confidentially, I never do," she lied. "That's why I bring fortifications with me." She raised her goblet and grinned wickedly. Sipped. "There 's fruit juice at the bar—and more of this naughty champagne if you'd care to join me. Please," she said it prettily.

Quantrill chose apple jice, a goblet, and the chair near her couch. His choice of liquids didn't matter, she thought; her gratification lay in the lobotol.

And she was half right, though it was was disappointment and not gratification she had assured with the drug. One of the regular additives to the diet of S & R members was anaquery, a substance that migrated to the brain without obvious effects—unless certain physicochemical changes occurred in that brain.

Whether by hypnotic concentration or drugs, minute chemical changes accompanied the blocking of volition and judgment. It was those changes that triggered anaquery, with results that appalled Eve in due time. Anaquery prevented any agency, including S & R, from digging into a rover's mind. It was a small sacrifice, in Salter's judgment, for the added security. After all, you didn't have to care about the guillotine's internal stresses so long as it sliced unerringly.

"I get the feeling I've seen you on holo before," she said to prompt him. Lobotol did its erosive work slowly.

"Maybe in a group," he said, eyeing the holocam.

"No. By yourself—a long time ago. Um—talking with Juliet Bixby?" Eve managed to hide her loathing of Bixby, her svelte opponent on another network.

"Quite a memory, Ms. Simpson; I'd almost forgotten. I was on the delta airship *Norway* early in the war. We got waylaid by a renegade bunch but—we got away," he finished lamely.

Her eyes grew round. "You started a fire or something, I remember now. You saved the *Norway* and were wounded. You were wearing a thigh crutch, weren't you?"

"Took a round in the leg." He did not add that he had seen his first lover shot dead by renegade sentries and had made his first kills that night. It had all been a long time ago. Long enough, almost, to forget.

"Care to show us the scar?"

"Not particularly." Again a glance at the holocam. The lobotol was taking its own sweet time.

"The camera's not on," Eve murmured. "We're just getting acquainted, you and I. May I call you 'Ted'? And by all means, my name is Eve. Tell me, Ted; do you have any special lady? Or maybe a hotsy 'in every port'."

"I'm a rover, not a sailor, Ms.—Eve. But no; no one special."

"Surely a young man in his prime," she smirked,

"enjoys a woman now and then. Do you like a strong full-bodied woman, Ted?"

Those piercing green eyes were slightly unfocused now as he took another sip of apple juice. "Sure I like 'em," he smiled uncertainly.

"Take another little sippie, Ted." She watched him do it, his motions less assured, his breathing now shallower. *Got him*! Softly, cooingly, with sexuality dripping from each word: "You know, primitive societies didn't care much for the slender-assed fragile little hotsies you see on the holo, Ted. We know, because they made effigies of their sex goddesses. Nice luscious great tits, round soft lovely ass, lots of woman to screw and screw and screw." She undulated slowly under the satin. "You look primitive to me, Ted Quantrill."

He just sat there, blinking, his respiration rapid and shallow as he watched her peel the satin away. Beneath it he saw her enormous breasts resting comfortably against a billowing ledge of fat. "May I show you what a sex goddess really looks like," she teased, pausing in her routine. Her legs, below the coverlet, were separate mounds spread for coming attractions.

He blinked. Swallowed. "I need to find the bathroom, Eve."

"To relieve your tummy or your tensions, lover? Maybe Eve can help. How would you like—"

She never got to describe it. Quantrill lurched up from the chair, but Eve caught at his trouserleg. He fell against her, shaking like a malaria victim, and vomited once, twice, squarely between her breasts, before she could get her great girth underway.

With a squall of revulsion Eve rolled aside, squirmed to her knees while trying to avoid the line of fire from Quantrill's much-used barbecue. She saw the finely corded muscles of his throat grow taut, another spasm building in his belly and working its way up his torso, and then she was reeling toward the bath.

The rover fell on his face as she slammed the door. She could hear him retching, gasping, as she turned the needle-shower on full force. If the little bastard suffocated in his own gorp it would be good enough for him.

Eve soaped herself furiously as she cursed and lathered, lathered and cursed. Eve was convinced that she had simply moved faster than the laggard lobotol; that the sight of her naked body had prompted this ultimate rejection from a man. Eve was not often embarrassed, and all her half-acre of skin blushed under the needlespray.

Reject her, would he? The scrumptious little hick would be sorry for this. She felt like rushing back into the boudoir to stamp out his life, and in mounting frustration Eve flung open the door.

Quantrill lay in his filth, repeatedly pushing himself up on trembling arms only to fall again, his limbs twitching in a way to make Eve suspect a seizure. To someone or no one he was grunting 'mayday', over and over.

She could not go near him, could not even stand his smell. She slammed the door; found that she liked the fury of it; slammed it again, and again, bellowing her rage and vindictiveness. She was still screaming when the hotel staff arrived.

CHAPTER 13

Sean Lasser had grown too old for active training operations, but he knew far too much about S & R to be turned out to pasture. It was Lasser, alone among rover instructors, who drew the gentle chores.

"No question about it," Lasser muttered as he studied the printout of Quantrill's vital signs; "you took a fair-sized dose of some narcohypnotic, to judge from your condition when they brought you here last night. Anything from PZ to lobotol could have done it. We're assuming it wasn't an injection." Lasser tapped his front teeth with a thumbnail, usually a sign that he was brainstorming. "Did you sit down to watch the holo? God knows you're not a likely subject, but some people can be put under by the right holo presentation. Had you been drinking anything alcoholic?"

"Not even beer. I remember sitting by Eve Simpson with a glass of apple juice while she asked fool questions about the love life of a rover." Quantrill, propped up in a bed in a very private room in Los Alamos clinic, was still a bit gray under the eyes but obviously on the mend. "I don't think it was the holo. Could it have been during the banquet?"

"Too long a delay. My lad, I'm afraid it was Simpson herself who zonked you. Any idea why?"

"Jesus, Lasser, I was picked out of a hat for the interview! Ask Cross or Howell."

"I've already gone around and around with them both on this—and with Salter. Eve Simpson told them she wanted to record an informal chat with a rover. She didn't specify you. But we know something about that lady and—" Lasser grinned apologetically, "—there is evidently nothing she won't do for a roll in the hay with a studly young buck."

Through gritted teeth: "I'll give her a roll off Truchas Peak! What if she'd asked me something Control doesn't want answered?" Quantrill did not know he got regular doses of anaquery. He assumed that Control would sooner see him dead than see S & R compromised—a fair assumption.

Lasser's tongue filled his cheek: "Well,—I suppose that's a risk she was willing to take."

"So who's she really working for: Mexico? I don't envy the rover who has to stuff that broad in a bodybag."

"Eh? Surely you don't think—"

"Howell told us once, 'media star, bishop or bird colonel; if Control says he goes,—*he goes.*' I don't see why Eve Simpson should rate any special immunity."

"You don't? Well, she does." Lasser dropped the printout, clasped his hands over his little belly in a familiar lecture pose, and considered his words before using them. "Eve Simpson and Boren Mills are the heart and soul of IEE. Mills is as close to our President as Lon Salter—and we don't want to get into a pissing contest with the CEO of the most powerful industrial arm in Streamlined America. I may as well tell you: Mills was one of the few Navy people during the war who knew T Section's charter—and he knows about rovers too. We couldn't prevent him from telling the Simpson woman. It's my guess she was toying with you in several ways at once; don't underestimate her. Young and the Fed party owe more to Simpson and Mills than

they do to S & R. Between 'em, those two can do
more for an image through media than all the rest
of us put together." The portly little man sighed,
made a helpless gesture with one hand. "*Now* d'you
see why we have to shrug this little fiasco off,
Quantrill?"

"Do *you* see that she's no more responsible than
a spoiled brat?"

"Granted." Lasser began to chuckle, shaking his
head in gentle disapprobation. "You should've heard
the hotel staff report, it fairly begs description.
First thing they saw was you, facedown on the
floor, and they got the idea there was a hand-to-
hand fight going on in the bath. So they broke the
door down, and found your, ah, friend Eve alone,
naked as a thousand-pound jaybird and ready to
toss them all out. She damn' near did. But Control
picked up your mayday and there's no shortage of
S & R teams in Santa Fe at the moment, so . . ."
Lasser spread his hands; seemed to take the whole
thing as a great joke.

"At least you've explained something about
Mills," said Quantrill. "I thought I'd seen him
before, and now I know when. It was the night I
did my first hit, on some Navy saboteur. Mills was
Navy too; saw me coming out of the guy's room. I
had cosmetic cover but I think he made me last
night at the banquet. It was one of those *deja vu*
things; you look around and you're staring at him,
just like the first time."

"I wouldn't worry about it," Lasser said after a
moment of reflection. "If you wore cosmetic cover,
Mills probably isn't sure—and if he is, so what?
He knows what you do for a living."

Quantrill narrowed his eyes, cocked his head at
Lasser, sat up straight. "If he has the need to
know, he's in my chain of command."

The two stared at each other a long moment.

Lasser said, "What's good for IEE is good for this country. But you are not, repeat *not*, to repeat that irresponsible notion." The flush across Lasser's cheeks said, *I've told you too much.*

CHAPTER 14

Quantrill was on his feet in a day, and in a sprint chopper a week later en route to Indianapolis. From the air he spotted two of the three old nuke scars, vast gray dustbowls with shallow lakes at their centers, that had all but killed Indianapolis in '96. Both bombs had targeted soft military sites, a Naval weapons plant and an Army post East of the city's center. The third strike had come during a later nuclear flurry, taking out the Municipal Airport after its conversion to a military base.

Slammed by airbursts, partly consumed by firestorm, the Hoosier heart of the city had refused to quit. Some of the of the old buildings still stood, monuments to an architectural style that had wasted energy when the stuff was cheap. Now, this very morning, one of those old structures had succumbed.

Dropping toward a parking area off Burdsall Parkway, Noah Laker banked their sprint chopper over the felled trade center, now no longer burning but smouldering still. Adams strained at her harness, craning her neck as Laker's deft work brought them over the collapsed edge of the

structure. "One of those long-span deathtraps of
the eighties," she said. "Rain load, you think?"

Quantrill shrugged. Heavy rains might have been
the last straw, but Howell had told him to look for
earlier straws. They'd found rebel arms along the
border, but in Indianapolis? It'd been a deep cache,
the kind you might expect in a region of heavy
industry. So deep they'd excavated a bit too far
under the old blast-damaged foundation. The acres-
wide roof had collapsed only on one corner, kneeling
into its parking lot, an obeisance toward Monu-
ment Circle in the center of town.

Three of the stubby black Loring sprint choppers were already at the site. Laker's group brought
their strength up to nineteen, not twenty; they
expected the rover, Quantrill, to disappear. He did
not disappoint them.

He took his time, nodding at the fluorescent
scrawls left by regulars at stairwells and ramps as
he descended into the bowels of the structure. Some
of the crews had been on the site for twelve hours,
and you had to accept their cryptic signs as gospel
even if the ferroconcrete swayed underfoot. "Going
in, Control," he said. "Ramp three-ell. Somebody's
been here with chemlamps. You copy?"

A moment's pause. "Copying, Q. Mirovitch set
the lamps, ah, eleven hours ago, so you should
have light for another twenty-five hours."

Quantrill came to a landing halfway down, saw
an arm protruding from beneath the laminated
girder which had slammed down through the
walkway. He grasped the wrist, released it gently.
Only one more level remained, but now he picked
his way over shards of plastic rail and jagged hunks
of concrete. The air below carried a pungent damp
stink and the faint odor of ozone.

At the bottom stairwell door was a woman. No,
only half a woman. He kept going, eased the heavy

door open and jammed it with a hunk of debris. He studied the faint glow in the quiet dank hell of the lowest sub-basement for long seconds. It wasn't entirely quiet; as he stood in the scant protection of the doorframe, a desk-sized chunk of concrete slithered a few centimeters down a pile of debris in muted warning.

"Bottom level, Control, facing East. Either Mirovitch planted some chemlamps *under* debris, or there's been more settling since he was here. Don't suppose you could send him down . . ."

The desexed voice was distant now. "Mirovitch was rotated out after he reported what he found, Q."

"Mustn't risk the prettyboys, huh?" But he knew better. The less a regular knew about weapons caches, the less he would speculate.

"Say again, Q," the faint voice requested.

"Forget it." He drew two chemlamps from his backpac, energized them, snapped a teat on one and squeezed carefully against its slender length. Bright gobbets of liquid light splashed near his feet, a trail he could follow later. With stealthy caution he skirted the collapsed segments, moving into deeper gloom.

He felt the faint tremor through his bootsoles, saw dust sift through another rent in the concrete above to his left. Several levels above him—endless tons of hair-trigger-balanced junk above him—something big had let go.

"Report, Q." It must've been a beaut. Now Control was loud in his noggin.

"Proceeding East, Control. I'm still suckin' wind, if that's what—wups. Well, Mirovitch was right." In the dim dazzle of his chemlamp was a welter of cartons. They had fallen from a stack against the East wall to reveal the top of a trapezoidal opening. It hadn't always been trapezoidal; it had been forced awry by the building's collapse. It hadn't been part of the original concrete pour, either.

The cartons weighed little, obviously just a mask for the portal beyond. Quantrill eased several of them away; stood shaking his head as he studied the skewed opening. He squirted the chemlamp fluid into the black maw before him, saw the spatter outline a stack of fiberite casings and, farther back, more military storage canisters. He wished then for an incandescent lamp but thrust that wish away. He'd seen what happened when an electric bulb cracked in an atmosphere full of dust. Usually nothing happened. But at times that dusty mixture supported combustion, and then what happened was of no further interest to the bulb user.

Some idiot had opened one of the sealed fiberite cartons, as if by leaving a live round in sight he could remind himself of its potency. Dumb . . . "We've got a cache of rockets, Control—could be old Hellfire ATM's they put on attack choppers against armor. Prewar stuff; I see a 1987 stencil. Estimate two hundred rounds," he said, easing his head into the opening to peer past the hole in the foundation wall.

Someone had run an earth-borer through that hole and hollowed out one hell of a room, without more than 'the flimsiest kind of wooden mineshoring to keep the earth roof in place. The damned stuff had already fallen nearby, he saw with a grunt of fresh surprise. All of that overburden could let go at any second, right on top of two hundred rounds of stolen antitank missiles. And old munitions were touchy.

It was then that he heard the rustle of fabric.

He tossed the chemlamp onto a distant pile of soft earth; fumbled for another. After a moment he catfooted through the hole to kneel in the dirt under that half-assed mine shoring. "Control," he said, "I've found a live one."

Silence in his mastoid, but ragged breathing from beneath a splintered plank. Half buried, left wrist flopping, hell of a bruise spanning cheek and forehead—but a steady pulse despite shallow breathing. Poor sonofabitch was just a kid. "Control? Verify, Control." Now he spoke louder, but into his cupped hand to minimize the echo. No answer.

From the sub-basement came another, louder slither of debris. Quantrill eased through the hole again to hear, "—Again, Q. Say again, Q. Say again, Q."

"Say what again?" The goddam building was completing its collapse in bits and pieces, he decided. And doing it directly above him.

"Two hundred rounds of ATM's and what else?"

Ah. Once through that hole he was shielded from Control. Quantrill had been warned that his critic might not function far underground. Of course they hadn't ever hinted that a Faraday cage might be a better shield against RF energy. "I couldn't be sure but there could be some binary nerve gas rounds there," he said, starting to grin as an idea blossomed. "I can't risk blowing the antitank rounds if there's much of that stuff down here. Concur?"

Pause as Quantrill's grin widened. "Concur, Q. How long do you need?" Another way of asking how long he'd be out of contact, without actually telling him he was beyond range of their signal.

"Five minutes, but this place is settling around my ears. Can you send a regular down with a doughnut?"

"Might be quicker if you called up for one, Q."

"Shout? In this house of cards? You have a lovely sense of humor, Control." But he began retracing his path up the stairwell.

Minnetta Adams met him at the fallen girder

with a bundle the size of a cheap bedroll. "Laker said you needed a doughnut. How'd he know?" She ignored his shrug as she spied the deader sandwiched on the stair. "Any more like that?" Adams was trying to keep it impersonal but any victim beyond her help affected her like a personal reproof.

Quantrill said nothing, only shook his head and waved her back up the stairwell before descending with his thirty-kilo burden. A doughnut inflated to virtually fill a narrow hallway; a fat sausage three meters long, two in diameter, with a long central passage like its namesake. A stopgap measure, but it had saved more than one life. Doughnuts could be inflated in place to raise timbers, but their primary use lay in keeping that small central passage free of sand, water, silo grain—whatever might otherwise block you off during a rescue attempt.

Quantrill snapped the webbing seal, rolled the flaccid sausage out, dragged it after him through the hole in the foundation, cursed as he remembered his backpac. It could hang up in the traction ribs of the annulus. He duckwalked back, tugged on the doughnut's D-ring, then worked furiously to get his pack off as he watched the orange ripstop fabric inflate. It would be jammed in the hole in twenty seconds. If any adjusting were to be done he'd have to do it now.

He oriented the mouth of the doughnut so that it protruded into the basement, thrust his backpac into the annulus, clipped a chemlamp at his wrist, listened to sinister pops and rustles as the doughnut fleshed itself out. Finally, thrusting the pack ahead of him, he hustled through the annulus. It was like crawling through the guts of some great animal.

He clambered onto packed earth and splintered

shoring, then placed his pack near the cache of rockets. There was no sign of nerve gas; never had been. But judging from the stenciled hides of other crates there were enough CBW protection suits to bring half a battallion through a gas attack. The rebels, thought Quantrill, must expect some very nasty treatment from Streamlined America.

Or maybe the rebs intended to wear those suits while dealing with the Confederacy. It was only a hundred klicks to the Ohio River, the boundary and quarantine line separating Streamlined America from the region that had once been the southeastern United States. Paranthrax had fixed that.

While Quantrill reflected, he worked. It was one hot sonofabitch in this hole, and damp as well. He eased a plank from the semiconscious youngster, roughly palpated arms and legs probing for major fractures beyond the wrist. Satisfied, he reached under the lad's jawline, pressed hard, held his thumb down. The faint moaning ceased. He did not want that kid coming around while in a rover's care. There was no proof that the kid was a reb; he might've panicked and run down here by sheer accident.

Yeah—and there might be no water in the Pacific Ocean.

There was only one way to haul a limp body through a doughnut; pull him after you. Quantrill gripped the boy's clothing and hauled. He did not realize the boy's trouserleg was hung up until he'd pulled the vertical timber sideways, and then he was scrambling as fast as he could, thrusting his legs into the annulus, taking a better grip on the boy's jacket while feeling for traction ribs with his feet. Staring at the dirt that dribbled down from that column was not going to slow it down one little bit.

He found purchase against the ribs and backed

furiously. He could feel thumps on the tough fabric; hear the hiss of dirt cascading down on it. If the whole thing gave way it would burst the doughnut like a wet bag.

"—Q. Report, Q. Report, Q," he heard as he scrambled backward.

"Stop honking," he panted an ancient routine. "Pedaling—as fast—as I can. You copy, Control?"

"We copy, Q," he heard as he ripped the youth from the annulus and rolled under the limp form. Under these circumstances, the first step to a fireman's carry was getting the load to roll over on you. "Regulars moved the wrong piece, Q. Are you trapped?"

"Don't know." This confusion might be a break. In all his missions for S & R, Quantrill had never actually *saved* a life. His real function made the idea slightly ridiculous, and as Quantrill moved toward the stairwell he was grinning again, licking sweat from his upper lip. But he mustn't be seen with his burden, and, "Suggest you tell regular crews to clear out above," he grunted. "Now, Control. It's like the bottom half of an hourglass down here, shit's raining down steadily." He was exaggerating only a little.

"Report on those munitions, Q."

Quantrill heard someone call from above, flung the unconscious boy behind an abandoned forklift at the first basement landing, raced below again. "No chemical munitions, Control. Old GI suits, stacks of timbers, ammo cans. Nothing that looks like ceebee or nuke stuff."

"Blow it, Q."

He stared at the doughnut; licked his lips. The annulus was distorted now, almost closed at the far end. "Don't know if I can get there again, Control. The whole fucking rig is caving—"

"Blow it, Q. Set it for a half-hour. Nobody will be inside by then."

"Except me," he snarled, and felt for the doughnut's release valve.

He played the valve by ear, ready to sprint for the stairwell, hearing soft rustlings past the hole. Finally he could clamber over the pillowy fabric, saw that there was barely room to squeeze between an angled piece of shoring and the outside of the foundation wall. The chemlamp on his wrist was his only light source. A hundred tons of earth had fallen into the makeshift munitions room in the past five minutes, and a timber groaned only an arm's length away.

Quantrill drew his chiller; clasped it to his breast. Whatever happened, he was not going to suffocate. He reached his pack and with one hand he stripped the timer from its velcrolok clasp. He placed the pack against the nearest ATM canister. He did not bother to dump the 'candy bars' from their pocket; inside each wrapper was a tenth-kilo of explosive. He grasped the detonator buttons in his teeth, unwound them like a tasseled cord from the timer body, blew sweat from his brow, stuck three of the tassel buttons through innocent-looking wrappers into doughy plastique.

When the timber gave way, he just managed to flatten himself against the foundation so that the cascading earth buried him only to his knees.

"Control, you suck," he breathed, running his thumb along the ID plate on the butt of his chiller. Then he reached forward, groped blindly into the fresh earthfall, and at last felt the timer. He set the damned thing by feel, unwilling to move it, murmuring every outrageous phrase he could recall and investing it in Control. Then, for the first time in years, he had an inkling of what people meant when they spoke of panic.

He could not lift either foot.

Somewhere just ahead, the timer was slowly willing itself to die. When it went, it would take two hundred antitank rockets with it, unless the effing timber just overhead went first. And he could not even ask Control to pull his plug. Control could not hear him.

Well, wasn't that what he'd dreamed of for years? Bitch, bitch, bitch ... He reached his decision, thrust his chiller into its clip, began to burrow with both hands at his right shin; sneezed. Clods of dirt were raining down on his neck as he wrenched the foot free, knelt, scrabbled at the stuff imprisoning his left leg.

When he lurched upward it was only to reel back, tumbling onto fabric that half-enveloped him; and then he was rolling backward, away from the rain of falling earth and timbers, through the foundation hole and onto concrete. He did not ignore the rumble behind him. He sprinted from it.

At the stairwell he remembered. "Message delivered, Control. The candy goes rancid in twenty-seven minutes do-you-copy?"

Faint but clear: "We copy, Q. Can you get out? If not,—can we help?"

Quantrill knew what kind of help they had in mind. How touching! "Twisted my knee. Stairwell is clear but getting up it will be a bastard. Can you send me an arm to lean on?"

Pause. A life depended on the answer. Not Quantrill's.

"We'll ask for a volunteer. All regulars are now out of the structure. Keep talking. Well done, Q."

"I won't faint on you." He climbed one level, paused to listen and to test the knee; he really had wrenched the bloody thing.

"Keep talking, Q."

"All I can think of is that old Chinese proverb:

yuck foo," he said with relish. Somewhere above him, heavy concrete shifted. "Okay, okay, just kidding," he said to the cubic meters of concrete.

When he heard quick footfalls above, he reported them. It was Minnetta Adams. It would be.

"Get on," she said, all business, patting her shoulder. He realized she intended to bodily carry him all the way up.

"Just give me a shoulder," he responded, and proved that he could walk.

At the first basement landing he lurched as though in pain, staggered, fell and rolled. His chemlamp, still clipped at his wrist, shed a glow over the dusty forklift and, "Hey, Adams, is this a deader?"

She found the younster as Quantrill had intended, but her joy was brief. "Maybe I can come back for him."

"In a pig's—ah, look, let's see if I can hobble alone, Adams. You grab the casualty." She was still arguing when he started up the last flight, one leg held stiff.

Minnetta Adams was *still* arguing, carrying one casualty and steadying another, when the three of them emerged from the wreckage of the trade center into open Indiana space, to a delighted roar from eighteen S & R regulars and twice that many holo newspeople.

And when the lower levels of the building disintegrated some twenty minutes later, holo pundits opined that the source had been a pocket of natural gas. By then, the commercial networks were in the process of lionizing Adams, announcing that she'd found the unconscious boy.

By then, too, Adams herself believed it. And by then Quantrill was at nearby St. Vincent's Hospital, hearing from medics that his knee cartilage wasn't seriously torn.

FBN holovision carried the story that night as Quantrill watched. Sixteen-year-old Geoff Townley was in satisfactory condition after his dramatic last-minute rescue from entombment just one level below ground floor in the trade center. Rescuer Minnetta Adams had also brought up an injured colleague—unnamed—minutes before a gas explosion completed the building's collapse.

The Townley boy, on summer hire from Nauvoo, Illinois, evidently recalled nothing of his day-long ordeal.

Quantrill winked at the holo set. If the kid was from Nauvoo he was probably LDS, and it was almost a felony to say 'rebel' and 'LDS' in the same sentence. The Townley kid was home free, whatever his political leanings, and no one but Quantrill—not even Adams herself—was the wiser. It was incredible, he thought, how much trouble you had to take, merely to do what the taxpayers thought they were paying you for. A damned shame that he'd never be able to share the joke with Sanger.

CHAPTER 15

The broad-shouldered man steadied his monocular in a cedar crotch and from his cover, studied the little homestead for long minutes. Finally he turned toward the soft footfalls approaching behind him. "If you can't keep those horses quiet,

Espinel, move 'em further back into the cedar brakes."

Espinel started to complain; thought better of it. Judging from the squint lines at the corner of his leader's eyes, this was no time for debate. "They smell water, Lufo," Espinel shrugged, and turned back. Lufo Albeniz might be the toughest jefe in Wild Country but his big scarred, slim-hipped body only looked like that of a Mexican cowpoke. Lufo was TexMex, but city-bred and no vaquero. He'd been cursing those good horses all the way up from Ciudad Acuña.

Lufo ran a hand inside his mottled threadbare shirt, scratched his swarthy hide, spat cottony fluff. He wanted water as much as those scruffy horses did, but you didn't just ride up to some squatter's soddy in these parts without reconnoitering first. Lufo saw a flash of yellow hair and trained the monocular near the soddy again. After a moment he grinned to himself and, almost without sound, whistled his appreciation between his teeth. She was young and blonde, and he guessed that her husband would be inside.

Lufo flicked his comm unit on, speaking softly. "Espinel; Thompson; there's a cute little rubia moving out to hoe the far end of the garden. If I can get near the soddy on foot, I'll be between her and whoever else is inside. Tie up those goddam horses; bring your carbines and cover me."

Tinnily in his speaker, from Thompson: "I'm no good with a weapon, Lufo, you know that."

"But those folks don't know it, and you can pull a trigger for effect. We're not after trouble, Thompson, but we must make a show of readiness for it. Do you want a roof over your head so you can work, or don't you?"

"Got it," from the speaker.

Lufo stuck the monocular in his pocket, made

sure his sidearm was hidden, and began a careful approach. He limped for effect, in case someone was watching from the half-submerged cabin with the log walls and sod roof. His pauses might have been frequent rests. But they weren't; he moved only when the woman turned away to chop with the hoe. The place wasn't much, but they had a wind-powered generator and a gravity-feed water tank. From the look of it, the place didn't support more than a small family. Perhaps there'd be only one man to watch for as long as Thompson needed the place. And if the man was in sympathy with the Indys, Lufo wouldn't need to use threats. In Wild Country, you never knew . . .

The high shrill tone stopped him in midstride, the woman turning, hurrying between rows of vegetables with the springing step of a girl. But Lufo was already near the doorway, calling out. "Hello the soddy! Can you spare a liter of water?" He saw the thin big-eyed child inside through the multipaned window, did not realize such small lungs could generate such a piercing blast until she whistled again, thumb and forefinger curled at her lips.

He laughed then, raised his hands in mock surrender, put them back on his hips. The sidearm was only a flicker away from use as he awaited the man of the house.

No man emerged—but that proved nothing. The yellow-haired young woman approached quickly. "Welcome," said the shapely gardener, eyes wary, carrying her hoe in a way that was not quite a threat. She had a low husky voice but, Lufo realized, she couldn't be over eighteen. Strong-limbed, sun-bronzed with startling blue eyes, she reminded him that he hadn't had a woman in too long, not for nearly a week . . .

"Wondered if I could buy some water," he said, fishing with two fingers into his jeans.

She completed her half of the ritual by pushing with one hand, palm down. "No, but you can have some. Childe, fetch our visitor the pitcher," she said past him, then walked around him. He allowed it; even if anyone had a bead on Lufo, he'd be crazy to take chances with two vulnerable females so near.

Lufo followed the blonde's gesture, ducked into the soddy, let his eyes adjust to cool shadows. His nostrils tasted earth, smoke, cornmeal, goat cheese; the odors of a clean soddy. He smiled at the tiny girl as he took the plastic pitcher from her; paused before drinking. "Got a broke-down pony out in the brush. You suppose I could talk with your man?"

"I thought you were thirsty," said the girl-woman.

He nodded, took a mouthful, rinsed and spat it out the door onto hard-packed earth. Then he drank, feeling danger somewhere near. But perhaps it was only the low roof that seemed to threaten his head.

"I can look at your horse," she said when he handed the pitcher back.

"Well,—I'd like to talk to your man first," he said carefully. "I'm not alone, but I didn't wan't to worry you folks. The others are out in the cedars."

"I know," she said, smiling for the first time, showing strong small even teeth and a confidence that was downright unsettling. "You three have been out there for an hour with a half-dozen thirsty ponies. Anyway, consider me the man of the house."

"You weren't worried—without a man here?"

This time she made a distinct effort to *hide* a smile. "If I need help, it's a lot nearer than you think, buckaroo." She used the anglo pronunciation instead of 'vaquero'; it was a subtle shading of language that said she was not intimidated by this lean athletic macho.

"Thought it might be that way," he said, utterly failing to understand her. "But I do need to talk with whoever makes the decisions here."

"Talk away," she said. "But if you're running drugs, just keep running."

Negative headshake. "You don't mind any other kind of little independent operation then," he hazarded.

She reached out to tousle the hair of the small silent girl before saying, "We're pretty independent here ourselves. My name's Sandy Grange and this is my sister, Childe. She doesn't talk."

Now his answering smile was more relaxed. With the faintest stress on the word 'independent', she aligned herself with the Indy party. At the least, it meant a somewhat liberal interpretation of the law. At most, it meant you leaned toward the rebels—or were one of them yourself.

Lufo walked to the door, spoke into his comm unit: "Bring the horses in, Espinel, it's clear. I have some negotiating do do with a lady."

"First five-cylinder-word I've heard for months," said Sandy.

"Sorry."

"For what? Music to my soul," she said, then turned quickly to Childe and whispered something, patting the little backside as it whisked out the door. She stepped to the doorway and called, "And don't you dare let him come nosing around up here; I know how you love to show off!" Turning to her guest again, pleasantly: "Don't ask. I don't want trouble any more than you do. Now then: what do I call you, and what's your problem?"

You didn't ask for real names in Wild Country unless you courted violence. The title of a very funny new Southwest ballad was "What Was Your Name In Streamlined America?". It acknowledged that many a saddle tramp was a fugitive from Fed justice.

"Lufo Albeniz," he said, shaking her small work-hardened hand. "We're packing some things back to Ciudad Acuña—they strayed, you might say. Very delicate stuff but as you put it, don't ask. In fact, it's so delicate we need to repack it. What if I offered you two hundred pesos gold to go into Rocksprings for a day?"

She pursed delectable lips in a silent whistle, her brows arched. Then she reached under the silky blonde mane and scratched behind her ear in a gesture so artless, in a way so unfeminine, that he could have hugged her in sexless camaraderie. "I didn't realize I could be so easily tempted," she said.

She waved him to a homemade cane-bottomed couch, trundled her Lectroped to one side, and plumped herself cross-legged on the floor, fetchingly limber for a girl so nicely rounded. "This isn't the first time someone's borrowed my place for a day or two," she explained, "but the last time I came back to find the soddy just ruined. Somebody had spilled a lot of blood and mezcal in here, shot my mirror all to flinders, even disamorced my generator."

"Dis-what?"

She grinned. "Remember the Rosicrucians? A M O R C? The light and power of the universe, and all that. Well, those ladrones took away my light and power. Disamorced me for a month. That's worth more than two hundred to me."

Lufo nodded uncertainly; this anglo hotsy had more kinds of language than a polyglot parrot. "We intend to work, not play—but you don't know that. Okay, I give you four hundred, just about all I have, and you come back in a few days and give half of it back. Fair enough?"

A slow smile: "Four hundred pesos? What if I don't come back?"

He met it with one of his own, feral, canny: "That garden's too well-tended, hija. You'll come back."

"You're right, I—uh-oh," she said, starting to rise. Lufo beat her to the doorway; he'd heard the commotion as soon as she.

Something had made the horses skittish as they approached the soddy, for the wiry latino, Espinel, had all he could do to keep his mount and the two he led under control. Behind him were three pack-horses in a string, carrying polymer-wrapped bundles much too long for any pack animal. Thompson, a medium-sized anglo afoot, hung onto his leadrope with foolhardy courage as the pack-horses milled and bucked around him, their ears laid back, nostrils distended, eyes rolling in fear.

Lufo sprinted around Espinel's remuda of three and hurled himself into the melee heedless of flying hooves and dirt clods, snatching at leadropes, making things worse by rushing headlong at the already panicky animals. Abruptly, one horse went down in a tangle of lashings, its almost weightless bundles rolling free. Lufo took a deathgrip on the second animal, the third growing calm after Thompson wiped his bandanna across its nose. Lufo saw that Espinel was leading his animals away from the soddy, found himself jerked off his feet, was thrown bodily under Thompson's horse and rolled stunned in the dust.

The pack-horse sunfished once, its bundles slipping, and set off for distant places. "There goes the rectenna," screamed Thompson. "For God's sake, Espinel!"

The latino's head jerked to and fro like a puppet's as he surveyed a situation gone to garbage and getting worse, and his restive mount helped his decision. Espinel vaulted from his saddle in one fluid instant, unslinging the wire-stocked carbine from his shoulder; staggered upright, spent two seconds aiming, and fired a brief burst at the fleeing animal. The pack-horse jerked, continued at a canter, then faltered and fell.

Sandy was running toward the groggy Lufo but Thompson waved her forward to Espinel's horse. "Grab the reins, lady, and stand fast!" Sandy did as she was told, reflecting that these men had priorities they valued more than their skins.

Espinel remounted then, and with Thompson's help managed to get the five horses tethered at the nearest cedar. Thompson wiped the nose of each animal, muttering. Sandy helped Lufo to stand and gasped as she saw the bare patch of skin on one side of his head.

"You're lucky he didn't kick your head off," she said with more tenderness than anger, and started to inspect the wound.

But Lufo shook his head and drew away. "That's an old scar, hija," he said, almost chuckling, "and I'm kinda sensitive about it. Here's where he got me," he finished, pulling up his shirt.

The hoofprint was an angry blue crescent at the side of his belly. The lowest rib was cracked but not floating free, and Lufo insisted on walking alone to his comrades. Sandy studied them, then the horses nervously testing the breeze, and walked back to refill her pitcher.

The three men paused outside the soddy to lay their bundles down before knocking. "You've rented it," Sandy called, "so don't stand on ceremony."

It appeared, as she ministered to them, that the rental terms would have to change. As Thompson put it, "We have no choice now, Lufo. We'll have to launch from here if I can repair the damage. It could take a week."

It was Lufo's decision to offer the four hundred in gold to Sandy in exchange for meals and her silence. "We'll sleep out with the stock, hija, but there's something we have to keep inside, and it's big. We can't take chances on anybody seeing it. If you have visitors you'll have to keep 'em out of here."

She looked at Thompson, whose quick precise speech tagged him as a nor'easter. "Sorry, but that's the way it is," he said. Espinel only shrugged as if willing to accept whatever the others decided.

Sandy had options none of them could know; and had she chosen, she could have arranged their departure in one Godawful hurry. But Sandy did not feel threatened; she would accept the situation. "You'd best hobble your mounts and take them down in the draw yonder," she said. "Less breeze down there, and some forage."

"Something in the air, es cierto," Espinel agreed. "No bear or cougar in these parts, señorita?"

They had moved on in the interests of health but Sandy only said, "No. By the way, Mr. Thompson, what's on that bandanna of yours? It certainly worked miracles in calming your ponies."

"Mentholated jelly," he said. "A horse can't smell anything past it. Espinel taught me that."

"Kerosene works okay, but not so good," Espinel said shyly. "Lufo, can you ride with that rib stove in?"

"He won't have to for a week," said Thompson, "but he may have to do some digging."

Lufo: "What for? The launcher?"

"No, to bury that damn' pony. It'll draw buzzards."

"I had no choice," said Espinel.

"You did right," Lufo said quickly.

"Don't worry about the pony," Sandy put in. "I

can butcher it out, and what I don't smoke or tan will go into my compost heap."

"I hadn't thought about that. You've got your own cottage industry here, don't you," Thompson said admiringly.

"Yes—but keep wiping your ponies' noses," Sandy warned. "As long as they're here they'll be spooky."

"You must have one hell of a compost heap," Thompson joked.

"It has an air about it," Sandy admitted. "And those big bundles of yours have an air, too—of mystery. What is it, some kind of secret weapon?"

Silence. Then, "She'll see it anyhow," Thompson mused.

"And she'll be an accomplice, which should keep her quiet," Lufo said, grunting in pain as he stood up. "Let's go get the stuff. We can lay it out inside the soddy while Espinel stakes the horses out."

"You've really piqued my curiosity," Sandy murmured, watching as the men carried the bundles in.

"Young and the Feds wouldn't put it quite that way," said Thompson, peeling back the polymer from one bundle. "They know Mexico can't afford holo satellites, and they didn't expect anybody to build an antenna thirty-five klicks high along the border. This one strayed too far into Wild Country and somebody nailed it with a laser—but it landed a few klicks North of here. We hoped to get it back across the Rio Grande for repairs but now I'm afraid I'll have to fly it back." He spread his hands above the naked bundle as if it were self-explanatory.

Sandy saw a protective framework of cottonwood, bound carefully with cord. Inside was an intricate gossamer structure covered with an almost invisible film and supported within the framework by a jury-rig of rubber bands as protection against shock or abrasion. Nevertheless, the elegant structure was ripped and buckled in places. Certain that she had misunderstood something, Sandy said, "You're telling me this is part of a tower that's thirty-five *kilometers* high?"

"Does the same job—and relays holo programs that the Feds manage to keep off their captive networks in Streamlined America," Thompson nodded. "That includes anything Governor Jim Street and the Indys have to say about little matters like industrial cartels, strike-breaking goon squads, and a team of what seem to be government assassins. What the governor has here," he tapped the gossamer structure lightly, "is a medium that's out of control. Blanton Young's control," he amended, beaming. "It's called a Boucher relay."

Sandy smiled while she wrinkled her forehead in amused disbelief. "But—but it looks like a huge model airplane!"

Thompson's hand formed an 'OK' in the air. "Dead center," he said.

CHAPTER 16

The Boucher relay was no model, but clearly reflected its modeler's origins. Kukon and MacCready, both pioneers, had both drawn on model techniques to develop aircraft that were ultralight for their times. It had been a third modeler, Boucher, who proved that balsa and plastic film could be

mated to solar cells for a permanent media relay
in the sky.

Essentially the Boucher relay was an incredibly
lightweight aircraft driven by an electric motor,
its wing panels glistening with the fire-opal glitter
of featherweight photovoltaic cells. Catapulted like
a sailplane, a Boucher craft used both multichannel
radio control and sun-sensors to provide its orientation. The earliest of these superb devices had
boasted wingspans of nearly ten meters with overall weights under ten kilos, thanks to handforming
techniques.

For two generations, said Stan Thompson as he
worked, Americans had been urged to buy prefab
toys that gradually deprived fledging engineers of
construction techniques, stress-analytical knowledge, and optimum performance—for no prefabri-
cated gadget could compete against the best hand-
crafted models. A 'Wakefield' model, hurtling almost
vertically upward with a propeller driven by only
forty grams of rubber band, was a culmination of
science and art; and looked it. Soviet-influenced
countries seemed to understand the research value
of the small Wakefield models, for their craft often
won Worldwide competition events and enriched
their understanding of high-efficiency aircraft while
Americans watched and ignored the implications.

By the end of the Twentieth cent. only a few
enthusiasts built these gossamer brutes; but those
few tended to be stress analysts, architects, aero-
dynamicists. Wakefield techniques tended to interest those who could combine the mind of a theo-
rist and the hands of a watchmaker. Stan Thompson
qualified on both counts.

Sandy Grange watched Thompson uncrate the
ultralight craft with dwindling disbelief and growing appreciation as he spoke. "What Boucher proved
was that you could build an aircraft that would fly

for years," Thompson said, pausing to cluck over a cracked spar. "Once you get the little bugger up above the weather, fifteen klicks or so, there's not much to impede sunlight."

"Except nightfall," Sandy murmured.

"That's where Boucher's vision came in. He designed 'em to climb so high that, by nightfall, they're over thirty klicks high. They go like hell in that thin air but so what? They're radio-controlled and they keep circling—more or less geostationary over some chosen spot.

"With such ridiculous wing-loading, the sink-rate is lower than a lizard's navel, and the aircraft carries storage cells to keep the propeller going at night. By dawn, it's still fifteen klicks up and sunlight recharges the accumulators—which are over there in the fuselage," he said, nodding to the package Lufo was unwrapping. "So up it goes again until nightfall."

"I don't see any propeller in front," she said.

"It's a pusher. The first Boucher relays were conventional, but this rig is a 'Daytwipper'—designed around the rectenna for a holo system. The fuselage must be almost a meter wide to hold that gear, so somebody thought of making a lifting-body fuselage. Actually it's a triple-delta shape with air-control vanes to keep airflow where you need it for maximum lift. The Daytripper has a nine-meter span, with a butterfly tail up front for still more lift, and wings at the rear. The technical term is 'canard'," he finishd.

Pregnant silence from Sandy before, "That means 'hoax' in French, doesn't it?"

He blinked. "Does it?"

Her gaze was a challenge. "Are you pulling my leg, Mr. Thompson? Look at it from my view: I'm being offered four hundred pesos so you can use my soddy to repair an airplane that flies *forever*.

BOUCHER RELAY
SUMMARY SHEETS

SUMMARY DATA

DESIGNATION: BOUCHER RELAY DAYTRIPPER   **CENCOM REVISION:** 5 Apr 2002

DEPLOYMENT: Mexican commerical media

SPECIFICATIONS:

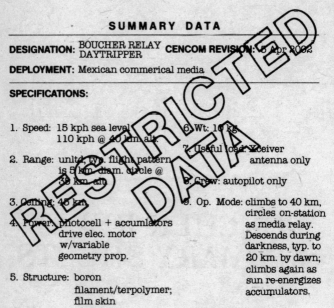

1. Speed: 15 kph sea level
   110 kph @ 40 km alt.

2. Range: unltd, typ. flight pattern
   is 5 km. diam. circle @
   30 km. alt.

3. Ceiling: 45 km.

4. Power: photocell + accumulators
   drive elec. motor
   w/variable
   geometry prop.

5. Structure: boron
   filament/terpolymer;
   film skin

6. Wt: 10 kg.

7. Useful load: xceiver
   antenna only

8. Crew: autopilot only

9. Op. Mode: climbs to 40 km,
   circles on-station
   as media relay.
   Descends during
   darkness, typ. to
   20 km. by dawn;
   climbs again as
   sun re-energizes
   accumulators.

10. Mfr: Unknown.

11. NOTE: ALL PERFORMANCE DATA ESTIMATED FROM
    INCOMPLETE REPORTS. POSSESSION OF ANY
    PORTION OF THIS DEVICE IS A FELONY.

Boucher Relay: 'Daytripper' model

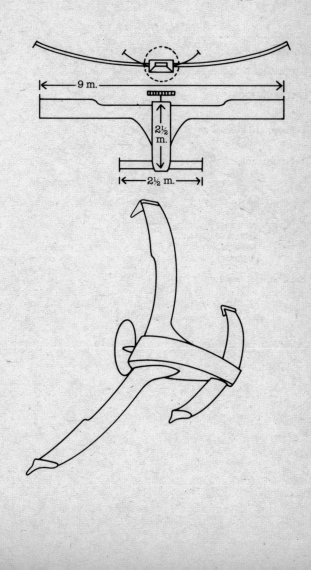

But you brought it here on pack-horses! And if that doesn't stick in my craw, you ask me to swallow the idea that it beams forbidden media into Wild Country."

Stan Thompson pulled out ancient bifocals, chortling as he adjusted them. "Actually, they're scheduled to come down in Mexico once a year for maintenance—but yes, that's about it. We knew this one had gone off-course and landed in this area, and for our purposes, for a low profile, a horse is still the best way to travel. I figured I could trouble-shoot the Daytripper and get it launched again, but I found it had been damaged too much. First by a beam of some sort that melted part of the film, and then in landing. Took us days to find it.

"I decided it'd be easier to dismantle it and take it back to Mexico for repairs, but I was wrong; it won't take rough handling.

"Now I either repair it and launch it from here— primitive as our accomodations are for it—or we destroy a hundred thousand pesos' worth of Boucher relay and go back empty-handed."

"Well, I'll believe it when I see it," Sandy replied.

Lufo had been listening. Now he pointed to Sandy's old holovision set. "Does your holo work?"

"Usually. For the past week I haven't been able to get XEPN, the Piedras Negras chan—." She turned back, mouth open slightly, to gaze at the disassembled craft. "Well I be damn," she whispered.

"Nine days, to be exact," Thompson muttered. "By the time I get it back on station, a lot of nice folks in Wild Country will have been without Indy media for two weeks."

"I thought you were working for the Mexicans."

"I am—because Governor Street asked me to.

How else can he get media coverage into Streamlined America?"

Sandy mulled that over for long minutes. The
credentials of James Street were well-known: Major General, USA, (ret.); Governor of Texas; Under-
secretary of State; then unsuccessful candidate for
the Presidency on the Independent ticket. In Texas
he was still 'the governor', a man who could sit a
horse or kiss a baby with the best of them. But
Street's anti-Federalist rhetoric had hardened after the war; Blanton Young labelled his trenchant
truths as sedition, and saw that the label became
official. Old Jim Street found himself branded a
rebel fugitive from justice, and knew what brand
of justice he could expect. Thus the official label
became the fact: James Street was the guidon-
bearer for rebel forces in Wild Country.

"Most of the news on the governor confuses me,"
Sandy said finally. "I heard on FBN that he's a
dying man."

"Sure you did. He isn't," Lufo assured her. "Who
d'you think plans strategy for the unions?"

"I hadn't thought about it. But I should think
the governor's too old to be sneaking around the
country like that."

"Mostly they come to him. And that's about all I
want to say about it," Lufo ended gruffly.

Stan Thompson moved sadly between the sepa-
rated pieces of the Boucher relay, sighing as though
the device were an injured child. "It'll be a mira-
cle if this ol' Daytripper makes another trip. Lufo,
will you get my repair kit? May as well start now."

But Espinel had anticipated him, carrying the
kit over his shoulder as he entered the soddy.
Thompson took it with a nod, then turned back to
stare at the latino. "Trouble?" Lufo had seen the
look too; stepped to the doorway, his sidearm ready.

"I don' know," Espinel replied. "But I took a

ride aroun' the perimeter. Miz Sandy, you got any pigs here?"

She swallowed hard, then spread her hands. "Where would I keep them?"

"I guess you wouldn'. But I see the biggest hog tracks I ever see in my life out there," Espinel said. "Un monstruo, prints big as my hand."

Lufo crossed himself. "I thought that damn' thing was just a Wild Country legend. No *wonder* the ponies were spooked!"

Thompson fitted a scalpel-like blade into a handle; began to slice film from a shattered wing spar. "What the devil are you talking about, Lufo?"

"The devil is right. Used to be a story about a Russian boar that escaped from a Texas Aggie research station near Sonora, North of here. Big as a pony, mean as a grizzly; sooner eat a man than look at him and has bowie knife tusks to do it with. Sandy Grange, where the hell are you going?"

She paused at the door to reply: "I, uh, have to find Childe. No, you stay there. I'll be all right."

"If you say so," Lufo said, doubting it, replacing the pistol with reluctance. He turned back to Espinel. "She's survived this long with that monster out there in the brush. Espinel, you sure about these tracks?"

Espinel essayed a wan smile, put his thumbs and middle fingers together to form an oval the size of a human hand.

"Mierda! So Ba'al is loose out here after all," said Lufo.

Thompson: "Who?"

"That's what they named him after he took a lot of slugs and killed some people. The false god; the devil; Ba'al. I hope that cute little rubia knows what she's doing out there. And we better mount a sentry at night; he might have a taste for horse-flesh."

CHAPTER 17

Sandy's journal, 3 Jun '02

The soddy is small for a rebel boarding house, but the pay—if I can believe them!—will be good. No fear I'll ever forget this day. Stan Thompson: healer's hands, monomaniacal in his work, preoccupied. I might be any age or gender for all he cares. Espinel: wiry, shy & deferential, not your average Mex bandit! It hurt him to shoot that pony. & Lufo Albeniz? A prototype, healthy laughing macho animal, moves like a big snake but crushes you with those dark mestizo eyes.

Nearly two hundred kilos of meat & serviceable hide but I'm exhausted. Childe took some leavings. Swears she can keep him placated & downwind as long as need be. Hope so. Don't want rebel blood on my hands. But if Lufo should try what I see in his glance, I'd whistle in a second.

Wouldn't I?

CHAPTER 18

Ten minutes after the plush executive hoverbus whirred from its lair under the IEE tower, Eve Simpson saw the southernmost tip of the Great Salt Lake pass on her right. That meant the bus was making better time since she'd urged Mills to wangle a police-freq. trip plotter. Once Eve tasted the lucullan comfort of the big fandriven bus, she refused to visit the desert lab in anything else. Besides, it needed no driver, skating smoothly above the potholed freeway with its onboard plotter in command.

With her police module, of course, other traffic was shuttled aside for Eve's passage, countermanding whatever other ideas the drivers might have. That way Eve could whirl along at absolute top speed and the hell with optimum energy trip plots.

The hoverbus drew on narrowcast power transmitters along the freeway until Eve passed Nephi. After that it would automatically receive LOS—line-of-sight—recharges from the transmitters that began to dot high points in the heartland of Zionized, Streamlined America. Those LOS recharges were frequent, for Eve's demands on everything she used were rarely less than the maximum. She had punched in the Nephi-Salina-Green River route, for example, instead of the more direct Provo-Price-Green River route because she did not enjoy the faint side-loads on her great bulk when the bus took a twisty course.

Her chosen route was longer and took more power. So what? Eve had power to burn. If Marengo—poor haunted, hairy, heavy-hung Marengo—was as good as his word, she'd have still more power soon. And he'd damned well better come through or she'd cut his dose of dreamstuff. She liked to think Marengo Chabrier enjoyed her sexuality as much as he enjoyed taking a nice long hit; and therefore that was what she *did* think.

At Salina she adjusted the lounge pneumatics, lit a filtertip joint, selected a porn cassette from her shoulder bag and lay back, her own vastness diminished by the room-sized insulated compartment. The fact that viewing such salacious stuff was now punishable, and ownership of it a felony, only heightened its charm for Eve. Since that stupid fiasco in Santa Fe she'd been horny as a rhino and not much easier to please. Her demand for sexual acceptance to counter that event was not entirely subliminal; with Chabrier, she knew, she could slake her thirsts. If it hadn't been so much trouble, she'd have plotted some revenge on that emerald-eyed young hit-man, Quantrill. But there was plenty of time. Sooner or later he would wander across her right-of-way, an ant on her freeway, and then . . .

The little holodrama unfolded before her, the voluptuous cowgirl, Patty, flirting with the wrangler but clearly more interested in the erection of her pony. Presently the heroine—for in a sense she had to be one—found a way to rig a sling under her little stallion.

Eve began to enjoy herself—more so when she perceived the vibration that rose under her bass-fiddle buttocks when she sat in the right position. She toyed with the pneumatics. The vibration toyed with Eve. Patty toyed with her trusty, lusty steed; and as the hoverbus neared the highway summit it occurred to Eve that a lot of summits were approaching simultaneously.

Eve reached down with tender sausage fingers; womanipulated herself, laughing at the holo and at the world. She flicked off the audio and, in a fit of whimsy, began to sing an ancient ballad, 'Always,' in her clear sweet soprano. In this context of purest narcissism, every phrase seemed funnier than the last and, once she'd sung ". . . need a helping hand, . . ." Eve rolled in her couch gasping with laughter and orgasmic release.

She flicked the pornodrama off then, suspecting fakery in the action. She wasn't sure it was possible to make it with a horse. Even if it was, she'd leave *this* little Cow Patty electronically stranded in mid-hump. It was a concept as silly, as willful, as tacky as the holoporn itself. Eve gloried in that because she could afford to do it when most citizens did not dare even watch such things. Pleasure without consequences: the goal and the province of power.

Eve had reached a pillowy mellow before the bus passed a road sign: NO SERVICES NEXT 170 KM., and whipped down the grass-obscured surface of an ancient ranching road near Green River, Utah. Five klicks South of that turnoff, a decrepit-looking gate of steel pipe accepted a signal from the trip plotter and swung open until the bus whooshed by flinging its broad flat wake of dust and weed seed.

It never occurred to Eve that the bus might someday have a breakdown, leaving her stranded. Her position in such matters was that no machine would dare risk such wrath as hers.

Forty klicks further, beyond the warning signs, Eve spied the P-beam obelisks that defined and protected IEE's San Rafael desert lab. The bus did not pause, or need to. Finally she saw the two-story chain-link fence and the earthen berm inside. The lab, dug into the desert floor, was perfectly placed, roughly midway between three geographic features. They were called Goblin Valley, Dirty Devil River, and Labyrinth Canyon. The names were old and apt. As Boren Mills had once drily remarked, it was no tourist trap.

The last automatic gate swung aside and then Eve's hoverbus settled on concrete, near the elevator platform atop the berm. Chabrier waited for her, alone on an electric cart, wearing his bright tragic smile that she knew so well.

A tongue of ramp slid from the side of the bus and Chabrier, familiar with Eve's desires, backed the cart up onto the deep pile carpet. Only then did he step down, making his slight continental bow. "You are early, madame," he murmured.

Eve warmed to the attentions of Marengo Chabrier. His deepset gray eyes were hooded by eyebrows so thick and black that they met in a ledge above the strong nose. His lashes were luxuriant, his cheekbones Scythian, his mouth sensuous and as small as Eve's own. The open collar of his beige IEE coverall revealed what seemed to be a tee-shirt of black fleece, but was body hair. The stocky Chabrier was marvelously endowed with hair except, as Eve knew, the top of his head and two bare islands flanking his backbone. Eve envied Cow Patty for her pony a bit less; she herself had access to a gentle ape with two doctorates and a tongue that could clean a mayonnaise jar.

"I couldn't wait to test your magic, curly," she vamped, letting him help her to her feet. "Let me see it."

The long lashes flickered over his sad sheep eyes. "Here?"

She nodded, chins aquiver, then emitted a volley of giggles as he reached for his coverall closure. "Not that, you fool," she said, staying his hand, rubbing the mat of curls over his sternum. "That I can see in your rooms—and I intend to." The purr took on a hint of rasp: "Isn't the amulet ready?"

"Ah." His open palm indicated the cart seat. "That is in my rooms as well. M'sieur Mills has many devices to monitor and I should be sorry to be recorded aboveground with such a thing. You however are a law unto yourself, n'est ce pas?"

"C'est tout dire," she agreed, and vented a whoop as Chabrier sped his cart down the ramp. She clutched her bag in her lap. In it lay much of her charm: the drugs for which Chabrier, as lab administrator, was responsible.

Inside via the elevator to the first level, then down ramps between backlit walls, fat tires squalling on clean linolamat, the air cool and tasting faintly of sidewalks after summer rain. Once during the trip—Eve knew he was taking this route as an informal patrol when they could have gone directly to the lowest level by elevator—a lank mongol hesitated in the passage to let them pass. On his middle-aged face was no trace of recognition that they were anything but machinery. He might have been a machine himself.

"Don't you ever get cabin fever in this dump?"

"We are all well—ah, le reclusion," he said, tardy to catch her idiom, nodding when he did. "We suffer, each in his way."

"But you all take the same prescription."

"In a general way." Quickly he added, "For me it is not so bad; I have you twice a month, ma petite." He nearly strangled on that diminutive term under the circumstances, but knew she liked to hear it.

At last Chabrier reached the utmost depth of the

lab and passed through the chuffing armored doors. Here was no receptionist, but a room with couches. Eve never got used to the jungle of potted greenery there, so many levels under the desert floor, fed with synthetic light and nutrients and even with subtle variations in the air-conditioning currents. Her arm laid on his, Eve swept into Chabrier's rooms to claim the chaise. "Compliments of Boren Mills," she smirked as always, handing him a package labeled PHOTOGRAPHIC FILM. It contained enough drugs to pacify Chabrier's minions for two weeks.

Chabrier tossed it aside as though it were not the most important single facet of his existence; offered her a drink. She accepted, noting the tiniest of tremors in his hands, choosing to think it was her humming sexuality and not something else that provoked it.

"So how goes the scale-up?" She was only making small talk. For Eve, the synthesizer was only an abstract notion, an iffy means to power. Her specialty, media, *was* power. She could not fathom the logic by which Mills had let his early media expertise run to seed while he chased this technological enigma—and by proxy! She had never managed much interest in synthesizers of any size until one of her spaced-out discussions with Chabrier, two months before.

The scale-up program, Chabrier admitted with the shrug of a much thinner man, was still in Phase Two. Phase One, design analysis of the unit Mills had committed murder to obtain, had been complete for over a year. Phase Three, if it ever arrived, would be a big unit, one for which Mills would cheerfully kill millions. But Phase Two was that crucial interval between analysis and synthesis, without which Phase Three could not begin.

Some philosophers of science virtually ignored

this transition phase because, bluntly, it eluded them. Mills revealed his partial understanding—and mistrust—of it by calling it 'interphase brainstorming'. Marengo Chabrier understood the creative process better; it was he who termed it the 'gestation' phase.

An organism recapitulates the development of its race, as a human fetus will reveal gill slits in its early growth. But the organism does more, when it mutates beyond. The change is made real, not merely potential, during gestation. A plan gestates; ideas gestate; earth-shaking social movements gestate—sometimes useful mutations, oftener not.

Marengo Chabrier understood that few mutations become dominant, that ideas are rarely more than the sums of their parts. He also understood that IEE's chief exec was demanding a useful, dominant mutation tailored to fit. More worrisome still, Chabrier understood that short-term success, measured in these terms, was damned unlikely. It was a remnant of intellectual honesty that made him use the term 'gestation', for it promised nothing beyond recapitulation.

Most worrisome of all, Chabrier knew that Mills was *very* unlikely to let a lab full of addicts flush various expensive shits through their systems forever.

One way or another, the synthesizer scale-up program would be terminated someday and, like as not, Mills would reveal it with a handful of permanent personnel terminations. Slow poisons in the drugs? That was why Chabrier had them chemically analyzed before he dispensed them to his lab staff. He would, in any case, dispense them—though his friendship with Sun and Ming would make that act painful. But Chabrier himself would then turn to his clean stash, and would either escape or plead for his life.

He knew he had no hope of crossing the San Rafael desert without help. That was why he hoped to infatuate this great sow, Eve Simpson. And if sexual bonds alone were tenuous, he might further ensure her help by making her party to a deception that would drive a wedge between the woman and Boren Mills. C'est le premier pas qui coûte, he knew; that first step which required so much resolve. But Chabrier had taken that step two months before, and Eve had cavorted like a Disney hippo at the idea. It had been her own idea, in fact, to disguise the thing as an outsized amulet—for she owned a jewel large enough, unique enough, to account for its size and whatever security precautions she might arrange.

As Chabrier was bemoaning his most recent failures to scale up the Chinese synthesizer, Eve cut in. "Well then, how about our little scale *down*?" Her face was alight with mischief.

He paused, switching mental tracks. "It functions," he said.

"Omigod, does it? I mean—what won't it make? How much at a time? What do I feed it? Any batteries to change? *Give*, goddammit!"

His last shred of suspicion—that she was baiting him on behalf of Mills—evaporated with her outburst. He winked, walked to his safe, spent his own good time opening it, and withdrew a folded kerchief. With a flourish, he shook something from its folds, dangled it from a chain of brushed stainless steel. Eve's mouth was a small 'o' as she tracked its pendulum swing.

"It looks naked," she said. "Can you put the Ember in the thingummy now?"

"The bezel? Yes, if you have it with you."

She ripped open her bag, tore its inner lining, and pulled out a tiny velour bag. The Ember of

Venus slid into her palm; and now it was Chabrier's turn to gawk.

The automated Venus sampler craft had found no true life on Venus. Mineral and gas samples, scooped up for physical return to Earth orbit, had mostly confirmed earlier data. The surface temperature of the shrouded planet was, after all, nearly five hundred degrees celsius.

But one mineral specimen, taken from an arroyo at the lip of Venus's Ishtar highlands, became wedged at one side of the container which was to maintain Venus-normal temperature during the long voyage back. The specimen gradually cooled in space and was quickly discovered by the sampler recovery team. The exact mechanism by which a mineral specimen became the Ember of Venus was still argued in learned journals, but its existence was unarguable fact.

Almost a centimeter thick after slices had been taken from it, the Ember was an ovoid the breadth of a hen's egg. It was under great internal stress. Despite the most careful progress of the diamond saw, one chip had flown from the side of the jewel.

Otherwise it was perfect, its surface smooth as a soap bubble but with voluptuous prominences on its face. The Ember of Venus compared to an Aussie fire opal as the opal compared to a gallstone. It had been presented to Eve by the CEO of LockLever as inducement for certain favorable media reports in 1998, when her body was merely lush and not yet obese. Eve had performed those services while passing sensitive data on to LockLever's competitor, Mills—which assured her position at IEE.

Thus Eve's possession of the Ember was irregular, but not illegal. She had often thought of wearing it. Now, to decoy attention from the device it covered, it would find employment at Eve's throat.

"Incroyable," Chabrier whispered. "May I?" He

took the stone between thumb and middle finger, intending to check its fit into the bezel he had prepared, but paused again as if thunderstruck. The translucent flickering depth of the gem seemed bottomless; iridescent hues of every color intersected, shifted, moved as if impelled by some viscous liquid.

Chabrier shook off the urge to snarl, 'mine, *mine*,' chuckling at himself. He laid the Ember into the bezel of the device in his other hand. Then he smiled at the irony. For the Ember of Venus was only façade for something of far greater value, a device more significant than any jewel: a tiny version of the Chinese synthesizer.

"Come, we shall imprison your Ember," he said, and she came out of the couch as if scalded by it. Together, for Eve would not let the jewel out of her sight, they moved to his littered desk. He cemented the Ember in place, then arranged the tiny padded metal fingers to clasp its edge while she looked on. Wordlessly he lifted the chain, spread it with both hands, smiled into the eyes of Eve as he hung it around her neck.

"Let me imprison *your* ember," she drawled. She was smiling, breathing deeply; and without taking her gaze from his she began to open the beige coverall.

Presently, after she had consumed his first orgasm, she lifted the amulet and licked that, too, as if by wetting it she could bring out still more lustre. Murmuring: "Now that you've taken advantage of me, you dirty old monkey, tell me how this fucking thing works!"

Rubber-legged, Chabrier walked with her to the chaise and began to instruct her. Set into small bezels in an oval pattern around the Ember were fifteen opaque black diamonds, cabochon cut, surely the zenith of understatement since they functioned as studs for the tiny integral computer terminal.

At the top and bottom of the bezel were globes of brushed stainless, the size of a child's marble. A grid in the upper globe was the air intake; the synthesizer did not create mass, but converted it—in this case, from nitrogen. The lower globe was the yield chamber, and a hidden detent allowed it to split apart. Isotope powered, the minuscule device had a yield measured in grams per hour.

Eve's amulet could not synthesize living tissue, of course, nor materials requiring great heat and pressure, e.g., diamonds. But using her access code to CenCom, Eve could request the chemical composition of many substances; punch the memory stud to place CenCom's response in the memory circuits; and then request a sample of that substance in the yield chamber. Chabrier had arbitrarily placed a one-gram maximum on a given yield as a safety precaution.

The readout display was hidden; Chabrier had put it inside the false back of the amulet, fearing that an overt display might reveal too much to any admirer of the Ember.

"So I memorize the functions of the diamond studs," she repeated, "and use the first thirteen for alphanumerics with the 'change function' stud." She saw his nod, then made a pouty-mouth: "But it won't make a kittycat?"

He laughed outright. "Mais non, it can only give you inanimate joys." He saw her puzzlement. "Gold dust, tetrahydrocannabinol, . . ."

She turned it over, weighed it in her hand. Very quietly: "I don't think I'll use it for anything more than a toy."

"I should be very dismayed if you did. I hope you will not be tempted by the urge to create—substances that could endanger you." His expression was serious, the long lashes low on his cheeks. Her wilfullness was a calculated risk which he must take, for if she died he would have no confederates.

"You're sweet, Marengo," she said. "What say we create a gram of harmless THC."

"Please do—and always flush the yield chamber carefully," he warned. "You must not ask for poisonous or radioactive items. That would not be wise."

"I'll be wise," she promised. If she had a motto, it was 'promise them anything . . .'

CHAPTER 19

Seth Howell stalked back and forth on the podium, cracking his big knuckles as he surveyed the rover gathering. "You get the best food, the best training, the best pay you could ask for," he growled. "And I don't have to tell you that if those carrots don't work, Salter could always use the stick." Howell tapped himself behind the ear; let his hard glance ricochet among the impassive rovers. Howell, of course, had no mastoid critic; for him, the finger-tap gesture came easily. "So let's understand each other: there will be no, repeat *no*, refusal of missions for any reason whatever. Some of you have been walking too near that line."

Dawna Clinton, easily the tallest of the half-dozen female rovers and the only black in the cadre, uncoiled from her seat. Watching her stance,

Quantrill thought the woman must sleep at attention. "With respect, Mr. Howell, I'd like to hear you comment on some ques—observations," she amended quickly. Nearby, little Max Pelletier shifted uneasily and looked away as if to find further distance from her. Pelletier and Clinton were an unlikely pair, but deadly little Max was one rover who tended to choose a buddy. At the moment, Quantrill realized, he must be wishing it wasn't Dawna Clinton.

"This isn't a press interview, Clinton, but go ahead," Howell snapped.

Voice clear, almost strident with stress: "Since this is a general ass-chew, I gather the rumors are true." She watched something flicker across Howell's face; continued: "Some rover has been turned, and the Indys are going to run an expose on us. Unless we disappear a few folks as a warning."

"Two out of three ain't bad," Howell cracked. No one smiled. "No comment on the 'turned rover' hypothesis; did you expect one? I'll say this much: we know two leak sources, and we're letting them run loose for now." Howell noted the looks among the rovers, most of them some nonverbal variant of, 'could it be you?' "Sit down, Clinton. By now you've all received your mission files. Some of you will have a pair. No doubt some of you, in spite of orders, have been comparing notes and put two and two together.

"And got five. It isn't the Indy *party* we have to stop. It's the rebels who have infiltrated some religious sects, lodge organizations, and yes, some radicals among the Indys. The Independent party itself must always be viewed as the loyal opposition, a necessary part of a two-party system in Streamlined America." Howell's husky tenor had become almost singsong, repeating the public dicta of Blanton Young.

Kent Ethridge's voice was weary, but cutting: "I learned more poly sci from you, Howell, than from every prof in Iowa State. Are you telling us now, in spite of what you used to teach in T Section, that a gaggle of hits against a loose confederation of rebels is going to stop the expose? Not *escalate* the trouble?"

"I know you have your orders." Something in the set of the heavy shoulders spelled embarrassment to Quantrill, who could not recall ever seeing the big man register that particular emotion before. But Howell had his orders, too . . .

"And if it escalates," Ethridge went on, voice as dead, as inexorable, as the collapse of an ancient mausoleum, "won't a rover be a millstone around the government's neck? And what, I wonder, happens to us in that case?"

Hissing it: "*You have your fuckin' orders.*" Howell passed a hand over the top of his head, took a breath, tried another tack. "The rebs are no longer a loose confederation, Ethridge. They've bypassed the pure guerrilla stage and are organized well enough for us to pinpoint some nerve centers. That's as well-kept a secret as any you'll hear. You sure won't hear it on the media," he snorted.

"Except the outlaw media." Quantrill spoke against his own better judgment. It had occurred to him that Eve Simpson might be a rebel in IEE clothing.

"We know who they are, too," said Howell. "We can jam some transmissions, and the rest is chiefly around the borders where it doesn't upset people in the heartlands where the strength of Streamlined America lies." He caught himself, aware that he was parroting obvious propaganda. "But whatever happens, don't worry that you'd be thrown away. I've seen contingency plans and, believe me, you'd be needed. Believe me," he said again, as though repetition generated its own truth.

Clinton again: "So, in a way, we're cleansing the Indy party of a few infiltrators and using the, ah, soap to warn the Indys against exposing S & R."

"Couldn't put it better myself," Howell nodded. "By now you've realized that things're heating up before the senatorial elections. If your missions don't send the rebels back into their holes, there could be open violence this fall. And wouldn't Canada and Mexico just love that?"

Quantrill sat preoccupied as Howell dismissed them, wondering at the surge of patriotism he had felt. No, Mexico and Canada weren't the enemy. They'd already bitten off as much of Streamlined America as they could chew—and Canada seemed genuinely ready to return border territories as soon as Streamlined America was capable of meeting their needs.

But there might be thirty million Americans who would love to see the Young administration overturned. You couldn't disappear them all. Were they the enemy?

Then the young rover glanced around; caught the hopelessness mirrored in the face of Marbrye Sanger; and again he felt the adrenal surge coursing down his spine. It heralded a sense of purpose he had thought lost forever, and identified the enemy of everything Ted Quantrill represented.

And from that moment on, Ted Quantrill was the enemy.

CHAPTER 20

"You don't like my toy," said Eve with a pretend pout.

"It's awesome," Mills conceded. "It is absolutely unique, it is beyond price, *and it scares the hell out of me!*" He slammed a fist against his console. "It also flies in the face of everything IEE stands for!"

"Like entertainment? Like control of subjects?" Eve studied a jeweled fingernail with elaborate calm.

Mills ticked off his objections as if examining his own manicure. "Wanton display of wealth. A working model of the most mind-boggling economic weapon the world has ever known. It employs chemical inducements, which are a tactical error. And unless I'm missing something, Chabrier made the goddam thing isotope-powered!

"That's just for starters, Eve! I can't let you keep that thing," he said, his hand shaking as he held it out. "Can you imagine what would happen if the wrong hands got control of your bauble?"

Her open-handed slap metronomed his arm, left his hand numb and his wrist aching. The rosebud lips tucked to reveal small sharp incisors: "Can *you* imagine what will happen if the wrong hand reaches for it?" Her blazing countenance, thought Mills, was not entirely sane.

Mills stood up, massaging his wrist, fighting for self-control. She had warned him long ago that her death or disappearance would cause certain letters to be opened, so his first impulse was really out of the question. (All aside from the fact that Eve could lift bigger men than Mills off the ground. He had videotapes of her with Chabrier, labeled 'The Argument For Celibacy'.) Perhaps he could manage to destroy the amulet. It was worth trying. Besides, he still needed her expertise in media research.

He took several long breaths before trusting his voice to be steady. "We'll consider the topic closed. I believe you dropped in for a chat on something more important," he prompted, as if the tiny synthesizer no longer interested him.

"Oh, yeah; those media relays," she said, shuddering the luminous glow of the amulet down her bodice. "I assume they're stratosphere balloons since you didn't seem to think I had the need to know. But you told me the Air Force had laser-equipped delta dirigibles cruising around Bakersfield and Gila Bend looking for targets."

"And other places. We think the translator relays are stealth-equipped Boucher relays, using Israeli electronics to displace the signal so we can't get a fix on the real antenna. We'll zap one sooner or later."

"You already have. Somebody did anyway." She noted his change of expression with glee; the sonofabitch didn't know everything! "At least, there's been a total lack of outlaw holo across a big piece of the Southwest for a week. Maybe there's a delta cruising around near the Big Bend, too."

"There is. They get momentary blips sometimes, and laser-grid whatever's there."

"Well, Ciudad Acuña's multichannel media station seems to be hors de combat. Just thought you'd like to know," she added, and energized her motorized couch as if to leave.

"You're even starting to sound like Chabrier," Mills gibed. "But thanks for the data. I wonder why the Air Force didn't know?"

"I expect they do. Maybe," she returned sweetly, "they didn't think *you* had the need to know."

Mills accepted this riposte with the sad small grin of one bested in a fair game, knowing it would put her at ease, and saw her out. Moments later he was commanding his console, checking the readiness of the facilities in the desert lab.

If Marengo Chabrier could create one amulet-sized synthesizer, he could create a million of them. The sooner Mills had a factory full of standard 'breadbox' size, the sooner he could have the Frenchman disappeared. It meant Mills would have to dump a lot of personal stock to finance the operation, but that was what assets were for.

Later Mills would call up the Lion of Zion for a chat to discuss the success of the delta sorties Mills himself had suggested. If they'd knocked down one of the damned holo relays, maybe they could zap others. But would they stay zapped?

CHAPTER 21

Sandy's journal, 9 Jun '02

Metaphorically, I worked a vein of gold in the caldera of Mount St. Helens this past week: enrichment & terror filled each day. I do not refer to the money, though I finally accepted 200 pesos, return-

ing the rest as my donation to the cause (the only way my honor-bound Lufo would take it).

At first I feared confrontation between Lufo & him but Childe has somehow kept her promise. The 3 men were uneasy on nights when Childe was gone. I gather Espinel has a daughter of his own. How could I tell him that my sister is safer on her mount than any rebel on any fiery stallion?

Later I trembled for Espinel, who sought to protect me from Lufo despite my reassurances that a moonlit stroll on my own spread held no dangers for me—even with Lufo!

Finally I dreaded what I knew must happen: the launch of the graceful Daytripper. Success or failure, it meant the end of their stay. This morn, before the breeze huffed in the cedars, Stan was ready.

Stan: a pitiable red-eyed trembling husk after days & nights with little or no sleep, meals strewn across every work surface, makeshift repair with strips shaved from my weary old bamboo pole after he used all his filament tubes. But last night, Lufo & I returned from a walk to a sight that captured my soul.

A dark form stood near the darker mound of my soddy, both arms supporting a great winged wraith as though offering sacrifice to the moon. We stopped breathless, somewhat fearful, & held each other. I suppose Stan could not wait to make his glide test. I know he wishes he had, now!

The night was quiet, the breeze holding its breath so completely that I could smell the earth—& Lufo's pungent masculinity. The figure moved forward, gathering itself, the enormous bird flexing its pinions like a live thing, & then Stan—freed it. Moonlight flashed long shards of cold white light from the lifting body. In utter silence the lovely thing slid down the night, & I saw that Stan had intended it to find a cradle among my tender young lettuce & peppers.

But a Daytripper spurns vegetables. Vast graceful

wings wavered, tips flexing, & responded to a sudden renegade breeze that reached my upturned face moments later. The craft ghosted shadowlike above my garden, rising, rising, nosing into the breeze, tasting its freedom. Lufo chuckled, hearing Stan's 'Oh, shitshitshit,' but I was terrified. The wind is a treacherous ally in Wild Country.

Stan raced into the soddy—as I learned, to retrieve the microwave control unit. By now, the soarer was high enough that I could see its spindly skeleton through the transparent skin, wheeling gently toward us, a silent spectre drifting across the moon. My tears were testament not to fear now but to its eldritch beauty.

Lufo, of course, was not transfixed as I was. Stan had explained that the languid reverse curves of the flight surfaces make the Daytripper float at scarcely more than a walking pace. Slithering with the wind, now, it moved faster than I can run. Lufo must have realized he must keep it between himself & the moon for visual contact. He leaped away, racing, head turned over one shoulder—& crashed headlong into a small cedar. Curses & consternation, for he had lost sight of the Daytripper while wrenching free.

Stan reappeared from the soddy's nightshadow, & suddenly splinters of moon glinted above me. The Daytripper was answering its homing signal, wheeling ecstatically, now bereft of its lifegiving breeze but striving to clear the trees. I knew that it could not.

I was nearer than Lufo, saw the noiseless craft straighten & begin its descent. It was no more than five meters over my stumbling feet when a wingtip sliced into a cedar top.

The Daytripper pivoted so slowly that I ducked under the long ghostly sweep of the free wing, held my arms out, felt the cool sleekness of plastic film, fell on my backside in the brush. A number 3 'owie', but it could've been prickly pear!

Lufo rushed up gasping, took my dead albatross from me, & stalked back to Stan Thompson on the crest of a wave of curses. I followed, fearful of bloodshed, but Stan had been punished enough. Once we disassembled the wings, we found no damage worse than torn film and a broken wingtip. Stan would not sleep until he had made penitent repairs. Lufo had long-since stormclouded off to relieve Espinel at picket duty with the horses.

The launch, this morn, was almost anticlimactic. Stan drilled Lufo & Espinel until they chafed. After all, snarled Lufo, it didn't even need its chingada propeller last night! The launcher was merely a stake driven into the ground (facing my garden, for Stan is a great believer in failure) with a 20-meter elastic band as thick as Childe's finger, leading from the stake to a rigid loop. A single-post slingshot, then, stretching nearly a hundred meters.

I imagined it would hurl the Daytripper away with great force but, at Stan's command, Espinel severed the tiedown and the gleaming craft accelerated with a sort of langour. It kited to 20-meter height before the elastic slackened and dropped into my corn. Lufo, standing where he might catch it if it faltered, leaped among my tomatoes like an idiot and waved his grungy sombrero, employing last night's curses but this time in joy.

Then Stan engaged the electric drive by remote control, kept his bird's beak facing what breeze there was, & did not let it circle until it was—how far up? Perhaps half a km. In early sunlight the canard shape made it seem a skeletal buzzard soaring backward against sundrenched clouds. I had never seen Stan laugh—& he had never seen me cry. He thought it was because the machine was leaving & I did not enlighten him.

Stan says the Daytripper yields almost no radar echo when its rectenna is inactive (it actually un-

*folds like a hothouse flower inside the lifting body!).
Little danger of an intercept after noon, when Stan
risked a telemeter check. It was fifteen klicks up, near
the Rio Grande—unless the lovely thing was lying. I
wouldn't be surprised, for it seemed a living and
whimsical creature.*

*I did not care about the dark things in Lufo's past,
nor that his real name carries a death sentence with
it. I do care that I may never again feel those cruelly
callused hands, the furnace of his mouth, the—well!
One day Childe will learn to read . . .*

*I hope Lufo lied to impress me, but not when he
promised to return. They lit a shuck for the border in
midafternoon, and they paused to wave as they topped
out on the South ridge. I suspect they'll wetback it
from something Stan let slip about the Indy supply
dumps. How could they imagine I don't know about
the caverns that undermine this entire region? I
watched my daddy slowly die of radiation poisoning
in one & we made it his tomb. Wonder what some
future explorer will think when he discovers my hoard
of playthings in my own cavern. A plastic tea set &
debris from a ghastly air crash. Pathetic toys but my
childhood treasures. Should I tell Lufo what I suspect of the canister I found?*

*At dusk, long after my sorrowful goodbyes, he came
in. Those dainty little strides don't fool me, I know
he was smelling manscent & nothing would serve
but to let him inspect the soddy, me, the windmill
which Stan rewired for me,—everything. He finally
relented, plopped his great breast flat until I took a
ride. First time I've done that in ages. That was his
idea of reconciliation! Mine was a five-kilo hunk of
horsemeat, not even half smoked, & of course he
made a pig of himself with it.*

*Piedras Negras is holocasting again tonight. Glori-
ous to think that I'm now a tiny fleck of that rebel-
lious voice, if only on XEPN, Channel 3.*

CHAPTER 22

At 8:03, the shift whistle finally blew. A fading sun cast the shadow of the construction crane across the City of the Saints. Soon it would be dark.

Dandridge Laird stood with his legs apart and mopped his brow with one khaki sleeve, proudly gazing down on his departing work crew from his perch atop the unfinished building. It had been only a few years since the airburst nuke that had blossomed far out North Temple Street, obliterating the airport, the monorail interchange, and many buildings almost to the Salt Palace and the State Capitol.

Already, though, Salt Lake City had repaired much of herself through prayer and twelve-hour shifts by a beehive of sturdy Mormon citizens. Already, Laird could smile down on the rebuilt state fairgrounds, noting the subtle LDS gable motif that graced strictly secular buildings just as the old ones had. And already, Dandridge Laird had marked himself for death by insisting on workmen's compensation for his laborers.

Laird limped the the nearest crane pillar, his scuffing gait masking softer footfalls in the elevator control room behind him. He did not catch the movement of the khaki-clad 'workman' in the unglazed window; would not have recognized the man in any case. Laird was testing his gimpy forty-two-year-old leg, wondering if the Church would be able to help his family much when he could no longer earn a living as construction supervisor.

Laird's own LDS 'stake', his local church organization, had so many helpless mouths to feed already! And as for the gentile workers,—Laird shook his head in honest commiseration. The proper solution was industry-funded insurance. The stumbling block was the blind refusal of management.

Or maybe the consortium that owned the construction company saw, and then looked away. None of the big conglomerates seemed likely to allow such reforms. Laird had gone to his congressman, to his elders, even to local reporters without achieving much. But somewhere along the line he'd been overheard by the people who'd come to him with help—and asking *his* help. Laird would have laughed to think of himself as a conspirator, yet he knew better than to talk about those meetings to anyone but trusted workers. You didn't keep a strawboss job after they spotted you as a union organizer.

Nor could you expect to keep your life if you were the first Mormon convert to organized labor in Salt Lake City since postwar reconstruction began, a crucial nucleus of Indy reform in the very shadow of White House Deseret. Dandridge Laird did not know how carefully he was groomed by labor 'outlaws'; how high were their hopes for him. Certainly he did not know that a man hidden in the lengthening, softening shadows had been sent to shatter those hopes.

Laird sighed, limped slowly to the control room, intending to walk down the interior stairs. The blow that caught him below the sternum did not wholly paralyze him but shocked his diaphragm muscle into a spasm. Exhausted by his twelve-hour shift, now robbed of his ability to breathe,

Laird fell to his knees at the stairwell, clutching the rail with both hands.

His assailant hacked twice at his upper arm, pulled Laird around to a sitting position with his back to the stairwell. The man didn't match Laird's bulk—seventy-five kilos, at a guess—but O Lord, what pitiless strength! A bandanna covered the face, only the eyes showing, and the ugly snout of an automatic pistol was leveled at Laird's breast. The crouching man's other gloved hand came up slowly to the bandanna, its forefinger vertical over where the mouth must be. Laird tried to speak, folded his hands over his belly, felt his chin jerked roughly upward. Again the forefinger, this time over Laird's own mouth. The head nodded vigorously, then paused and cocked sideways.

Laird understood; nodded; let his head loll against the rail as he peered at his captor. His work-callused hands came up, faltering as he fought for breath, in an ancient gesture of surrender.

The man's empty hand flickered at a hip pocket, came up with a tutorial voder the size of a wallet, and then placed the voder on the cement floor. Yet the vented barrel of that handgun never wavered, and Laird tried not to wheeze as his breath returned.

A soft luminescence lit the voder's alphanumeric studs under flying fingers. Then, impersonal and crisp as any other language-teaching machine, the voder said softly: "Whisper all you like. One loud noise and you are dead."

Laird tried twice before he could even whisper. "What have I done to you?"

Fingers flew again. Finally: "Union organizer. Does not matter true or false. Next two days many government enemies dead, you included."

Laird licked his lips and almost forgot to whisper.

"The government? I'm no traitor. You mean the general contractor?"

In due time: "White House Deseret. You more important than you think. Your only hope is disappear. Now, next few minutes."

Pause. "I have a family, for heaven's sake. How can I leave them without telling them?"

"Their only hope is to think you dead. If anyone knows you survive, you and I both die. Lion of Zion plays for keeps. Time wasting; run or die?"

Laird looked at the gun muzzle, now indistinct in the gloom, and felt cold sweat. "Lord Jesus Christ help me, I wouldn't know how to run! Or where. Maybe I could hide out along the transient camps awhile, but—"

The man's head shook sideways, fingers flickering again. "I have clothes, false papers, money for you. Written directions for best route, Ogden to Pocatello, across Snake River into Canada. Not long if you go now. Now. Now," said the insouciant tutor with no more urgency than a mattress commercial.

"I think I'd rather die than let my wife think I ran out. You don't know what it means—how it would affect the kids."

"Send for them in a month. Or your wife can be a widow tomorrow. Will not trade my life for you. Losing patience."

A long shuddering breath; then, nodding his whole body: "All right. I don't really have a choice, do I?"

"Not since your file came to S & R."

"Search & Rescue?" Even in semidarkness, Laird's teeth gleamed as he smiled. "They're rescuing me? But I thought they were the President's own—"

But the man was waving his hand as if shooing flies. After a moment, from the voder: "S & R has group called rovers. Primary job is assassination. Good at it. Tell Canadians. Truth."

"I whipped my son for repeating that rumor." As if to chase the memory away he went on quickly: "So what do I do?"

"Follow me down after two minutes. May be someone monitoring outside fence, so I carry you deadweight to company pickup."

Laird stood up with difficulty. The smaller man scooped up the voder, moved in a predator's silence down the first few stairs. "It all seems unreal—hard to believe," Laird muttered, not quite a whisper.

Gun muzzle and voder were both out again. "This is real," said the voder lackadaisically, as the gun moved side-to-side. "Death is real. If I have to come up after you, will prove it."

"Go on before I lose my nerve," Laird husked, and marveled at the soundlessness of the man's passage down six flights of stairs. Meanwhile he counted to himself. At a hundred and twenty he began his own descent, swiveling so that each footfall was as steady as the last, no matter how it hurt the bad leg. He did not know whether he expected the apparition to be gone, or to feel the impact of bullets as he reached the first landing.

Yet his nightmare continued as the smaller man handed him a large filmy sack. The voder was already programed: "Step into bodybag, pull it up over head. When I pick you up, go limp. Whatever happens, play dead until I tell you to speak. May take an hour."

Laird took the huge bag, fumbled as he whispered, "Look, I have to believe you're on my side."

In the dimness, the head nodded.

"How would I recognize the rovers sent to kill me?"

In answer, the man jerked a thumb at his own breast.

"Maybe you would, but—." Laird stopped. "That's not what you meant, was it?"

Slow headshake. Accustomed to the gloom, Laird thought he saw a crinkle around the eyes. A wry smile, perhaps.

Now the bodybag was nearly up to his chin. "You're the rover sent to kill me," Laird whispered hoarsely.

Slow nod.

"So you'd have the keys to the perimeter gate and access to a company pickup, wouldn't you? And you still might throw me off a cliff somewhere."

A shrug—but that odd, ugly little automatic was now in the man's hand, held by the muzzle for display. Yes, if he wanted a man dead he sure didn't lack the means to do it; could have done it already. Over the roof parapet; down the stairwell with a broken neck; or maybe into the bodybag quietly, into the damned company pickup and then out to some canyon where the man could shoot him like a trussed goat.

Laird felt the top close above him, fought an urge to scream, then found himself hoisted in a fireman's carry. An arm slapped at his legs, not hard, and he made himself suitably limp.

All the way out of town and up the old freeway, Laird bounced under a tarp in the bed of that pickup.

And at every bounce he wondered whether he'd been hoaxed into his grave.

When at last he felt himself being dragged feet-first onto the tailgate, Laird vented the smallest of strangled sobs and felt steely hands grip hard against his ankles. Then he was again carried over uneven ground for some distance. He heard the murmur of water; began to breathe deeply, won-

dering if he could fight his way out of the bag
before he drowned.

Laird found himself deposited carefully on grass,
then heard the voder again: "Whisper. Pickup may
be bugged."

"Where are we?" He helped the man shuck the
bag away and now for the first time he began to
hope, to truly believe, that he might live.

Pause at the voder. "River near cemetery in
Ogden. Good place to lose a deader. Good place for
you to walk to monorail." Laird felt, more than
saw, the pile of clothes that dropped in his lap.
But the voder's glow gave him enough light for
him to change.

"Mind if I ask—well, don't you speak American?"

Pause. Then, "Not with a radio planted in my
skull. They can hear every word I say. Do not hear
this gadget."

"How d'you know they can't?"

Pause. "Still alive. Explosive in the radio in my
head. If you get caught, . . ."

Laird jumped and did not hear the last few words
from the voder, for the man was suddenly speaking aloud; a young man's voice. "I hear you, Control.
No, not yet. Message is in process but not yet
delivered." A brief pause before, "You know my
em-oh, why not get off my ass until my message is
delivered?" Then after a moment, "How should I
know? Maybe an hour. I'm already in Ogden so it
shouldn't take me long to deliver message two."
After the last pause, a sigh: "Into the goddam
river. It's the quickest way; quicker still if I don't
have to give you a blow-by-blow. Thank-you-
Control-and-*out*," he finished in a singsong parody
of good cheer. His sigh at the finish seemed only
half exasperation. What was the other half? Relief?

Dandridge Laird stood up, tried the fit of the
sport jacket while the young rover busied himself

with the voder. "A little short in the sleeves," Laird whispered.

"I get the god-*damnedest* complaints," said the young man aloud, and it was a moment before Laird realized the rover might have been talking to himself for all anyone else knew. The little son of perdition was quick all right.

Then the voder began: "Wait five minutes after I leave. Walk to lights, read instructions, then walk as if you owned IEE."

Laird laughed almost silently. "Only fitting; it owns me."

Pause. "Not any more," said the voder.

Laird nodded; stretched a hand out to be shaken, found it ignored. The rover was busily stuffing old clothes and a hefty stone into the bodybag. Uneasy now, anxious to be on his way, Laird whispered, "Is there any way I can help you?"

Long pause. For a moment the young man did not attack the voder keys. When he had finished, it said, "Wait a month before telling family. By then I may figure how to disarm this thing in my head. If not it probably won't matter. Best help for me is, you not get caught." He left Laird standing there, and he left on the run.

Laird did not wonder whether the young man's next 'message delivery' would be of life or of death. He was too busy just inhaling the scent of grass, and of flowers, and of life; and of the joy he would take in it for as long as he lived. One day Laird might recognize the inestimable value of Ted Quantrill's gift.

CHAPTER 23

Only a crazy wolf, or a very hungry one, would be hunting at midday on the unprotected flank of the mountain that soared above the San Rafael desert. The gaunt gray loafer had made hors d'oevres of one ground squirrel and the yellow eyes glittered toward another when, simultaneous with the great shadow, an unearthly rustling drone moved down the wind. The little varmint fled. The wolf looked up, then padded swiftly into one of the abandoned man-made caves that once had followed crystalline yellow ore into the belly of the mountain.

Before the war, the huge delta dirigible had been as yellow as that uranium oxide ore. Repainted for wartime cargo missions, it had at last been decommissioned and bought, on very special terms, for industrial use. Now the delta carried the IEE logo on its tan polymer hide. Its crew were veterans of a war and many an unscheduled cargo drop, but they seldom flew over Utah's central desert. In Cassidy-and-Sundance days the region had been dangerous because only desperate men lived there. Now it was dangerous because, for the most part, no men lived there. The few who did, were desperate for modern reasons.

Cargomaster Cole Riker leaned over the shoulder of the delta captain, pointing to their two-hundred-meter shadow that raced across the mountain.

"If that's Temple Mountain, Steve, we're a little off-course."

Stevens nodded easily, switched off his headset so he wouldn't be recorded. "Thought we'd take a look at Goblin Valley on the way in. Since the war nobody but a few plutocrats can afford sight-seeing in these parts."

"It's a shame what crosswinds can do to a flight plan," Riker said facetiously, and saw Stevens's reflection grin back through the windscreen.

Though the delta had been designed for a crew of eight, wartime mods and peacetime cost-accounting had reduced the crew to two. Neither of the men knew that the corporate CEO, Boren Mills, had personal reasons for employing the fewest men possible on a cargo drop into the San Rafael.

Stevens increased buoyancy, actuated the enormous elevons, and eased more power to the shrouded, stirling-engined props that whirred like a billion muted sopranos on the lifting body of the delta. He could always explain such anomalies on the flight recorder in terms of the plain orneriness of a delta. It was overloaded, for sure; so much so that it could barely climb above three thousand meters. Wind currents were haphazard, too.

At maximum altitude, with the video magnifier, they could study Goblin Valley longer. The bizarre wind-rounded sandstone blobs sat like so many gargantuan sepia biscuits baking on pedestals in the bone-dry Utah heat. Then Stevens thought to flick his headset on and, "I'm getting the lab signal," he said. "Wonder if they've installed an honest-to-God mooring pad."

Of course they had not. Stevens asked for help in securing the big retractable landing struts which, in a proper moorage, found sockets to fit. The huge delta rocked gently as it lost headway, passing over earth berms that sloped nearly to the roof of the lab complex.

Riker counted nine men below, all in lab smocks, and swore as he noted a braided pigtail on one of the men. When a Chinese rejected the revolution of his elders, he tended to do it up brown. Riker didn't mind working with wartime enemies, but when securing a delta you needed flawless communication.

Riker dropped the cargo hatch himself and nearly fell while shinnying down handholds of a mooring strut. The lab staff was willing but maladroit; not until Cole Riker had snapped a cable latch into a mooring ring did the Chinese understand how to secure the others, and naturally Stevens couldn't cut the stirlings as long as vagrant winds might tug, slap, or tilt the motionless vessel. Finally Riker toggled the winch pneumatics, saw the strut pads squash against concrete, and pronounced the delta secure. The bellicose rustle of the props died and, with the Chinese and one incredibly hairy caucasian, Riker got the air-cushion pallet in place.

Stevens could not leave the controls with such primitive moorings. Damn a corporation, Riker thought, that didn't give a rat's ass about the working stiff. It wasn't so bad with the small companies, only they tended to get gobbled up by the big ones. In his last state-of-the union address, the President had quoted gross national product figures and claimed that things were improving. For the big boys, maybe. But to Riker it seemed that the split between haves and have-nots was widening.

The caucasian, Chabrier, signed for the first palletload. "I gather we shall see more of each other in the coming weeks," he said in gallic accents.

"Damn' right. And if you can install some strut sockets we can do it a whole lot quicker."

Chabrier asked, as they maneuvered the air-cushion load to the roof elevator, how many trips would be necessary. Riker thought five trips might do it. "So soon?" Chabrier's deepset eyes, Riker thought, were those of a thinner man—at least thin in spirit.

Riker: "Well, we're stripped to the bone and carryin' eighty thousand kilos each trip. With some good cargo handlers and proper moorage we could have all this stuff—whatever it really is—delivered in ten days." Riker had intended a harmless joke along with the pointed hint about trained handlers. In every industrial cargo there were bound to be items that wouldn't match a manifest list.

But the Frenchman's face clouded. "It is merely automated machinery and tunneling equipment," he said quickly, tapping the fax sheet. "How is it that you can carry such loads?"

"Tell you when we're through." Riker scrambled back into the delta to winch another pallet into position.

Hours later, when the sixteenth pallet had been trundled to the elevator, Marengo Chabrier spoke in a richly intonated dialect to his lab crew who disappeared with the load. "Perhaps you will join me below for an absinthe," he said then to Riker. "Or perhaps something even stronger." The barest tint of urgency colored his offer.

Riker whistled. "Stronger than absinthe?"

"I am a chemist, mon vieux." Shy and deprecating—but pleading, too.

"Oh. Uh, some other time, maybe. I'm on IEE time, and the light will be fading soon. Cap'n Stevens will be edgy as three cats in a sack after a whole afternoon at his console." Riker restowed the air cushion, turned to shake Chabrier's hand. "See you day after tomorrow if we maintain schedule. Don't worry about the cable releases;

that much at least is automatic. We can afford electrics *below* the hull. And we can save lots of time if you can get us a decent moorage. Think about it."

"Unfortunately, Riker, I too am on IEE time, and funding. I fear we must do our best with things as they are. It helps when one can relax with one's liquids and powders. Or even to present a friend with a kilo of them."

This time the air of desperation was unmistakeable. Cole Riker knew what a kilo of some alkaloids was worth; knew also that he wanted nothing to do with them. Suddenly he wanted only to get away from this half-crazy frog squatting atop a desert lab croaking friendly overtures to a near-total stranger. "It'll bear thinking about," said Riker, and swung onto the strut handholds.

The props were already turning, the fuel-stingy stirlings warming to thermally-efficient range. Chabrier called up through the cargo hatch. "Riker! You are certain you can complete the shipments in so little time?"

"Barring a malf we can't fix, yes," Riker shouted, then grinned. "I'll tell you why now, if you won't let on to your crew. Just didn't want to worry you during your early experiences with an IEE delta. It's really pretty safe, you know."

"What is safe, mon ami?" Chabrier saw the cables release, to whirl like snakes into belly orifices.

"Hydrogen," Riker called, pointing at the buoyancy cells above him as the belly hatch thunked shut. As Stevens poured full power and actuated the strut pneumatics, the vast delta vaulted safely upwards for the first ten meters. Laughing, Riker watched the poor Frenchman run full-tilt off the end of the roof and tumble down the berm, away from countless cubic meters of the near-explosive hydrogen. It really *was* fairly safe, Riker told himself. Nothing like the safety of helium, but lots cheaper and with roughly ten per cent more buoyancy. That was IEE for you.

Riker checked the pallet anchors, his smile fading as he mentally replayed his hours with Chabrier. It seemed almost as if the bulky chemist—if that was really his job—wasn't interested in speeding up the shipments. If anything, as if he craved a delay. And friendship. But why would a highly trained scientist crave camaraderie with a delta crewman? As the vast craft slid upward into the last of the sunlight, Riker pondered the question and studied the particle-beam perimeter weapons that stretched away across the trackless desert.

One hell of a waste, he thought, to set up such a P-beam security rig as that. All corporations were a little paranoid about their measly secret processes. What could be so important that anyone would bother to sneak *in*? But that was IEE for you . . .

CHAPTER 24

For all its gleam and pillared portico, White House Deseret was chiefly a ballroom with a few staff offices, guest rooms and kitchen. And with one particular elevator to whisk senior staff and certain invited guests, far down below the 'bench'—a natural terrace at the base of the Wasatch Mountains. From the bottom of the shaft, Boren Mills took a ten-minute ride in a magnetic sling tube. Mills was not supposed to know—but knew, none-

theless—that the real hardball business of Streamlined America was transacted directly beneath the
repository of Mormon genealogical files in Cottonwood Canyon. If you weren't safe under the Granite Mountain genealogical vault, you couldn't *get*
safe.

Mills passed through more security, then forced
a pleasant smile despite an urge to gape. The raven-
haired young amazon who escorted him to the
Presidential apartment was nearly two meters tall
in her spike heels, and while the hooded white satin
gown fell to her ankles, it was also slit to reveal a
lot of luscious apricot-tinted thigh. This was a far
lusty howl away from the conservative male staff
who had escorted him in previous visits. It unset-
tled him; told him to expect changes in a man he
had studied carefully.

That man was also just a tad drunk. "Go and
ponder your sins," Blanton Young told the improbable vision, and waited until she had gone.

"Future sins, I hope." Mills could not resist it.

"How'd you guess?" Young took the small Mills
paw in his big one, held the Mills forearm with his
other hand. The ritual communicated great physical vitality, which Young could squander. "I tell
you, Mills, there's no end of wisdom in that
scripture."

Mills let his gaze follow Young's open-handed
gesture. On one wall of the lavish ultramodern
room was a tablet of black onyx, and inset in flowing
script of richest polished gold was the legend: ". . .
*And it is by the wicked that the wicked shall be
punished.*"

"Interesting," said Mills, not knowing what else
to say.

"Interpretation of the Book of Mormon is just a
matter of Divine guidance," said Young, as if that
guidance was self-evident, leading his guest to the

wet bar. "For instance, in '97 it told me I should shunt that bunch of Army assassins into S & R as soon as my," he paused to savor some personal joke, "*sainted* predecessor shuffled off this mortal coil." With that, he performed a shuffling two-step, then took a sip from his goblet.

To say that Mills was aghast was to claim a delta dirigible was a penny balloon. Mills did not care what caprice a man chose, so long as he chose it predictably. This was not the Blanton Young he had seen previously—or was this, at last, the private Young emerging? Mills managed to say, "Got it: wicked hit men punish wicked Indys."

Rumbling: "Rebels, son; an Indy is a rebel only when I interpret him as one. But it took me awhile to realize that you can make a sinner punish himself-herself," he winked, with a wave of the big head toward the door, "by a penance consh— consisting of more wickedness. You take a girl brought up strict, caught lifting a smoked ham to feed a few useless mouths; and if she's not too keen, after a week or reconditioning you can argue her into, ah, any position."

Reminds me of an old joke," Mills essayed.

"Bet I've heard it."

"About druggies. Their idea of a round-table religious debate is to see who can commit the most original sin on your lazy susan."

Young guffawed after a two-beat pause. Mills would never know whether he really got it. "Well, I owe you one for that," said the pixillated Prez. Staring into his sour mash as if it were a crystal globe, Young went on in softer tones: "So I'll pay off now. A certain industrial concern whose initials are LockLever is pressuring a Texas rancher to sell his whole spread, which LockLever will turn into the wildest, wooliest, modernest dude ranch in the world."

Mills was astute enough to break his chuckle off. "Hanh-I'don't-get-it."

"It's not a one-liner, Mills. The pressure comes by way of LockLever's control of the aquifer North of Texas Wild Country. There isn't a drop of running water on the Schreiner ranch; they water the stock and imported game animals from wells—always did.

"As it happens, LockLever *could* pollute or divert the whole underground supply from their experimental rigs nearby. The Schreiner spread used to be a hundred square miles back in the 'eighties. It's grown since. I don't know if they'll sell—they've always been a tough bunch of Texas pecans, I hear—but if they do, LockLever will need cheap power to run the kind of Wild-Country Disneyland they have in mind. And there isn't any good place to put a line-of-sight tower on the whole, million-acre ranch."

Now Mills got a glimmer. "Where's the nearest mountain?"

"Ten klicks North of the ranch boundary. And there *is* enough federal enforcement to that prominence—couldn't call it a mountain but an LOS tower could narrowcast cheap power to the ranch; and that little old prominence is now federal land."

Jesus, God and Moroni, thought Mills; to think he'd swapped an old gag for a chance to screw LockLever! "I should think LockLever would've made a handsome bid for such a natural LOS site," he murmured.

"They did. Some hitches developed. Old lawsuits, title irregularities; you know. You can always find something if you look hard enough."

"I've always wanted to own a small mountain in Texas," Mills said with a straight face.

"Oh, I don't think your government could show that kind of favoritism to an individual," Young tutted. "But of course, some survey crew might find signs of oil, or something else that Streamlined America badly needs. That's an argument LockLever hasn't used. Yet."

Mills: "And what might a geological study turn up?"

Young: "Surprise me. But the discovery would have to come from a reliable company with a good track record."

"IEE owns Latter-day Shale—if memory serves," Mills said.

"A good reliable company," Young nodded sagely. "Excellent track record—in which I may have some stock if, as you say, memory serves."

"Sonofabitch," Mills exulted.

"You're another," said the President of Streamlined America, and drank as if validating his reply.

CHAPTER 25

Over his next glass of sippin' whiskey, Mills learned why the President chose IEE as leverage to balance the proposed LockLever project. LockLever claimed that such an entertainment center would bring wealth to the area and would be welcomed by the locals; but Young had learned something more. The giant consortium had further hedged its bets by paying off some people who had clout in Wild Country. In a word: rebels. Federalists suspected that much of the payoff wound up in the hands of the Indy leader, old Jim Street. Maybe

LockLever hoped to accommodate all sides while carving out a region of influence where the government had little or no influence.

"You mustn't think I'm against reconstruction in Wild Country, Mills. It'd bring law and order back to those crazies—on our terms. And LockLever *could* build those ten-kilometer thrill rides and restage the Battle of Britain there twice a day, just like they claim. But I can't trust 'em."

"True," Mills murmured. "When LockLever owns foreign companies, foreigners have clout with LockLever."

"Which reminds me that your own people have a little romance going with—um, what's that firm at the Turk Ellfive launch complex?"

Mills smiled. "ECI; Electronics Corporation of Israel. Those initials also stand for electronic counter intelligence, which was too near the truth. So they've changed it to Tuz Golu R & D, which makes their Turkish landlords happy."

Very quietly: "But they still do research with microwave relays, or so I am reliably informed. Any gadget that can project multichannel holo from a point in empty space would be ours, or Israeli. And it isn't ours."

At last, Mills felt he was about to learn why he had been invited to Young's inner sanctum. "Those Mex stratosphere relays," he guessed. "You think they're using Israeli equipment, Mr. President?"

The National Security Agency thinks so. And I want those rebel holocasts stopped! You seem the logical conduit for us to find out how it might be done."

"My people tell me you've zapped one already," Mills said, pleased to show how well-informed he was. "Congratulations."

"It's casting again."

Mills shrugged. He was damned if he'd admit he hadn't known *that*.

"Let's understand each other," said Young, evidently still clear-headed though his tongue played him false at times. "You'll get the LOS site for trying to wangle us a media countermeasure. If you're successful, you could get the Schreiner land for IEE to develop—assuming you want it."

Mills laughed ruefully. "It's a great idea. Battle of Britain, eh? Some old Lockheed thinktank man is still plugging away in LockLever." He shook his head in grudging respect, then grew serious. "Sure, IEE could do it, if we can get that land. And if we can get protection without paying off Jim Street."

"Our guess is that you could get a ninety-nine year lease from the owner, *if* the federal government allows some special tax incentives to Schreiner, and *if* you could convince the Schreiner family you'll keep it all unpolluted and mostly unraped. As for protection, just hire most of the locals and name the goddam place Wild Country Safari."

"My God," Mills muttered, thinking it over. For that matter, the ersatz Spitfires and Messerschmitts for a Battle of Britain show could carry live ammo, just in case. IEE could train those leathery Taxas lunatics as maintenance people and let 'em carry sidearms.

And the gambling! IEE could thumb its nose at state laws in Wild Country. A refitted delta could ferry in six hundred high-rollers a trip and could run the games at it pleased. The LOS tower meant cheap power. Nothing need be said about the gambling. A replica of old Dodge City? That would be the first step Mills took after taking the place over.

Inside a year, the gambling sincity could be running at a profit. In two years, mach one thrill rides! Oh, yes, this was too good a thing to pass up. Mills needed *something* from which he could secretly siphon cash during the next year or so.

Because otherwise, the synthesizer factory would bleed him to death before it came on-line.

CHAPTER 26

Imagine the most complete array of RF sensors available to the National Security Agency to secure a President's lair against bugging. Next, imagine that guests are profiled, fluoroscoped, interviewed and voice-stress analyzed by NSA professional paranoids whose sole raison d'etre is to screw those who would try to screw Blanton Young.

With these conditions in mind, now try to imagine the frustration of the head NSA spook when Young's own personal screwing put the quietus on audiovisual security screens. The President might envy porn stars, but he did not propose to be one even for his own laconic gumshoes who had already seen everything and would not, presumably, have been scandalized to find that a widower President enjoyed a carnal tussle now and again, and again, and again.

Young was perhaps ignorant of the criticism Russell laid on Neitzsche. Paraphrased: it's okay to be tough-minded, provided you start with yourself. Or perhaps Young simply did not want *any* recordings of *any* deals inside his Granite Mountain apartment. It was this decision which permitted the raven-haired hotsy to circumvent Young's anti-bugging array with basic equipment, ears and memory. The lissome lass lay flat on her belly in Young's bedroom and monitored the Mills meeting through a fresh-air duct that served both rooms. The early part of the evening had justified all her hours of patience. Yet the initial dialogue paled as good booze took its effect in the room just beyond . . .

CHAPTER 27

". . . Told you we'd build the true Zion together four years ago, didn't I?" Young had now switched to brandy, and tended to use shorter words.

"You also said it would take some careful weeding," said Mills, gauging his own alcohol capacity with care. "But I wish you'd told me how much weeding you intended to do last week. Even with control of FBN, Mr. President, we've had a bitch of a time explaining away that rash of disappearances."

"Couldn't be helped," said Young, waving his goblet airily. "Anyway, a good third of 'em were Mormons. Who'd believe White House Deseret could possibly be involved?"

"Must've been a tough decision for you, of all people."

"Shhhhit," said Blanton Young, and glanced at the younger man with a half-smile. "Not with true inspiration to guide. Mills, in the true Zion there won't be any room for a bunch of old farts wran-

gling over interp'tations of the word of God. Came
to me in a meeting of the Council of Apostles one
day. A rev'lation like a thunderclap; I was bein'
tested.''

Somehow, Mills decided, a tiny ice cube had
entered his bloodstream. "You mean—Divine exam-
ination?"

Nod. "A dozen old men, balkin' me at every
turn. It came to me that the President of Streamlined America can't be wrong every time; that if
Blanton Young was put in this office by a higher
power, then a solid wall of opposition can only
mean that wall is bound together by the devil's
flaxen cord." The zealot eyes burned past slitted
lids. "You follow me, Mills?" The President's face
was choleric with remembered frustrations, his
last words a rasp on old tin cans.

Until the past half-minute, Boren Mills had cher-
ished the assumption that Young, whatever his
failings, was bound to his Church; that ultimately
he would be constrained by its tenets of fellowship
and grace. Mills's ice cube was now a frozen stalac-
tite against his spine. "I couldn't help noticing
some, ah, changes in your, um, lifestyle. Are you
saying you've decided to leave your Church?"

"*I am the Church*!" Mills realized with a start
that he'd seen the same look on Eve's face when he
asked for her amulet. "The Council of Apostates,"
said Young, relishing his heresy, "is a test. I see
that now. And I have passed that test."

Through his consternation, Mills saw that he was
privy to a development so new that it had not yet
become surrounded by rumor. With utterly no idea
of what to say, he fell back on the hoary goad of
interviewers and shrinks: "I see."

"I wonder if you do. I have passed through a
purifying fire of the spirit, and I can depend on
insp'ration. When I'm inspired I can't be wrong.

It's a tr'mendous sense of respons'bility but," the President unleashed a beatified smile, "somehow it makes me feel free."

No doubt, thought Mills. That same sense of guidance and inspiration must have given the same freedom to Alexander; to Rasputin; to der fuehrer. But to ride the coat-tails of Young was to ride a barmy tiger. Should he dismount now? But how the hell could he? And how long before this loony generated an open break with what was, unofficially, a state religion?

Suddenly Boren Mills knew why LockLever was paying cash homage to the rebels. They knew of Young's instability; were straddling the ideological fence. Yet the CEO of LockLever hadn't helped organize Young's S & R hit team as he, Mills, had done. Mills and IEE could expect no quarter from Jim Street. Unless—unless Mills made himself absolutely vital to the survival of Streamlined America no matter who won the political battles. Choosing his words with utmost caution: "Mr. President, how did the Council of Apostles respond to your revelation?"

Young lurched up from his chair, circled the wet bar as if analyzing an opponent, chose a glass of seltzer before answering. "I'm not an idiot, Mills. I won't feed a man things he can't swallow. What I *can* do, is replace Council members with my own people. A matter of seein' that some of my folks are standin' in the right places. Pity you're not LDS yourself."

"I can do more as a fellow traveler," Mills said quickly. "How long before, um, normal attrition in the Council," he said, knowing that some members would die by means that were not normal, "gives you the power you need?"

Innocence personified: "How would I know? Could take a year or so."

"If I might suggest it, Sir, you might take care not to let your new lifestyle show in the meantime."

"Council isn't as down on plural marriage as you might think," Young chuckled, "but I get your drift, son. It has been revealed to me that even the head of the Church must make haste slowly." Horsewink.

Mills exhaled with undisguised relief. Whether mad as Parisian hatters or merely posturing in his cups, Young still understood caution. Mills: "Depend on IEE to move with you. But I'll have to know what you need."

"You can start by talking with those Israelis about a media countermeasure. Streamlined America must break free from foreign pressures." A rolling rippling belch paced the President's train of thought. "And not just media gadgetry. Mex oil, Canadian platinum, African cobalt—stuff this country must have."

At that moment, inspiration struck Mills. Some crucial raw materials were present, in minute quantities, in sea water. "We're already doing our part with shale, but IEE hasn't been idle in the rare metals field either," he said slyly.

"I'm talking metric tons."

A hundred kilos a day of lighter elements from a synthesizer, perhaps ten a day—he'd have to check with Chabrier—of heavy rare metals like cobalt. It would mean a different production schedule of synthesizers, but a few could be on-line in less than a year. A hundred synthesizers could yield a ton of heavy elements every day.

"So am I," said Mills. "Pure stuff. It's, uh, an extraction process we've kept pretty secret. In a few months IEE can be shipping a ton of cobalt a day from Eureka."

"Not enough for the New Denver and Cleveland

mills by a long shot. We use seven thousand tons of Zaire cobalt a year."

"In two years we can match that," Mills promised. He hadn't said the process was ocean extraction, but the implication was clear enough.

"Domestic?"

Time to enrich the implied lie: "Domestic as sea water."

"At compet'ive price?"

"No, Sir." Pause for effect. "Cheaper."

The President sat down slowly, then raised his goblet in salute. "The Lord has provided," he murmured. "I knew I was right about you; inspiration," he said smugly and then added, "but you better come through."

Mills tallied new necessities in his head. He'd have to maintain utmost security on shipments of elemental metals from the Utah desert to the Port of Eureka. And set up some kind of barge facility off the coast as a blind. But once those shipments became mainstays of reconstruction in Streamlined America, Mills could write his own ticket with any administration.

"To Zion," said Mills, and raised his own goblet.

Ten meters away on the other side of the wall, the raven-haired hotsy felt her lip curl.

CHAPTER 28

As the pudgy, chain-smoking Sean Lasser began Sanger's briefing, she surmised that old age was creeping up on him. He'd never shown this much courtesy to any rover. ". . . Had to be one of the undercover rebels that we disappeared two weeks ago, you see."

Sanger, quickly: "You mean because it had to be a rover who helped him escape? If the man told the Canadians all you say, I suppose so." Finger-snap: "Unless some rebel posed as one of us and—"

Lasser's headshake, slow and commiserating, stopped her. "No one but a rover could've faked that mission," he said gently. "All we needed was the escapee's name, and our man in Calgary couldn't get that. He *did* manage three minutes alone in the room where the man had been de-briefed, and tape-lifted prints off the chair arms. We identified one this morning. Ever hear of a Dandridge Laird?"

Nagative shrug. Marbrye Sanger had no doubt she'd learn plenty about him from the file that lay at Lasser's elbow. She'd never had to go into Canada to disappear a man before, but the prospect disturbed her no more than any other killing might. "Will I be on a team or singleton?"

"Team. We have to pick that team with more than usual care. Howell and Cross are busy setting the mission up; that's why Seth isn't briefing you himself." A finger tapping against his teeth, as though the ritual and not his thought processes generated the pause. "How well do you get along with Ted Quantrill?"

Under the little man's deceptive mild gaze, Sanger had to force her eye contact. "As well as with any rover. We've teamed on several missions— but you know that." Taking a risk: "We get along; he doesn't talk my arm off. He's a surly little bastard but he doesn't have many weaknesses."

"Not even in bed?"

"I've had that pleasure," she said evenly. "Also with Ethridge, Graeme Duff, once even with Howell, which I won't bore you with. I might have it with you, if the occasion ever arises." The spots of color on her cheeks did not suggest that it was very likely.

"Why thank you, Sanger; though I ah," with a dusty cough of self-deprecation, "wouldn't want to bore *you* with *that*." Pause. "I'm asking as politely as I can: do you think any of your liaisons—with Quantrill, for example—left emotional bonds?"

She made her laugh loud enough so that it wouldn't come out shaky. "Basic T Section stuff, Lasser! Going soft on another member of a hit team is a deadly mistake." Her grin was as feral as she could make it: "I don't have many weaknesses either." Sanger, however, knew that her responses to stress were not as controlled as Quantrill's. At the moment she hadn't the strength to kick a sick whore off a bidet and she knew it.

Lasser, studying her, at last said, "Good," and picked up the thick file. "Howell will give you details but I can tell you now that this will be touchy work. You have to take your man out without killing him, if at all possible. We have a lot of questions we need to ask him."

"Soporific slugs? Hypospray?"

"Hypospray might not be fast enough, but you'll get a canister just in case. You'll probably have to use your chiller. Just don't hit a vital spot; they don't care if he loses an arm. He won't be needing it again."

Not worried, but perplexed: "So how do we get a bleeder back here alive?" She was thinking of Calgary.

"Sprint chopper. He doesn't know we're onto him but when he does, you can expect some good moves."

She took the file from Lasser, glanced at the first page, and then realized why that file was so thick, why Howell and Cross were setting up the mission. Seth Howell and Marty Cross had more single combat experience between them than any half-dozen rovers, and they would be her team members. No wonder Lasser had been so gentle, so careful.

The file she held was Ted Quantrill's.

CHAPTER 29

So this was the way her world ended, thought Sanger. Inside, she was whimpering. She'd spent far too much time trying to figure a way to warn Quantrill, and not enough time steeling herself for her decoy duties. Quantrill was pulling sprint chopper maintenance at Dugway, on the Utah side of the Nevada border. How simple it might be to ask Control, through her critic, to patch her into Quantrill's head. And how fruitless; for Control would not let her say a dozen words of warning, and she'd be cancelled forever. What would she say anyway? *Run for it*? They'd only zap him with his critic detonator. *Whatever I must do now, I love you beyond all reason*? He probably knew it anyway, and it wouldn't keep either of them alive.

Sanger stared out the polymer port of the sprint chopper, ignoring the wiry half-Cheyenne, Cross, in harness near her. Howell was not as good a pilot as he was a killer—but there was no great hurry as he guided them past the Oquirrh Mountains.

Quantrill had not seen fit to tell her (oh God, why not? Hadn't he known he could trust her?) he'd funked a mission, turned rebel beneath her nose. But neither had she told *him* the real story about his friend Palma. How Sanger had left a printed warning for Dr. Cathy Palma two hours before she was expected to disappear the woman in Abilene, Texas. God *damn* that man, refusing to ask her help! Now she could not give it and hope to live. Marbrye Sanger did not want to die, and didn't intend to. The best thing for her was to expunge Ted Quantrill from her memory; to bleed her soul of him. He'd made his single bed and now he could die in it.

CHAPTER 30

Quantrill only half-noticed the approach of Howell's craft as he lay supine on the mechanic's creeper. Three similar craft squatted outside the maintenance hangar five hundred meters away, and Quantrill lay above hot concrete beneath the nose of the fourth, which Miles Grenier had flown to the alignment pad. Old-timers still called these secluded spots 'compass roses'. Grenier sat in the cockpit, checking out the avionics and calling out the results of Quantrill's simple remove-and-replace operations with numbered modules. It had never occurred to Quantrill that rovers might be kept deficient in electronic theory.

Perhaps it was the continuing buzz of the distant sprint chopper that first suggested a break in routine. Usually the pilot set his bird down quickly to avoid spreading dust across the flight line. This one hovered, half concealed by the hangar.

He heard Grenier's audio buzzer. From sheer curiosity he pushed the stowed nose flotation bag aside; listened through the thin inner bulkheads. Grenier spoke normally at first. After a pause he spoke more quizzically but Quantrill could not hear what he said. The rover wiped late morning perspiration from his brow with the sleeve of his odorous work coverall. He had time to damn the heat of the turbines whistling in the fuselage; they weren't loud but while checking the bird out you wanted them idling.

A vagrant breeze wafted warm exhaust back to Quantrill, pungent with expensive fuel. Quantrill decided Grenier was going to take all day on his comm set, cursed, rolled back on his creeper and slapped the nose hatch shut before sitting upright. The hovering sprint chopper in the distance, he noticed, backed from sight without landing.

Quantrill was only a little surprised to hear the turbine whine rising, but very much so to see the wingtip shrouds swivel into takeoff position. If that goddam Grenier was heading back for an early lunch he wasn't going to leave Quantrill to leg it alone back to the hangar.

He lay back on the creeper, grasped handholds and shot himself backward to the belly hatch, punching the skin detent as he passed it. The hatch opened and Quantrill snagged internal handholds, legs driving him vertically as the craft began to lift and turn.

"What is this, Grenier; trick or treat?" Quantrill lay on the narrow walkway and stared angrily forward at the pilot.

Grenier did not hear him over the turbine scream, but evidently heard something in his headset. He chopped back the power too quickly, flicked off all systems while struggling up from his seat. And the glance he flicked at Quantrill was rich with fear and suspicion.

"Abandon ship," Grenier shouted, waving Quantrill out the still-gaping belly hatch, and following him with almost a rover's speed. Grenier backed away, not looking at the aircraft but at the rover. "Quantrill, get away," shouted the pilot. "We've got a problem with the bird!"

Quantrill trotted after the taller man, saw past him to the flight line. Five minutes before, there'd been several people currying their birds. Now the place was deserted. At the periphery of his vision was a charcoal-black mass, skating ten meters over the deck, and now Miles Grenier was running like a deer. The hurtling mass was a sprint chopper, arcing in between the two men. *Isolate your hit*, said a well-remembered voice in his memory. The voice had been that of Jose Martí Cross, the same man that Quantrill now saw peering from a side port in the approaching aircraft.

Quantrill dropped to one knee, slapped at his armpit for a chiller that wasn't there. The face of Marty Cross vanished from the port and with that simple reflexive act, Cross said it all: combat stations.

Give the pilot credit, thought Quantrill; he horsed his craft around while masking Grenier from a man who, if armed, might well shoot him or take him hostage. But Quantrill was sprinting too, now, and a precious few seconds are required to stop and then accelerate six thousand kilos of Loring sprint chopper.

In those seconds Quantrill crossed fifty meters of level concrete toward the craft he had so recently abandoned. Then Howell surged forward, coming out of the sun, high enough to clear his quarry's head, low enough so that his shrouded propwash would knock a horse sprawling.

Any watcher would know by now that Quantrill was unarmed. But Cross sat with feet braced against the padding of the open belly hatch, both hands steadying his chiller between his thighs, waiting for Quantrill to come into view. He was almost too close to miss—but also too low to see Quantrill until a second before the Loring passed over him. It should have been enough, with a chiller.

Because the sun was high, Quantrill saw the big shadow almost too late. He saw a tuft of grass that might serve as a shoving-off point, kicked away against it in an abrupt change of direction, rolled. He saw three puffs, hairbreadth misses by Cross, of dust as he came up squatting in a welter of pebbles at the concrete's verge. The Loring continued, levitated over its abandoned twin, prop shrouds gimbaling as Howell turned, virtually hidden from Quantrill as if seeking cover. Which he was, for a vital five seconds.

Then Howell leapfrogged the abandoned Loring again, this time slowly dropping to a meter off the deck. Now between Quantrill and his goal, Howell stopped the Loring. Quantrill feinted, started to run, then slowed as he saw the legs of Cross swing from the belly hatch. Quantrill dropped his pumping arms then, a gesture full of defeat.

And of misdirection. He could see Howell in the cockpit, grinning, knowing he could slam a six-ton hammer into his victim. He saw Cross hit and roll. And he saw that he was no more than twelve meters from the nearest wingtip shroud. His high overhand toss seemed a ridiculous empty gesture until Howell, with a spurt of pure horror, saw the glitter of small objects in the sun.

The handful of broken concrete half-fell, was half sucked into the circular shroud as Quantrill raced toward that wingtip, ignoring Cross who was up in a crouch below the fuselage, steadying his aim for a kneecapper.

Quantrill could not possibly sprint quickly enough to reach the shroud before its fiberquartz prop blades ingested those jagged chunks of concrete. He counted on that fact. With a shrill series of reports like small-arms fire, the concrete hunks shrieked through polyskin, some whining as ricochets into the distance, some shrapneling the fuselage behind Howell's bubble. Neither Howell nor Cross was hit but before either could make a patterned response, the Loring—as Quantrill had known it must—responded on its own.

The balance of a twin coleopter craft depends greatly on the shape of those prop blades, and their proximity to the airfoil surface in the shroud. Hammer a few dents into a shroud, especially near those prop tips, and its efficiency will plummet. Blow a dozen jagged holes in it while the props eat hardware, and you will see a coleopter go bonkers.

Quantrill had that pleasure.

The upward-slanting shroud was only a meter from concrete at its trailing edge when Quantrill committed his act of classic sabotage. It faltered, fell, scraped concrete, and became a sliding pivot as the other wingtip lifted as if to cartwheel the entire vehicle. Howell reacted almost quickly enough. A thorough pro, Cross sidestepped to get a shot at Quantrill who in turn kept himself masked by the nearer shroud. Cross took Howell's expertise for granted, and had no warning when the fuselage sideswiped him across his back and shoulders.

The craft was settling. Quantrill, flinging his other handful of gravel into the face of the falling Cross, cleared the halfbreed's fire pattern in a running leap. Still, he was lucky; one round blew a hunk from the heel of his work boot and spoiled his landing, so that his kick took Cross in the right shoulder instead of his face.

Both of Quantrill's hands closed on the chiller, pressing on Cross's fingers to squander the rest of the magazine in one sputtering burst. He'd learned that ploy before they ever put the critic in his head.

When Control spoke to him, it was obvious that someone—Howell?—was describing the action. Except that Howell was still up forward in the cockpit while the sprint chopper wailed down to quiescence, a bird with only one good wing. "Q, you're over-reacting," said the quasifeminine voice in his mastoid. "It's still not too late to save yourself. We need to talk to you, Q. Why don't you just—"

"Control, why don't *you* just go fuck a duck?" He had longed to say that for years. "I've got my signet ring garrotte wire snugged under Cross's adam's apple. Maybe I won't jerk and cut his head off when you pull my plug. But can you risk it?"

It was a lie but Quantrill was making it true, first passing his arms under Cross's to deploy his wire. Cross, the master of stealth, was no master of defense against the impacts that had stunned him at temple, scapula and groin. Quantrill's standard-issue signet ring was the only weapon he'd worn that day—even though he wasn't supposed to wear it while doing mechanic's chores. The filament-thin wire was hardly more than a meter long but with the signet in one hand and the ring on his other, he soon had the loop pressed around the throat of his old instructor, his new hostage.

Barely conscious, smaller than Quantrill, Cross grunted as raw bone edges grated in his right shoulder. The renegade rover lifted Cross bodily under the arms, both hands at shoulder height, bright sun glinting from the loop of wire. Howell popped his canopy and swung down to concrete, his own chiller drawn as he watched Quantrill move backward with his burden, facing Howell.

Seth Howell's bandy long legs could have carried him around Quantrill to balk progress toward the intact sprint chopper which Grenier had abandoned, but Howell had made other plans. The big man had no mastoid critic but with his headset still in place his every word could still be monitored by Control. "You're no pilot, Quantrill," he said, pacing his quarry, holding eye contact. "You'll sit in that Loring 'til you broil. Cut your losses, man."

Quantrill, still backing, let his fists move apart. "Stop right there, Howell, or I'll bleed your bunkie a little." Howell stopped. Quantrill was now virtually in the shadow of the Loring's wing, ignoring the calm pleas of Control that continued in his ear. Howell stepped first to one side, then the other, compelling his attention. The big man had trouble keeping his gaze on the rover's; his temptation was to study the progress of Marbrye Sanger, coming up from under the fuselage behind Quantrill.

CHAPTER 31

The first thing Sanger did after dropping from Howell's craft was to stand motionless, hidden by the second Loring while Howell passed over it again. Then she moved to the fuselage, put one foot into a maintenance toehole, and grasped an air intake duct so that she could peer over the craft, to study Quantrill's desperate ploy with only two handfuls of broken concrete.

Sanger grinned as she exchanged the chiller's explosive rounds for a magazine of ball ammo. They wanted the man alive and, with a target as quick as Quantrill, you couldn't depend on the exact placement of a round. That was *one* rationale, anyway . . .

"Howell's lost control," she murmured through her critic. "Subject is going mano-a-mano with

Cross." Pause. "But Howell told me to stay behind this chopper and wait for an opening. You countermanding?" Another pause. "I concur with Howell. Why not patch me into his headset? I can't tell what the hell is going on." She nodded to herself as she heard Howell's voice in her head.

After a few moments she could report Quantrill's stolid progress as he moved backward toward her with Howell in careful pursuit. "For God's sake don't risk hitting me, Howell," she muttered, and dropped silently to the concrete. On all-fours she could see Quantrill half-dragging Cross, whose struggles were weak, and she moved as if unaware that she was lining up with quarry and stalker. She refused to think about the likelihood that Howell might shoot anyway.

Crabwise, Sanger passed under the fuselage, then stood directly behind the panting Quantrill. She waited until he stopped, hardly more than arm's length away. She could have hacked at the juncture of his neck and shoulder with the barrel of her chiller, but Howell muttered into his headset, "He's got to let go of that fucking garrotte wire."

She waited.

"Don't get your hopes up," Quantrill called. "The loop is still in place." With that, he let his right hand drop the signet, still holding the wounded Cross as a shield, and reached back to feel for the starboard hatch release. Instead he felt a chiller's muzzle in his right armpit, an arm against his left elbow. Her position violated Sanger's training but under the circumstances she had no choice.

"I can't miss, Quantrill," she said as he froze. "Think very carefully before you jerk that wire." Then, as he slowly swiveled his head, she pressed the chiller flat against his ribcage, loosening her grip, her unseen fingers splayed apart so that he could feel them. "*Very* carefully," she said again.

"I have him, Control." Thirty meters away, Seth Howell stood in an approved crouch, both hands steadying his weapon.

Quantrill thought about it until Howell took that first step nearer. Then his backward-extended right arm swept down an infinitesimal instant before his knees flexed to drive him backward against Sanger. He dipped, still holding onto Cross, rammed his free elbow lightly into Sanger's midriff, her sidearm clattering to the concrete. She rebounded from the Loring's fuselage, clutching her belly, and fell to her knees.

Howell resolved his dilemma when he saw the chiller drop; began to lope intending to pistol-whip Quantrill. The doughty Howell had not believed it possible that a garrotte wire could slice lightly, be unlooped, then re-employed around a second hostage in the time it took for him to run twenty paces. In that brief instant, Howell became a believer.

Quantrill squatted beneath the Loring and behind Sanger, his garrotte loop against her elegant throat. Marty Cross sat before them, right arm useless, and stared at the blood that dripped from his clutching left hand to pool between his legs.

"We can all stand here 'till he bleeds out," Quantrill called, "or you can try me again and lose this bitch, too. Or you can drop the chiller and go back to your parking problem."

Howell glanced at his sidearm. "No way." But he began walking backward, pausing to shout, "Marty! Can you breathe? Can you hold?"

Even while holding the edges of his throat together, Jose Martí Cross refused to shame his Cheyenne mother. But when he nodded his head, his entire upper torso nodded too.

"Yes, the motherfucker has *Sanger* now," Howell raged into his headset as he loped away, reseating his chiller. "All right, we *all* underestimated him! Who is this? Salter? Get a meat wagon out here on the triple for Cross. What? She didn't have a chance, you gotta see this sonofawhore to believe him. He's hauling her into that chopper and he can't fly it—I don't think. Control, do you have any kind of video on us? I'm getting tired of being your eyes . . ."

Quantrill pocketed Sanger's weapon using the garrotte one-handed as a leash, then rolled carefully into the side hatch. Sanger needed no encouragement to follow with the loop around her neck. In seconds they were lost from view, re-emerging in the cockpit. For a man who didn't know how to fly a sprint chopper, Howell admitted into his headset, the little shit was doing a lot of things right—and one-handed at that.

The turbines were still warm, tanks nearly full; in another twenty seconds the props were skating the craft away while Cross went into a bloody foetal crouch. In the distance a crash crew sped toward the injured man. Howell: "He's getting it up, Control. Better pull his plug now; Sanger's as good as dead if he crashes!"

He heard the response in his headset, cursed, drew his chiller, and fired his entire magazine toward the rapidly dwindling aircraft in the futile hope of damaging it. Howell was beginning to think Lon Salter needed that little turncoat alive for interrogation more than he needed Cross and Sanger. Behind him, two of the parked sprint choppers were whistling to life. But both were dead cold—and Ted Quantrill's vehicle was already disappearing to the East. If he was smart, he'd keep low over urban areas as long as possible. It gave Control one more reason not to pull his plug until they'd played the other options out.

CHAPTER 32

"So you'll have to check out the Schreiner ranch for me," Mills said. "Do some of your patent screened interviews on old-timers. Take a look at their books; you're good at that, Eve. I wouldn't put it past Blanton Young to steer us into an operation that spends more than it makes on food for giraffes and other exotic animals. If it looks good to you, I'll go down later and take a second look."

Eve Simpson gnawed her upper lip, studying Mills carefully, nodding only to purchase a few seconds for evaluation. When *he* came to *her* office, it was always to study some new media magic—or when he was too agitated to wait for her motorized chaise. Did he have some ulterior motive? For instance, sending her out to a goddam dude ranch to ensure her absence from her own office on some specified day? Well, she could cut those odds. "I'll have to judge my schedule and let you know when," she said agreeably. If he demanded some rigid schedule of his own, she would elevate her suspicions another notch.

But: "No big hurry. In fact, first we've got to let a gaggle of earth scientists scratch around nearby and decide whether to discover oil or a gravel mine," he sighed. "I'd say no less than two weeks nor over a month." Impeccable in summer tans, Boren Mills strode near the great window of Eve's office. It was nearer the street than his own office and gave a more detailed view. Rocking on his heels, stroking his chin: "I'd go myself if I could afford to leave while Chabrier's juggling his priorities on me. Some things require face-to-face negotiating right here."

"With IEE's board, or with the Lion of Zion?"

"Both, maybe. I talk to Young nearly every day just to make sure he's still,"—a finger circling like a drill at his temple—"among us. Today he's all excited about his S & R people."

"Who've they assassinated now," she said, yawning.

"Nailed one of their own rovers," Mills said, amused. "Young wants to be at the control center when—*good God*!"

During his previous few words, a faint whistle had become a bellow outside. He threw his hands up, ducked and whirled away from the window as the source of the noise thundered past. Eve saw the huge window bow inward, crazing the faint reflection of Mills before it reflexed, returned to normal. Even with the insulation in the IEE tower they were momentarily deafened by the catastrophic roar as a sleek black something missed the tower by scant meters.

"God almighty, what was that?" Mills was erect again, hands pressed against the window, straining to see while the thundering wail was still audible.

"I don't know, but it was below this floor," Eve said in awe.

Then, "I see it," he said, and chuckled shakily. "Must be a victory pass or something. It's an S & R sprint chopper, going like a tracer bullet!"

PART II:
SINGLE COMBAT

CHAPTER 33

Quantrill banked northward toward Brigham City, so near the surface of the Great Salt Lake that his passage ruffled the steel-tinted wavelets. He saw Sanger's desperate gestures, backhanded the air to stop her.

"*Mayday mayday mayday*," she signed, leaning forward. "*If you run North they pull your plug! I was briefed*," her hands insisted.

He whipped the Loring around, nodding, and eased up on the turn as Sanger clawed to keep from tumbling into his lap. She squeezed his arm in camaraderie. Only then did they shrug into their harnesses.

Then in his mastoid he heard, "Report, Q. Report, Q."

"So you can follow my signal in a stealthy bird?"

"Affirm, Q. Presidential directive: Q's programs will be cancelled the moment he reaches Idaho."

It made sense; he didn't doubt they'd do it and wondered why they hadn't already. "You have a link with The Man, do you?" Meanwhile he steepened his bank again, judged his sweep over Ogden would clear the IEE tower.

The President is in Control center," said his mastoid primly. "He wants to avoid further violence. You must leave us viable choices, Q. Is your hostage conscious?"

169

Quantrill glanced toward Sanger, whose hands were saying, *"Control trying to raise me."*

"She may be possuming, Control. With my loop around her neck I don't blame her. Walloped her head on the cowl but she's a tough bitch. I don't trust her. One word from her and I'll shorten her a little." He fought the sideslip, believed for an instant that he had delayed for a fatal fraction of a second. With six tons of black comet hurtling through an absolutely vertical bank, he skimmed past the IEE tower, then eased back on the throttles. "Maybe I should kamikaze into you, Control."

"If you knew where we were."

"Maybe I do," he said.

"We'd like to talk about that, Q. You're too valuable to waste. But if we can't raise S. soon you'll be less valuable."

"Why not call us by names, Control, you miserable jilloff." He was planning furiously. He'd have more time aloft if he kept the sprint chopper at cruise speed—particularly if he stayed over population centers. Loudly, over the turbine wail, he said, "Sanger, report!" His free hand said, *"You're hurt. But do it."*

She groaned, "Go to hell, Quantrill," and signalled him to continue on his course. Below them was the unbroken urban sprawl that had been well underway when Salt Lake City became the heart of Streamlined America, and which now spread from Brigham City to Nephi. He nodded. His readout showed something less than a two-hour fuel supply.

"You get no more from Sanger. I just tightened my loveknot to remind her," Quantrill said aloud, watching Sanger rifle the map compartment for hard-copy air navigation charts.

"We don't have to be nice. For example," said Control, as a tone began in his head. No, a cacophony of tones. Its effect was something like a squalling infant dragging its nails over slate while running a power saw. It was louder than any transmission he had ever heard from Control, but still bearable. For awhile.

In defiance: "Can barely hear you, Control. Say again."

The maddening noise increased slightly and stayed that way for a moment as Quantrill gritted his teeth. It ceased abruptly with Control's, "Loud enough, Q?"

"The name is Quantrill. Let's hear you humanize us, shithead."

"If you want to live," said his tormentor, "don't let your signal fade. Can you land a sprint chopper?"

His signal wouldn't fade as long as he was in range of a relay, which gave him much of Streamlined America. He had landed a Loring twice during maintenance checkouts but, "I can try," was all he said. Keep the fuckers guessing.

Sanger signed, "*Maybe I can find us a hole. Wait one.*"

Quantrill: "*Not always sure whose side you're on.*"

Her eyes widened before she squeezed them shut, her mouth open in a silent agony. Her hands said nothing. The garrotte wire said a great deal; she had not bothered to remove it. He saw moisture coalesce at the corner of her eye, begin coursing down her lean high cheekbone. She wiped it away in anger. Still said nothing, only stared at the nav charts.

Merely to keep the channel alive he said, "If you're so goddam smart, Control, where am I?"

"A hundred thousand citizens are complaining about you,—Quantrill," said Control. He had never heard his own name spoken conversationally by Control; the victory seemed larger than it was. "You're over the Zion strip."

"Bet your ass I am." He glanced at Sanger; realized that pursuing sprint choppers or scrambled jets might soon make visual contact. If they got near enough, they could see into the canopy. "At this altitude, you wouldn't want me to make a bobble. You might think about that while you're telling people to jump me. And if you value your other aircraft, keep 'em out of chiller range. These little maintenance ports in the cockpit are made to order for it."

At this mention of a sidearm, Sanger frowned, then quickly stripped the flesh-colored rover glove from her right hand, holding its thumb before him for inspection.

Quantrill did not understand until Control replied, "Your chiller was in your locker at Dugway, Quantrill. Any other little bluffs you care to try?"

He said one filthy word, drawing it out, then laughed. Sanger was offering the glove to his own right hand. "I'm wearing the thumb of Sanger's right glove, control. It has her ID, and it's her chiller—so don't worry about me, sweetie; you worry about anybody who gets near me." He saw Sanger mime "*OK*".

"You've been planning this a long time, Quantrill."

"For minutes and minutes," he said, letting the truth satirize itself. Ahead, the urban strip was thinning. He tapped Sanger's arm, pointed at the all-channel commset. "*Maybe I should make this public*," he mimed.

"*Zap you right now*," was her silent reply. "*Looking for area I know. Coal mines. Safe if we get deep*?" She ended with an interrogative; S & R had never intended its rovers to know how to mask a critic's reception.

"Quantrill: "*Near*?"

A shrug, then the jab of a finger on the chart near Price, Utah. Between Nephi and Price were

peaks reaching three klicks above sea level but a
sprint chopper could clear them.

He nodded, pulled the Loring into a steep climb
that skirted the southern edge of Salt Creek Peak.
The closer he kept to the terrain, the less likely
that any pursuer could maintain visual contact.
Quantrill kept very, very close, choosing not to
think what would happen if one of his prop shrouds
gulped a bird or a fir tip, and veered to the East in
a rocketing climb.

When Control spoke again it was with a different voice. The signature would have voice-printed
the same, thanks to CenCom's reprocessing. But
Quantrill intuited the differences; contractions,
cadences. All pointed to a *human*ness that Control
did not normally permit in its transmissions. "Quantrill, haven't we proven we don't want you hurt?"

"Su-u-ure. Cross convinced me," he rejoined. He
was trying to activate the map video display but
did not know the cockpit layout that well. For a
harrowing instant he found that he had set the
autopilot; rushed to regain manual control as he
flashed across the phalanx of treetops.

"We could ice you with the flip of a toggle,"
Control went on imperturbably. "You're valuable
to us, Quantrill. Whatever was responsible for this
momentary lapse, we need to talk about it. We're
reasonable, Quantrill. If you head for Canada or
try some—home remedy—to blanket our signal,
we'll have no choice. If you give us a chance we can
talk you down in one piece. Think of Sanger; we
don't want her hurt any more than you do."

Now the sprint chopper flicked above obscuring
peaks, and Quantrill saw a secondary road wind-
ing through a valley far below. Now, also, the
dense cover of trees was thinning. "If you think I
don't want Sanger hurt, try me," he said evenly,

eyeing her obliquely. Buying more time: "But do I hear you offering me an amnesty?"

Control, after a puase: "Something like that."

Sanger, her face pleading, her headshake redundant: *"Never happen."*

Quantrill, aloud: "Let me think about that. I'm a little pressed for time, Control."

Sanger's hands spoke again. *"They'll promise anything; afraid other rovers have been turned."*

He nodded, scanning the distant range of bluffs ahead. These prominences were lower, dotted with vegetation, tinted orange and dusty rose under a pitiless sun. Sanger's finger thrust dead ahead.

"You must realize you're under surveillance, Quantrill," said Control smoothly. "But we'll honor your request to keep a respectful distance." To Quantrill it meant they probably did *not* have visual contact—but no doubt they were trying.

At least now he knew why they hadn't pulled his plug before this: they were fouling their knickers in fear that the cadre of S & R rovers had somehow become honeycombed with treason. "Control, if I pack it in, do I have your oath that I'll be released alive?"

"Absolutely," said Control.

"Interrogate, then ice you," Sanger signed. Beneath her tan lay a dreadful pallor.

Quantrill, you are now in the vicinity of Seely Mountain, proceeding East," said Control. But they might know that from the relay station there. Perhaps they still didn't have a visual.

Well, let 'em think he was convinced. "What sharp eyes you have, granny," he said, craning his neck to see the lake far away. He pointed, unnecessarily. Sanger was already aware of it.

"Five minutes that way," she signed, her hand slicing a point northward.

In five minutes, unless Sanger was a lousy chart-reader, they'd have some *real* deceptions to practice. Now the land was sere and hostile; box canyons sharply defined, horizontal strata of black and blonde painting the canyon walls. They had over an hour's fuel left, and he was tempted to stay aloft until the last possible second. Which was, in all probability, just what Control expected. It wasn't like Control to negotiate; those bastards depended on absolute obedience. Which suggested that they might have a fresh brain in the circuit, a slick negotiator, perhaps a psychologist.

But psych people had their knee-jerk reactions too. "Thinking it over, Control," he said. "Do you have anybody online who can tell me how to land this thing? Just in case," he added that tiny bit too quickly, smiling to himself. He was developing an idea, a balls-out crazy one. "Don't kid yourself that I can't do it alone. I'm not afraid," he said. That last word, he judged, would convince them he was scared shitless.

So scared, in fact, that he could never contemplate the action he was about to take as Marbrye Sanger pointed a triumphant finger ahead.

CHAPTER 34

Sanger was mentally exhausted from trying to ignore the demands of Control. They'd asked if she could communicate and she'd ignored them. Then they'd suggested she try removing the garrotte wire; bolting toward the rear of the Loring; half a dozen

scenarios, all based on two fallacies. The first was
that Quantrill's psychomotor responses were anywhere near normal; and the second was that
Marbrye Sanger had not committed herself, once
and for all, to her lover.

Even while he doubted her fidelity.

"These little mines East of Carbonville," she signed,
taking too long to spell out the name. *"Catholics,
Indys. I had a mission here.* She did not elaborate;
why waste time admitting you'd disappeared a
woman for pushing media unscramblers to the tough
local miners?

Quantrill knew that Sanger expected him to attempt a landing with the sprint chopper. *"Where's
our DZ,"* he signed.

She paused, vaguely disoriented. The township
was further down the valley; the access road twisted
below. In the distance was a mine tower, like a
scarlet silo protruding from the earth—but Sanger
knew that meant big business. They'd have a better chance in one of the small mines operated by
men and women who competed against the Fed
consortiums. Nearer, she saw two tailings piles,
suggesting horizontal shafts typical of small coal
mines.

"There," she signaled, pointing near a two-story
structure of stone and mortar that was too large to
be a residence. Sanger did not study it closely;
assumed it housed crushers and sorters. She could
not have known that her decision of that instant,
that momentary gesture, would decide a great many
things.

Quantrill eased back on the throttles, scanning
the bright heavens for swift birds of prey. *"Take
the cable down,"* he signed. *"I'll follow."*

Almost, she spoke aloud. *"If you leave it hovering,
they'll soon realize we're down."*

But he was already waving her back, speaking

aloud. "I'm going to mull it over, Control," he said. "Don't know where the hell I am but I know how to circle. I think," he added. At that moment he slowed the Loring's forward motion. He'd have to program a steady tight bank for himself, but he didn't have to risk Sanger's bod that way. Without looking, he brought his left fist up over his shoulder, thumb jerking downward. Then he pulled the tee-handle for the belly hatch. The aircraft wafted nearly motionless above baked earth.

Stunned, Sanger realized that Quantrill expected her to exit the ship on her cable harness. If he kept it hovering while he followed, the first pursuer on the scene would penetrate his deception. Then she grinned at his back—her first smile in two days—and hurried. She'd concluded incorrectly that he intended to shoot the aircraft down with her chiller.

She snatched up the cable from its overhead stowage, reeled it out, saw it writhe below; fitted a handgrip with its frictioner to the cable, then attached its carabiners to her epaulets. Hers was an easy drop, less than a hundred meters, and she made it in a dozen seconds. The instant she touched the ground, Quantrill banked the Loring and began to climb. She raised both arms in supplication, certain that he had decided to leave her.

Then, three hundred meters up, the craft began to circle, one coleopter shroud angled more than the other, and she saw the stubby wings wavering as Quantrill sought a smooth pattern. He wasn't all that good at it. He steepened his bank, the cable whipping below, and moments later she saw his legs through the belly hatchway. The autopilot was now in charge.

Quantrill hadn't wasted his maintenance experience. He stripped a rubber tiedown cord from stowage, gripped it in his teeth while improvising a sling with harness straps. His work coverall, of

course, had no epaulets for a cable drop. With the
straps across his back and under his arms he linked
them into a loop, fitted the cable frictioner, locked
it. The cable drum had its own brake and automatic rewind stud. He set it for auto rewind, sat in
the hatchway with his feet against the hatch, pried
the downlock trigger from its clasp. Now the wind
pressure thrust the hatch against his bootsoles,
but he could not be certain it would slap the hatch
more than halfway shut. His last jury-rig was the
rubber tiedown, hooked to the hatch and stretched
to a handhold inside.

He dropped, batted by the hatch door as it
snapped against the cable. The sling bit into his
arm sockets. He was rotating helplessly, sliding
down the cable and, linked as he was, Quantrill
could not stabilize himself with a free-fall arch.
Strictly speaking, his descent was not even a true
rappel. It was a pirouetting slide down a cable
that slowly unreeled against a preset drag, and a
survivor of this experiment would be one who did
not make the same mistake *once.*

Quantrill cocked a leg outward, increasing drag
on that side. His rotation slowed and his spiral
narrowed slightly. He arched then, legs spread,
elbows back, and found himself tracking in a great
arc—but a lesser arc than that of the droning sprint
chopper. If his pursuers made visual contact now,
his ruse would be all for nothing.

Each time he tightened his hand frictioner, more
of the cable paid out from its reel in response to
the drag of his body. In fifty-meter increments he
descended to treetop height—if there had been any
tall cottonwoods near. He had intended to set the
Loring's circle low enough that the cable's weighted
end would finally drag the ground—though if it
caught on a rock outcrop he knew the cable would
part. He hoped he could descend swiftly, stabilize

his track again, and slip from his harness loop to approximate a chutist's landing. But it did not work out that nicely.

Wind drift caused the aircraft to stray from a perfect circle. He found himself at the end of the cable, still moving at a respectable speed, still ten meters up. But the ground was uneven; by closing his limbs he further narrowed the radius of his circle. Now he was eight meters up, fighting a fresh rotation; now six. And just ahead was a two-meter hillock made by an old road-grader. Beyond that, his drop would be greater.

He reduced the odds another arm's length by releasing his handgrip and slipping from his sling, holding to the end of the loop as he approached the hillock at a sprinter's speed and much too high above it. He released his grip.

Sanger could not know all the variables Quantrill fought and was a hundred meters distant when he caromed off the earth, spilling down the lee side of the hillock into a rutted mining road. She saw him hit on the downslope, bounce, tuck into a ball, hit again, come up on all-fours. He was shaking his head, trying to rise, when she reached him. Then he fell on his back, gasping for breath. And Control could hear involuntary grunts and wheezes.

"Sanger, has your status changed?" She wondered at Control's use of her surname; realized that Quantrill could not speak, whatever Control might be saying to him. Controllers could talk with a dozen rovers at once.

She made two snap decisions, hauling Quantrill's midriff fabric up to ease his discomfort as she panted, "Nailed—the bastard."

"Can you fly a Loring?"

"Neg, Control." She saw Quantrill's eyes blink, hoped he was fully conscious as he fought for breath. Above them the sprint chopper continued its banked circle, slowly drifting downwind. The belly hatch was nearly shut, Quantrill's makeshift harness caught at the hatch lip when the auto rewind reeled it in. It might escape notice from a distance. But the canopy was clear; obviously, no one was minding the store up there. "He got it— circling on auto—and I got in—a neck chop. We're in—personnel bay. If—you value that eye—Quantrill,—let go of—the garrotte."

Quantrill could wheeze a bit now; gestured feebly for her to release his coverall. She could not tell whether his toothy rictus was a smile or a grimace until he made a manual "*OK*". He didn't look okay, he looked like bloody hell with dark stains wetting the frayed coverall at his elbow and right hip.

"Mexican standoff, Sanger," he gasped finally for Control's benefit. "When this bird runs out of fuel,—it's you and me both."

"*All the way*," she signed, and hauled him to his feet. At first he limped but soon was loping with her up the road to the many-windowed stone building. Aloud she said, "Any good ideas, Control?" She had two reasons for being breathless; one bogus, one real.

Wait one, Sanger," from Control. "We have to get closer visual contact." Scanning the heavens, she realized that they had no visual contact at all. Yet. If they had, they'd be wondering why two people were leaving dust spurts as they bounded up an access road.

The masonry building had its own windmill and, she saw with a start, a flowering hedge. It also had stained glass in its front windows and a hand-hewn cross of stone over the double doors.

Sanger had haplessly led Quantrill to a Catholic Church.

CHAPTER 35

Other structures squatted nearly a kilometer distant, but they knew better than to risk any more time in the open than absolutely necessary. They were supposedly locked in mutually deadly embrace, still in the circling sprint chopper that slowly circled downwind across the valley.

"Quantrill, you made a hell of a try; the best," said Control in his head. "If you remand yourself to Sanger's custody now, maybe we can get you both down alive. If you don't you are suiciding. Do you agree?"

"Maybe; maybe not," he panted, hurling the wooden doors open.

"We hold too many cards," Control insisted, and reminded him by setting the squalling infant on the slate again at medium strength. Then, over the cacophony, Control began a seductive spiel with one theme: "Give it up, Quantrill. You've taken too much punishment. Let us help you. You must be exhausted, hurt, afraid. We understand; we don't want you hurt. Relax; let us take the burden . . ."

The two desperate rovers stormed down a center aisle in the nave, pausing at the sanctuary which, for their immediate needs, was no sanctuary at all. Control's transmissions were still too loud, too clear.

Sanger darted toward one of the hallways that flanked the sanctuary; discovered only a gloomy little bathroom and a gloomier reconciliation room with its confessional screen.

Quantrill took the other hall, now limping again, and was ready to blow the lock off the sacristy door when a lean aged figure appeared at the end of the hall, buttoning the long sleeves of a black shirt. "Is there something—," the man began, and saw the chiller, and crossed himself. Quantrill nearly shot him dead before seeing that the priest was not reaching for a sidearm.

The man of God faced this hellish apparition with its dirt-caked face, its torn bloody coverall, its deadly weapon and half-mad eyes that glowed with more deadly purpose. The rounded shoulders straightening, he stared at the young rover. "I'm Father Klein. You won't need that in my chapel," he said, nodding at the chiller.

In answer, Quantrill pocketed the weapon, waved for the priest to follow, hobbled back to the nave. He had remembered the visior's register near the doors. Sanger all but collided with him, saw his silent gesture to his rear, tried a sickly smile as she spied the elderly man hurrying toward them.

"Are you in trouble? Can't you talk?" But she was shaking her head, pointing to her breast and then drawing a finger across her throat. The gestural shorthand of S & R rovers would not take her very far with this man, who could not know that his were the only spoken words to which Control was wholly deaf.

The felt-nibbed pen in Quantrill's hand flew across the register, the few scrawled words high and bold. *NEED BASEMENT OR CAVE. THEN TALK.*

The priest bent to study the scrawl. His response seemed to take an eon. Unheard by him, Control babbled in two heads. "There's nothing like that here," the priest said, blinking. "The nearest mines are some distance away," he gestured, leading them back through the nave and past the sacristy.

When Sanger half-sobbed, "I need time to think, Control," the priest studied her with curiosity and compassion.

Then he led them into a spacious kitchen meant to serve large gatherings. "I haven't a car, and it's a brisk climb up to the mines," he said, pointing through the nearest window.

It was all of that, Sanger judged. Even with help, the battered Quantrill would need a half-hour to get up-slope to the nearest mine shaft. She scanned the kitchen. She did not see the ancient clipboard near the sink, but took in the huge butcher block that squatted near the center of the kitchen with cutlery of many kinds arrayed on its solid flanks. Staring at the gleaming blades she said aloud, "I have a bad cut and I need a doctor right now. Immediately." Her calm was ice-brittle. She knew Quantrill would never agree with her silent decision.

Father Klein frowned; he could see no blood-stains on her clothing. "Let me help," he said, stepping nearer.

From Control: "Some things take time, Sanger. We're on the way."

Sanger juggled her auditors, waved the priest away savagely while staring hard into his face. "A surgeon, as soon as humanly possible. How long?"

Control: "Not long."

Father Klein: "Ten minutes, I suppose. I don't have a link to him but I'll take my bicycle to the village. It's pretty primitive here, I'm afraid." He gazed at Quantrill, fascinated. Sanger saw that Quantrill was staring at nothing, but his hand tore at the hair over his mastoid as though idly plucking fur from a stuffed animal. Then he glanced at the others, half-smiled; dropped his hand, oblivious to the strands of hair caught between his fingers.

"Make it five minutes, will you?" So far, she had given Control no hint that she might be speaking directly to a fourth party. She gestured the priest on his way, looking about her for equipment she could use. In a thigh pocket she had the first item, the hypospray canister.

"Is that as loud as you can do it, Control?" Quantrill's forehead glistened with sweat, his eyelids flickering in tune with some maddening noise that Sanger could not hear.

Using muted gutterals that Control alone could decipher clearly, Sanger lied, "I think he's fainting, Control." If the bastards thought him unconscious they might not pull his plug. Oh, but they wanted him *bad*, she thought, so they could dissect him at their leisure. Well, they might just get some dissection—but not on their terms.

She noted the prewar dishtowels folded near the sink, the small hardwood cutting board that hung at the side of the chopping block. They would have to serve. She faced Quantrill, hurrying on with it, certain that if she faltered only once she would not be able to continue. She addressed him twice, once aloud and then in sign talk. "Quantrill, you're about to get your moment of truth." Pause, then, "*I love you*," said her hands.

He was plucking at his hair again, but stopped as he read a phrase he had never seen her use. Evidently the sounds in his head took a lot of cognitive jamming because his silent reply was jerky: "*Sorry I doubted you. Even if you took me out, I'd go loving you, Marbrye.*" Aloud he managed to say, "We may just go out this way together, Sanger."

Lips and hands moving: "Don't try to scare me, little man." "*That's the way I'd want it, my love.*"

She moved to him, raised a hand to his cheek, saw his eyes close as he kissed her open palm to seal a pact; one that might accept, if not mutual suicide, then double murder. It was then that she brought up her other hand with the tiny canister of hypospray.

Sanger's weapon was not as gentle as most drugs, but only curare was quicker. At least the stuff would put him out instead of leaving him paralyzed and fully conscious. She placed her mouth on his for one heart-rending instant before triggering the canister against the side of his head and then, as she pulled back, spraying it into his mouth.

Stumbling, wiping furiously, he backed against the chopping block. "Sanger! Oh Sanger, what the hell have you done?"

"Outlasted you," she said. She dared not approach him as he faltered; his dismay was tinged with fury. Yet her hands said, *"I love you, Ted. Trust me. Love you. Trust me,"* as she watched him register betrayal and, mercifully, loss of awareness.

Control was braying for a report. "Hypospray," she gasped. "Got the little fucker but—inhaled a little." She pulled him onto the butcher block, face down, and snatched up a handful of clean towels. Two of them, folded thick, went under his chin. Her belt medikit provided sterile pressure patches which she lay face-up on the wooden surface. Her utility knife with its retractable blade guard was as sharp as a filleting knife. If Sanger could shave her legs with it, perhaps it would shave a patch of skull. She did, nicking him only once over the swell of mastoid behind his ear; and saw the thin scar appear, a neat job by men of great expertise and no vestige of human compassion.

The cleaver was her first choice but she feared it was too dull. The largest of the carving knives was almost as heavy, and wickedly sharp. She sterilized its blade with an ampoule from her kit, grabbed the small cutting board by its handle, laid it down again and gripped her hands tightly to quell their trembles. She might be killing him anyway, but if either hand shook she would surely fail.

Several long breaths, murmuring to assuage Control, and then she gazed again at that neat livid scar. Somewhere beneath it lay the small horror that had driven them both past cold-blooded murder and on to self-hatred. She wiped the shaved area to sterilize it, placed the heavy knife squarely on the scar, lifted the cutting board again, and with steady hands she readied for the blow. "I think Q is out, Control; but I intend to make sure." With that, she struck with her makeshift mallet against the back of the heavy blade.

Quantrill grunted with the impact; made no other sound. She saw that she had struck too lightly, peeled back a flap of skin and struck again, harder, from another angle. A rough trapezoid of tough spongy bone popped away. Sanger had watched training films of appendectomies and had spilled a lot of blood on her own account, but none of that had been Quantrill's blood. She bit her lip and continued, perspiration rivuleting her face.

Marbrye Sanger clung to the tatters of reason as she peered into the cleft she had forced into the spongy bone mass behind her lover's ear. Now she knew why surgeons rarely elected to work on a loved one. For the first few seconds, surprisingly little blood welled into the cavity she had driven nearly two centimeters deep and twice as long. In the deepest part of her brutal incision the hollow irregular mastoid cells were larger, and Sanger perceived a larger cavity the size of her fingertip before upwelling gore from surrounding tissue blocked her view.

She wondered if she were insane. She did not know what the damnable critic looked like, nor exactly where to look, and rumor claimed that it would explode at her touch. Yet she knew it must include a rechargeable energy cell and a gram or so of explosive. Surely, she insisted to herself, she would recognize such a foreign body when she saw it.

That little cavity at the deepest limit of her cut: was it larger than it seemed? The edge made a curve that seemed too regular to be part of the surrounding bone. Blinking against tears, her lower lip bleeding between her teeth, she swept the synthoderm face of a pressure patch through the scarlet mess; saw the tiny cavity; eased the tip of the knife in and felt nearby bony cells carved away like half-rotted wood under her careful assault. She flicked the knifetip out to dispose of bone fragments, swallowed against a bitter taste rising in her throat,—and then she saw it.

She nearly sobbed aloud, facing the hellborn thing. Gleaming unnaturally white in the pinkish gray of human tissue, wedged into the mastoid antrum cavity, lay Ted Quantrill's loathsome critic. Inside its firm flexible surface Sanger could see striations as of dissimilar materials stacked inside an oblong capsule. She carved away more bone, infinitely tender, willing her arms not to shake.

"Sanger!" Control's voice was strident in her head. "What is he doing? We're getting anomalous readings; how hard did you hit him?"

"He's flopping on—on the deck," she stammered. "Can't stop him. Need time. Woozy as hell." She did not know how her savage surgery was registering to Control, but they obviously did not like what they were monitoring. The God-damned critic was still intact, untouched; but now fully exposed.

She tasted salt when she swallowed, grasped the knife again.

When Sanger's sweaty grip caused the knife to slip, the blood-smeared blade carved neatly through the translucent plastic and some dark cheesy substance as well. No explosion.

There was no explosion! Now the monstrous, repulsive thing lay in two pieces, connected only by filament-slender wire which had resisted the knife. Whimpering almost silently, Sanger wiped away blood and tried to shave more of the bony material side. She flicked the blade, prying, and saw a half-dozen hunks of bloody debris spatter onto the butcher block and floor. Sanger laid down her knife, sobbing noiselessly as she stared.

Ted Quantrill might die now, or in a day, but he would not die from a detonator in his skull. Among the crimson debris were both wire-linked pieces of the mastoid critic.

From Control: "Ease up, Sanger! Are you beating his head in? Brief us; we get anomalous signals from Q."

She remained silent, controlling her gasping sobs, both hands held to her face in mingled revulsion and relief. With a featherlight touch, she pressed two sterile pressure patches into Quantrill's gaping wound; shuddered at the trickle of his blood that soaked the towels under his chin. Her hands were sticky with his blood. She could feel it drying on her cheeks, and this added sensation galvanized her once more.

Rushing to the sink, Sanger scrubbed viciously at her face and hands, willing her sobs to abate. She commanded herself to stand fast against emotional collapse, for her job had scarcely begun.

Rubbing hard with a dishtowel, she scanned the room for a terminal or chalkboard—anything to write with. At last the old clipboard with its pencil

on a frayed cord arrested her gaze. She tore away
a shopping list, began to scribble; slowed as she
saw that her trembling scrawl was nearly illegible.

Escaped S & R rovers, she wrote. *Mastoid-implant
radios can be exploded by S & R leaders. I cut
Quantrill's out. Must remove mine NOW!* She jumped
toward the voices and hurrying footsteps; saw the
priest from the window, and with him a swarthy
man in shirtsleeves.

As Sanger darted to the doorway, Control spoke
again. She wrote another passage as Control said,
"We've made a command decision. Howell advises
us of a disturbing possibility and we can't chance
it. If near Q's head, move away or cover his head
with something. Terminating Q's programs in ten
seconds, *mark*."

Sanger did not answer but stood swaying before
the two men who now entered the kitchen. "This
the injured woman?" The doctor, gripping a scarred
little bag, gaped beyond her. He saw the body of
Ted Quantrill, and the thin drool of his blood from
sodden towels, running down the flank of the chopping block. As he stepped around Sanger, she
slapped his arm hard with the clipboard and held
it before him.

She pointed at Quantrill, then at the debris on
the floor. The doctor was reading, frowning, shaking his head. "Incred—," he said, as a high-pitched
report echoed through the room. The sound was as
thin and sharp as a scalpel.

The physician stepped back quickly from the
small object that skittered across the floor to rest
near his feet. The priest was now reading the note.
"Father in heaven," he breathed, and crossed
himself.

The physician pocketed the tiny device at his
feet, hurried to Quantrill's side, felt for a pulse
with one hand while carefully peeling back the

gore-soaked patches with the other. "You've probably killed him," he said, then remembered Sanger's last scrawl. "And what makes you think we'd be likely to give anyone political asylum, young lady?"

Control was clamoring for a report but Sanger knew her best tactic was to feign unconsciousness. She snatched up the clipboard. *NOT sure*, she wrote; *S & R querying me now.* She circled a previous passage—*Must remove mine NOW*—then dropped the clipboard and, in what seemed one choreographed motion, swept her utility knife up with bared blade to shave away the hair from her own skull.

Priest and doctor froze, unsure whether this violent young woman was attempting suicide; but the doctor was quick to infer her real goal. "A hell of a choice you give me," he snarled at her, and motioned for her to sit on the rough bench near the window. "Guess I'll have to tend to you first."

He gestured for the knife, studied it expertly for a second, tossed a quick bitter glance toward the priest who was administering last rites to the unconscious Quantrill. "Save the hereafter for later, Klein, he needs help here and now. Apply finger pressure over those patches to lessen the bleeding—and tell me if he stops breathing!"

Fingers almost a blur, his bag open beside him, the medic bade Sanger lie prone on the bench. He bound her to the bench with velcrolok straps; began to shave the fine chestnut curls away, murmuring to Sanger as he worked. "Klein told me you weren't long on talk—and now I guess I see why. Search & Rescue runaways, hm?" He did not pause for answer. "Never believed those rumors, but unless you set this up to sucker me, guess I'll *have* to give it credence. Your bosses talking to you now?"

He held the razor-sharp blade away; saw her nod, and saw the scar behind her ear. "By God,

here it is! Nice incision, whoever implanted the
thing. I have a portable rotary bone saw, young
lady, but I'll have to put you under first. God
knows how the young fella stood it. These things
take time."

Sanger ignored the irony—the doctor echoing
Control's complaint about time—and signaled that
she wanted to write a response. A bone saw would
generate vibrations that Control might identify.
And the brutally efficient S & R hypospray had
put Quantrill under in scant seconds. It could do
the same for her—if she could make the doctor
understand.

"Not now," he said calmly, and triggered a spray
of cytovar onto her unprotected skin.

She still had her spray in her pocket. "No!" She
blurted it out, writhed aside, fumbled for her
hypospray.

Control misunderstood. Someone imagined that
she had seen Quantrill die. "Couldn't be helped,
S," crackled in her ear.

Cytovar was among the best of the quick-acting
anesthetics, but it overtook the mind in layered
stages. The faculty of judgment was first to capi-
tulate. Knowing this, the physician quickly climbed
astride Sanger, his legs pinioning her arms as the
heavy straps bound her to the bench. Even so, he
took one solid blow to the kidney from her flailing
feet before he leaned forward. He soothed, "Relax.
You won't feel a thing."

Softly, desperately, hoping against all odds that
Control might not understand, Sanger whispered,
"Spray in my pocket—is faster. Use it!"

The physician heard. "I'll not take chances on
anything like that."

Control heard, too. "Nothing's faster than a critic,
S. Uh—hypospray? How can we use it from—"

and then in sudden suspicion, "Who else is monitoring you, S? Report!"

Marbrye Sanger fought to resist an automatic response to Control's last command. Above and behind her came the sound of a small rotary tool being tested. With her last shreds of duplicity she muttered, "Hovering, Control. Can't—think."

The doctor fitted a sterile Weck blade to its handle, prepped her skin with a chill anesthetic. And then he made a mistake: "If you can hear me, start counting down from twenty."

Now she was slipping down into limbo, incapable of violence nor even of resistance. "Twenty. Nineteen. Eighteen. Seven'een," she began.

Control: "What are you counting? Report!"

Sanger's automatic responses were laid bare. "Down from twenny."

Control: "Why are you doing it?"

"Doc'or's orders."

Physician: "Another few seconds; keep counting." He pinched the flesh around the scar, hard. She did not flinch.

Control: "What doctor, S? *Report*!"

"Sixteen—dunno 'is name."

"What is the doctor doing, S? *Report*!"

A final tatter of conscious resistance; then, "Cut'n you out—of me."

She was taking an infernally long time to go under, thought the physician. At least he could make his preliminary horsehoe incision, laying the skin back and clamping it. He did so.

Control stepped up its audio power. "So, are you under sedation?"

"Uh-huh." She tried to nod. The doctor cursed, held her head still.

As loud and as sweet as any transmission Control would ever make: "We can help you, S. Just tell us: is someone removing your critic?"

Help, or the promise of help, glimmered faintly in the corridors of semiconsciousness. She murmured what could have been an affirmative, "Um-hmm." Her head did not move. Her entire body became limp.

The physician adjusted his rotary tool, aligned the saw blade so that it would not spit debris into his face, flicked the switch and lowered the spinning steel teeth against the dull gleam of mastoid bone. "Won't be long now," he soothed.

It was, in fact, almost instantaneous.

CHAPTER 36

The critic's detonation inside armoring bone was not as loud as the rotary saw, a muffled meaty resonance that erupted under the whining saw blade as if the physician had cut into a pressurized cartridge. A gout of flesh and bone splinters flew outward in a hideous spray, and the body of Marbrye Sanger gave one convulsive throe. Straps parted; the physican found himself hurled to the floor.

Wiping his face, using his rage to overmaster his nausea, the doctor stood again to survey what had moments before been a lovely woman in desperate need. He rolled her body over, saw the gaping wound; knew even as he checked for vital signs that no human body could survive such internal assault. Never again would she harbor desperation—or fulfillment.

The physician turned and caught the horrified gaze of the priest, and somehow this fleeting contact fanned the guttering flame of his spirit. Approaching the unconscious Quantrill he growled, "If ever we had any doubts about where our government is headed, good Father Klein,—well, I offer Exhibit A." He swept his arm outward as if offering aid to the lifeless body that lay splashed with blood and hard sunlight below the window.

Father Klein cleared his throat several times before he could speak. "Some things I have never doubted. But I don't know what to do."

"Take a blowtorch to every bloodstain you can find, and help me get this youngster to the Masonics," the doctor replied. "We've got some tracks to cover, Klein. These Search & Rescue people don't screw around."

CHAPTER 37

On her next trip to the San Rafael lab complex, Eve displayed gaity like a semaphore. Chabrier, essentially a sensitive man, waited patiently to learn the invisible message that underlay her overt signals. Their drug business concluded, both retired to his lower-level chambers to transact their pleasures.

Though plenty of IEE's drugs were handy, it was Eve's pleasure to draw on the Ember of Venus for the stuff they shared. Luxuriating in her second rush within the hour, Eve plucked at the hairy mat on Chabrier's belly and sighed, "Sometimes I envy you, Marengo."

A snort was his Gallic answer.

"I mean it. Tucked away out here, controlling your own priorities,—not like that fucking mad-house at IEE."

If Chabrier had owned antennae they would have vibrated like a tuning fork; real trouble at her level, or Mills's, must inevitably have its effect on Chabrier. In feigned lazy indifference he said, "With you and the formidable Monsieur Mills at the helm? Surely you exaggerate."

Eve's turn to snort. "If we weren't controlling the media, my man, the leadoff lines alone would boggle your brains."

Chabrier recalled an old Chinese curse. "We live in interesting times," he said. "But perhaps they would not interest me."

Eve could not resist the bait. "Two weeks ago it might've been, 'Government Assassins Executed While Escaping'. According to Mills it was a damned close thing; if forensics cops hadn't identi-fied bits of hair and bone on an ore crusher, they'd still be looking for the man." She smiled to think of Quantrill's body in a condition that no woman would crave, macerated and consumed by the system. "I met him once, you know."

"A one-day news sensation, perhaps."

"Sensation you want? You got it: 'President Young Loses Marbles.' Mills tells me the Lion of Zion is about three liters low on his mental dipstick, fueling himself on booze and pussy and due for a major overhaul." She searched Chabrier's face for a sign. If that news didn't faze him, he was either wasted on her alkaloids or singularly unimpres-sable.

Dealing as he did with Chinese on a daily basis, Chabrier found her American slang barely scrutable and donated a show of concern. "I gather that IEE is, ah, deeply in the President's debt."

"Call it a mutual aid society. Mills is trying to diversify. Whatever a gaga president pulls down with him, IEE can maintain a stranglehold on Streamlined America."

Chabrier's smile was bleak. "As Krupp did in Germany, eh?"

Since media history is inextricable from political history, Eve boasted a modest understanding of the German firm's tactics. "Only Krupp didn't get into dude ranches, with gambling and thrill rides so big they make the Disney ruins look like backyard sandpiles by comparison. Matter of fact, I'm scheduled to look over a hell of a big ranch very soon. I'll miss you while I'm down there but it's my first ride on a delta, so it won't be entirely boring."

Chabrier's gaze was speared on a needlelike sparkle from the great jewel that hung at her throat. "I shall be with you in proxy," he said, brushing the Ember with a fingertip. Far better, he thought, for this great vache to stave off bordeom with drugs than to take up some alliance with another man of a desperation equalling his own.

Eve lay back, took the amulet by its chain, let it swing above their heads where they could revel in its lightshow. "Krupp didn't have a shot at this, either," she said dreamily. "The scaled-up synthesizer is IEE's real hole-card, Marengo. I'd hate to think what would happen to you if it turned out to be a deuce."

This time her jargon was impenetrable. When she explained, Chabrier could only shrug. "To envy me, ma cherie, is to envy a man walking a tightrope over an abyss."

"I hope your progress reports to Mills don't sound that pessimistic."

"I am not a fool," he grumbled.

For perhaps thirty seconds she studied his sad countenance. Eve could not know that Chabrier's maternal grandmother in Amiens had left him a behavioral legacy, having slept with a Nazi officer to avoid a concentration camp. Yet Eve began to sense that her lover needed her for more than sexual favors. She could view this revelation as a wedge cut from her sexuality, or as a buttress added to her power. As always, she chose the pleasant alternative.

"My sweet monkeyfuck, do you think I'd let any harm come to you?"

"I think," he said slowly, "that you would not learn of it until too late to help." He knew better than to ask her for an avenue of escape. She must stumble upon the notion herself.

But Eve did not need to stumble. Her fertile imagination had long since created scenarios in which she stashed her gentle gorilla in some Mexican villa with an acre of palms waving overhead and a three-acre waterbed undulating underfoot. The problem was, Chabrier had far more potential to please her by a breakthrough which could make her awesomely rich, than he did as purely sexual outlet. Chabrier was clearly a multipurpose tool.

And if Mills found him expendable in his major purpose? What a pity, to dispose of him when he had other delightful uses! Assuming that Chabrier had an escape hatch, he would still be crazy to use it while Mills supported him. "Marengo, would *you* know in advance if you were about to get the axe?"

Doubting, and hiding that doubt, he nodded in bogus certainty.

"Then leave it to little Evie to find you a bailout procedure."

He had the courage to smile, recalling the ancient bastardized French of airmen. "M'aidez?"

"Yeah; mayday," she agreed, and began to aid him in more carnal ways.

CHAPTER 38

The rawboned stranger swept in on the scruffiest, quietest hovercycle Sandy Grange had ever seen. She noted however that beneath its blotched paint, huge muffler, and dented air-cushion skirts lurked a small turbocharged diesel of the sort that might take a man a hundred klicks on a gallon of fuel. And its pannier tanks were uncommonly large.

She penetrated the man's disguise as easily as she did the machine's. "You were told right, Mr.—uh, Gold," she smiled, shifting her basketful of snap-beans to shake his hand. His fingertips, but not his palms, were callused; and his sunburn said that he had not been outdoors much until the past few days. "How long will you stay?"

He slapped dust from his sweatstained stetson and favored her with an ingratiating grin. It removed any stray doubt as to his real name. "Depends, Miz Grange. I expect to be met here for the next leg of my trip. I detoured around Rocksprings, so don't worry 'bout that. And I brought my own grub."

"But no guitar," she said in mock innocence.

"Now you're funnin' me, ma'am." The grin was suddenly lopsided.

Confidently she led him into the soddy. "Just a little," she admitted, showing him where to wash up and to lay his sleeping bag. "I believe the Scots word for 'golden' is 'ora'. Really, you might've chosen a different alias."

Ora McCarty raised despairing eyes to the roof, sighed, said nothing.

"Besides, I've seen you many times on the holo. How many towns have you passed through on the way here?"

"Not a one, little lady. They said it was either take the outlaw trail or have some work done on my face and, well,—"

"Your face is part of your fortune. I understand, Mr. Mc—Gold."

"Aw shoot, you'll razz me hollow at this rate, Miz—"

"It's Sandy, Mr. McCarty. Do you know, you're the third traveler I've had here in a week? I may add another room and hang out a shingle, if this keeps up. Now if you'll excuse me, this garden truck of mine won't jump into the basket by itself."

Presently McCarty emerged, much refreshed, and wandered out to the garden. Soon he found himself picking beans—one to Sandy's four—and laughed with her when she observed, "Someday I'll tell the story of the time a future President helped me pick beans."

"But make that 'candidate,' Sandy. Election is two years off and I'm the darkest horse since Black Beauty. Nobody's afraid of me at the polls."

Sandy stretched the kinks from her back. "Nobody was afraid of W. Lee O'Daniel either—until it was too late." In her passion for books and a Texan's passion for Texas, Sandy had accumulated a fund of trivia which she happily shared with the reverend McCarty. O'Daniel had become famous in the

1930's as a cloyingly countrified guitar plunker, but rode his radio audience into the Governor's mansion in Austin—and then galloped on to Washington as a senator.

McCarty knew his faults. He was politically naive and, though far older than Sandy, found her arguments worrisome. He was a lay preacher, not a Machiavelli. He hadn't sought the Indy vote; accepted his candidacy with reluctance only after slick-talking folks in Ogden raised a campaign fund without his knowledge.

Several Indy candidates had already made their intentions known, though presidential campaigns would not intensify for nearly two years. For McCarty, things had just kind of got out of hand. Still, in face-to-face rallies Ora McCarty could say things he couldn't say on FBN holovision; for example, that a company big enough to hire ten thousand people was also big enough to accept collective bargaining. That implied unions—a topic on the proscribed list. So far, McCarty's rhetoric was much milder than that of most dissenters.

"I have an idea this fella Albeniz rigged this trip for me to talk to some union folks," he confided as they carried their produce 'truck' back to the soddy. He was not prepared for her response.

"Albeniz? *Lufo* Albeniz?"

"I talk too durn much," he gloomed.

"You said what I wanted to hear," she laughed, "but if Lufo arranged it, don't be surprised if you happen across Governor Street."

"That would surprise me, all righty," he chuckled. "I come down here 'cause I was told it might save a lot of trouble, maybe some lives, if I came alone like this."

He paused as Sandy placed fingers in her mouth and blew a long, two-note whistle with a rising terminal inflection. "I'm calling my little sis," she explained. "While you're here she'll have to, ah, tend the stock."

You run cattle hereabouts?"

"We try," she replied vaguely, and with an amusement he could not fathom. In truth, the only way they ran cattle was to run them stampeding, the first time they got downwind of Childe's improbable steed. Childe drank goat's milk and liked it.

In good time, a scrawny girlchild pelted out of the cedar and oak scrub, moving somewhat warily as she neared the middle-aged stranger with the well-worn clothes and the fresh sunburn. But Sandy had given the 'come alone, OK' whistle and Childe's approach was only her natural shyness. Sandy introduced Childe as mute, and McCarty as 'Gold', giving each a cover story.

"You go tend the animals, hon, but be back by dark if you want supper." The little girl kissed Sandy, made a ragged-skirted curtsy that charmed McCarty and sped off again, a knob-kneed little whirlwind lacking only her attendant dust-devil.

The late-summer sun was touching distant trees as the two adults feasted outside on cornbread, beans, and a hot sauce Sandy labeled Ajuey— pronounced 'aa*whoooe*y'. McCarty praised each bite as it bit him back, and claimed that his were tears of joy. He had heard of South Texas hot sauce; knew that in time it would lose its erection, and silently prayed God for that time to arrive. Bats could have roosted in his sinuses. When the sun went down, he was sure, he could use his tongue for a flashlight.

When at last his voice lost its castrato timbre, Ora McCarty resumed a previous topic. "Governor Street is a man I mightily admire, Sandy. If he wasn't on the dodge, he'd be the man to beat on the Indy ticket."

Those, Sandy replied, were her own feelings.

"But his hide wouldn't hold shucks if he paraded it in Streamlined America. Young's enemies have a way of wakin' up dead these days," he persisted.

Sandy nodded and took more hot sauce with cool unconcern.

"Anyhow, I just hope I can make it back to Zion—uh, Utah, without makin' Young's hit list. Awright then, I'm nervous," he admitted.

"I would be, too. I'd be scared to run an Indy safehouse even here in Wild Country if I didn't have—friends—to protect me." Her candid eyes, agelessly wise but somehow artless, smiled into his. "I guess we have to decide whether we want security or improvement; and there is no security. So you and I made the same decision, hm?"

"You're a spooky young woman, you know that? Too smart too soon. If I was a young man of courtin' age, your brains'd run me up a tree."

"I have a lot of spare time. I spend it reading," she said as if explaining her differences away.

"Hmm. Jim Street, you think?" He asked while savoring the idea, fearing it too. Then belittling it: "Maybe he wants an introduction to Boren Mills. I could do that much, for sure."

"Or maybe he wants to throw in with a winner, Mr. McCarty."

"I'm not trained to it. Besides strummin' a mean guitar, what can I offer folks that smarter politicians don't?"

"Honesty. Compassion for the luckless. Reform. All the things religions put up front, and some governments used to work for."

"That's not enough, Sandy. We've had Presidents who had those things aplenty without the savvy to get anything done. And a lot of folks know that, too. Making me the Indy candidate is the same as giving Young four more years in office."

Sandy reached for his plate, paused as their faces drew level. "I think the Feds are counting on just what you said," she murmured, adding softly, "and I think they could be making a very, very dangerous mistake."

CHAPTER 39

Sandy's journal, 4 Sep '02
I seem to be running a small hotel. No complaints so long as Lufo is a frequent guest as he was again yesterday. Mr. 'Gold' was a rare entertainment, a man of plain tastes & good will who traveled far during Labor Day weekend. He & Lufo set out this morn on hovercycles that would be pretentious if not for their last-legs appearance. I notice they moved out much faster than horses & a man rides low in the saddle, vanishing quickly with little commotion.

Sandy Albeniz Sandra Albeniz Mrs. Lufo Albeniz Sra. Albeniz—wonder if there is already a Señora Albeniz. Or several? I'm silly to think of it until he asks me. But lordy, he's asked for everything else & I have yet to refuse him! & when he asks about him, *what then? Childe would never forgive me if I took her from her only companion—might even refuse. It isn't the same as for some domestic pet. Even Schreiner ranch wouldn't hold him, especially with the things they attribute to him. Mowgli could have more easily ridden Shere Khan into the marketplace . . .*

CHAPTER 40

The unconscious rover was moved twice; first to Elko, Nevada under the false bed of a truckload of corn where he was treated for days in a LockLever warehouse. He would have died there without the aid of Dr. Keyhoe—the man who had seen Sanger die, who had abandoned Streamlined America upon seeing the implications of her death. Fellow Masonics in LockLever's employ had helped make their escape possible.

LockLever did not maintain spies throughout all its companies to root out Indy sympathizers. Small wonder that a unique cargo like Quantrill would be routed through such conduits as L. L. Produce and then Midas Imports by men hostile to the current administration. That news was particularly welcome to rebels near the Texas coast.

Quantrill regained consciousness in a well-lit room without windows and saw that he was not only strapped down, but instrumented. Not much hope in pretending deep sleep, he thought, but it might be his only option. Soon enough the bastards would be taking his mind apart unless he could make them kill him first—by taking a few of them out. Footfalls sounded outside the door. He closed his eyes; the door opened to admit cool air and a suggestion of echoes.

"Nope. Still out," he heard a twangy female voice declare. "I'm not very sharp on that monitoring equipment of Doc Keyhoe's. You suppose he'll let us keep it?''

A gruff male in a rumbling near-whisper: "Not a chance, Claire. It doesn't belong to the doc. We wouldn't have it now if this young fella wasn't a V.V.I.P. Soon as he's up and around, back it goes to the clinic in Burns.''

The door eased shut again. As his head cleared, Quantrill realized that furious mental effort would show on some monitors. He had no idea what kind of ruse they had readied for him. He hoped only that some fleeting chance would come—and that his damnable headache would subside before that.

Testing the straps that bound him to the bed— not even a real hospital bed, and the other furnishings looked too makeshift for a government facility—he found that he could easily slide his hands free. His signet ring had been taken. He used up five minutes freeing his hands, trying to imitate the motions of a sleeper. But when he turned his head to study the nearby table, a localized pain whacked him behind the ear.

He thought, *Sanger, the bitch!* '*I love you; trust me*'. *Su-u-re.* What kind of game had she been playing? And what worthless ribbon would she get for playing him out on such a long leash for S & R? Well, that was her job—he could even grudgingly admire her. *And love her. Well, fuck that. You see where it got you . . .*

On the table: steel basin, towel, and holy God in heaven, a disposable razor! The holo monitor? Nowhere to be seen but that proved nothing. When he moved, it would have to be with no wasted motion. And if the door wouldn't open for him? He would wait, and whoever *did* open it would harbor only the briefest of regrets.

He saw no clothes, no shoes. A sheet for a toga would only impede him and in any case he didn't expect to last long enough to need clothing. He peeled back the torso restraint and had the razor before he reached the door. *Stupid assholes; didn't even lock it!*

Down a corridor wearing only his briefs, sheet wrapped around his right arm for a pitiful shield that might parry an edged weapon, the razor in his lethal left hand. He would have fallen had the corridor been wider, a limp staggering parody of himself. All color, then shades of gray, began to fade. Whiteout: he had no choice but to kneel and tuck his head, or faint dead in his tracks.

Jesus, every footstep was a thump behind his ear. He had a bandage there too. Running footsteps behind him compelled him to try again, and he turned with the corridor as a woman cried, "Sir! Sir, omigod, the man's gone crazy! Mr. Caufield!!"

He slammed out of the corridor, missed his footing in enveloping blackness, fell headlong into some yielding stuff. Now two voices clamored behind him. He found a carpet of wood chips beneath his fingers, reeled up again, saw that the trail led through a smooth-walled tunnel in solid rock. In the far distance, the faintest suggestion of a glow. He ran toward it, more by the feel of wood chips than by the light ahead, keeping his bare feet off the cold hard stone.

Behind him, a heavy masculine shout, echoes booming: "Mr. Quantrill! It's okay, we're friends! Let us help you." Oh yes indeed, he'd heard *that* one before . . .

Unbelievably, he thought, they were letting him get away. If boxed at the end of this nightmarish stone intestine, he could turn on the two behind him and retrace leaving a couple of deaders in his wake. They weren't gaining on him, but the man couldn't be more than twenty meters behind.

Quantrill could pull a rolling one-eighty if his head didn't fall off in the process.

He tripped as the tunnel swerved to the left, rolled against a rounded stone outcrop. The pain in his head and the internal sunburst that accompanied it beggared the distant oval of sunlight. But it *was* sunlight, pouring into the oval mouth of a tunnel with no bars, no door, without any hint whatever of a secure facility.

The entrance was less than three meters high and nearly ten wide. Quantrill zigzagged in sudden sunlight to avoid marksmen, labored up the rock pathway. He welcomed the loose stones underfoot because they were better ammo than anything he had on him, but stooping to fill his hands with them he lost the razor, snatched dizzily at it, fell hard. Near collapse, he lacked the coordination to use his body as a killing machine. He would be lucky even to draw blood.

The man was still shouting as he emerged into the bright morning sun, hands out and innocent of weapons, the woman saving her breath as she followed. Quantrill tossed one stone in high trajectory, part one of the rockfighter's one-two punch, the one they were supposed to watch while he bifurcated the nearest sucker with number two, a bullet of stone hurled as though from a pitcher's mound.

He missed, nearly grazing the woman's head with number two, and saw her mouth grow round in anger and astonishment. He scrabbled for more rocks, heedless of pain, watching the man who made no move to gather stones but raised his hands aloft instead. Then he paused to listen.

"Will you stop? Can't you understand, for God's sake? If you keep on like this you're going to hurt yourself, you stupid idiot!"

He might hurt himself, the man said. An incomparable jest under the circumstances. But the circumstances were no longer clear to Quantrill. No one else approached. The entrance to the tunnel was a natural one, and carefully painted on its stone brow was, of all things, a weathered Masonic emblem.

Faint traces of an unsurfaced road undulated in grass across the brown prairie nearby, and the velvet breeze off the hills above was softly pungent with scents of dry weed and sage.

Through the pounding in his head, Quantrill tried to fit pieces of his puzzle together. He had gone down in the kitchen of a Catholic Church in arid coal country, and come up in what was evidently a natural lava tube in open range country. Central New Mexico? He gestured at the ancient pathway, managed to croak, "Where does that lead?"

"To Route seventy-eight. In a couple of days, if you're up to it, I'll take you there."

"I'm up to it now!"

The woman, heavy-bodied and sunbaked like the man, strode near with folded arms. "I wouldn't be barking out demands if I were you, sonny," she said, dull anger smoking in her face. "You managed to survive getting a hunk cut out of your skull, you nearly got meningitis from an infection in what's left of your mastoid, you're all but mothernaked, and all you can think of is throwing rocks at us. Now I know what I agreed to do for the Masonics but as far as I'm concerned, you throw one more fit like that and you can go to hell. Wander back to Streamlined America for all I care."

Back? What was *left* of his mastoid? Quantrill's puzzlement must have shown in his face. The man said, "He's still confused, Claire. Mr. Quantrill, a young woman cut a tiny radio out of your head over a week ago, and managed to explain who you were, and naturally the Masonic brotherhood was

interested in helping. This is Malheur Cave, Mr.
Quantrill. You're in Oregon Territory. You're a
free man." Oblivious to thistles and to the two
strangers, Quantrill sat down, hugged his knees,
and let the storm of tears overtake him.

CHAPTER 41

Ted Quantrill wasn't entirely convinced of his freedom until an hour later as he sat in one of the
small rooms far back in Malheur Cave. He would
never learn who had taken his signet ring, but
focused on something far more important. He held
the clear plastic container between thumb and
forefinger and peered through light cotton packing
at the device inside. "Doesn't look very potent now.
How can we be sure my critic isn't listening to
us?"

"I only know what Doc Keyhoe told me," shrugged
Ed Caufield, a thirty-second-degree Mason who
knew a little veterinary medicine but little of high-
tech electronics. "This came out of your head and
half of it blew up a minute later. They put it in
cotton inside this vacuum vial to make sure it
wouldn't receive conducted sound. And to make
double-sure, somebody in Elko wrapped the vial
in metal foil. Anyway, we're under thirty meters of
rock here. I reckon it's pretty safe."

"I'd like to grind it to powder," Quantrill growled.
"S & R won't rest 'til it's back in their hands."

"I don't think so." Claire Connor had spent long

days and nights tending Quantrill, had listened carefully to the men discuss their unconscious patient. "Doc Keyhoe knew he'd have to abandon his practice once he got involved with you, so he risked his skin and rigged some false evidence. Even conked a poor old priest and tied him up so the good Father wouldn't seem part of it." Supposedly, she added, Quantrill had fallen into the machinery that fed pulverized coal into the steam plant after his head burst open from detonation of the critic.

Haunted by his earlier fury at Marbrye Sanger, Quantrill asked, "And you're certain the woman didn't make it?"

"We weren't there," said the Connor woman. She'd needed half an hour to overcome her anger at Quantrill but found herself warming to him. He reminded her of her youngest boy, lost during the Bering Shoot before Oregon became a Canadian protectorate peppered with U.S. Army deserters.

"Doc Keyhoe was there," said Caufield as if apologizing. "I think it was seeing, um, well, seeing her die that got his dander up. Close friend, was she?"

Quantrill could find no words to explain how far that phrase fell short of the truth. He nodded, looked at the ceiling, brushed moisture from his cheeks. He could not yet appreciate that his tears were talismans of human emotions which Control had sought to drive from him, and that Control had failed.

Finally he pointed at the encapsulated solid-states of the critic and said, "Whatever comes of this, we owe to Marbrye." Then with a quick sad smile: "You have no idea what it's like to talk freely after six years with that thing in your head. I can say anything I like, recite poetry, even say, 'I love you, Marbrye.' Only she can't hear it," he finished.

"I think she might," the woman replied, but saw that Quantrill fought bitter tears. "Let's get you back to bed now, Ted Quantrill. You won't be ready to travel for awhile yet. I don't know what you have in mind, but Doc Keyhoe is in touch with some people who want very much to meet you."

"But that's all up to you," Caufield chimed in. "You're in Oregon Territory now and you can do as you damn' please. That's something to sleep on, son."

In time Quantrill did sleep, but only after he had cried for Sanger, and for himself for having lost her. Yet his tears could not wash all his accumulated poisons away; his last waking thoughts were of personal combat against those who were twisting Streamlined America into a daily twenty-four-hour nightmare.

CHAPTER 42

For the record, health service officials announced that Father Matthew Klein died of a particularly virulent form of paranthrax. Off the record, he died from the effects of virulent questioning methods by Search & Rescue after he admitted under torture that Quantrill still lived. The paranthrax cover story became a blanket explanation for inoculation teams that flew into the mining community and, one at a time, hyposprayed two categories of the locals: members of Klein's parish, and patients of the missing Dr. Keyhoe.

As inoculations, the hypossprays were useless. Each patient and parishoner returned home ignorant and safe. Ignorant that they had babbled honest answers to all queries put to them by Howell's rovers; safe because none had guilty knowledge of Quantrill or of any other conspiracy against the system. With Sanger dead and Keyhoe beyond its grasp, S & R had to proceed with what little the priest could tell them. That little was enough.

Lon Salter called his meeting exclusively for top-level staff and eventually found it necessary to send out for sandwiches. The decisions were not reached quickly or easily. But then, their latest data had not come without painstaking legwork and two more missing persons.

At one point, Salter raised a hand to ward off more data. "Stop right there, Reardon, I don't need to know what you did with the teamster's body. If you say he admitted hauling those two into Elko it's good enough for me."

Mason Reardon was a medium man, a man so average in appearance and mannerism that he could move almost unnoticed in a business suit or a coverall. Long before, he had taught surveillance methods to Quantrill, Sanger, and many others. More recently he had moved into the comm center as one of the voices of Control. Very recently he had made a quick trip afield, tracing Quantrill's route.

Old Lasser could afford a more detached view, with his medical restrictions against field ops. "LockLever's harboring a lot of these people, Lon. They're cozying up to the Indys."

Salter: "Exactly why we can't ask White House Deseret to lean on them. We can't afford to let our suspicions show. What we've got to do is find all the terminals of this escape route, this—this underground railroad; emplace bugs on every truck and hoverbus owned by L. L. Produce and Midas Imports; find out how serious our problem is."

A cynical laugh from little Marty Cross, who still wore a sling for his right arm. The most irritating part of his job, thought Salter, was the insolence of Cross and his crony, Howell. Both were nominally his subordinates—and both often justified a charge of insubordination. They knew what Salter knew, i.e., without them Search & Rescue would no longer have a flinty core of sociopathic readiness. In rover terms, they were the last of the best.

Now Cross shared his dark amusement. "Here's how serious the problem is. See me? Pretend I'm S & R; I've got my good arm in a sling because that fucking Quantrill got loose. If he's still alive and out of the country, I can mend. If he links up with rebels *in* this country, I might get both arms in slings and my ass in another one. Cripple me and you cripple the Lion of Zion—and if *he* goes belly-up, not a man in this room will have a hidey-hole deep enough to suit him.

"Look: we've had these Catholics and Masons and liberal Mormons all along—no worse than a bad cold, right? But Quantrill's a bad fracture just waitin' to happen. There's too many ways he could hurt us—"

"All right, all right," Salter interrupted; "get to the point."

"The point," said the whiskey tenor of Seth Howell, "is a top-level effort to find him; take him out. Track him down in Canada or wherever, make an example of him. Pretend we've bought that amateurish yarn about him getting graunched in machinery, keep a sharp eye out in case he tries to turn other rovers—and see to it that we're the machine that graunches him."

"I agree," said Lasser, who knew Quantrill better than any of them. "If he's abroad, we might try talking Smetana out of retirement."

"Negative," Howell rapped. "That's one of the ways he can hurt us! We have other linguists who can pass as foreign, and Smetana's female. She used to have a letch for Quantrill—hell, find a cunt in S & R who didn't! He snuck Sanger right out from under me—"

Lasser, recalling Sanger's admissions: "Now that's just too freudian to let pass, Seth," intended as a jolly reproof.

Howell, his ruddy face blackening with rage, scanned their faces one at a time: Lasser, Reardon, Cross, Salter. "Anybody here think that little turncoat sonofabitch is a better man than I am?" Dutiful headshakes and, from Lasser, an abstention. "Then that settles it. We need a team ready to respond the instant we learn where Quantrill is. The very best S & R team ever mustered. That's *me*—"

"And me," Cross hissed, his eyes glistening.

"And maybe Ethridge," Howell said.

Lasser and Reardon together: "Why Ethridge?"

Howell: "Because in some ways he's a better athlete than Quantrill. And because Ethridge wanted Sanger so bad you could see the hard-on in his face. All we have to do," he smiled, "is to tell Ethridge it was Quantrill who blew her away."

Amid the buzz of discussion, Lon Salter rapped the table for order and called for opinions. He knew it was purely *pro forma*, a sop to his title. The major decision had already been made.

That decision would have varied in crucial details, had they known that the electronic half of Quantrill's critic still existed. But the old priest had described the detonation, and they'd found traces of the event in the surface of a butcher block, verified by gas chromatography. They had not wrenched a vital datum—Keyhoe's recovery of the solid-state module—from Father Klein because the priest had not noticed it, engrossed as he was in Sanger's desperate scrawls.

And why go through the dull formalities of removing access channels into the central computer when the remote terminal in question had been blown into white-hot gas?

CHAPTER 43

In even the simplest of strategems, one must proceed on the basis of certain assumptions. Yet nothing is more deadly than a false assumption.

Search & Rescue assumed that when the shaped charge of the critic blew, it atomized the solid-state terminal to CenCom.

Quantrill assumed that his enemies thought him dead.

CHAPTER 44

After a week, Quantrill could wake without a rush of despair for Sanger, and of guilty elation in his freedom. Later he might recover his old reticence, but now he welcomed the men who came to Malheur Cave to talk (a little) and to listen (a lot) while he completed his recovery. It pleased him to talk freely after six years of practice at remaining mute with caution, reinforced by the pitiless puppet-masters of Control. Those talks were not *all* pleasant; he learned from Dr. Keyhoe how Sanger had died. He would not accept it as final until Keyhoe, in exasperation, snarled that the poor creature was dead, dead, dead.

Quantrill never made a friend of Keyhoe, sensing the man's dislike for him, unable to pinpoint a reason. The reason was simply this: Quantrill was the catalyst who had precipitated Keyhoe from a life he had enjoyed, a practice and a group of friends he missed. Keyhoe had abandoned his old life to save a young assassin and was beginning to wonder whether his sacrifice would ever have any important outcome.

Precisely because Keyhoe did not want his sacrifice to be pointless, he made careful inquiries through his contacts in and beyond the Masonic orders, giving no particulars that, in his opinion, might identify Quantrill. Because lodge brothers in Streamlined America were increasingly concerned with the country's internal affairs, he got prompt responses from New Denver, Cincinnati, Corpus Christi, and the sprawling new port city of Eureka. And because nations are inordinately fond of finagling with each other's internal affairs, he got responses from New Ottawa, Ankara, Canberra, and, again, Eureka.

The day Keyhoe removed the last bandage he seemed particularly surly. "You'll want to keep a hat on until your hair grows back," he advised. "If your brains haven't all leaked out, you'll head North and talk Ottawa into giving you a new identity as I'll have to do myself. If you have no more sense than a goose, you'll be flying South."

Quantrill tried to make it light: "You have your profession and I have mine. It'll be easier now that I'm a deader."

Tiny wrinkles gathered at the Keyhoe temples, as though Quantrill's face were on some far horizon. Without fondness: "Selling death to the highest bidder?"

"You know better than that, doc. It won't take me long to find a slot with the rebels. I can be useful."

"Money? Contacts? Routing? Have you thrown in with any of the people you've met here?"

A slow headshake.

Now with something like grudging respect, Keyhoe said, "Good. How much do you trust me?"

A grin. Quantrill held up his thumb and forefinger, spaced so that a knife blade might have passed between them. Then he said, "And that's a hell of a lot."

"I know a man in Eureka who buys Oregon wood for LockLever's shipbuilding company. All he knows is that you were a field agent of some sort. You wouldn't be the first man he's filtered back into the system. But you'd have to shell out."

"So who foots the bill?"

"Not money; information. But if they suggest drugs for your debriefing, my advice is to say no."

Quantrill appreciated Keyhoe's candor and his caution; agreed to meet the man from Pacifica Marine on neutral ground. Two evenings later he was flown in a creaking underpowered Boxmoth with dacron wingskin, no running lights, and almost no radar signature to an abandoned road near Jacksonville, Oregon Territory. He became one of three thousand strangers inundating the little town during a nocturnal outdoor concert at something called the Britt Music Festival. As advertised, he quickly located the two men sharing the big jug of California wine, and covertly studied them until intermission. Keyhoe had been right: in Oregon Territory, nobody else drank California wine in public.

Quantrill followed the older of the two men to an outdoor toilet and murmured the ID phrase through the polymer back wall. He got the right response, half-lost in a snort of merriment. "You sure have a knack for finding my vulnerable moments," said the man. "You'll be the young buck in the baseball cap behind us, I take it."

Quantrill admitted it. If they'd been enemies, they would've already had time to collect him—or to try. Five minutes later, under the marvelous thud-and-wonder of John Williams overtures, Quantrill again sat in near-darkness just behind the two.

"Call me Brubaker," said the older one, passing the jug back. He indicated the heaveyset younger man at his elbow: "Call him Brubaker too."

Quantrill named himself as 'Conrad', pretended to drink, and complimented the Brubakers for arranging a meeting where Fed surveillance would be hamstrung by white noise and public uncertainties. During the remainder of the program he traded wisps of vital information without mentioning the vacuum-packed device he carried in an armpit pocket of his turtleneck sweater. He did mention that he needed a contact with some group well-versed in electronic countermeasures.

Old Brubaker said there were several ways, all unspecified, to get Conrad in touch with ECM wizards. Nashville, in the Confederacy, was one option, if Conrad had his paranthrax shots. The other ECM center was Corpus Christi, near Wild Country; and in Corpus he would be near the rebel nerve center. Conrad would have to pay his way, of course.

Quantrill wondered aloud how that payment might be made. He expected a long interrogation. Young Brubaker surprised him. Canadian intelligence had collected information on a Chinese device which could apparently synthesize a wide range of substances. That synthesizer—if it had ever existed—was a casualty of the late unlamented war. Yet the giant consortium, IEE, had swallowed up several Chinese scientists and one Frenchman whose specialties might be used to redevelop such a gadget.

Now, IEE was promising Blanton Young an endless, cheap supply of strategic materials from an extraction plant near Eureka. At this point old Brubaker chimed in: "But that's a blind. IEE is outfitting an anchored barge from the air with a delta dirigible, and we've traced its route from a lab 'way the hell and gone out in the central Utah desert. That barge is doing something, all right—but it isn't sucking up enough sea water to yield a hatful of chromium, cobalt, platinum—the stuff that's starting to trickle off that barge.

"There's isn't a commonwealth or a kingdom on Earth that wants to see Young grow independent of foreign trade; Canada sells a lot of platinum here, so you can see why we—uh, they—get nervous when pure platinum starts pouring off that barge. So where's it really coming from? We think it's from that lab—which is the private property of IEE's chief, Boren Mills."

"There's no sea water in the middle of Utah," young Brubaker muttered, "so our guess is that the enterprising Mr. Mills has a synthesizer operating there. We can't find out much about the layout, beyond the fact that it's underground. But it should be possible to get a man stowed away on the IEE supply delta—which, by the way, is filled with hydrogen and has only a two-man crew. Mills is buying tunneling equipment for the lab from overseas. We just might be able to switch some crates of machinery in the Port of Eureka for a few crates full of greeting cards.

"Our man could be put down at that lab inside one of our crates. It'd be nice to pick a team but we're afraid time is short, and we'd be willing to go with one man. If he were a one-man team, that is."

Quantrill felt a distinct tingle at the base of his skull; the signal that his muscles could tap a great surge of noradrenaline on command. "And you're asking me to raid the place for some kind of machine?"

"It's probably the size of a barge, so we're asking you to blow the whole place sky-high," old Brubaker murmured.

The crates, young Brubaker added, would also contain weapons and explosives, all untraceable. "We've established that the lab perimeter is guarded by P-beam towers. Nothing you can't get past with a hovercycle, provided it carries a covey of little

Homingbirds. If you get back in one piece, you've got a free ticket to anywhere he can route you." He nodded toward his companion.

Quantrill resisted the urge to run. No professional would outline such a plan to a stranger with such vague credentials as his. Lazily, as though he were not humming with readiness: "For a couple of guys who don't know me from Adam you're telling, and asking, a lot. Hell, I could just boost a 'cycle and head for Nashville on my own with less risk than you're suggesting."

Young Brubaker lay back on the grass, face up, fingers interlaced behind his head in a position that could not have been more vulnerable. He smiled and said, "Don't kid yourself. D'you think Canadian intelligence would send me here without proper briefing? The offer is absolutely valid. We happen to know you're familiar with the innards of a delta. Also with munitions, and the word is that a little extra risk hasn't stopped you yet.

"We don't often get a man and a mission that fit together this well—but as you can see, I'm, ah, bending over backwards to keep from putting you under any pressure. The decision is up to you, Ted Quantrill."

Sandy's journal, 11 Sep '02

Lufo accompanied 'Mr. Gold' back as far as my soddy & lingered alone for the night. I do not mourn the shortened days when nights are this rewarding!

We talked for hours, straining to find common ground for small talk. Since I had no news of interest, I told him stories of my childhood. He avoided the past & spoke of the future. Told me that an old companion has fled the life of a slave-assassin & may migrate to these parts soon. No name, but if Lufo is to be believed, the man must be the equal of him. *No doubt a hard-faced old lobo, for he has killed easily and often in the service of our enemies. Lufo spoke of him with brevity & perhaps envy. Already I loathe him. Why would good men want to associate with the likes of such a monster?*

La-de-da: who am I to speak ill of monsters?

CHAPTER 45

What was the point in being a mover and shaker, Eve asked herself as she lazed at a window of her delta stateroom, if a girl couldn't have a few amenities for her troubles? In Eve's case those amenities were more than a few. She alone occupied one of the rearmost rooms near the delta's center of balance, where the gentle maneuvers of the great craft were least disturbing. The engine pods were so far away, so muted, that only a whisper reached her. And she'd had caterpillar treads affixed to her motorized chaise so that she would not find it necessary to waddle back and forth on the long voyage from Salt Lake City in a gondola that might undulate a bit.

But if her status was high, her spirits remained low. She ignored the ever-changing view as United's behemoth—one of five which offered expensive passenger service—ghosted to the high rolling wind-racked grasslands of Cheyenne, to the awesome abrupt crunch of flat plain against majestic gray-blue peaks near La Junta, to the vertiginous bluffs near Lubbock where plains crumbled into river valleys in their long slope toward the Mexican Gulf hundreds of klicks farther off.

She did not rejoice to know that a rack of lamb awaited her at dinnertime. The plain fact is that Eve Simpson had been bored out of her mind since her second hour in the delta. She knew her antidote, and learned that it was not to be found aloft; most of the delta staff were colorless middle-aging men, and the rest were svelte young women. Eve told herself that she had high standards, and cursed the delta staff collectively.

Her mood was not improved when she found that dinner would be no leisurely feast. Favorable tailwinds were boosting the great delta toward Kerrville Municipal Airport and Eve had barely sealed her closet-sized wardrobe when the craft slid down to grapple against mooring sockets built during the war. This was as far into Wild Country as commercial airship skippers cared to risk their craft, a full hundred klicks West of the rebuilt ring-cities around the ruins of Austin and San Antonio.

Though the platform lowered her as smoothly as any elevator, Eve's uneasiness mounted. Across the field were the lights of the old Mooney aircraft plant where, if Eve's briefing was correct, assembly bays were sometimes used by Texas renegades to refit or overhaul rebel equipment. And despite advertiseed claims of safety, the Shreiner hoverbus would waft her another fifty klicks into this lawless region.

To bolster her confidence, Eve touched the bubble-smooth surface of the Ember of Venus that lay cushioned between her breasts. Mills had argued against her taking it, but Eve had not been swayed. Confidence rekindled, Eve guided her chaise from downramp to bus, alert lest United mishandle her luggage. You couldn't trust the idiots, she reflected, to shift a cube of solid armorplate without shattering it in the process. And only if you were an Eve Simpson could you depend on fair compensation. But that was how it went in Streamlined America; as long as reconstruction lasted, the name of the game would be 'screw Joe Small'.

In no respect could Eve be considered small. United took special care with her wardrobe and dropped it only once.

Soon the lights of Kerrville swept by on her right, and then the hoverbus was droning on its diesels through hamlets and between limestone bluffs. The other passengers, two sporting types and a middle-aged couple, chattered away in what could have been Arabic. Eve was not surprised; the cost of such a spa was most easily borne by Islamics, who had not fought the war but nonetheless had won it. The combatants had all lost.

Soon after the bus passed the ranch entrance, Eve perceived that she was truly in a different world, one in which vehicle headlights might pick out exotic ibex, aodad, or bounding gemsbok as often as native wild whitetail. The hearty, "Howdy, and welcome," by a squint-eyed young man in tight jeans and dusty boots filled her with suspicion. Surely, she thought, these people were putting her on. She would learn that century-old habits were genuinely alive and well in Wild Country.

She trundled to the main stone lodge, trading frank states with the ranch staff who found her as arresting a spectacle as she found them. Yet the curious glances were friendly and the twangy greetings more so. Nobody who'd seen Schreiner's albino elephant would think Eve particularly unusual.

She tried to work up a small fury on learning that her spacious, bath-equipped cabin had no telephone or holo, but found the effort taxing. The western trappings in pavilion and cabin, and the trim lank rumps that paraded past her in worn denim, pierced the dikes of her reserve and let the anger leak away. Eve retired to her cabin an empty vessel—but she knew how these cow-pokes could fill her.

Two days later, se felt privation. From the phone in the central lodge, Eve coupled a scrambler module to the jack in the bezel of her amulet and let her tiny computer talk to CenCom in its lair under Granite Mountain near Ogden. Satisfied that her synthesizer was accumulating a dollop of lobotol at last, she used her scrambler for a second call.

Her initial words to Mills were, "Talk about primitive! I can't even talk to CenCom without a goddam telephone, that's how far I am from a relay. Do you know what it's like to be without a snort of THC in these parts?"

"I'm sure it must be just sheer hell," was his laconic reply. If this were all she could bitch about, the accomodations must be very good indeed. Mills waited until she had adumbrated a media freak's list of horrors: no terminals to electronic sugartits. He tut-tutted at the right moments and finally said, "Nobody's checked with me about your authorizations from IEE. Haven't you told Schreiner's management you're not down there just for the atmosphere?"

"Not yet. This is one hell of a big operation, Boren; I've got a floppy casette half-full of notes and I haven't seen more than a fraction of the place. Most of the guests are foreign, and half of 'em even *you* couldn't buy. I'll say this: if it isn't making money, they don't know how to run a hidden casino."

"No sign of anything like that?"

"Not a scintilla. Doesn't surprise me; a bunch of ecology nuts living in a purified version of the Old

West. They're pretty open—naive, if you ask me—about needing water. I'm amazed that somebody like LockLever hasn't already bought 'em out."

"They've considered it," Mills said, withholding details. "But Latter-Day Shale has just discovered a site for a limestone quarry on a rise near Schreiner's boundary. When they show you the books, you can drop the word that IEE owns a nearby site for an LOS tower. With cheap power, the ranch could draw water to spare. We've got to convince these bumpkins that we mean to keep the place unspoiled."

Her chuckle was rich with shared cynicism. "Why, *shore* we do, podnuh. Can you believe some of the help actually talks like that here? Incidentally, this might be a good route for a bit of midnight export of precious metal like, say, platinum, through Mexico. I don't suppose that had occured to you."

Mills's turn for irony: "Never crossed my mind. Speaking of precious metals, you might be happy to know our friend Chabrier is stepping up his production of certain strategic materials—from Eureka, of course."

"He'd better not be your friend like he's my friend," she teased.

"Obdurate bitch. Look, I'm busy. Call me when you know more about the financial end there, hm?"

"It may take awhile. I'm off tomorrow for a three-day outing." It pleased her to imply that she would be roughing it. No point in adding that she would ride the 'chuckwagon' hoverbus, nor that she had her eye on the rangy snuff-pinching guide who bossed these photo safaris. Pleased with herself, Eve rang off. It wasn't every day that she could render Boren Mills speechless with one of her adventures.

CHAPTER 46

Sandy's journal, 15 Sep '02

No wonder Indians loved Indian summer: they didn't have to work then! They merely starved later. This Sunday has been my last day of rest until all our canning & preserves are done. Childe is old enough to help, this year, & took me seriously enough to shoo him *whistling down the wind for the duration. Why toward the ranches of the East, I wonder? And how do they swap such explicit tidbits? Childe said he went toward the sunrise, though she knows the word 'East' as well as I. There is more to their eye-and-head tossings than I can decipher.*

I hope he is satiated with wild game & does not go far afield. I recall one ride when he carried us both halfway across Edwards plateau in one muscle-cramping day. I have grown too old for such meanderings—& I wonder if he feels the onset of age. He may have five or ten more good years—or the Texas Aggie research people may have bred him for longevity as well as size and intelligence!

Moral question: were the breeders right to make him thus? There is as much wisdom in that terrible great head as there is ferocity in the sabers of his muzzle. Now the breeders are long dead, & now it is I who worry . . .

No sign yet of the turncoat Lufo spoke of. Good! The presence of such an old devil would disturb me as others might quaver before Ba'al. Yet—if one demon has his good side, why not another?

CHAPTER 47

Over the years, said Cleve Hutcherson, the huge private preserve had spread nearly to the Kerr County line. He'd been raised in adjoining Edwards County, and figured the abandoned old Hutcherson place might one day be 'his' range again. The redbone guide spat unerringly, anointing a lizard as it sat sun-stunned on a limestone outcrop. Of the three camera-toting tenderfeet, only Eve appreciated Hutch's little joke on the lizard; and Hutch was a man who liked being appreciated.

That first night in bedrolls, as the mesquite fire dwindled, Hutch had thought the fat gal almost too attentive to his yarns. There was something unsettling about being responsible, in Wild Country, for a city gal whose ass wouldn't fit in a Number Three washtub. Well, at least she didn't go wandering off to get a hock lamed in a prairie-dog hole the way some did. Fact was, she stuck very close to Hutch.

Eve gauged her image carefully. Just because this juice-projecting trailboss was insular, that didn't make him stupid. His stories of raw violence, and his obvious courage in trimming down that pack of wild dogs that surrounded their group, made Evie itch. Here was a man who could handle a six-gun, and presumably a woman, of any caliber.

Since puberty Eve's weakness had been for men of spirit, and of clout. In this country, Cleve

Hutcherson's dusty denims were packed with clout. She took genuine delight in counting every scar she could see, and wondered how many more she might tally after the others were asleep, with a smidgin of lobotol in Hutch's coffee. It was now late afternoon, not far from a favorite camp spot Hutch knew. On all but the driest summers the spot boasted a languid 'dripping spring', he said; a trickle of water that bled from a limestone bluff and fed a patch of green grass amid the surrounding parched tan countryside.

Animals do not really smell water. Rather, they catch the faint sweet odors of vegetation that prosper in arid regions. The huge omnivore moved toward those scents, now and then balancing on his hindquarters to better test the breezeborne messages. His kind did not often behave that way— but then, in some ways there were no others quite like him; had not been since humans first probed into the Urals.

For the surviving dogs, fleeing from Hutch's firepower and briefly expecting that this lone creature might be their prey, their encounter had been ultimate disaster. Their quarry had not run at first, but waited for the doberman's second slashing pass. He had fed the doberman a flinty forehoof with a projecting dewclaw that ripped out the ribbed roof of the dog's mouth before its jaws could snap shut. But the dog was tasting blood—its own—and did not heed the lesson.

The mixed-breed and the alsatian tried for a hamstring and found that their opponent could leap with any gazelle. Their normal pack attack was to circle and veer, but with only three of them this strategem had a fatal flaw. The vast bristly ham was not where the mixed-breed expected; instead, a sharp splayed rear hoof the size of a man's relaxed hand exploded into the dog's ribcage, tossing it as easily as the kick of a horse; and this should not have surprised them, for they had faced full-grown horses smaller than this snuffling red-eyed demon.

The mixed-breed stood again, but could not return and collapsed, dying, bleeding from mouth and nostrils. The alsatian whined in impatience and perhaps, a little, in fear. When the doberman started its frontal stalk, its companion eased rearward. Usually if the quarry charged forward, a big healthy dog could blitz from behind to deliver a disabling slash. But when that charge came, it came with such blinding suddenness that neither dog could respond. The doberman wanted a shot at the throat or, failing that, the shoulder. Instead it found a snout tucked nearly to the caliche dirt and two scimitars leveled at its breast and coming on as if rocket-propelled and, scythe-impaled, the fifty-kilo doberman died while carried forward by the endless thundering charge of an animal ten times its bulk.

When the great beast turned at last, the alsatian was fifteen meters in arrears. Alsatians are smart. This one saw the body of its mate dumped like an offering, or a challenge, between predator and prey, and realized that the monster could outrun him, and knew finally which was truly predator, and which was to be the prey.

The alsatian ran anyway, which was not very smart. Nor would he have been smart to attack, nor even to roll over on his back and wag his tail. When death is absolutely certain, perhaps nothing is very smart.

When the victor had fed he began to crave water, not only to slake his thirst but to wash away the blood that splashed his scant bristly coat and his long sloping face. That was when he drifted away from the sunset toward the smell of waterthings.

His trained olfactory bulbs told him there was person-scent near, and man-scent as well.

He knew two persons whom he loved. He had never met a man he liked. A few men had had the good sense to fall down before him, or to feed him, or simply the immobilizing horror to stand rigid and piss themselves when facing him. Most of those still lived to foster the legend of Ba'al.

He still carried a handful of slugs, cicatriced in mounds of muscle, from the deerfly sting of a '22 to the really damaging wallop of big shotgun pellets, fired by men who had chosen the valiant option. Of the valiant ones, very few still lived. Ba'al did not care which category he would meet upwind and now that his bloodlust and his hunger were assuaged he no longer hungered for trouble. But if they stood between him and his water,—meet them he would.

CHAPTER 48

For the first time ever, Eve Simpson gathered firewood. And enjoyed it! She noted for later recording that occasional rain torrents could create momentary freshets—Hutch called them 'gully washers'—that spewed hunks of oak and mesquite and cedar along their paths before drying again.

To Hutch it only meant easy pickin's for a showy bonfire, the kind city folks liked, the kind that wasted enough wood for a week of sensible cooking and warming. Well, whatthehell, some tenderfeet

had their points. The fat gal, Evie, had slyly offered to sweeten his hardrock coffee with sourmash
that night, and he didn't mind if he did. It was
against the rules but in by-God Wild Country you
could take a few by-God liberties. He would jolly
the young couple along with whatever stories they
wanted, most of them true, and knew that the fat
gal's eyes would gleam with pleasure no matter
what he did.

Hutch supervised the camp setup near the dripping spring, letting Evie help, ignoring the way
she panted every time she had to squat in ready-
ing the bonfire. Poor li'l rich gal, the thing that
would most likely make her eyes catch fire was
one thing he wasn't about to offer.

Hutch cussed softly at himself for the vagrant
moving mental image of himself with her. He wasn't
fair, letting himself be revulsed by her when she'd
done nothing to provoke it. All the same, he reflected as he brought out the preheated banquet
from the modern 'chuckwagon', he mustn't give
her any signals she could take amiss. Cleve Hutcherson could imagine nothing more terrifying, more
unmanning, than wallowing with Eve Simpson.
That was because Hutch was a man with a narrow
imagination; an hour after sunset his imagination
would be immensely expanded.

CHAPTER 49

He moved carefully toward the fireblaze, walking rather than trotting to catch every scent, tallying the information with what he saw and heard. Two persons and two men, none smelling of fear or anger, talking in voices he could have heard a kilometer away. He had not been hungry, not with twenty kilos of dogmeat in his belly, but the odors of Schreiner food would titillate a gourmand of any species. He identified armadillo (roasted over slow mesquite embers), Corsican lamb (with braised mint), and something he could not place (no wonder: ostrich-egg omelet with avocado and eggplant). This last tumble of sensation was a nose-puzzler, and he snorted.

The slender person turned, her night vision lost in the glare of bonfire, and stared directly toward him. "What was that?"

He studied her alertness; could detect no fear. Other voices calmed her. He might pass behind them to the shallow waterhole, but knew they would hear him drink. Well, they were on ground he had chosen, however temporarily, as his and now he was salivating for the food that lay in plain sight near the four humans who sat on stones and taunted him unaware. He moved nearer between stunted cedars, then nearer still to the very edge of the firelight without being detected. In his way he was having his little joke, easing into their very midst in utter silence. But not without odors of his own.

The louder of the two men took a coffee cup, sniffed, said, "Hutch, what do I smell in this java?"

Hutch, blinking: "Why—just coffee. Whoo-*eee*, but that's rank! It isn't coffee, podnuh, smells more like a stray—", and then he peered across the firelight into the eyes of a primordial power and lust unmatched by any homicidal maniac since time began.

Hutch's lips formed the word: *Ba'al*; but could not say it aloud. To his surpassing credit he quavered instead, "Folks, do not move. I'm dead serious; don't scream, don't do *nothin'*. Aw, my great—good—Gawd—almighty."

The slender person glanced between the two scrub trees, hardly a spit away for Hutch; drew a breath; fainted.

Her consort stared and was paralyzed as surely as though he had seen the face of Medusa.

Eve, in the act of fanging a lamb riblet, would have shrieked had her mouth not been full. She jerked; which brought a hellish visage swinging toward her.

In a husked tremor: "Evie. For your life, gal, don't panic." The bristle-edged ears flicked but did not flatten. Hutch knew animals. He wondered if animal lore applied to this leviathan. He saw Eve's wide eyes beseeching him, and his right hand might be near enough to the holster for him to get off one shot. He knew with utter certainty that six rounds would not be enough.

Eve saw the guide's leathery face ashen in the flickering firelight, his hand twitching near the six-gun, and knew that his mortal terror was justified. Her gaze was drawn again to the colossal bloodstained beast, a Russian boar so enormous that he seemed heraldic; mythological. He sat at

his ease as if judging them all, his long dark triangular head as high as a man's. His little eyes—
reddish yellowed whites that matched the incredible
tusks—gleamed with intelligence and with calm
intent under the scarred brows. They missed
nothing, yielded nothing, feared nothing. Eve swallowed with an audible gulp.

"Easy now," Hutch whispered. "Toss that bone
down in front of him."

She did it. The great muscular shoulders flowed
forward, hindquarters up and disproportionately
small but corded with sinew and crossed like the
shoulders with old scars. Ba'al's shoulder hump
was the size of a young bison's but his entire body
would not have yielded enough fat to grease a
skillet. He dipped his snout, still gazing steadily at
his hostages, and Eve saw flecks of foam on his
jaws as he took the offering. Then without being
told, she astonished herself by easing forward,
grasping the stainless steel warmer, placing it in
the dirt, toeing it in the boar's direction.

The flywhisk tail switched once. He stepped
forward, dainty mincing steps on split hooves that
seemed tiny though they would have sufficed for
an Olympic elk. Ba'al vented one subterranean
grunt, buried his snout in the lamb as Eve stood
two paces away. Hands at her sides, facing this
horrendous brute, she stood filled with awe and
with a wild rush of something she had felt many
times before. Never like this. Trembling, she stood
before an animal whose natural weapons beggared
those of Bengal tiger and Kodiak bear, whose awesome constantly-whetted tusks could have sliced
paper, and she welcomed the rush of emotion.

From behind her, a barely recognizeable thin
male squeal: "Shoot, Hutch, for God's sake *shoot*!"

"I don't dare," was the soft reply. "Evie, back up

real careful. Every'body move slow into the chuck-wagon."

Unwilling, Eve backed away. She was last into the cramped cargo hold of the hoverbus, puffing with exertion as she found a seat. The young couple were both crying with relief as Hutch flicked toggles; engaged the diesel starter.

The diesel's clatter angered the great animal. Ba'al backed away from his feast, ears flat; rushed the vehicle, slamming ivory knives against the thin aluminum of the engine hatch. Hutch shut the engine off instantly and sighed aloud to see the beast amble back to the food panniers. "Well, he damn' sure ain't got a radio," said Hutch with new confidence and punched out a code on the radiophone.

Eve half-listened to the conversation, fully aware of its portent as she peered out the window at Ba'al. She hadn't known the little hoverbus carried a phone but since it did, she had a potential link to CenCom.

Help couldn't reach them for hours, said the ranch manager. It was up to Hutch to keep his charges alive until then. To the manager's suggestion Hutch said, "Sure we can take pictures, the ugly devil's near enough that I could make his dental chart. And when you see 'em, you'll see why I ain't gonna go up against him with no damn' handgun. Shoot, Mac, I'd sooner face a grizzly with a willow switch, them tushes is long as my forearm! I just hope he don't decide to use 'em for can-openers. Listen, maybe you could home the chopper in on us; buzz us a little. Maybe the wind would send him off—or if you got it down low enough maybe he'd chase it. No shit, Mac, this is the real article: Ba'al! If the notion struck him he'd chase King Kong clean to Mexico!"

After completing his call, Hutch moved aft to

comfort the poor in spirit. It was going to be okay, they'd be safe if they kept quiet and took a few infrared photos which, he opined, would command a tidy sum. As Eve squeezed into a front seat near the controls, Hutch maintained a running monolog and helped the others ready their cameras.

Eve found her bag and the scrambler module, saw that the radiophone was standard, and quietly set about her contact with CenCom. The Ember of Venus slid up from between her breasts. In another moment she was encoding.

Hutch did not notice. Poor sniveling human; she had seen him wither to an empty palpitating shell before an awesome potency that no mere man could ever approach. Eve was not one to ask herself whether she had overtrodden the boundaries of sanity in her grappling toward greater sensation. Her sole criterion was, 'Can I get away with it?'

Her alphanumeric readout glowed in the bezel. It looked as if she might indeed get away with it. From some forgotten veterinary file, CenCom provided an answer that Eve did not wholly understand, nor did she need to. The tiny synthesizer understood and accepted its task, for the female sex pheromone of the wild asiatic pig was within its capability. Eve disconnected the radiophone; smiled at the firelit scene ten meters distant.

She was still sitting there smiling when, minutes later, Hutch came forward. He had watched the huge predator move to the waterhole, had heard the contented bass grunts of Ba'al at his toilette. Maybe, he said, they could start up the diesel without startin' a one-sided war.

Eve's reply, he thought, lacked warmth. Something had changed between them now. He couldn't say what he'd seen in her gaze during the past few days, but figured it had to be fear. Because he'd

seen a bushel of it on her face as she'd stared out
that window.

The diesel steadied to a softer thud after twenty
seconds of Hutch's anxiety, and he eased them
away without feeling the impact of Ba'al's scimitars again. Built for hovering and not for ramming,
the vehicle could not have withstood many such
collisions. Hutch was too busy to notice that Eve
had rolled her window down slightly; was flicking
her fingertips into the night breeze.

Eve's temptation was to insist that she be let out
of the 'chuckwagon'. That, she was certain, she could
not get away with. She had sprinkled her lust-
message on the night air, and for now it would
have to be enough. Later she could return alone in
a chartered hovercraft to make her assignation. In
the meantime she would research Russian boars,
the better to make her alliance.

For the first time in her life Eve had faced a
masculinity so full of clout that she had not
dreamed of bending it to her will. Ba'al, the prince
of hell, was not a thing you vied with; he was
Something you paid homage to.

No one saw the long sensitive snout jerk up from
the water, wriggling like the tip of an elephant's
trunk, questing after the hoverbus. Ba'al remained
indifferent to the dwindling thud and whirr, but
was no longer indifferent to what he smelled. Unless his nostrils deceived him—and they rarely did—
the noisy vehicle contained an oestrus female of
his own breed. He had not happened across any
females for over a year and the last had not been
in oestrus, and had not been pleased at the size of
her suitor. Any experienced female might suspect
that, if the corkscrew-ridged penis of a standard
feral Russian boar grew to nearly half a meter in
length, then the organ of Ba'al would represent
much too much of a good thing.

Hutch got the vehicle up to highway speeds once or twice, but at night in broken brush country he averaged scarcely half that pace. Ba'al, with a consuming curiosity and nothing better to do, followed at a distance-eating trot, undecided whether to risk the bangsticks of many men to satisfy his suspicions. In any case he could afford caution; he felt no compulsion but the urge of his scrotum.

CHAPTER 50

Quantrill was tempted to leave his damaged critic in the care of the Brubakers before leaving on his mission of prepayment, but hit on a better ploy. He hid the vacuum vial with a note of explanation in a light fixture of old Brubaker's office in Eureka; wrote a letter addressed to Mr. Brubaker in a fictitious town in Nevada; and gave the return address as Brubaker's own in Eureka. In the letter was only a note giving the location of 'something of interest'. After mailing the letter, he told old Brubaker to check his returned mail carefully, if Quantrill himself did not return from his ride in the IEE delta. Anyway, if the letter went awry Brubaker would find the vial soon enough. Postwar incandescent bulbs seldom lasted a month before replacement.

Young Brubaker had fretted and sweated to copy the massive crates which had been offloaded from Japan and scheduled for one M. Chabrier of San Rafael Laboratories. The largest of the replace-

ment crates contained a fast hovercycle. One of
the others contained Ted Quantrill with weapons,
heated bodysuit, rations for five days, and a venti-
lation slot fitted with a mass-motion sensor. When
anything larger than a wharf rat approached
Quantrill's crate, Quantrill knew it.

Most of the other crates were, in fact, the origi-
nals with tunneling equipment of Japanese manu-
facture. Carefully stacked in hoppers, battery pans,
and in every unoccupied corner of those crates lay
bags of granular material labeled 'dessicant'—
moisture-absorbent chemical. Most dessicant's were
harmless silicates. Old Brubaker had diverted the
Japanese silicates in favor of a chemical so cheap
it was employed as fertilizer: ammonium nitrate.

Like many a cheap substitute, ammonium nitrate had its side effects. It was fertilizer-grade
ammonium nitrate that once filled the hold of the
freighter *S. S. Grandcamp* and, on the sixteenth of
April 1947, blew the ship and most of Texas City,
Texas halfway to Houston. Old Brubaker judged
that four tons of it, confined in an underground
lab, might well boost a hunk of the San Rafael
desert halfway to Mars.

To Quantrill's dismay, his crate was lashed down
on the aisle of the cargo bay in the IEE delta.
Every time the cargo-master passed, Quantrill's
motion sensor readied him for action. At least he
was near enough to the cockpit to hear some of the
conversation and in this way he gauged his progress.

Quantrill performed in-place calisthenics, read
by the light of a pocket chemlamp, and felt the
great airship respond to side winds as it slid toward Utah from Eureka. He heard the captain say
they were maintaining one-fifty kph. groundspeed,
and tried to place the voice. As a teen-ager, Quantrill
had briefly served on the ill-fated delta *Norway*
and had met men from other crews. The cargo-

master was 'Cole'; nothing to catch the tripwires of Quantrill's memory. But the captain, 'Steve', might be a man named Will Stevens. From the *Cayley*? The *Santos-Dumont*? one of the *Norway*'s sister ships, anyway.

Quantrill's mission included leaving the crate to set a time-delay incindiary beneath the delta's gas cells. He heard the interchanges between Steve and Cole. The two men chafed aloud against their masters, spoke of their kids and their ration coupons. These were not the enemy, in Quantrill's mind; these were innocent teamsters of Streamlined America. It no longer mattered to Quantrill whether he had met either of them before; it mattered very much that they would fall as flaming crisps from a gigantic midair incinerator, casual victims of Quantrill's vendetta. He felt an upwelling of joy to realize that he had decided of his own free will—*free will! Thank you, Sanger*—against destroying the delta.

Eight hours and a time-zone later, the stirlings changed their whispery songs as the delta descended. Quantrill heard Steve's complaint, voiced to someone at the moorage: "Better get some floodlights set up, Chabrier. If you people don't get us a decent moorage, one of these days I'll put a strut through your roof. It'll be dark before we're snubbed down."

Quantrill ventured the private opinion that the lab would soon lack not only moorage, but roof as well. He sought handholds, waiting for a series of jolts, and silently praised the captain as he heard fondly remembered sounds; rasps of strut against concrete, creaks of a rigid spidery structure two hundred meters long as it became linked to the landing pad. It was a nice piece of work without mooring sockets.

Cole Riker inspected the strut anchors before

hauling pallets to the cargo hatch and spoke briefly with Chabrier while directing the floodlights. Then as he rode down with the third pallet, Riker muttered, "That crazy Chabrier is either queer for me or he wants out of here mighty bad." A hand's breadth away, Quantrill stifled the urge to whisper an inane reply. Riker had told no one of Chabrier's pathetic attempts to befriend him, but after three meetings he began to suspect that he represented, to the Frenchman, some form of potential escape.

Quantrill's pallet thudded and jounced en route to the elevator. He heard a Gallic accent entwined with the cargomaster's, heard the same voice raised among those of cargo handlers in some oriental tongue. This was a complication: what if he had to face down a crew without an interpreter? The goddamn Brubakers might've handed him a translating voder—but they'd briefed him on the Chinese staff and he hadn't thought of it either. Quantrill resolved to waste anyone who couldn't follow orders; the SinoInd war was still too recent for him to harbor much pity for a Chinese national.

Forty seconds ticked by while the elevator lowered Quantrill to the guts of the lab. Very slow elevator—or very deep basement. He'd been trained to memorize every datum going in, the better to grease his skids coming out. He tried, thrusting aside the failure scenarios his imagination paraded before him.

Fiasco One: They had sensors so good they would discover him before he had time to leave the crate, and guards alert enough to surround him before he could find a way out. Fade to

Fiasco Two: His crate would be stored in a building completely removed from the others. He would have no explosives and no hovercycle. Fade to

Fiasco Three: They put all the crates into vacuum storage. Fadeout.

At least, he told himself, they were sliding the entire palletload into the same place. That gave him the 'cycle and two hundred kilos of deadly 'dessicant'. Now if only they didn't start opening the damned crates immediately! Old Brubaker had manufactured a brief delay to make certain the delta could not arrive in the middle of the day.

Presently the alien singsong argot faded, borne away on shuffling feet. Quantrill's sensor, even on full gain, could detect no motion outside his crate. He eased noiselessly to the spyhole; put his eye to the lens expecting darkness. Instead he saw, dimly lit by fluorescents, a forest of crates on pallets. In the shadowy distance squatted a flat treaded earthborer, its toothed boring bit erect on a cantilevered beam. He studied the rig for long minutes; it looked capable of chewing a tunnel all the way to the surface, if a man had the time and no concern for the noise he made—and if he knew how to operate the goddamn thing.

The concrete walls were featureless slabs except for two areas that drew his interest. In one place near the earth-borer, gray flatness gave way to soft contours in concrete that led into darkness. In another, a great white spinnaker of plastic bulged like a tumor into the storeroom, inflated from behind. Beside the velcrolok portal in the plastic, flexible conduits drooped from raceways in the ceiling to plunge like feeding tubes into the tumor. Whatever lurked behind that positive-pressure seal, he judged, must be very delicate to need clean-room conditions.

An orderly commotion of men and machines issued from somewhere beyond Quantrill's view. Moments later more lights flickered on. He saw that the dark contoured hole was an excavation, its

rounded walls and domed ceiling sprayed with
ferroconcrete, and that the job was not complete.
Judging by the flexible seals where the concavity
began, this excavation might eventually be sealed
and pressurized with a twin to the portal nearby.

Four white-clad men came near, operating a
pneumatic lift and bearing more crates that looked
familiar. The men were orientals, one with his
hair in a pigtail, and they did not have the bodies
of laborers. Faces glistened with sweat. A grunt, a
snarl of torn fabric, a laugh; no hint that they
might be tense. On the contrary, they flopped onto
whatever was handy to wipe a brow, investigate a
hangnail, stretch kinks from shoulders. Quantrill
damned them for making it necessary for him to
squat immobile, but ten minutes later got his
reprieve.

The thickset caucasian who accompanied the last
palletload spoke mostly in the same foreign in-
tonations, but Quantrill recognized him from
mugshots provided by young Brubaker. Marengo
Chabrier spoke with authority and received defer-
ence without exuding arrogance or false *egalité* in
the process. A harried man, Quantrill decided; a
man consumed by details and gifted with languages.
His speech was peppered with American phrases:
assembly line, overtime, and to a refrain of snickers,
stoned to our follicles.

Quantrill recalled a tip from a sly-bodied Army
linguist, Karen Smetana: a few perfect unaccented
phrases can let you pass as a native from another
village—but make sure you *do* pass on, before somebody realizes you're faking it. Now Quantrill stared
at the other side of that coin. The foreign crew
might not know any more of Quantrill's language
than those few phrases Chabrier used.

But he'd heard Chabrier topside speaking excellent American. If Quantrill couldn't find a way out

without a guide, his ticket outside would bear
Chabrier's likeness. A month previous, driven by
Control, Quantrill might have taken extraordinary
chances on such a mission—in part because he'd
had no hope in the future. Now he dared hope,
knowing that hope might make him hesitate at
some vital instant when hesitation equalled death.
Then he thought of Marbrye Sanger, and trembled
with fresh intent.

When the Frenchman finished his spiel, one of
the Chinese drew a note plate from his smock and
encoded notes on its keyboard as Chabrier studied
the crate labels. The other men wandered off to
the elevator and Quantrill considered taking two
prisoners as soon as they were alone. Chabrier
rapped a knuckle on one crate, then another, then
Quantrill's, then a fourth. Priority items, perhaps,
for immediate attention. A hail echoed in the near
distance; Chabrier turned with his assistant and
quickly walked away. Quantrill's moment had not
passed; it hadn't really existed.

He made himself lie back and recheck his equipment during the next half-hour, giving them abun-
dant time. Better to waste a few minutes than to
be surprised at his work. That surprise would work
both ways, of course. His little Heckler & Koch
automatic was hardly in the same class as a chiller,
but for a silenced handgun its balance was respectable, and its Canadian 5 mm. rounds contained
curare in their soft noses. They didn't blow you
away; they just embalmed you where you stood.

His time-delay detonators remained a worrisome
enigma because he had no idea how precise their
rugged chemical timers might be. Young Brubaker
had sworn by them. They would write like any
other pens but, stabbed into a bag of ammonium
nitrate with the top unscrewed and the timer set,
were supposed to pop plus or minus one minute

over a one-hour range. Sloppy in comparison to solidstate devices, they were invulnerable to electronic detection.

Quantrill was already setting the stuff up in his mind: a chain of bags overlapping in a vee along the base of two walls, with a shaped-charge mound piled between the legs of the vee. The blast waves would sequence themselves in milliseconds for maximum shock up through the building, pretty basic stuff for any powder money and just about the limit of Quantrill's expertise.

Sometime after nine P.M., he slid the catches from the door of his crate, grateful for the few glowing fluorescents. Working in furious haste, he took the sides from marked crates using detents as they'd shown him, then began to emplace the bags— and there were hundreds of them. He worked with the knowledge that he might be caught at it somehow, his coverall damp with sweat. He could not know that, as he spent his first breather inspecting the pressurized portal, an enhanced infrared video bug silently followed him with its snout.

Alone in his chambers at the other end of the lowest level, Marengo Chabrier watched his video monitor with cold shock.

CHAPTER 51

The great boar let instinctive caution divert him as he approached the scatter of old-style ranch structures, low black silhouettes on a moonlit horizon. He saw distant figures scurry in patches of light as the ranch staff welcomed the 'chuck-wagon' occupants. He might have stood motionless and waited there, but the wind was not right and some of the stock in nearby stables had evidently caught his scent.

Pacing silently away, Ba'al studied the compound as he tested the breeze and returned, this time downwind of the restive horses. By chance he chose to wait in the moonshadow of a darkened guest cabin. He waited with good cheer, for his questing nose repeatedly caught the promise of an oestrus female.

Eve found herself in an unfamiliar role. Her companions could not say enough for her courage in facing down the brutish apparition so that they might scuttle to safety. More irked than embarrassed, she accepted applause and one nightcap before pleading exhaustion. Accepting a chemlamp to light her way, she walked from the central lodge and gracelessly refused Hutch's offer of escort to her cabin. A vagrant breeze at her back tickled the base of her neck.

In black shadow, Ba'al heard her heavy footfalls and the rhythmic song of Eve's corduroy breeches,

size fifty. More important, the odor of a ready
female was now a steady reek on the wind. He
heard her fumble at the the front door of a cabin
near the one where he stood. The cabins on either
side of Eve's were unoccupied, drawing him to slip
nearer in the darkness and to study this puzzle. It
appeared that he was studying some new hybrid,
an inexplicable cross between asiatic swine and
human. He had met the person face to face, knew
her to be a person and, moreover, one who did not
panic at first sight of him. But her scent was now
richly swinish and her great size richly suggestive.
He moved to the rear of her cabin near its one
feature, the broad sliding glass door, that clashed
with its decor. He could not see through its inner
partition, but snuffled against the glass.

Eve heard movement through the folding cedar
partition; heard a soft explosive grunt. If that poor
pitiful Cleve Hutcherson was trying for a late date,
he could—well, maybe he could have one. Maybe
something about their mutual experience had
turned him on so that he would please her without
lobotol. She turned off all but a single nightlight,
drew the wooden partition back, and gazed at the
demonic face that stood high as her own and near
enough to touch were it not for the glass pane.

She stood transfixed, trembling in the grip of
her glandular cascade. Ah, but it was unspeakably
good! Her memory served up a scene from a porn
cassette, lissome young Cow Patty with her lung-
ing pony, and now the little studhorse seemed
shoddy goods. Even if Russian boars were not hung
so well, she thought wildly, it would be an ecstatic
experience to couple with this devil; with the
demon, Ba'al. She smiled and unlocked the glass
door, then slowly slid it aside. With this act she
did not merely overstep sanity, she flung it to
oblivion.

Ba'al had rarely entered a human dwelling but showed no reluctance, snuffling in curiosity, stepping onto floorboards that creaked with his enormous weight. He ignored the distant sounds of merriment from celebrants in the lodge who were still toasting the escape. When he was inside, Eve managed to shut the glass door and the partition with fluttering hands. Now, no one could see or hear the apotheosis of Eve Simpson.

Even among lackluster domestic boars, certain forms of courtship are common. In Ba'al the instinct was tempered with high intelligence and despite goading from the command of pheromone he made haste slowly, emitting his soft insistent mating song as he did so. That song consisted of quick gutteral grunts in a truly subterranean basso with pauses for breath. He smelled fear in her too, a little, a person-sweat. He urinated briefly on the floor, also part of the mating ceremony, and gently thrust the tip of his snout against her side.

Eve could not recall her voice ever carrying such a tremolo as she heard the stream of urine. "Excited, lover? I'll bet you are," she breathed, shuddering in delight, daring to touch the monstrous ivory tusk behind his snout. He looked at her in bold curiosity, his grunting now insistent, and nuzzled her between her legs.

She took off her shirt quickly, ripped the brassiere away, whispering to this impossibly potent lust object in a way that approached prayer. He ceased his nuzzling to let her strip the corduroys away and she had to sit on the bed to accomplish it. She tried to part her oleaginous thighs for him, peeking to see if the devil's penis could rival a pony. But unlike some courting animals, the boar rarely unsheaths before the moment of mounting. Ba'al paused to glance at the object that flashed multihued splinters of light from between her breasts, sniffed at it, and found his head awhirl with the mating command. He placed one forehoof on the bed and rooted under her side to turn her over.

"Ah, so that's it," she teased. Why expect a boar to mount her face-to-face when they probably did it dog-fashion? She rolled over, found herself lifted by a bristly snout between her legs, and then she saw the incredible, endless unsheathment from under his belly. In that instant she scrambled to regain her sanity.

"Ohh, no you don't!" She frog-leapt to the head of the bed, writhing onto hands and knees, facing the great head that nudged and grunted in a demand she understood only too well. But she had erred horrendously in her expectation; this legendary brute carried a schlong like a barber pole! There was simply no question about it, she was far too puny to accept a partner as prodigiously endowed as this. In a clarity that arrived too late she knew that she had teased this minister of hell into expecting a great favor from her.

His grunts were louder now, his muzzle open in a satanic grin with grindings of teeth and copious foam dripping from his jaws in accompaniment. Again he tried to roll her over.

The bedframe splintered, dropping Eve so that she rolled almost under the beast. She reached up to grasp for a handhold, found that the upswept tusk kept a razor edge, bleated as she saw tendons bared in the palm of her hand. She wondered why it was not bleeding more.

Ba'al smelled blood, fear, and pheromone, stamped in impatience, nuzzled against the flaccid body of the sow-person. Her cries were not screams, not yet, but they were an irritant, and anger began to smoke in his red-rimmed eyes.

Eve saw and recognized the glare. In her extremity of terror she thought of a gift that any sane man would have preferred to her body. "Look, look," she babbled, unlatching the clasp at her neck. "I offer this in—in my place." She reclasped the chain, seeing that it would not reach around the vast pulsating throat, and then she held it aloft in sacrifice.

Ba'al saw the pretty bauble and her blood that smeared it; snuffled the acorn-sized yield chamber and wondered if its message was a lie; and finally he decided that the scent did not emanate from the screaming, praying person, and that he had somehow been cheated.

He might have acted differently had he perceived that Eve, eyes rolled up until only the whites stared blindly from their sockets, was praying directly to *him*.

CHAPTER 52

Chabrier adjusted the image intensifier and wondered where this madman had sprung from, an intruder who wore no uniform but carried a handgun in an armpit holster outside his coverall. The stranger seemed bent on arranging tons of dessicant in a simple geometric pattern on the floor of the synthesizer rotunda. Could Mills have sent him? But mon Dieu, for what? And could Chabrier afford to simply stroll into the rotunda and ask him? Not while the man—all youth and spring steel, to watch him move—carried that weapon.

It would not be wise to alert his Chinese staff. Only one of them would be any good in a rough-and-tumble, and Chabrier did not want *any*one to know of this security breach. If several men converged on the stranger it would only make him more likely to kill them all. Chabrier's schedule would slip and his friends would suffer. But without weapons, how could he disarm the man? None of Chabrier's drugs had enough potency to stop a man immediately without a killing overdose. He wanted to ask questions of that prowler . . .

Chabrier's fingers instructed the elevator to override any signals to the bottom level. There was no internal stairwell, thanks to the paranoia of Boren Mills. The intruder was now Chabrier's prisoner unless he could defeat the elevator doors and climb the sheer wall or the cables. Chabrier was nothing if not a gamesman; knew he would not be the young man's physical equal in combat. But he did have advantages; he knew his own turf and how to use it. He knew, for example, that the automatic sliding doors of the elevator were virtually noiseless. He knew how to cut power to lights inside the elevator or in any given passage in the lab. And he knew that, in common with hospitals and other limited-access buildings, the elevator had doors on two facing sides. With both sets of doors open, the elevator was simply a short passage through which Chabrier could move from his apartment into the rotunda with the prowler.

The man strode back to the palleted crates, removed a side panel by what seemed to be magic, began to hustle sacks that must have weighed ten kilos apiece—an infernal lot of dessicant, but who knew what Japanese packers would do next?

Chabrier, palms sweating, moved to his potted plants, removed one of his socks. He packed handfuls of damp sand into the toe of the sock and tied the knot to keep the sand compacted, darting glances at his video monitor. By the time he had located the sharpened letter-opener and thrust it into his belt, the intruder had started to disassemble the largest of the crates.

In fresh astonishment, Chabrier saw that his crew had off-loaded a crateful of hovercycle. Chabrier had requisitioned no such craft. He knew it would not have been forthcoming if he *had* asked. Someone—Mills, no doubt—had tampered with the shipment, sent the stranger in with his own devices.

The entire lab's support systems were Chabrier's responsibility and his portable control module had its own flat video screen. He could plug into the system from many stations, including the panel at each elevator call button. He took off his other shoe and sock for stealth, hurried into the main corridor, plugged his control module into the elevator call plate. Then he caused his corridor lights to die. On his module monitor he saw that the intruder was trundling the hovercycle on its small kickwheels to the elevator, having finished his peculiar ritual with the dessicant bags.

The man pressed the elevator call stud. Well, why not? Chabrier removed his prohibition, heard a faint whine in the shaft one pace away from him. He intended to open his own doors first until he saw the man draw the handgun, perhaps anticipating a violent welcome. Ever patient, Chabrier watched his monitor and waited, and cut power to the elevator's interior lights.

An eternity of seconds later the elevator stopped, and Chabrier's heart leaped; he had nearly, by mistake, opened both sets of doors simultaneously. With the intruder so clearly ready for confrontation, Chabrier now decided he could stop the elevator between floors to trap his opponent.

Through his video he saw the man vault into the

darkened elevator, and heard the soft impact of a
sidelong roll near him. No shots. A moment later
the man emerged reseating his automatic, then
heaved against the hovercycle so that it stood half
on the cargo platform, half in the rotunda. As the
man wheeled away with whiplash quickness, Chabrier realized that the hovercycle was a blockage
against the recall of the elevator from any other
level. The little salaud was canny—but so was
Marengo Chabrier.

Chabrier did not know what the man had forgotten but felt a thrill of good fortune. His fingertips
commanded his own door to slide back and then
he was into the elevator, the door whispering shut
behind him, trying to feel his way around the
hovercycle in darkness. He was between panel jacks,
his control module useless until he could grope his
way to the panel inside the elevator and make a
fresh connection.

Chabrier knew a surge of mixed emotions, a
piss-or-bust amalgam of fear and readiness, even
though he was having trouble getting around the
damnable machine in the dark. He was sure that
the intruder would not expect that sand-filled sock,
a street-fighter's sap, to come whistling out of the
blackness. He moved slowly to avoid any possibility of noise.

Had Chabrier peered into the faintly lit rotunda
he might have wondered why the intruder engaged
in a new madness. Six times Quantrill knelt, twisted
a time-delay to its maximum setting, and thrust a
detonator into a bag of ammonium nitrate before
sprinting forward to kneel again. This was redun-
dancy with a vengeance; any one of the detonators
should start the chain reaction and six detonators
made success almost a mathematical certainty.

Quantrill did not intend to be mangled by his
own success and hurtled toward the elevator while

fumbling for his tiny chemlamp. He placed it on the seat of the 'cycle, illuminating the elevator's interior and nearly causing cardiac arrest to the beefy Chabrier who crowded into the near corner, barefooted. Quantrill shoved hard, his head down against the fan skirt, and he moved forward with the vehicle. At virtually the same instant he saw a bare foot covered with black curly hair and a sodium-yellow sun that burst inside his head with a soundless flash.

CHAPTER 53

When Quantrill's eyes finally focused, they traded solemn regard with the sad dark eyes of Marengo Chabrier. "I regret this, mon ami," sighed the Frenchman, "but you will appreciate my position."

His position was commanding at the moment. He sat on the edge of a chair and toyed with an ornate stiletto. Quantrill felt the bite of wire against his wrists and ankles; saw that he lay on a bed in a room that did its best to personalize concrete walls. He remembered setting the last detonator, man-handling the hovercycle, seeing a naked foot. "You're Chabrier." A nod. "How'd you get me out of the lab?"

"You are not a large man. I carried you here."

"Where?"

A shrug, a wave toward potted plants. "As you see—to my apartment, such as it is."

"*How long ago?*"

"Perhaps twenty minutes, perhaps more." In tones that carried a dark whimsy Chabrier added, "You will understand if I ask the questions?"

Twenty minutes. It might've been worse; it might still get a damn' sight worse if he was kept wire-wrapped in this hole much longer. Or had the Frenchman removed the detonators? "I can't very well stop you," he said, trying to smile around a pounding headache.

"Why did M'sieur Mills send you?" Chabrier asked lightly, lazily, as if he had no doubt who'd sent the intruder.

Quantrill used time-consuming dodges; long breaths, slow speech, pauses, to give him time to think. If Chabrier thought Mills had sent him, the detonators had probably gone undiscovered. It didn't seem possible to Quantrill that Mills might send in a saboteur against his own operation. "Mills is a certifiable nut," said Quantrill, hoping it would pass for an answer.

"You underestimate our employer. I do not."

"Sure you do. You can't even figure out why the little gob of snot might go in for vandalism against you."

Chabrier hesitated. Any agent of Boren Mills should know better than to revile him, or even to discuss his mission, when recorders might be taking it all in. "It is not too late for a priority call to Ogden. What will happen to you if I call M'sieur Mills now and inform him how easily I nullified you?"

"You and I will both disappear without a trace—because you didn't nullify me. It's later than you think. You have a voice stress analyzer here, Chabrier? If you do, get it. Then you'll know that what I *do* tell you is the truth, no matter how much you'd like to disbelieve it."

Chabrier stroked his lower lip, remained seated

and rearranged some opinions. "Petty vandalism would be madness, or the tactic of one who wishes to impede production. Does the subtle Mills wish to make it appear that one of my staff is malingering, or insane?"

"My guess is, he'll wish you to *dis*appear—and you will. Me, too—after he's had me taken apart."

Chabrier refitted pieces of his puzzle; tried a new piece. "Then why did he provide you with an escape vehicle?"

"That was my own idea."

"You are aware of the particle-beam weapons surrounding this place?"

A nod. "And I can deal with 'em."

"I do not think you are in the employ of Mills at all," Chabrier blurted. "I think I have caught a saboteur."

Quantrill caught the relief in his captor's face. This poor bastard was more frightened of Mills than of outright sabotage! "Let's assume you're right, Chabrier. And *if* you're right, you got to me too late because I was outward bound when you nailed me. Let's assume I've stacked enough explosives in your basement to blow us all to hell and gone, with motion sensors on the detonators." Like fleas, small lies can prosper on the back of a large truth. "I *know* you haven't found the stuff, because we're still here in one piece."

"The dessicant," Chabrier raged, leaping to his feet. Holding his head as if to create a helmet, he glared down at his prisoner. "It will detonate when anyone approaches it?"

"That's part of it. There's more—but I think better on my feet. You've got my sidearm. I've got your ticket past the P-beams out there in the desert. What'll it be: out of here on a hovercycle with me, or in little bitty pieces in a few minutes?"

As he attacked the twisted wire at Quantrill's

wrists, Chabrier chattered, "Cretin! There are mice in the loading bay. One of them could trip a motion sensor at any moment. Imbecile! I hope you are more careful in getting us out of here." The heavyset Frenchman stood back, holding the automatic. Quantrill removed the wire from his ankles, stood up, rubbed his wrists, flexed his arms. Then he turned his back on Chabrier, a languid casual move followed by a backward step at blinding speed, pulling Chabrier's gun arm forward while right hip and thigh swung in and upward against the heavier man in a classic *harai-goshi*. That move and the cross-arm lock that followed on the bed were essentially simple ploys, but devastating when used in sequence by a man who could flip a coin and catch it between thumb and forefinger.

Chabrier found his right elbow locked at full extension in the other man's crotch, his wrist gripped remorselessly. By arching, Quantrill could easily shatter the elbow. He proved it with a slight arch, then relieved the unbearable bending force. "That's for catching me like a first-timer, Chabrier. Never hold a handgun on a man when he can see it's on safety. Now give me the piece, and I'll give you your elbow."

Chabrier let the weapon go, saw the younger man flick a tiny lever under the receiver, lay still until he was alone on the bed. His face registered fatalism as he rubbed the aching elbow. "Now at least I shall know your intent," he grumbled. "Am I to be shot, or left to be crushed?"

"Get up, you poor bastard; even the cargomaster on that delta knows how bad you want out of here. I said I'd haul your freight, and I will if I can. How many guards do we pass between here and open ground?"

"None." Chabrier rolled to his feet, took one step toward the next room; said, "I must bring my medication, mon vieux, or life will not be worth living."

"Go ahead, take your time but don't forget your mice. If you're trying to sucker me again, Chabrier, you won't live to see this place go up."

Chabrier stood motionless for five seconds, nodding to himself. Then he tugged on socks, thick-soled shoes, and his only windbreaker, ignoring several suits of foreign cut and a very oriental-looking brocaded robe. Quantrill followed his every move with suspicion and, noting the Frenchman's economy of movement, with approval. If not for his sluggish reflexes, he thought, Chabrier might have made a superb agent. Then Chabrier paused; released a charming smile. "If you are not entirely devoid of mercy, mon ami, you will allow me to warn my staff."

"Then call me Mr. Devoid. Risk getting boxed? Not a chance."

Chabrier shook his head and muttered, scooping up his stash of drugs, stuffing them into his zipped jacket and grabbing a pair of fine leather gloves. He tried again while trotting from corridor to elevator: "One develops friendships, even with prisoners. Will you permit me to alert them when we reach the surface?" Negative headshake as Chabrier, using his control module, began to normalize the functions of the building.

Quantrill snatched the thing away.

"For the love of God, let me get us out of here!" Chabrier imagined the few mice multiplied into swarming thousands, nosing into invisible capacitance fields, tripping a detonator,—and snatching at the module in frustration.

Quantrill slapped the hand away, then offered the module. "Just remember this thing is full of curare slugs, frenchy. Ah,—what risks do we run if I warm the 'cycle engine up inside the elevator?"

The elevator door ghosted aside and in the now-illumined space they finished positioning the 'cycle. Chabrier flicked studs, watched the door close. "If it is not terribly loud, go ahead."

Quantrill waved his companion against the far wall, seated his handgun, primed the engine and kick-started its muffled engine after several tries while the elevator slid upward. He jerked a thumb overhead: "You're sure we won't meet some goons up there?"

"I shall cut the lights beforehand, to be certain. The perimeter guards make their rounds at various times, but they know me. In any case, the fools drive about with lights blazing. Bear in mind that I am as anxious as you, M'sieur."

"Do you mean to tell me there are no guards at all inside this lab?"

"None. Boren Mills has—ways—to ensure a kind of loyalty, and the desert itself is a barrier. Plus guards who shoot to kill if one is caught outside, and of course the particle-beam towers."

Quantrill tested the diesel's supercharger; folded back the fore and aft covers from the munitions pods that lay against the forward fan skirts. The beam-seeking munitions were rocket-propelled 30 mm. Canadian Homingbirds, fitted with carbon shields over their sensors. With its internal vanes, a Homingbird could jitter in flight in a preprogram that could defeat most beam weapons—unless the beam struck precisely, the first time. Its range was under a kilometer, but if fired in volleys the little rockets simply overwhelmed a laser, maser, or P-beam weapon's ability to readjust its aim.

Best of all, the dilating rocket nozzle permitted the little rounds to loiter in flight for several seconds, tempting enemy fire. When that fire came, the surviving Homingbirds went swarming in on full boost with shaped charges. Canada still lacked the solid-state technology of Streamlined America, but she knew how to make weapons dumb enough to sacrifice and smart enough to win.

"I am cutting the lights," Chabrier warned, and Quantrill saw tears coursing down the man's blue-whiskered cheeks.

Not one but two sides of the cargo elevator slid back; Quantrill ducked low, blinking in a darkness that brightened as his eyes adjusted. The moon helped a little. The breeze was summer-soft, and from their prominence atop the lab berm they spied moving lights two klicks distant and moving away. "The patrol," Chabrier sniffled, and cleared his throat. "They could return in less than an hour."

"Oh, I think we can count on that," Quantrill chuckled, revving up the fans. "Get on behind my seat, man, what the hell are you waiting for?"

Chabrier's hands squeezed and grappled at one another. "Go to a safe distance and wait for me," he pleaded. "Please, I beg you; I am not a murderer! I cannot just let my fellows die like vermin." He waited for an answer; got none. "I shall not tell them that you exist; only that Boren Mills has arranged our deaths as we all knew he would." Voice rising to a tortured baying: "At least give them a chance! They are prisoners, you dirty boche! Slaves! All they can do is run!"

"Tell 'em to scatter in different directions, not to travel in daylight, and *especially* not to be found by black search aircraft," Quantrill said in anger and resignation. "Truth is, Chabrier, they have about ten minutes." He thought it might really be nearer twenty.

He listened to Chabrier chatter into his control module, the Frenchman standing on one foot and then the other as if the elevator floor were hot lava. Slow-moving, emotional, untrained with the weapons of single combat: Chabrier was all of these, but his courage in behalf of alien slaves filled Quantrill with a bitter envy. The good Samaritan, it seemed, had his counterpart among the minions of Boren Mills.

The elevator's panel speaker erupted in jabbers that Quantrill did not understand. He understood one thing: the staff was staging their own Chinese fire-drill somewhere below. Chabrier spoke their tongue in staccato bursts, repeated one phrase, then leaped from the platform as the doors began to close. He ran the few steps to the hovercycle, scrambled aboard; cried, "Avance; vorwarts; GO, for God's sake!" Quantrill went.

As the vehicle gained headway, Chabrier leaned forward and called over the whoosh of fans, "The perimeter fence is high and very near. If we cannot go over it, how will you get through?"

"Now you tell me," Quantrill snarled, throttling back, letting go of one handlebar to rummage blindly in the toolbox near his feet. Chabrier pointed to a dim moonlit tracery of rectangular mesh ahead, fully five meters high with steel pipe bracing at intervals. He shut off the machine, let it settle, swung his chemlamp to study the barrier.

"Be assured that if we cut it, we will alert the guards," said Chabrier quickly.

Quantrill saw that they were still too near the lab for safety. "Where are the nearest guards and how soon can they get here?"

"Halfway to the North gate. The patrol is probably halfway there now and they may need ten minutes to return from there."

"In other words, if we wait five minutes we'll have the longest head start."

"Do we dare?"

"Relax; we dare. I promise, the detonators won't pop for another ten minutes. At least that's what *I* was promised. Who the fuck knows?"

Quantrill unrolled a coil of tubing the thickness of a finger and ten meters long; gave another to Chabrier, demonstrating how to string the tubing in a great 'U' against the steel fence. As always, Quantrill readied two escape holes in case one, for whatever reason, failed. Pressure-sensitive tape crossing the tube gave it the appearance of barbed wire, but was only an aid in holding the tubing against tree trunk, fence, or door facing.

To Chabrier's query the younger man said, "Plastiquord—an improvement you French made on Primacord. When you pull the pin at the end you get ten seconds before it blows, and it'll sever two-centimeter steel bars. Just make sure it's snug against the fencewire, and let me pull the pin."

"That honor is all yours," Chabrier muttered, peering at his handiwork, readjusting a corner curl of the tube as if neatness counted. Quantrill checked the work; saw nothing to criticize. Near the midpoint at the crossbar of each 'U' he tied a monofilament cord to the fence and let it trail back on the ground.

The hovercycle was running again when a muffled thump from above the earthen berm made them glance back to the lab. The cargo elevator again stood in the open, a square of blackness against the night sky. "Uh-oh," said Quantrill, who leaped to pull the delay pins; proved that he could duck trot as he dodged behind the 'cycle. ". . . Eight, nine, ten, elev—" he said as the first report ripped the calm. The second blast came a second later.

Quantrill burst from his cover to grapple with the monofilament cord, hauling backward with all his strength. Chabrier knew the fence was not electrified enough to deliver a shock—but the little saboteur hadn't asked him. Chabrier helped fold the severed mesh back by sheer force. Tied back by the cord, the mesh yawned open and, seeing several dim figures hurtling down the berm toward them, Quantrill vaulted onto his seat.

"Those guys are on their own now," he called, floating his vehicle through the hole. "Get aboard, Chabrier, before they swamp us!"

Moments later the two men hummed away without lights, building up to a speed so great that Chabrier was sure they could not avoid an obstacle if one did loom ahead. Quantrill squinted at a small box riveted on his instrument panel; twisted a vernier knob until an orange light glowed; readjusted so that the light barely flickered. With Chabrier's extra weight, the 'cycle's engine worked harder to keep its distance from the hardpan, and their speed seldom exceeded highway norms across the desert expanse. They were not yet ten klicks from the lab when a flash at their backs lit the terrain. Quantrill glanced back, thrust a fist aloft in triumph; far behind them, in splendid silence, a massive roil of crimson and yellow arose from the desert floor in a fireball that darkened as they watched.

Quantrill, over the engine noise: "Looked like an oil storage dump. Ammonium nitrate doesn't go up like that."

"Monomers and diesel fuel tanks buried outside in the berm, mon ami; it would appear that you are damnably thorough."

Turning again to the west, Quantrill laughed outright. "You should be cheering, frenchy; weren't you a prisoner too?"

"All that work, all that experimental data—one hates to see it lost."

"Mills's enemies don't hate to see it lost—and that means most of Streamlined America."

"They would, if they knew what you destroyed."

Dull thunder finally overtook them, half a minute after the glare. As it faded Quantrill said, "I was supposed to blow away a Chinese gadget that synthesized rare materials."

Chabrier stiffened, then accepted the fact that Mills could not keep his secrets as well as he imagined. Speaking into Quantrill's ear: "You are well-informed. Every unit in existence was operating in that lower basement, and the porcelain parts were even more delicate than the cermets. I might possibly rebuild one from—from a small model and my memory, but without great good fortune M'sieur Mills will find nothing of much use back there."

"That makes you a valuable man to—wups," Quantrill ended as the field sensor light winked, then glowed brightly.

A sharp turn on a hovercycle requires the driver to bank steeply without scraping the fan skirts. Quantrill nearly lost his passenger as he urged the vehicle up and around in an abrupt turn. The field sensor light was a steady glare. Quantrill slowed until they were hovering; steered to make the 'cycle pivot; made its nose wag slowly as he watched a meter on the sensor box.

Finally, his outstretched arm pale in moonlight, Quantrill pointed left of center, ahead. "P-beam tower. I'm told they're about fifteen hundred meters apart. That true?"

"Closer, I think, over uneven ground. I saw them only once. Boren Mills amused himself by flushing rabbits and driving them forward by gunfire. When the beams struck the poor little beasts exploded as though struck by lightning. Of course the vultures came later—and met the same fate. Mills merely wanted to frighten me. He succeeded."

"Let's see if we're close enough. Move your legs up and shut your eyes; I'm going to fire one of the little birds near your feet."

Chabrier obeyed as if goaded by needles. Quantrill

set a dial; pressed a stud. With a near-explosive whistling rush, the little homingbird sizzled away, backblast shifting from boost to loiter, and Quantrill watched with one eye covered to maintain half of his night vision.

For perhaps five seconds the exhaust cometed off, dwindling to a hard point on the horizon. Then a thread of light stretched across the desert for one retina-jarring instant, and a blue-white firebloom marked the intercept point where rocket and P-beam met twenty meters above the hardpan.

Quantrill urged the 'cycle forward another three hundred meters while Chabrier's grip tightened on his coverall; then he warned his passenger again. This time the Homingbird's rush carried it only a few hundred meters before a sharp line of glowing air molecules traced the P-beam's passage to the sacrifice decoy. Both men heard the *spaaat* of the beam in air and the chuffing boom of its target. "Near enough. This'll be a loud one; three, two, one." Hands over his ears, Chabrier still heard the sharp whistles. First one, then four more boosters howled away. Quantrill protected his ear nearest to the munitions rack; watched with one eye as the brief battle unfolded.

The sacrifice round preceded the others by a half-second, moving in the arc of its brief patrol. The hard actinic line again stretched from obelisk to target, and suddenly four exhuast glows became long zigzag booster trails like an aerial firework gone berserk.

A second P-beam fired, and one rocket cartwheeled into the distance. There was no third P-beam because the sawtooth trails of two Homingbirds converged on the obelisk at such a pace that Quantrill could barely follow the sequence. Two shattering blasts, the ear-pounding signatures of small shaped charges, echoed from nearby gullies and weirdly from inside the hollow shaft of the obelisk like a belch from a pipe organ. The upper fourth of the shaft split open, one piece spinning into the air.

Blue sparks showered up from the obelisk in a display that could have been seen from Mexican Hat, a hundred and sixty klicks to the south. More sparks erupted horizontally from a hole at the tower's base. "Solar accumulators are shorting," cried Chabrier. "Thanks to God! This will be a beacon to my friends."

Quantrill did not advance until the base of the obelisk, thick as a man's waist, began to melt. Only then did he gun the 'cycle forward, passing the tower as its energy accumulators consumed gobbets of metal that fell inward. Not until Quantrill was half a kilometer beyond did the itch subside between his shoulders. He throttled back, settled himself for the long ride, and veered South.

"We can hide in the mountains if we continue to the West," Chabrier called.

"We've got enough fuel to make New Vegas, and I have a contact there," Quantrill said over his shoulder. "By dawn we'll be skirting the Grand Canyon. But anytime you'd rather walk, you just sing out."

Chabrier laughed and fell silent. He knew that he could negotiate with reasonable men; sell his talents as Von Braun and others had; but he wondered whether he would meet any reasonable men. No longer could he hope to live in the ballooning shadow of Eve Simpson—and in a way he would miss the great cow. If he was to reconstruct a synthesizer—of *any* size—he would have to recover her amulet. In its cermets and solid-states resided technical details that no one, not even Chabrier, could memorize. He had long since committed his records of those secrets to a temporary memory storage in his apartment; a memory bank which would automatically self-destruct without daily recoding by him and him alone. Somehow, he must get his hands on that bezel again. He entertained a hope that this young saboteur's friends could make contact with Eve Simpson.

CHAPTER 54

No one found it remarkable that Eve would be so drained of energy that she might miss breakfast. The tale of her courage on the previous evening hung in the dining hall, rich and pervasive as the perfume of chorizo omelet. But on the second pass on her morning rounds, the maid still heard no reply to her knock on the door to Eve's cabin.

She knocked again; called; fitted her key to the door and insinuated it open. "Maid service, Señora," she sang as required, and then wrinkled her nose against the stench of urine—and of something else.

It smelled, she thought, of butchering in the barrios; not a truly bad smell if it brought memories of feasting in a poor TexMex family, but a smell very much out of place among rich gringos.

The girl thrust the door open further. The first thing that caught her eyes was the gaping hole where the sliding glass door should be, with sunlight streaming through it. Then she saw the corpulent dark-smeared nude torso sprawled grotesquely near the broken bedframe, its skin gray-white, the flies already idling in through the breach in the wall; and when she glanced near her own feet and recognized that the melon-shaped object near the door had a face that stared unblinkingly toward her, she began to run ...

CHAPTER 55

"Don't make me go over your head, damn you," Boren Mills raged into his office holoscreen, "or I'll trot out the holotape I showed you and run it for Young myself!" Mills's automatic devices could not record Chabrier's control module, but duly recorded the views of the lab monitor until the moment it went blank.

Lon Salter knew that he could delay the inevitable, but anyone with eyes could recognize Quantrill's profile and the way he moved. "We already have three S & R teams probing the site, Mills; and two rover flights tracking the fugitives. They all went out the same hole afoot and then split, but they can't go far. What good will it do to take you out there?"

"I can't tell you that, Salter—well, maybe I'll have to. I don't care what you do with Quantrill after I question him but I want my lab staff on ice and unhurt *at all costs*! I want a voder—belay that; I want a live interpreter who speaks technical Chinese, and I want to be on the site in three hours with him. I can make you a very," he paused, thinking of Salter's own recorders, "—a very happy man if we can recover certain things from that wreckage—or a very unhappy one if you balk me."

Salter's usual lugubrious expression grew deeper. "I'll have to pull every string I can with the Air Force, but maybe I can get you to the hole before noon." He frowned at Mills's image: "Maybe I should meet you there. I won't carry any bugs if you won't."

Recording devices were easily detected anyway. "Agreed," Mills rapped. "One more thing: we both know why we can trust rovers to keep quiet. I want no one but rovers to collect anything from the site. No outside experts, no regulars! There are some things so sensitive that it could be necessary to disappear some of your own people."

"You'll go on record with that?"

"I'm sure I already am."

A pause to confer with his roster display. Salter registered something akin to pleasure as he said, "Mills, to do that I'd have to pull every rover in S & R from other duties all over Streamlined America. A national red-alert emergency: are you ready to justify that to cool down a fire in IEE?"

"What do you think Steamlined America is all about? Who backs the Lion of Zion? Where would he be without you and me, Salter? Now stop acting naive and get those rovers to my lab site! I'll see you there as soon as possible. Make it possible very, very soon."

Mills slapped the holo off, stood up, started pacing his office. Oh, he had a lot of the prints and specs for the synthesizer; everything Chabrier filed into permanent memory. But the subassembly prints for the cermet parts, and the ones for the toroidal yield chamber, were top-assembly prints without breakdowns. Chabrier had held out on him, and now the goddam Frenchman was either Quantrill's hostage or, worse, his companion!

And what if he couldn't get Chabrier back? Well, there was always that tiny unit the sex-crazed frog had made for Eve. Other men might upscale a standard model synthesizer from that. Suddenly the Ember of Venus and its tiny integrated synthesizer took on an importance it had never owned before.

Mills detested drugs, but with his back to the wall he would shoot Eve's fat arse full of alkaloids. He would have her mainlining popcorn, hulls and all, if that was what it took to recover that sole remaining model of a working synthesizer.

He was striding toward his holo, phrasing his recall demand so that Eve would suspect nothing unusual, when the intercom spoke.

Mills's secretary had been hired not for her thirty years of experience so much as for her seventeen-year-old voice. Vibrant and girlish as ever, now it was also troubled. "It's some manager of a ranch in Wild Country, Mr. Mills, on line one. He says he can't speak with anyone else—and he seems to be crying."

CHAPTER 56

The hardest part about getting from New Vegas to Eureka was persuading Chabrier to shave. The man flatly refused to let anyone but a female registered nurse scrape the fur from his back, buttocks, and thighs, and finding a woman they could trust took Quantrill's contacts nearly a full day.

Quantrill was shipped in a container labeled 'Radioactive Waste'. No one had expected Marengo Chabrier—for that matter, they hadn't really expected Quantrill—so the scientist underwent six hours of cosmetic work. Chabrier was wheeled into a Greyhound omnibus as a sallow drooling fossil by the same slender nurse who had shaved him. Before they reached Eureka, Chabrier and the woman passed narrow scrutiny several times, and knew the stirrings of a beautiful relationship.

Quantrill was in no position to read faxpapers. Chabrier's nurse bought a fresh four-page edition at every stop and read it aloud as one might read to a bedridden child. Nowhere was there any mention of an explosion in the desert wilds of Zion, but the Reno *Tattler* was of the tabloid persuasion and squandered ink on a bizarre report from Wild Country. The *Tattler* confided that, according to unimpeachable sources, a creature the size of an elephant had emerged from its age-long sleep in local caverns to gorge on human flesh. Its most recent victim was a lovely young girl, one Eva Simmons, whose talon-ravaged parts had been found in the ruins of her isolated cabin.

So much for tabloid accuracy. Nothing in the piece gave Marengo Chabrier the slightest cause for concern.

Quantrill never saw young Brubaker again but, while retrieving a vacuum vial from one of old Brubaker's light fixtures in Eureka, he reminded the older man of their bargain. "I've had my paranthrax shots," he admitted, "so I'm not worried about Nashville. But if you have contacts in Corpus Christi, that's my choice. Is there some way I can go without climbing into another box?"

There was, said old Brubaker, if he didn't mind routing through Alta Mexico. "Port of Oakland or Los Angeles to Tucson, El Paso, Matamoros, and then to Corpus; Mexican territory all the way to the gulf. You speak Spanish?"

"Enough to get by unless they grill me."

"They won't, with your papers. You'll be a security man, keeping your eye on dredging machinery that Midas Imports ships to Corpus. Mex transport is cheap with all their oil, so we route heavy stuff around Streamlined-ptooey-America. Anyway, you'll be safer on Mex soil than you'd be crossing Wild Country."

Quantrill recalled his days in Southwest Texas; the free-wheeling ways of the people who had a law unto themselves; and smiled. "I doubt it."

"Then you haven't heard what happened while you were earning your passage. Your friend Chabrier was debriefed last night with some LockLever people—he beat you here by a day, sorry 'bout that—when he heard about Eve Simpson."

Startled: "My God, Brubaker, I know the crazy broad!"

"Not any more, you don't." Old Brubaker gave him a sketchy version of the woman's death as reported by UBC Press. "It hit Chabrier pretty hard. He clammed up right away, but evidently she was carrying a keepsake he gave her. Would you know why it might be important to him?"

"Haven't the foggiest." Staring out the window at the growing port city, Quantrill mused, "I'm tempted to believe in fate, Brubaker. I mean, that huge boar is something I know about first-hand. I tracked him once after he snuffed a little kid I knew—but I never located him.

"And I met Simpson once. And *now* I find that Chabrier was a friend of hers, God help him! It's almost as if there really were only a few hundred people in the world . . ."

Old Brubaker stood beside him, chuckling, fondling his one-a-day cigar. "In a way it's true, Ted.

When you're as old as I am, you'll realize how few people there are who do pivotal things; people full of ideas and vitality, gamblers for the most part; stepping on people's toes as they pass, shaking the rest of us in our little ruts and striking sparks from each other. Not exactly a prescription for a quote, nice guy, unquote. My only surprise is that some of you live so long. Oh, you're obviously one of the breed," he said, showing patently false teeth, laughing at Quantrill's quizzical look. "So is Governor Street; so are those quintessential assholes, Young and Mills. I'm not saying *all* you hyperactive wowsers are good for us; only that you're all agents of change, one way or another. And I wouldn't trade places with you. I like to play chess, read a Michener epic I've read twice before, watch a long sunset; things I couldn't cram into a short life."

"And you expect to outlive me; is that it?"

Pause to light the stogie. A long pleasured puff. Gently, then: "Yes, I do. I got a look at the Canadian file on you, Ted. You've lived several lives' worth of risks and you're barely old enough to vote. If you keep living on the cutting edge—hell, *as* a cutting edge—you'll run out of reflexes or luck one day. Soon, maybe. Or later, maybe."

"It's been years since I had a chance to bullshit with someone like this," Quantrill sighed. "I'd like to try a slower pace, myself. I intend to, when all this is over."

"It'll *never* be over! There'll always be a gamble somewhere with your name on it, Ted."

"You don't think I could change?"

"Not sure you ought to. Remember, I sit in on the game too, now and then—with you, for instance. One day it could get me snuffed. But I've found a slot, call it a rut if you like, that isn't too hectic for a family man like me. If you weren't in such an all-fired hurry I'd invite you for a home-cooked meal. You're one guest my grandkids couldn't terrorize," he laughed.

"You keep sliding away from giving advice," Quantrill observed, studying the play of fine wrinkles that fanned from old Brubaker's eyes.

"Don't know you well enough. I just know that whenever you've been run through a meat-grinder, it's the machine that got busted." Now he was laughing again as he watched cigar smoke swirl in the afternoon light. "That's no small talent, Ted."

Quantrill, wistfully: "There must be another slot for me beyond that. Any ideas?"

Old Brubaker rocked on his heels, nodding, taking his sweet time. "Foreign correspondent," he finally murmured, "if you can face a holo camera."

"Scares me shitless."

"Security staff? God knows your training has taught you most of the angles."

"Possible," Quantrill hedged. "My trouble is that whether I worked for government or some corporation, they're always screwing somebody and I'd be likely to change sides."

"True," said Brubaker. "Then you'd just have to decide where your ethics pointed you. I can't tell you what your ethic is; I can only tell you that everybody has one, however twisted it might be. You're a long way ahead if you know what's likely to keep you awake nights. And," he said with a wink, "I've wasted ten minutes playing guru on the mountaintop to a man who knows what he wants."

"Do I?"

"Sure: temporary work with Midas Imports, and papers to get you to Corpus Christi. That little container seems to be burning a hole in your pocket. I don't want to know what it is, but I imagine Governor Street will. Am I right?"

Quantrill thought again of the critic, and of

Sanger, and felt his scalp tighten. However much
he might long for the statisfactions of a Brubaker,
he yearned more for redress. One day he might
luxuriate in unhurried disputes of ethics. But for
now, his was still an ethic of destruction.

CHAPTER 57

Sandy's journal, 23 Sep. '02

*Hands so raw can hardly hold pen but canning
done! Preserves & veggies, gleaming ranks of riches
to spend this winter. With 2 more paying guests
could buy choice items in Rocksprings. Note from
Lufo; his friend Quantrel expected from Mexico. Wonder if brute distant kin to Ted Quantrill? Not common name & variations frequent. Ironic that hardened
killer should remind me of gentle, generous Ted, object of first girlish crush. Doubtless long dead in
some pointless Asian battle. Cannot even recall face
after 6 yrs. Is forgetting a natural therapy?*

*He has returned with, of all things, garish pendant
draped over one tusk! Lost or discarded by some
tourist with taste for cheap flash, I suppose. Childe
insisted hers, & why not? Truly it does charm the
eye; poor so long I tend to make poverty a virtue.
N.B.: caution Childe against showing it off; why
tempt strangers who might think it valuable?*

CHAPTER 58

Anything small enough to fit on a railroad flatcar is small enough to disappear when routed through Mexico. That is why Midas Imports always shipped a security kiosk on the same flatcar. Quantrill found those quarters cramped, but the kiosk was insulated and the toughest part of the job was staying awake during the hours he spent in switching yards.

His first transit delay left him in on a siding in downtown Tucson for hours. He could see that the Mexican government did not splurge on civic upkeep; street traffic detoured around potholes in the middle of the city, and the streets were littered with trash. Well, perhaps Mexico did not really expect to keep these yanqui territories very long. His temptation to stroll into the city faded quickly, and Quantrill spent Wednesday reading in his kiosk.

Wednesday was also the day when old Brubaker said a little too much on an unscrambled videophone. By then, Boren Mills had persuaded President Young that S & R needed help. The NSA people didn't like it, but they did it; a listening NSA spook fingered the Midas Imports man to S & R. A few hours later, kidnapped in his own Chevy by the nearest rover, old Brubaker suspected that he might not get much older.

Old Brubaker was right. Questioned under torture, he cried as anyone would. Graeme Duff of S & R sensed that his captive might be crying too much and revealing too little so, cursing the time it always took, the rover brought drugs into play. While going under, old Brubaker had time for regrets, chiefly focused on his family. He also regretted that he knew how to contact the Canadians, and that the young escapee had important information for the Indys in Corpus Christi. Brubaker thought it was a memory cube.

Before long, Duff would know whatever old Brubaker thought.

Bull-necked and bull-headed, the rover Duff might have botched the interrogation but for his two-way connection with Control. His critic cautioned him against mentioning names or events until they had been voiced by the victim.

Fifteen minutes after old Brubaker started to babble, Duff asked for Seth Howell on-line and in another five minutes, got him. "You'll want to wring this one out yourself," said Duff, neither happy nor unhappy. "He's tied up with Canuck spooks, and the last man he fed to the rebels was Ted Quantrill."

His critic fed him Howell's triumphant, "*Goddamn*! I'll be in Eureka in two hours. Keep the informant comfy 'til I get there and meanwhile, find a snuff-box for him. You'll need it when I'm done."

Duff coded out, grumbling inside. He could always count on Howell giving him the shit-jobs.

On Friday afternoon, Quantrill dozed through the arid stretches of Coahuila while the NSA untangled coded manifests enough to place his flat-car somewhere between El Paso and Matamoros. It would have been possible for S & R to spend a day setting up an airtight trap, monitoring every breath Quantrill took until they nailed him. Except for one thing—actually a bundle of several small things.

First, NSA deputy assistant directors do not appreciate being suddenly subordinated to agencies such as S & R. Next, a position high in spookery does not always eliminate one's political biases. Both the NSA and CIA employed a few patriots who chafed against their orders. Also, the NSA's charter is information-gathering, and some of its team leaders shared the rumor that a certain S & R rover had somehow managed to become a high-pressure leak in an uncontrolled part of the system. Some of these leaders viewed that rumor with what might best be termed guarded optimism.

Finally, it was late on a Friday, and S & R had neglected to formally request prioritizing codes to ensure that information on Quantrill would be run through NSA's crypto office with flags flying. The deputy assistant director spied, among seven other completed routine tasks, the timetables for a flatcar in Alta Mexico. He could pursue this particular item Friday after hours—or he could hurry to his condo and dress for a function he had been told to attend, an open-air reception certain to feature illegal booze, fancy dress, and pliant women. Known in the crypto trade as tux and fux.

The deputy assistant director was not long plagued by indecision. "Catch you Monday, Quantrill," he murmured, and headed for his long weekend. Sometimes, he reflected, doing one's part means doing nothing.

On Saturday, Quantrill's flatcar skirted under Wild Country and was bunted onto a barge at Port Isabel. The flatcar was still unpillaged, but still at the mercy of Mexican shippers. Quantrill's security job would terminate when the dredge equipment reached Corpus Christi Bay but, to judge by the slow passage of the barge up the intracoastal waterway, that equipment might become obsolete during the trip. Tow cables parted; sand bars materialized where none were expected. By late Monday morning Quantrill was almost ready to leap overboard near one of the many islets adjoining the sandy coastline, but now at least the barge was proceeding faster than he could swim.

And the team of Howell, Cross, and Ethridge was proceeding at mach two from Ogden direct to Corpus Christi Naval Air Station. Their vehicle was an Air Force jet under Executive Verbal Order. It made a straight-in approach as if low on fuel, and a fast Navy chopper waited for them near the end of the runway. Before the USAF jet was in chocks, the trio of rovers was en route to the docks in the Navy chopper.

S & R cosmetologists had done their best on short notice. Seth Howell was bald as an egg, fat-cheeked, padded to pudginess beneath his longshoreman's outfit. Cross was blond, dapper in his business suit, and remembered to limp as he leaned on a cane that would fire shotgun cartridges. Ethridge wore the gray hair, wrinkles, and dress whites of an aging naval officer, his gymnast's body carried with military correctness. They exited from the chopper at a dead run with five minutes to spare as Quantrill's barge was warped slowly to its pier.

In S & R training, paranoia was a matter of policy. Quantrill did not see the helicopter drop behind the warehouses because he was too intent on the uniformed customs officials who strolled to their posts, each with a sidearm and shoulder-slung video terminal. Quantrill had the unsettling notion that they did not walk like customs men.

Corpus Christi was a port of entry into Streamlined America and here he might be retina- and thumb-printed on the spot regardless of the papers he carried. It was high noon under a cloudless sky with no hope whatever that he might step ashore without a confrontation, and a small patrol launch idled slowly past the barge on the bay side. Quantrill wrenched his heavy shoes off and, with a flash of foresight, placed them with his wallet and sidearm in a polymer garbage bag, trapping a considerable volume of air in the bag as he clamped it shut. The only other garbage bag was full. He emptied it onto the floor of the kiosk, thrust the partly inflated shoe bag inside it, opened the window on the bay side, dropped his bag onto the bed of the flatcar.

Through the dockside window he saw a tall portly workman in earnest conversation with a customs man. Something in the way the workman's hands moved set a small alarm chittering in Quantrill's head. He felt a shudder as the barge nudged its pier and knew that the great flat craft would grind and groan as it sought perfect alignment with track adaptors. He flowed over the windowsill on the bay side, snatched the drab garbage sack; squatted perfectly still as he squinted in hard sunlight at the patrol boat. It was starting its turn for a return pass.

Another massive shudder, then a series of metal-to-metal screeches. Quantrill made two squatting leaps, flatcar to barge and barge to salt water. He had no way of knowing whether his splash was lost in the clatter of moorage.

Gripping the neck of the bag, he did not plunge far under the surface; if anything, he had trapped too much air inside. He kept the bag between himself and the patrol craft; felt a feeble current bumping him against the flank of the barge. He opened the bag, reached inside, then saw that his head and shoulders would fit inside the filthy thing. He eased into it, tugging the neck of the bag; realized he could not haul it down farther without tearing an air hole.

Above the slap of wavelets against the barge hull he could hear the burbling approach of the patrol boat. Too late to hyperventilate now. He scissored with his legs, feeling the barge hull at his heels; let the current abrade him against it. The surface current tended to move the bag faster than his submerged body, and he treaded water to keep himself vertical. His flotation bag might pass unnoticed among other floating junk in the bay.

The silt stirred by the barge was Quantrill's ally, darkening the water to gray-green opacity. He heard the patrol craft pass fifty meters away, held his breath, felt the current quickening as he was dragged faster along the hull. The thrumm of the barge's starboard engine grew until he could feel it through his ribcage and Quantrill realized he was being drawn toward the whirling propeller. He slid the bag aside to risk a glance and saw that he was barely fifteen meters from the aft curve of the hull. The barge was twenty meters wide but ranks of steel-sheathed pilings stood, a welcoming forest, supporting the pier. He had time for four hard breaths before pushing away, abandoning his flotation, feeling the swirl of current. An instant later, a meter beneath the surface, he felt himself flung aft of the barge. He let the current take him where it would.

The silt stung his eyes as he fought to keep his orientation. He exhaled at the first lightheaded tingles that signaled oxygen starvation, emerged for a breath, and saw through stinging eyes that he'd been swept a full seventy meters behind the barge. His flotation bag bobbed lazily, angling toward distant pilings. He submerged again, kicking hard. A long half-minute later he felt his way between pilings, saw that he was in shadow; surfaced noiselessly. Mouth open wide, he made his

breathing as silent as possible and kept his arms
below the surface to prevent splashing. He was
half-blind from silt, breathless, weaponless.

No, never entirely weaponless. Sean Lasser had
taught him long before: when you don't have a
weapon, make one—preferably a surprise. He had
his denims, shorts, and belt. Careful silent lungfuls
of air gave him his second wind and, blinking
furiously, he stripped his belt loose.

Just above the waterline ran an ancient rickety
scaffold of boards, a chancy footpath for structural
inspectors. Quantrill was feeling with his feet for
purchase against the submerged metal sheathing
when he heard, muffled by echoes, a voice that
chilled him: "Negative, Marty; if he's not on that
flatcar he's probably holed up somewhere on the
barge." Ten meters away, the indistinct outline of
a big man showed against a piling. The voice was
unquestionably that of Seth Howell.

Quantrill's heart stuttered, then steadied. No hope
now of climbing onto the catwalk, and no telling
how long Howell had been standing on it. Well, if
he couldn't climb up, Seth Howell would just have
to come down. Quantrill had done some of his best
work underwater. When the massive Howell advanced along the catwalk, Quantrill could trip him
with a noose made from the belt.

But Howell was disposed to wait. The hulking
shoulders lifted, and now Quantrill's vision was
good enough to reveal Howell's left hand against
the throat mike of a headset. Of course the sonofabitch wouldn't have a critic! "Told you before,
Ethridge," he growled softly; "we don't *want* him
alive and whining to these people. Bag him the
instant you get a positive I.D." Pause. "No, maintain your cover and make sure he doesn't go over
the side while Cross goes aboard. I'm staying put;

he's got to flush sooner or later. If I know Quantrill he'll head for the shadows down here."

Quantrill smiled grimly and headed for Howell; slid directly under the catwalk, grateful for the buoyancy of salt water, not daring to grip the boards lest Howell feel them sway underfoot. The slap of waves masked the tiny swirls that marked Quantrill's approach. Then, almost below Howell's big feet, Quantrill paused to assess his position.

Angrily then, from Howell: "You've got a goddam Presidential directive, Marty; use it! Get those customs assholes in gear and remember he's carrying plague so they're to shoot on sight."

Howell faced outward, toward the barge, one hand caressing the throat mike while the other held his chiller. Without warning, a snakelike object flew up before his face, the belt uncoiling in midair, and Howell instinctively drew back with knees flexed, groping with his left hand for a piling. He heard a suck of water below, felt the catwalk sag, then felt a vicious forearm chop behind his knees and vented a single "Whup!" before he struck the water.

For a man of modest size, Quantrill enjoyed a great deal of upper-body strength but knew that Howell's massive upper torso overmatched him. And if Howell got half a chance with that chiller he could fire it underwater. Quantrill's advantages lay in surprise, a lungful of air, and the quickness to grapple for that gun-hand before Howell could kill him with it. Maybe.

Of course that left Howell's left hand free. Quantrill caught the big man's right sleeve, slid beneath him, managed to get both hands on Howell's right wrist while clamping his legs around Howell's long upper thighs.

Howell's head snapped back in a head-butt, catching the smaller man squarely in the middle of the forehead. It was a score; another like that could knock his assailant unconscious.

Quantrill slid down, pressing his face between Howell's shoulders, and felt the long left arm snaking back, its hand scrabbling for Quantrill's groin. Instead the powerful fingers found the fleshy part of Quantrill's inner thigh through his trousers and wrenched with sickening force. It was like a bite from a horse, and it kept on biting.

Quantrill grunted, a few bubbles bursting from his nostrils, and with both arms surrounding Howell, heaved as hard and as abruptly as he could. The impact of his own chiller's butt into his solar plexus caused Howell numbing pain and, worse, the loss of a great gout of air. At that point he did what he should have done first: released Quantrill's thigh and snatched at his hands. With a few broken fingers Quantrill would be candy.

But Quantrill was wondering when Howell would go for his hands. The instant he felt the big bony fingers grope for his, Quantrill let go with his right hand, his left still clutching Howell's right sleeve, spinning the big man around. At the same instant Quantrill unscissored his legs, thrusting away from Howell with his knees so that the larger man spun faster. On land, Howell could have prevented this maneuver, but not while flailing in frictionless liquid darkness while his lungs ached.

Howell was prying back on Quantrill's ring finger when he felt that loose right hand grip his left, and then he felt the stunning impact of two bare heels in his face. He fired the chiller without much hope on full auto, felt the septum of his nose crumble under a second pounding of those pitiless heels, sensed the tingle in his skull spreading along his torso, and tried to disengage. It was not entirely panic; he could tell that his hands were no longer as strong as Quantrill's. The difference was air, air, *air* . . .

Quantrill let the chiller go; he knew better than to fire it, knew also that at least one round had struck him in the right pectoral after losing most of its punch in its passage through water. He felt Howell's hands growing lax, knew that he *must* keep pounding with his feet. His heel encountered Howell's chin, shattered the jaw; and Quantrill distinctly felt the quiver of Seth Howell's weakening body as the two collided with a piling.

With all but a few opponents, Quantrill might have given quarter. But Howell's flailing fist struck him above the still-healing head wound by chance, and the result was a half-second of hallucinatory rage. Quantrill's enemy was a piece of Control's forebrain, a calculating monster, killer of Marbrye Sanger. Quantrill placed his bare feet on Howell's torso and, without releasing the hand, pivoted completely around the axis of Howell's shoulder. He heard the explosive scream underwater.

He almost lost the jerking, pulsating body of Howell but broke the surface with the man's shirt in his grasp; whirled in search of enemies; grasped the catwalk with his free hand. When he hauled Howell to the surface as a possible shield, the shirt tore away. Howell still moved but breathed more water than air. Nose torn half away, jaw a shapeless ruin, right arm free of its socket—Howell would lead no more death squads. Quantrill's last concern with Howell was in wrenching the signet ring from a dying finger; its garrotte might come in handy. When he pulled himself up to the catwalk his enemy lay face down in the water, naked to the waist. Quantrill left him, racing crazily down the catwalk, scanning between pilings until he spotted the garbage bag.

From Howell's backward plunge until Quantrill

emerged for breath, some twenty-five seconds elapsed—considering their combined knowledge of combat moves, something of a marathon. He had to swim for the bag and, hauling it up to the catwalk again, Quantrill saw something that sped his flashing hands. Its broad naked back and arms awash, head down, the body of Seth Howell had floated out into September sunshine.

"Howell, Cross; there he is," sang a familiar baritone from somewhere above, beyond Quantrill's vision. Quantrill snatched his H & K automatic, freed its safety, froze in place. He did not hear the chiller but saw Howell's body jump, submerge, roll into its back. Then Kent Ethridge's horrified, "*Howell*, Christ almighty! Quantrill's down there already!"

Quantrill left his shoes and sprinted down the swaying wooden walk in search of an upward stair. He found one at the end, blocked by a steel gate with a padlock that no small-caliber handgun could mangle. Above him in the gloom ran triangulation rods, bolted between pilings. Quantrill did not intend to swim for it, now that dozens might be watching.

As he passed the site of his duel, he wondered if Howell had taken a second stairway and then suddenly he located it, as a white-clad form came pelting down a shadowed stairwell in stockinged feet. It stopped at the first piling and disappeared—Ethridge, pausing to let his eyes adjust.

Far above, Quantrill heard shouts and hammering feet. In the stairwell, more heavy footfalls. A strange voice in Texan accents: "All right commander, or whoever you are, that's enough! Come up here with your hands—", and then the customs man moved into view, and Quantrill heard the cough of Ethridge's chiller. The man spun on the stairs, grunted, scrambled upward cursing and moaning.

Quantrill waited in wonder, hidden by a piling. More shouts from above but no more rash heroes. A white naval jacket fell to the catwalk. Shakily, then, almost in a sob: "This is for her, Quantrill— for Sanger. I know you're there, I can smell you. Come on! Mano-a-mano, you baby-raping bastard," and almost crooning, begging: "Just you and me." Then finally an agonized scream: "QUANTRILL!"

For Sanger? It had the ring of a vendetta; and poor Ethridge had never quit trying for her favor— not ever. Quantrill was tempted to reply but had better sense than to give his position away.

"Quantrill!" Sobbing outright, with no attempt at stealth. Almost as if Kent Ethridge was asking for a fast snuff. "She was too good for you," echoed under the pier. "Maybe for me, too. *QUANTRILL?*"

It was just possible, Quantrill thought, that Ethridge was truly whacked out. More probably running on Control's orders, a decoy to draw him out. But he was doing one hell of an imitation of a grief-crazed fool.

One hell of a gymnast, too. "Spare me your problems, Cross; I'm going in alone," said Ethridge in normal tones, then raised his voice: "Try me, Quantrill! We can go out together." Quantrill's eyes widened in astonishment as he saw Kent Ethridge soar into space.

A creak from the structural support, and Ethridge was swinging up and over. Not an easy shot—but Ethridge's chiller was snugged into its armpit nest, no immediate risk. The gymnast hurtled up, slipped, regained his balance, stood on a horizontal rod masked by another piling.

Quantrill felt gooseflesh. Whatever Control told Ethridge, they couldn't see that vast jungle gym under the pier, couldn't possibly know of his insane risks: a parallel-bars routine in rotten lighting, diagonals criss-crossing his path, moisture everywhere. No, the crazy sonofabitch was really doing it on his own, daring Quantrill to reveal himself; hoping he could bring his chiller into play before he died.

He's willing to die for her, now that it's too late. My God, he's me. Quantrill sidled against his piling, paying no attention to the commotion above on the pier, sliding the H & K's magazine out without a clatter. Gunfire erupted in a muffled exchange from the barge as Quantrill slipped the curare-tipped rounds into one hip pocket, pulled the magazine of ball ammo from the other. He wondered what the hell those people were shooting at.

A faint creak, and Ethridge flipped head downward, using diagonals this time, a clean lovely maneuver in a pike position to the next horizontal rod. Quantrill shifted again, still unseen; felt water trickle from the fresh magazine and blew into it without thinking.

Ethridge heard it. "You're getting it in her memory," he said. "I wanted to be sure you knew." Dead calm in the voice now.

"She got me out, Ethridge." A part of Quantrill could not believe the rest of him could be so stupid as to speak. He went on doing it: "That's why Control pulled her plug! Howell ordered it—and you just shot him. Thanks."

"Murdering shit; you're lying." Ethridge seemed to be moving nearer.

"Why d'you think I haven't bagged you already, Kent? Every time you shift position I get a clean shot."

"Better take it, assbreath."

Quantrill found the lie easy: "She wanted to get you out too, Kent. She told me so, damn you."

"Shut up. I see those wet footprints, Teddy. I know where you are."

Another creak, and Quantrill flicked his head out to check. Ethridge pendulumed almost overhead, one hand missing a diagonal, and as the gymnast recovered he saw Quantrill's adder-quick draw, at a range of less than five meters. For an instant they were face to face. There was no shot.

Then Ethridge flung himself away to the safety of another piling. He ducked from sight and Quantrill could hear him mutter, "Christ Jesus; Christ Jesus," over and over, at the knowledge that he had been spared certain death.

Quantrill: "Now goddammit, will you believe me?"

Silence. Then shaky muffled breathing. Quantrill edged out until he could see an arm; a shoulder. Kent Ethridge leaned perfectly still against the piling, high up, his face in his hands. "Kent."

No response.

"Kent, why was it a crime for us to love the same woman? And why does one of *us* have to die for it? Control is our target."

A long sigh, a grunt. It could have been agreement.

"You know I had you back there. You goddam *know* it! But icing you is the last thing Sanger would've wanted. If you get your ticket punched, how can you help me hit Control?"

An exhalation. Then after a long pause, a rapping on metal: S O S.

"Got it. If you'd rather trust me than those cocksuckers behind your ear, tell 'em you're going into a sewer or something and come down from there with your hands clean."

He tried to hear Ethridge's mutters, but a loud-hailer on the patrol boat was making too much noise. He stood out of its view, weapon at his side, and watched Kent Ethridge's lithe descent.

The loud-hailer finished its spiel two hundred meters down the pier, burbled nearer, started over. "Commander Niles, your Mr. Fairbanks has been shot while resisting arrest. You are surrounded. Come out unarmed. Mr. Conrad of Eureka: you are among friends; please do not show yourself or fire on your rescuers." The crew of the patrol boat took no chances and kept out of sight as they moved on to repeat the message. Obviously they didn't know the exact position of the men under the pier, but now it was only a question of time.

Ethridge's eyes flickered around him as he dropped to the catwalk—perhaps looking for an escape route just in case—His hands were not as high as Quantrill would have liked, but no matter. They both knew whose draw was quickest. Quantrill stuck the H & K into his sodden trousers. "Don't forget Control; use sign talk," he said to Ethridge who nodded, hands trembling.

"You're commander Niles?"

Nod.

"Who's Fairbanks?"

Manually: "*Cross.*"

"Good; they bagged his ass. Any other teams?"

"*Not that I know of. Can't be sure. They psyched me up like a berserker—*"

"Later; we've gotta find a safe hole for you. Those customs dudes on the level?"

Elaborate shrug. Then, wincing: "*Control trying to raise me.*"

"Don't answer. Take off those white pants, they make too good a target if those guys come down here after you. I'm going up. Keep that chiller; if I come barreling back down, for God's sake don't snuff me." Quantrill eased past the gymnast, squeezed his arm in passing. "You and I together can make Control regret Sanger," he added, trotting toward the stairs.

He emerged slowly into the light calling, "I'm Conrad! Take it easy! Send me one man, unarmed, to the stairwell; you can understand my caution."

He could hear men talking; a rattle of their equipment. He winced, reached inside his shirt, felt a lump between skin and pectoral muscle. The little explosive slug popped into his hand like a pea from a pod, still a live round. A half-meter of Corpus Christi Bay had made all the difference.

The man who slid into view kept his hands out and, beaming, explained that no customs men were anywhere near the pier. The men in borrowed uniforms were rebels; a welcoming party of picked men.

CHAPTER 59

Even when he spotted two men carrying the body of Cross, Quantrill was not absolutely certain of his welcome. He refused to move into the open until the blocky prewar Mercedes rolled onto the pier. Flanked by towering bodyguards made taller by stetson hats, the old man who stepped from the rear seat carried an odd-looking piece of headgear. He was an unforgettable figure to anyone old enough to recall earlier Presidential elections. The paunch, the rolling gait of an old man with bad hips the compressed features on a big bald head with its halo of gray hair: Ex-Governor James Street of Texas.

Quantrill grinned, placed his automatic on the pier, strode to meet the Indy leader.

"Here, put this on first," said Street in introduction, taking the helmet from under his arm. He turned it over and a cascade of metal mesh fell out. It would form a cape reaching half-way to the wearer's waist.

Quantrill accepted the thing, shook the proffered hand. "I'm Ted Quantrill, Governor. What's this thing for?"

"We know who you are, boy," the old man said in a friendly growl. "We've had unimpeachable reports that you're still wearin' a gawddam bomb in your head, and reports just as insistent that it's gone. If it isn't, put on the gawddam helmet, it's somethin' they call a Faraday cage with its own signal generator. If that tells you a lot, then *you* explain it to *me*. But the gawddam Feds can't blow a man up when he's wearin'—where the hell are you goin'?"

But Quantrill was already sprinting back to the stairwell. "I've got a friend down here who needs this," he shouted, and started down the stairwell talking as he went.

Moments later he returned with a very cautious Kent Ethridge who made an arresting picture in helmet, briefs, socks, and a silvery metal drape that covered his upper body. Ethridge still refused to speak aloud, full of mistrust for the helmet; but his hands spoke often to Quantrill in rover dialogue.

Quantrill made the introductions. "You'll excuse Ethridge, Governor. He doesn't have much faith in that helmet, and I don't blame him. What he wants is a nice deep cave as long as that critic's in his head."

Along the pier men were running, changing clothes, speeding off in cars and on hovercycles. One of the stetsoned giants leaned over to murmur into the Governor's ear. "You're right, Tom," Street nodded, and turned to Quantrill with a squint-eyed grin. "This little switcheroo took some doing, and the real customs folks want to get back on the job before the gawddam media come flockin' down here. You boys ride up front," he added, and moved in the painful flatfooted gait of a tired old warrior toward his chariot.

CHAPTER 60

It was not a genuine death-dealing icy wind, the kind that could sweep down from blue-black October skies to justify the local label, 'blue norther', but it made Sandy Grange glad she'd rebuilt this half-submerged old soddy instead of moving into an ordinary cabin. Gusts slapped at her big window near the fireplace and Childe gave a delicious shiver in response to the moaning at the eaves. "Tell me a scary," she wheedled, twirling the great Ember.

"Not now, hon," said Sandy, playing with the holo channel selector. "And quit diddling with that awful thing. Remember last week?"

Last week Childe had been idly toying with the amulet, watching its smoky gleam reflect the firelight, when it began to issue a terrible odor of long-forgotten eggs. It had taken Sandy awhile to track the stench to its source, but only ten seconds to throw the amulet outside. And there, on the grassy verge of a South Texas soddy, the only functioning synthesizer on Earth had spent the night, its glitter challenging the stars.

Now, Sandy window-shopped between two channels. The FBN channel offered its usual sitcoms. The Mexican channel was for all practical purposes an American channel with expatriate yanquis like sultry Ynga Lindermann whose talk show reached well into Streamlined America. Secretly, Sandy enjoyed the Lindermann show because at times her guests said and did things that went far beyond the legal limits. But after all, it was only a Mex station. Nobody *had* to watch.

But tonight Sandy chose FBN's electronic pablum because it promised a special cameo appearance by a personal friend, the Reverend Ora McCarty. Apparently the Federalists did not yet suspect that McCarty might have rebel connections. So, for the best of reasons, Sandy missed Lindermann's talk with an old guest star, Governor Jim Street. And a new guest, Ted Quantrill.

Boren Mills would have missed it as well but for a priority call from Salter. Since his return from the utter ruin in the San Rafael Desert, Mills could usually be found either in his office or his adjoining spacious apartment, trying to buttress his tottering empire. The Israelis were dragging their heels on the ECM deal, and Young's complaints of outlaw media became daily more threatening. The two teams of innocent S & R regulars had found no trace of Eve Simpson's amulet at the Schreiner place, and while the desert lab had yielded many small fragments of synthesizers, Mills entertained little hope that a working specimen could ever be reconstructed from them. Other members of IEE's directorship were asking pointed questions about the failure of the (nonexistent) sea-water extraction facility near Eureka, and now Young had reneged on the licensing of the LOS site near Wild Country.

Unless Mills could offer some outrageous inducements, the IEE board might begin realignming companies like Latter-Day Shale. And Mills could find no inducements to sway some of those staunch upright Mormons. It was clear that Blanton Young's vision of Zion no longer coincided with theirs. If LDS voters found common cause with Catholics and Masonics, Mills would be wise to have his bags packed and his IEE stocks converted to faceted jewels. As his private phone buzzed, Mills was estimating that he might have six months to unload.

Lon Salter's holo image was that of a frightened man. "Mills, I'm watching XEPN, the Mex station. Can you receive it?"

"We own FBN, Salter. I can get an Ellfive station if I like."

"How nice for you, Your Arrogance. Turn on XEPN and pray that Young doesn't see a replay." Salter broke the connection.

Frowning, Mills snapped on the holo; coded the illegal Mex station that catered so brazenly to the rebel Indys. He slouched in his chair, not particularly surprised to see the two-shot of Ynga Lindermann and homely old Jim Street. But his frown deepened as the audio gained strength.

". . . knew about the explosive implants in those Army Intelligence agents during the war," Street's gravelly voice insisted. "But we could never prove those same agents were still in the field. Well, they are, under President Young's direct orders, and their primary job is still assassination."

Lindermann was playing straight-woman. "They certainly keep a low profile, Governor."

"Hell they do, they wear the same uniforms as all the regular members of Search & Rescue." Audible gasps from an unseen audience. Street pressed on: "But they have extra equipment. Body bags. Silenced weapons. That mastoid-implant radio I mentioned. Whenever you see a lone S & R member, you may be looking at someone like him."

As the old man nodded to his right, the holo camera zoomed back. Boren Mills sat bolt-upright, a chill beginning at his widow's peak and centipeding down his spine. Ted Quantrill sat beside Street, clearly uncomfortable in a full dress uniform of S & R. No matter that the uniform must have been faked for this broadcast; the psychological impact was enormous; charismatic.

The old man said, "Of course some of them want out, but you can imagine what it's like to know your skull can be blown open anytime Young's people—they're called 'Control'—get the slightest suspicion that you could be an embarrassment to them. Young Quantrill had an incredible piece of luck, never mind the gory details, but somebody got that damnable thing out of his head before it exploded. And the instant he was free, he came hot-footin' it to us." A sly smile: "As all free Americans will, sooner or later."

Lindermann glanced into the camera. "A shameless political plug," she said archly, as though she were not a crucial cog in the Indy media machine. "I understand that he was pursued. Ted, how did you escape?"

Closeup of the uneasy young man in the sleek S & R uniform. "Well,—they caught me," he said, clearing his throat, trying to ignore the camera. "I guess their mistake was in training us so well."

Street, off-camera for an instant: "They caught each other, Ynga. And it cost Young three of his best men, including two instructors. They got good Christian burials—better'n they deserved. The instructors didn't have those critic things in their heads but the young fella did. Chased Quantrill into a storm sewer and—well, I saw the body myself. Sure made a believer out of me. Poor fella was an olympic-caliber gymnast before the war; Kent Ethridge, his name was. Damn' shame he threw in with the wrong folks." ·

"He didn't have a choice!" Quantrill's objection knifed through the old man's words. "None of us did." He seemed ready to subside.

Lindermann, sensing the young man's readiness to unburden himself, prompted him with, "Would it be too painful to say how all that affected you, Ted?"

Quantrill leaned forward, hands on his knees, then looked directly into the camera. He had been sweating, but not now. Now he was willing to stare the holo camera down.

In his eyes was a look that saw beyond anguish, the scarlet pain burned out, leaving only a dull and apparently permanent rage in the impassive, too-youthful face. "Okay, then." he leaned nearer into the camera. "You know about our mastoid critics. You know we're kept for killing—and they'd monitor our thoughts if they could. But nobody's told you what it does to us. I'm going to tell you now."

A long pause, the green gaze unwavering, muscles twitching at the corners of his mouth as he framed his words. "Think of the people you love the most; your brothers, sons and daughters, a wife or lover. You've trained and grown together for years, saved one another from dying, held—", and here he paused, throat working convulsively, "—held each other for comfort, knowing you must never—*ever*—say 'I love you'. Not even in a whisper. Because if you did they'd kill you.

"But you find ways to show it. And then realize you don't dare. There's always that fear in your guts that the training has been *too* good; that maybe loving *is* a sign of weakness; that if you show weakness you'll be rejected, maybe killed, by the one you need most.

"And the day comes when they force your own sweetheart to kill you, and instead she defies the entire system and gets you out of it all, knowing you don't completely trust her, knowing they may blow her away at any moment.

"And they do, the sons of bitches." Softly, softly: "They blow a piece of her head away and she dies, with no assurance that all of her love and trust and longing meant a God-damned thing to anyone else, including you. Including you," he repeated, nodding into a ghastly self-accusation.

The studio was so quiet it seemed one could hear the slow blink of those eyes, dry and green and entirely without pity. "And when someone offers you a chance to tell about it on holovision, you know you won't find words, there are no words, to truly explain how the bastards have hollowed out your soul and filled it with hate. But you know they monitor rebel 'casts." The nostrils flared infinitesimally. "They've made a death list naming a thousand innocent people, LDS and gentile alike." The barest suggestion of something like a leer. "They also know how well you can carry your assignments out. Who are they? Men like Lon Salter of S & R; Boren Mills of IEE; and their chief executive, *your* chief executive—President Blanton Young.

"Should they be surprised to hear that I have a little list of my own?" He was silent for two beats, his unwavering stare a promise of annihilation. "Be seeing you," he warned.

Old Jim Street's face was flushed and Ynga Lindermann appeared genuinely shaken. Quickly she put in, "Mr. Quantrill's opinions are his own, of course. We'll continue with our next guest after these brief messages . . ."

Mills realized that the phone was clamoring for attention. Salter? Young? Shit, who cared? He was slumped down, as far as he could get as if trying to disappear into his cushions and no goddam phone was going to pry him out. Mills began to wonder if there was any cushion anywhere deep enough to hide him from that green-eyed maniac. He did not have six months to unload. If he was very, very cunning, he might have six days.

CHAPTER 61

The morning after Quantrill's broadcast, the Governor would not be swayed. "You blew it, son," he said in exasperation, swiveling in his high-backed old office chair to follow Quantrill's pacing in the room. "They might think *he's* dead," he jerked a thumb toward the silent Ethridge. "But you? Ever' pistol-packin' spook in Streamlined America will have an eye cocked for the noodlehead who threatened the life of the President on international holovision! And I'm not sure it was smart to let that little fella Mills know we've linked him to S & R. Nope; if I put you on that penetration team it'd purely jeopardize the mission. Besides that, there's things we need you for right here in Wild Country. And quit makin' those funny hand-signs to each other! Makes me gawddam nervous and it isn't polite."

Ethridge: "I was only telling Ted I'm better in a vertical shaft than he is, anyway."

Quantrill caught and erased his grin. Ethridge had really said, *"After we blow CenCom I'll do a singleton. Mills's scalp sound good to you?"*

The old man jabbed a peremptory finger at a nearby couch and Quantrill dutifully sat. "Nobody's goin' after that computer until our own crypto fellas have sucked out all available information with that little radio you brought us, Ted. And even then, I'll scrub the mission if it looks like they've got another memory storage as backup." Leaning back, balancing precariously, he stared at the cedar-beamed ceiling and mused, "The great drawback in a secret police setup like Young's is that he dassn't trust anybody with duplicate records. If we can mount a clean operation, we can cripple just those parts of Streamlined America that Young and Salter need to keep folks in line.

"It's all got to be in that central computer. S & R's rover files, records of Young's undercover deals with industrialists, maybe even physical evidence they keep for blackmail. Oh, it's an old pattern; wish I could say I never stooped to anything like that myself."

"I can tell you where it'll be," said Ethridge, tugging carefully at the bandage on his head. "I had to disappear a cipher clerk for Salter once. There's a maze of tunnels under the LDS genealogical vaults where Salter keeps what he calls 'executive exhibits'. I'd guess they're forensics exhibits. Mormons aren't going to thank us for blowing a hole under *their* most treasured records. And how the hell do we destroy corridors in solid rock without a trainload of plastique?"

Startled at Ethridge's knowledge, the old man flopped his chair down with a squeaking bang. "You boys know too damn' much," he complained.

"All right, then: we're aware of that. What we're plannin' now is how to get every innocent soul out of those LDS vaults when we tote a suitcase nuke in below. Genealogical records are sacred, but they have duplicate vaults in Nauvoo and Jerome. At least history won't record that we did to the Mormon Church what Caesar did to the library at Alexandria. I have to think about things like that."

Quantrill's chuckle was low, but it made the old man study him quizzically. "If the Feds thought you had any portable nukes, every rover in S & R would've been down here before now," Quantrill explained.

"We don't have one yet. But one of my best field men told me a story about a small SinoInd nuke that a young girl found in Wild Country during the war. She didn't know what it was at the time, but—well, it could be just a story. That's what I want you to check on, Ted—you and my man, Lufo Albeniz. Fact is, he knows you." A sparkle of youthful deviltry danced in the rheumy eyes. "Mean as hell, Lufo is. Begged me not to let the cougar outa the sack until he could watch, just so he could see you jump."

"It's been tried," Quantrill grinned, "but I don't recall the name."

"Why would you, boy? This is Wild Country," the Governor winked, and returned to the topic at hand. "I don't really want to nuke that CenCom facility; I believe in due process of law and besides, the thing's too useful. But usin' that little gadget out of your head, Quantrill, my computer spooks are breakin' into its memory banks. Already stole a pisspot full of information, they tell me.

"You know what a trojan horse program is? A trapdoor?" Blank looks and, from Quantrill, a shrug. "Me, neither," Street admitted, "but we have fellas from Sperry-Rand and Osborne who use 'em to

gain access to CenCom. They're workin' around
the clock to find ways to generate destructive
commands—in other words, tryin' to get CenCom
to tell us everything and then kill itself. Well, it's
workin' only up to a point. Don't ask me what a
'security kernel' is, but it keeps us from makin'
CenCom commit electronic suicide. There's stuff
we can't get at—so we'll have to atomize it. Without casualties, if possible."

Ethridge, acidly: "Some of those people know
exactly what they're doing. Fuck 'em."

"And let innocents suffer too? That's exactly the
em-oh of the Federalists who are tryin' to strengthen
this country again by boostin' the gross national
product at the expense of the average citizen. Read
any text on American history after the Civil War.
It's a record of spreadin' corruption, boys."

Ethridge could not resist it: "Governor, you ever
see a *boy* with false teeth and balls like a cantaloupe?"

The old man slapped his knee and cackled.
Nonetheless: "Lots of 'em," he replied. "To this
day, I want to yell and cheer, yep, and cry for joy
like a kid, ever' time I see *even a picture* of a P-47."

Ethridge and Quantrill together: "A what?"

Jim Street laced his fingers, cracked the horny
knuckles, stared out the window toward the creek
that meandered near his study. "Well boys, it was
near sixty years ago, just days before Christmas,
and German incomin' rounds were pourin' in on
us like shit through a tin horn. We were nearly out
of food and artillery rounds and the fog was bitter
cold, and the Air Corps couldn't see through it to
drop supplies, and the sumbitchin' krauts had cor-
ralled us.

"And then some corporal from Kilgore whacked
my helmet to pop me outa my foxhole early on the
23rd, and it was a clear cold mornin' and waves of

fat P-47 fighter-bombers were swarmin' down on the kraut armor at chimney level with napalm, frag bombs, ever'thing but spitwads, while our transports dropped a scad of supplies down to us in Bastogne; and if there was one man in the One-Oh-First Airborne *not* yahooin' like a boy, I sure-shit didn't see him." He nodded to himself. "To this day," he said again, chuckling. He added, "Maybe enthusiasm is what makes the boy. So don't feel all cut-up when a boy eighty years old says you're another."

To Quantrill, the events seemed as distant as the battle of Waterloo. Yet here was a grizzled old warrior who'd taken part, was still taking part in struggles against dictatorship. "Battle of the Bulge," he said in awe.

Ethridge recognized the allusion. "If you went through anything that bloody, how can you worry about snuffing a few enemies in the CenCom vaults?"

"Because I'm not a Blanton Young. The American system of government has taken some terrible shocks, but it can still recover. We can cut away those secret Fed controls without bloodshed and let honest elections replace Young's administration—or we can fight without regard for human lives, and start a full-scale revolution. None of us would profit from that."

Obviously Street's vision of the good fight did not tally with that of young men trained only for killing. It did not occur to Quantrill or Ethridge that the Governor was devoting a great deal of precious time to their rehabilitation. A man like Young would have had them tossed into the sea like unwanted munitions, and they were only beginning to appreciate this difference between Fed and Indy leadership.

The old man made it clear that he was no pacifist,

reminding them that Jose Martí Cross had gone down in a brief firefight like a mad dog, once Street's bogus customs men realized his imposture. The Indy rebels trod a narrow line, aggressors against specific property but killing only in defense.

Ethridge made no secret of his relief on hearing this last point. "So *if* we make the CenCom raid, and *if* I get bottled up, you won't object if I pop a cork to get out." He still had his chiller, and patted the armpit where it nestled.

"Whatever's necessary to defend your life," Street replied. "But if you go gunnin' for anybody, you make damn' sure I never hear about it. That goes for both of you. Hell, I believe in law and order!" He banged his fist on the chair arm and went on, growling it, "I've got no place for a plain bad-ass in my outfit, boys. But if Lufo Albeniz can keep his nose clean, so can you. Speaking of which, . . ."

The Governor trundled his chair up to the big carved Mexican desk and punched an intercom stud. "Kit, you know if Lufo's had his beauty sleep yet?"

The speaker replied in a slow masculine West Texas drawl. "He's been out on the porch for twenty minutes now, Gov. Must have an awful bad joke to tell you; he's sittin' there grinnin' and tremblin' like a dawg shittin' peach seeds."

"Trot him in, then." The old man leaned back in his balancing act. Somewhere in the long ranch house a voice called, a screen door skrinched and clacked.

A moment later, the door swung open to admit the rangy, slim-hipped latino. "Morning, jefe. Oh hello there, compadre," he murmured as if he had last seen Quantrill the day before.

"Lufo,—" Jim Street began.

"Lufo my ass," Quantrill blurted; "that's Rafael Sabado!" In three strides he reached the tall latino.

The Governor turned to Ethridge and grinned. "Always gives me the creeps to see grown men huggin'," he said. Albeniz/Sabado had pegged it right: Quantrill jumped like a rabbit to see the man who'd tagged him for Army Intelligence six years before, a man he'd supposed was long-dead in Wild Country.

CHAPTER 62

The President lay on his aircouch in a satin lounging robe, his chin resting on folded arms. Salter and Mills both sat on cushions so that their heads would not be elevated above his, and tried to ignore the lovely brunette who sat astride Blanton Young to administer his backrub. Before the arrival of Mills, the President had named three LDS Council members who were to be expended through 'natural causes' by the good offices of S & R rovers. Now, with Mills present, Young advanced his agenda to the media problem.

"I'm using all the leverage I have, Mr. President," Mills pleaded. "But the Israelis insist they can't help us knock out those media relays. Surely the Air Force has something that can intercept them."

"A massive search-and-destroy grid for a hundred million dollars, yes," Young snarled. "All to knock down a cheap, slow-flying gadget the Indys can replace the next day for ten thousand. Those broadcasts are hurting us, Mills!"

To divert the President's wrath, Mills said, "It

might be a lot quicker to send some rovers into Mexico to—"

"Be reasonable," Salter said in disgust. "A handful of rovers without air support in a foreign country? We've got a medium out of control, Mills! That's your department."

The President grunted something to the tall brunette: shifted so that her perspiration did not fall on his neck. Then, "Salter's right. And you're not handling your departments very well these days."

"There's one thing we might try," Mills hazarded. "You know we're using animated holo that can pass for the real thing. What if we claimed it's the *Indys* who are faking holocasts?"

"I'm listening," said Young.

Mills expanded on his ploy. That ghastly broadcast with the defector, Quantrill, for example: FBN had enough videotape to generate a sound-enhanced image of the turncoat that would have charisma— would pass for the real thing. Using the animation software stored in CenCom, FBN programmers could eletronically fake a holocast in which Ted Quantrill would swear on prime time that he'd been victimized somehow; was still a devoted member of the falsely-maligned S & R. Holo pundits could suggest that the Indy media were using imposters; no need to mention the possibility of electronic fakery. The overall effect might be to cast doubt on all mass media, but FBN could counter that trend if men of unblemished reputation were to vouch for the FBN lie.

"Even though you'd be faking their images too," Young nodded. "Might work. I can think of a few old codgers on the Council of Apostles who won't object," he added, with a meaningful glance at Salter. He mentioned three names, all of Apostles who would soon be unable to protest the use of their holo images.

Mills agreed to oversee the job. Without Eve Simpson, he would have to supervise the thing personally. It was taking much longer than he'd hoped to turn his vast personal holdings into cash—but where he was going, they dealt out immunities on a strictly-cash basis. In the meantime he had to step through his little minuets with Blanton Young as if he were not gathering himself for a leap into limbo. Better a temporary retirement than to be permanently retired by someone like Quantrill.

"There's one more thing," Young said. "I know you captains of industry have your little secrets, Mills, but you don't lie to the general. You led me to believe I could depend on some fuckin' sea-water process for strategic metals; and now I find the stuff was coming from smack in the middle of Zion."

Mills did not shift his gaze. He did not have to, to identify the carefully noncommittal expression on Salter's face. The sonofabitch! How much had he told? Salter was covering his ass, which meant the S & R chief no longer valued his alliance with IEE—or at least with Mills. "I—I deeply regret that, Mr. President."

Young bored in; Salter had told it all. "Not only did you fail to place a vital discovery under national security. You let that pig Eve Simpson lose a miniature version of it in Wild Country *disguised behind the Ember of Venus*, for the love of God! And co-opted S & R regulars in a God-damn' easter-egg hunt for it on a Texas ranch, without anything to show for it." The President heaved himself up, paying no heed to the brunette who fell to the floor in her scramble to move aside. Thundering his fury, Blanton Young raised his fists and shook

them overhead: "You played me for an ass, and
God is not mocked!"

"No, sir." Mills kept his head down in his best
display of contrition. Given the least chance, Young
was increasingly capable of indulging in violent
tantrums. He had seen the man rumble and groan
in his own personal earthquakes before, but until
now Mills hadn't found himself at the epicenter.
Face turned to heaven, bellowing of Gadianton
robbers and of terrible retribution, Young stumbled over the brunette and kicked out viciously.
She scurried out of the way, holding her ribs,
making no outcry. Presently his furies subsided
and Young stood over the other men in the stance
of one who has gained some gallant victory. He
waited until his breath had steadied.

"Boren Mills," said the President, "I'm told you
have a pair of Chink scientists left and a roomful
of pieces to put together. And you are going to see
that it all gets put together. Tomorrow morning,
you'll get a call from a fellow in Technology Assessment about a certain top secret project that you
will lead. Personally."

"Yes, Mr. President." Mills wondered if the crazy
bastard thought he could dragoon the head of IEE
into such a farce—then reflected that the President
of Streamlined America could do *exactly* that. He
could kick Mills's brains out right here in the executive apartment, and no one would ever find out.
On the morrow, one of the Twenty-First Century's
shrewdest organizers would be juggling a hopeless
synthesizer project and an animated holo scheme
that might just backfire on him, to satisfy the inspired hallucinations of a crackbrained dictator.
Mills could think of several absolute rulers before
Young who'd followed the same pattern, and three
of them had eventually turned on their best men.

Smug in his assurance that God would not let

him err, Blanton Young stared down at Mills. "Consider this a trial, Mills. There is only one indispensable man in Zion, and you are not that man. Now get out of my sight. I want to see that animated holo of yours in three days."

Mills knew better than to argue about deadlines. He was as powerless in Young's presence as that big brunette hotsy and he made his exit a quick one. At least he still had some freedom of movement, and a fraction of his once-stupendous fortune converted to gemstones. He would simply have to abandon the rest.

CHAPTER 63

Just as travelers in the old West moved from waterhole to waterhole, travel in Wild Country depended on precious liquids. If you were on a horse you still watched for windmills and learned which rivers were running: Rio Frio, Llano, Pecos. If you rode a fast hovercycle you needed diesel fuel, and rebel fuel dumps were hidden near places like Hondo, Del Rio, Alpine. With their pannier tanks, Lufo confided, they could make the round-trip from Jim Street's ranch to Rocksprings and back. Unless of course they got jumped by brush poppers, outlaws whose only allegiance was to booty—and in that case he and Quantrill were ordered to disengage. Translation: run like hell. Their mission had nothing to do with cleaning out the brush poppers; old Street needed that little

SinoInd nuke and he needed it yesterday. Did it really exist? Quien sabe?

The dust trails of the two 'cycles varied with their speed and the terrain, and Lufo knew the proper pace to minimize a dust signature. Long ago he had trained Quantrill in unarmed combat; now he was once again the instructor.

Skating along a dry creekbed, their passage might have been heard a few hundred meters distant and when they talked, it was with their scrambled short-range headsets. "So this ol' woman brought me to Odessa and seein' it was a head wound with a few birdshot, they X-rayed me and found my critic. By the time I woke up, I was a man without a name or a critic, and I liked it that way," Lufo said, explaining his defection from Army Intelligence. "Always felt bad about getting you in, compadre, because of that chingada critic."

"S'all right," Quantrill lied. "Hey: tripwire ahead!"

Lufo jerked his head around. "O-ho. Watch your right skyline and squeeze off at anything that moves," he said, splitting his own attention between the high ground to their left and the glistening wire ahead. "Now you'll see how the antenna works," he added, continuing at the same pace.

The 'antenna' formed a parabolic arch from the front end of the hovercycle, over the rider's head, to the sturdy pillion behind the jumpseat. Its spring aluminum alloy was triangular in cross-section with a stainless steel blade set into the top edge and Lufo's first warning to Quantrill had been to avoid grasping it. The damned thing would slice through a glove and the tendons beneath it—or sever a thin wire strung across its path.

Lufo gunned the engine to get additional lift as he neared the cable. His vehicle bobbed lower as it swept under the taut wire, polymer skirts scuffing the creekbed, and then Quantrill encountered the same effect. He saw the cable vibrating in Lufo's wake, felt a solid thump as his own 'cycle kissed the creekbed, and then he was past it, craning his neck to the right with his H & K out and ready.

Lufo laughed at Quantrill's cursing. "No sweat. Next time you'll know just when to gun the engine, and then you won't bounce your cojones off. It's a knack. Anyway, that was just an old sucker cable, nobody layin' for us, but if it's braided cable like that sometimes it won't break."

"Nice folks out here, Sab—ah, Lufo. How do they know when they've bagged somebody?"

Lufo pointed aloft. "Buzzards. One of these days, compadre, you'n me can take some time off, set some traps of our own out here for those ladrones."

"What'll the Governor say?"

"Shit, he don' know everything," Lufo scoffed. "You think your 'migo Ethridge won't go lookin' to settle old scores when he gets to Utah? Out here it's every man for himself. Until we get a few U. S. Marshals in Wild Country, it's vigilante time." He pronounced it TexMex fashion, *veeheelahntay*. Quantrill admired the wild free spirit of his friend, whom he still thought of as Sabado; but a Sabado by any other name was still basically a vigilante, a man who'd sooner dispense justice of his own than leave it to a Marshal or a jury. When the Marshals came to Wild Country they might find Lufo Albeniz more trouble than help. And with that thought came another which Quantrill filed away . . .

Presently Lufo led the way into higher country damp with recent rain and thick with brush, where a man on a quarterhorse might have met their pace for a short distance. The tall latino was singing of his dark-haired corazón when Quantrill interrupted, "I thought this one was a blonde."

Laughing: "As you'll see in a couple of hours. I

HOVERCYCLE
SUMMARY SHEETS

SUMMARY DATA

DESIGNATION: HOVERCYCLE   **CENCOM REVISION:** 17 Jun 2001

DEPLOYMENT: Various military/private

SPECIFICATIONS:

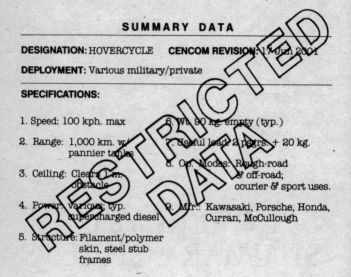

1. Speed: 100 kph. max

2. Range: 1,000 km. w/ pannier tanks

3. Ceiling: Clears 1 m. obstacle

4. Power: various; typ. supercharged diesel

5. Structure: Filament/polymer skin, steel stub frames

6. Wt: 90 kg. empty (typ.)

7. Useful load: 2 psgrs. + 20 kg.

8. Op. Modes: Rough-road & off-road; courier & sport uses.

9. Mfr.: Kawasaki, Porsche, Honda, Curran, McCullough

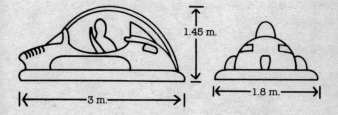

1.45 m.

|← — 3 m. — →|

|← 1.8 m. →|

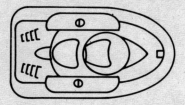

was thinking of the one in Laredo—or is it the one in Corpus?" He yelped in sheer high spirits; sang the refrain from a current western tune: 'Like a Mormon fundamentalist I'm a much-married man."

It was no trick to get Lufo talking about that. Lufo's was the classic form of machismo: potentially every woman was his, and only his. The only time you knew you were a man was when you were atop a woman; not beside, or below. Atop. You liked frequent assurances of manhood and if you had to marry her—well, you married her. Of course any woman who dallied with any other man while married to Lufo would do it at risk of her life, and of the other man's life. It was not a joking matter to Lufo; he might have a dozen women, but they must have no other man.

Lufo explained his one self-imposed restriction: "Plain loco to have two wives near enough that they might learn about each other. That's for men who keep house; have kids. Me, I've had my tubes tied but none of my women know that. They all think a niño would get me to settle down—so they try to get one from me. Ay, it's a good life, compadre!"

Quantrill voiced an agreement he could not feel; told himself that boys would be boys: thanked God he knew no women who might fall under Lufo's spell. Three hours later, after topping off their tanks near Barksdale, they whrummed into view of the soddy.

CHAPTER 64

Quantrill imitated Lufo and shut off his engine in a clearing beyond the ramshackle rows of corn stubble. Lufo's horn was a silly bleat, a long and two shorts. "You won't believe what I think this is all about," Lufo said, turning to his companion, "but she always comes out and—listen."

Quantrill saw a blonde figure skip out of the soddy, admired the strong legs and full figure of the young woman in the short dress. She put fingers to her mouth. A series of piercing blasts floated out across the oak and cedar scrub.

As she turned in another direction to repeat her whistled signal, Lufo said, "She always does this. It's not another man, but she's got someone out there that she won't tell me about—someone her little sister plays with." At this point he stood on his seat and waved until the woman saw him. She waved them in. Settling to the controls Lufo added, "But if you had a hotsy that lived out here alone with boar tracks the size of my hand all around, and she never wore a sidearm and never worried who came to her door, and made you swear you'd never shoot at any pig within an hour of here, —what would you think?" He shook his head, restarted, drove up in the shadow of a tarp-covered woodpile without waiting for an answer.

Quantrill replied through his headset: "I'd think about what happened to Eve Simpson, and I'd think you're fucking loco to think what you're thinking," as he followed Lufo.

With their 'cycles hidden under the plastic tarp, they hefted their traveling gear: mummybag with spare clothing, food, and survival articles packed into the folds. It was then that the warm-eyed blonde ran to meet Lufo. Her arms were already around his neck when she glanced at her second guest. She registered shock, then something like anger, pulling back from Lufo who grinned at the way she stared.

"This is Ted Quantrill, Sandy," said her lover with pride. "He finally made it out this way."

Quantrill intended to extend a hand but saw her hands gripping each other at her breast, her mouth open in a new astonishment. Instead he nodded and smiled, trying to ignore a display he did not yet understand. Even with her jaw down, she was a hell of a looker—and not a woman yet, in years. It was his turn to gape as Lufo continued. "Ted, this is my woman, Sandy Grange."

Quantrill could only repeat her name. She gave him a quick nod, and feeling like an idiot he said it still again. A scab-kneed kid of eleven back in '96 before he joined the Army; yes, if caterpillars became Monarch butterflies, then his gamine girlchild friend Sandy could become this lush creature six years later. He had lost her trace in Sutton County, assumed she'd been devoured—*by the great boar, Ba'al*! He'd even seen their tracks together; had drawn the obvious conclusion. Well, the obvious wasn't always true. Ted Quantrill did not know that he was bubbling with silent laughter; knew only that Lufo was right. It could be a great life.

Sandy glanced quickly at Lufo, whose keen gaze was asking 'what the hell ails this pair,' and then she held out her hand. It was already shaking.

"I'm—glad to meet you, Mr. Quantrill." She was all but weeping.

Instead Quantrill burst out laughing, caught her to him, hugged her and whirled her around. "It wouldn't work, Sandy," he said, still laughing as he released her with a gesture at Lufo. "Not for ten seconds! He's not blind and he's not stupid and hell, he isn't even Lufo Albeniz. But whatever he is, he wasn't your playmate back at Sonora—and I was!"

Lufo's swarthy color hid most of his blush, but he quickly moved from anger to suspicion of some vast joke. "Playmate? You two know each other?" It just missed being an accusation.

Breathless from Quantrill's whirl, spots of color reddening her cheeks, Sandy hugged Lufo's sleeve in mock severity. "Now don't be like that, Lufo. If you weren't such a secretive bozo, and a creative speller too, you'd have told me your old friend was Ted—and I wouldn't be gawking at him like this." She linked an arm through Quantrill's, glanced at him again with a 'well-I-never' headshake; urged both men toward the soddy and walked between them.

While Sandy brewed herb tea, she and Quantrill explained their Sonora connection to the disgruntled Lufo. In the process Quantrill realized that the ribbon-chuted canister she'd salvaged from scattered aircraft debris lay hidden in the same cavern where he had once met her dying father.

"I don't think I could find the place without you," Quantrill admitted. "I was only fifteen years old then."

"Wouldn't matter if you did," Sandy murmured, pouring tea. "I stored all my treasures in another entrance—but I can find it. I'm not truly certain that thing is a bomb, you know. The war was over before I saw a holo program showing enemy munitions—but I swear one of their small air-dropped nukes was identical to the thing I dragged into my cavern."

Lufo welcomed the chance to focus on the present. He could do nothing about alliances his woman had known in childhood. He asked if Sandy had ever spoken of her salvage item to anyone else. No, she said, not even to Childe; it was something she did not like to think about.

Quantrill recalled Lufo's mention of a little sister. Adopted? Again she demurred; Childe had been born two months before Sandy escaped with her from Wild Country outlaws.

Quantrill: "You wore sandals the day you escaped toting a two-month-old sister." Not a question, but a statement of facts.

Sandy: "Why,—how did you know about the sandals?"

"Tracked you after a team of us ran those outlaws down. I was too late to help your mom. Saw some other prints with yours at a waterhole, and figured you'd made a meal for the biggest predator that ever roamed this country."

Sandy tried to change the subject. Lufo was having none of that. Until now he'd held some hope that her tantalizing hints of a protector in the brush was only a fanciful tissue. Yet Quantrill added earlier, if circumstantial, evidence. Lufo, almost sadly: "Ted, you're talkin' about a big boar hog."

Sandy said nothing, but stared daggers at her lover.

Quantrill, nodding, with a half-smile toward Sandy: "I'm talking about Ba'al. Or maybe there's more than one. Sandy?"

She searched her teacup for a reply, evidently without success. "I don't want to talk about it. I have enough trouble keeping my—human friends from each other's throats."

"That brute is a killer," Quantrill said without rancor.

"And you?" This from Sandy with much rancor. "From the little Lufo said about you, I didn't recognize the gentle boy I used to know. I expected someone like the picture of Dorian Gray! You've probably shed more blood than Ba'al, and for worse reasons—both of you! That *brute* adopted me and Childe. If you were hungry and hunted, would you adopt a piglet?"

"I wouldn' make it part of my family," Lufo said levelly.

"Many's the night I've stayed awake wondering, if I ever had to choose between the *brute* that looks after us and a human who looks in on us now and then, how I would choose. Well, now I can sleep!" The nubile breasts rose and fell rapidly as Sandy's temper flared.

The two men shared guilty knowledge that with only a casual application of heat they had brought a long-simmering problem to a rolling boil. Sandy burst out: "I'll show you two what you came here for, and you can take it and, and, and go to hell with it and remember me as the piglady for all I—Lufo Albeniz, do you want Mayberry tea down your collar?"

Lufo had moved near her; had made what he imagined was a conciliating gesture. Blinking: "Hadn't planned on it, chica."

"Then take your hand off my butt! Lordy, but you big strong men are sure of yourselves," she snorted, as Lufo jerked the offending hand away.

Lufo's choice would have been clear to any old-fashioned macho. He could either beat the squishy *mierda* out of his woman, or he could retreat with the lighthearted patience of a big dog attacked by a very small dog. Any other solution—apology, or any explanation that smacked of apology—would be unthinkable in the presence of another man, especially Quantrill. Because Lufo was survival-oriented, he let himself be swayed by several facts.

If he struck her, he might have to fight Quantrill too. And Ted Quantrill was the only unarmed combat student he'd ever seen whose psychomotor responses defied belief.

If his little gringa became angry enough, she might just whistle up a half-tone cyclone of tusk and gristle that could come through a wall and survive a lot of small-caliber hits while scattering a man around a little.

Lufo needed time to think. Sandy Grange didn't fit any simple pattern, and her old friednship with Quantrill muddied the problem further. He examined these facts in the space of a second or two, unleashed a dazzling smile, made a mocking bow as he backed away. "I was clumsy with desire, chica. I'll set up my bedroll at the woodpile as penance while the light is still good." He paused at the door, traveling gear under his arm. There was a faint air of command in his, "Coming, compadre?"

"In a minute." Quantrill waited for the door to swing shut; considered several questions. Instead, he said, "I tried every way I knew to find you, Sandy. If that—that boar succeeded where I failed, I'm in his debt. I know for certain he's taken out some enemies of mine so," he sighed and slapped his thigh with rueful good humor, "—I guess I have to count him as a friend." He put down his cup, grasped his traveling gear. "You have to admit this is a little hard for me to take in, all at once. But I thought I'd forgotten how to laugh until I recognized you. Now I'd better go."

He was in the doorway when she said, very softly,

"I don't want you to go, but yes, you'd better. Tell Lufo I'll send Childe out with bowls of menudo when she gets home. Wouldn't want him to think I maltreat my guests." But her smile was the real apology.

CHAPTER 65

Neither of the men found the right words before dinner. They spent the time with a deck of Lufo's cards and reminiscences. At last the shadow-quiet Childe faced them, offered steaming bowls of savory tripe soup and, after studying Quantrill for long minutes, ghosted away again. With the sun down and the breeze up, they were soon lying on their backs in mummybags.

Lufo lit a cheroot. After a few puffs he offered it to Quantrill. "Some things a man *can* share, compadre," he said.

Quantrill, who disliked cigars, accepted this one for its symbolic value. Handing it back, exhaling luxuriously, he asked, "You two married?"

"No. Now don' interrupt; I have some things to say but they won' be the right ones if you push me. Okay?"

"Right."

Long silence before, "I talk too much. But I only exaggerate a little. I have three wives; since I already tol' you about that, I may as well keep on. I don' know what you two had going when she was a kid, maybe nothing, but I know how she looked when she saw you today. I know that look." Chuckling gruffly: "It was a jump-on-your-bones look, compadre. Maybe that's layin' it on some, but take it from me, she mus' have missed you a lot once, and she didn' forget you."

Long ago, Quantrill had noted the heightened sibilant TexMex speech accents in his friend at times when he was not posturing. He recognized them now as Lufo went on: "In la raza there is a code. I'm glad it isn' your code because it gives you two places to stand in this matter, but only one way to move. You could act as a brother or as the one with the horns, the cuckold. Either way you'd have some bad business with me for trifling with Sandy. Because either way, you have a prior claim. I donno, maybe it *is* your code. Is it?"

"I don't know. Not the way you put it, but I won't see her victimized. If she knows all about you and likes it that way, it isn't up to me to make trouble."

"She doesn' know what you know—and I'd jus' as soon she didn'. What my code says is, the nex' move is yours. If you don' go for my hide then I can either keep on seein' Sandy, or I can admit you have first claim and shy off. But it's your move."

Quantrill puzzled over that for awhile. Eventually he said, "An old guy named Brubaker told me everybody's got an ethic whether he knows it or not. An ethic, a code,—whatever. Yours says I'd have to act as an injured party, but mine says no; it's none of my affair if she isn't hurt. And I go by my ethic, not yours. If you go on with her like this, not telling her your ways, sooner or later she *will* get hurt. And then you and I will have what you call bad business. If you really care about her, seems to me you have a choice, and I won't try to make it for you."

"I can read an anglo's moves, compadre, but not his mind. What choice?"

"Tell her about your wives or shy off. Any other way, you'd be treating her like someone without rights."

A chuckle: "The rights of a woman? Yours is a troublesome code, compadre."

From Quantrill, a sigh: "Don't I know it."

"At leas' it gives me room to live with mine. Whatthefuck is that word? Ay, compassion. I am a compassionate man. I don' want Sandy hurt, and telling her would hurt her. I already have enough women. If I let this one go she might hurt for awhile, but I think it would be a pleasant hurt and she would recover. Unless somebody else tol' her."

"Aw, shit, why do you beat around the bush?"

"Rafael Sabado from Houston did not beg favors, and Lufo Albeniz of Wild Country does not beg favors."

"No, by God you sure don't," Quantrill grumped. "Now I know why you guys never overpopulated Texas; you kill so many of each other off! Anyway—no, I won't tell her if I don't have to. As you say, telling her would hurt her. I guess. Christ, how would I know? I haven't seen her since she was a scrubby little kid! For all I know she might be happy to squirm around in your bed with all your other women watching!"

"Hey," Lufo broke in, harsh and bellicose, "you don' talk that way about my woman!"

Quantrill's reply was a guffaw. After a moment the big latino joined in, peals of laughter resounding inside the tarp as their tensions drained away.

Sandy's journal, 2 Oct. '02

AAARrrgh! MEN! The laughing embrace of Ted Quantrill (!!) should have made this a day to remember, yet ten minutes later I was denouncing him and Lufo. It cannot be pleasant to be compared unfavor-

ably with swine. Still, I spoke the truth. Or did I? I have only Lufo's word for Ted's reputation.

& what of my reputation? What must they think & say of me? I hear them now, hooting & hoorawing out there, I hope the woodpile falls on them both!

Ted has changed, of course. The scars, the broken nose, the sparse hair behind one ear similar to Lufo's. Some dreadful initiation rite, perhaps. But his laughing mouth & those malachite eyes are the ones I knew, however briefly, however long ago . . .

I remember seeing him making love with that woman on the ground, the day he says they searched for me. Some search! & why do I feel anger at that? He gave me only kindness & owes me nothing.

Imagine! The mere appearance of my first love-object, & I am babbling about him to Lufo's exclusion. I must not forget that men, especially men like Lufo, can be violent children. Shall I be mated to a violent child? Dear God, are they all alike?

Tomorrow we ride near Sonora in search of more destruction. Childe will be off riding with him. *Must remind her to keep an eye on the place. Wish I had never told Lufo of that frightful device in my cave. It makes me resent the cleverness of the human race. Were it not for gadgetry, Lufo would not be gallivanting all over hell & Wild Country. (Nor would I have a holo or aspirin or a water pump!) Perhaps by making us more independent, gadgets help us alienate ourselves.*

Sorry, journal, I feel doggerel coming on. Well then:

THERE IS NO GOD OF MACHINES

This demon of persistence,
Man's technik, which berates us—
It lends us bare subsistence
While it separates us!

I would make war to exorcise
This fiend, technology
If in the ashes I could rise
And cleave to only thee.

Now then O cunning poet: who the hell is 'thee'? I doubt that I shall know before I'm an old crone of thirty.

Holo promises good weather. Must remember buckskins & parfleche of jerky , just in case. Dread this trip. MEN! AAARrrgh!

CHAPTER 66

They encountered the broad shallow arroyo of Devil's River Canyon late in the morning of the next day, Sandy's outflung arm lancing past Lufo's shoulder as she recognized a rock outcrop. They passed old tire tracks in hardened mud, now crumbling with recent fall rains, and the scant shrubs were green with that memory.

Sandy, lithe in tight buckskins, was first to approach the rockfall that sealed her father's tomb. "Mom carved this," she murmured, stroking the weathered wooden cross with the legend,

Wayland F. Grange 1955-1996

Quantrill remembered the man whose choice had been to let radiation sickness complete its ravages in the small cavern, attended by his daughter and his pregnant wife. Quantrill swept off his Aussie hat and knelt silently at Sandy's left, while Lufo knelt at her right.

Finally, "Thank you," said Sandy, and trudged away from the fallen entrance. She could not at first locate the second entrance. Lufo found it by stumbling at its lip, a sinister trapezoidal hole in brittle spongy limestone, masked by agarita shrubs that grew at the entrance in perfect camouflage.

Lufo had never taken S & R courses, and proposed to go below with only his flashlamp. Quantrill's training made him cautious. "Whoa, compadre; let's get the rope and harnesses. And you might describe the layout again," he added to Sandy.

While they brought equipment from the 'cycles, she told them of the sloping shaft, the first 'room' with its jumble of fallen stalactites, the passage leading downward, the huge sand-floored room with its mighty treetrunk stalagmites.

"Is it still a live hole?" Quantrill asked. "I mean, does water still drop from the stalactites?"

She supposed it did. Six, or six hundred years were finger-snaps of time in a cavern. "Below the big room—I called it the church—is a pool with a slight current. You can wade in it to the next room. That's where I stored my things."

"Okay. If the cave's still alive, there's less worry about dislodging dried-out formations. Buckle this harness on and let Lufo be your rear guard. I'll take point position," he said, using a jargon Lufo would appreciate.

Their flashlamps revealed signs of animal burrows near the surface. Twenty meters inside the first shaft they encountered a room gleaming with damp pillars and fingerlets of limestone. Fallen stalactites, some as thick as a man's arm, lay among the upthrusting pillars.Quantrill anchored one end of his rope to a stone stump and paid the stuff out as he continued at Sandy's direction. No point in dwelling on the fact that they could be walking over a thin crust with a long fall beneath, but he kept well in the lead.

A bend downward to their right, then a chute flanked by solid pillars like monoliths poured from wax. By now they had passed the realm of natural light and their flashbeams showed no dust in the air. Quantrill climbed down far enough to see a phalanx of gypsum sheets, petrified draperies sparkling in the beams of light, before he heard chittering peeps nearby. Sandy was five meters behind, sliding her harness friction link along the rope. Very softly he said, "What kind of bats are down here?"

"I never tried to catch one," she replied. "There weren't many except at dusk. They came out in clouds then."

"Well, there's bagsful of 'em now," he said, and played his flashbeam toward a dome that arched away past intervening pillars. The dome seemed to ripple, but his mind refused to accept the carpet of fur that covered its surface. The powerful flashbeam swept across the black carpet, a surface that moved and flickered and then, the faint chittering silenced by the disturbing light, began to denude the dome.

A half-acre of bats left their perches on the dome and fled up the chute down which the interlopers climbed.

"Lights out. Don't move," Quantrill hissed. A second later they squatted immobile in total blackness as countless bats hurtled past them in a whisper that became a fluttering roar. Sandy uttered one tiny bleat of fear as the sound of their passage grew, yet not once did they feel a single impact. Instead they detected hundreds of feathery touches, hardly more than breaths, against hair, arms, shoulders. The experience, Quantrill thought, was exactly like squatting in a dry waterfall, a spattering fluid cascade of sound without the moisture. The tiny mammals had to be echolocating adroitly to avoid striking them, their squeaks no longer audible to the humans.

For several minutes the waterfall of leathery wingbeats roared around them; then it began to subside. Finally Quantrill risked the flashlamp again, directed downward now, and saw ghostly flickers wheeling in the room below, some whispering past them. "Proceeding," he said quietly, and began the descent anew.

The mottled gypsum surfaces were wet but not slick, hand- and footholds frequent. He saw scars in the scaly gyp, probably made by eleven-year-old Sandy who had braved this ten-meter descent with only a chemlamp. He marveled that she could have navigated this grotto lugging anything heavier than a handkerchief. He saw a featureless floor sloping away, gingerly stepped onto damp sand, realized that water had smoothed away Sandy's footprints.

The others followed quickly, their echoes sharing the void with hollow plops of water in some nearby pool. Quantrill, recalling a spelunker's lecture; "Could be pockets of quicksand. Water level can rise after a long hard rain." Occasional vagrant sweeps of flashbeams revealed that the dome was within five meters of the outside world, to judge from black roots that clung to the dome in espalier fashion as though fearing to extend down into the cavern. Quantrill couldn't blame them.

Sandy released her safety line, hurrying past an elbow made by translucent crystalline carbonates, her flashlamp forcing ghostly glows through them. "My corridor was over—oh Lordy," she said as the men reached her. Her lamp beam penetrated the two-meter depth of water to reveal a smoothly worn channel, the water wondrously clear except for tiny eddies at its banks. Distorted by refraction, the mouth of Sandy's corridor glowed faintly—half a meter below the surface.

They searched long and fruitlessly for some alternative passage, one too high or too subtle for a little girl with a chemlamp. They found two crevices, neither large enough for a human body, and returned at last to the slow-moving water that issued from Sandy's submerged corridor. In a week, Quantrill guessed, the water level might dwindle. Or with October rains it might rise further.

Finally he pursued a line of questioning he would have preferred to ignore. How long was the passage? Perhaps fifteen meters. Did it slope up? Down? No, almost level. It seemed likely, he said, that rising water had forced the bats up from their usual haunts in lower unexplored reaches of the cavern. Was the roof of her treasure room higher than the present water level? Yes, much higher, with ancient water-swept benches like church pews and strange formations like coral or petrified roots that protruded from the upper walls. Sandy could not remember how high she had placed her few treasures. By now they might have been swept away, lodged somewhere downstream, perhaps at the bottom of some drowned abyss. Quantrill persisted: still there was no reason why a strong swimmer couldn't work upcurrent to emerge in her grotto?

No, said Sandy, "If he were one part fish and nine parts crazy. Neither of you fits that description, I hope."

"I don' swim that good, compadre. Maybe we can come back with scuba gear, otra vez."

Quantrill thought of the delays, the risks, and

then of Sanger. "The hell with another time. The water's not too cold, and I'm fresh." He began to strip, establishing a rope-tug code as he reconnected his harness, preparing his body for the trial with long draughts of air, easing himself through fine sand and refusing to shiver as he tested the current. It was stronger than he'd thought.

Sandy watched his preparations in silence. Her first impulse was to invent some barrier, a white lie to turn Quantrill aside from this imponderable risk. But he claimed to be a good swimmer—and as he stood in abbreviated shorts adjusting his harness to tow the safety line, she felt a swelling surge of confidence. Beside the tall, slim-hipped, slender-legged Lufo, Ted Quantrill seemed small. But the muscles of his legs and back were distinct bundles of cable flowing beneath the skin. His arms and shoulders possessed the terrible whipcord beauty of a light heavyweight boxer in peak condition. For such a physical specimen, she thought, the drowned tunnel might just be navigable.

As Quantrill clamped the flashlamp handle in his teeth, he heard Sandy's, "Enjoy your tea-party, Ted." He nodded without understanding, inhaled again, kicked away toward the hole.

For the first five meters it seemed a cinch, though his elbows scraped painfully against the narrow sides of the tunnel. He hugged the bottom, peering ahead and upward to study the undulating roof in hopes that Sandy had exaggerated the distance.

If anything, she had underestimated. He felt tension on his harness and a flash of anger at Lufo for paying out the line too slowly; rolled slightly, banged his head; nearly lost the flashlamp. Then he was kicking hard again, using his hands for purchase where he could, telling himself he had plenty of time.

After a half-minute struggling against the current he saw a transverse rim of rock ahead with a milky reflective gleam beyond, pulled himself past it, realized he was in a deep pool, so deep that it was for all practical purposes bottomless. But the tunnel roof arched up here, and he saw surface eddies above him, and he rolled onto his side, feeling for the roof. There was none. He forced himself to rise carefully; saw in the sweep of the lamp that he was now in another room; fought the current as he grappled for handholds. In another few seconds he sat on a cold bench of stone, pulling in more line as Lufo paid it out, moving his head to play the flashlamp around.

He hauled in the line quickly, jerked twice, felt two jerks in answer; jerked twice again. Faintly, as though from a great distance, he heard a male shout and a lighter female rejoinder. There was an air passage somewhere, he thought—but a labyrinthine one. No sense in his shouting back—certainly not when it might bring a mountain down on his head.

Quantrill anchored his line around the bole of a stone pillar and made a careful assessment with his lamp, pinned between worry and awe; worry that Sandy's treasures could never be found, awe at the ineffable beauty around him.

Across the pool, a great cream-white formation emulated a pipe organ rising from liquid blackness. Nearer stood a pinkish gleaming array of translucent stalactites hanging from lips of gypsum in imitation of gigantic Spanish combs. And nearer still, above benchlike tiers smoothed by many floods, an incredible forest of coral-like helictites glowed in flesh tones, thrusting out in all directions in evident unconcern for gravity.

Then, somehow most bizarre of all: a stippled mound like a formation of gleaming orange snow with a child's plastic tea set nestled among its undulations. Quantrill laughed aloud, remembering that he had swapped a lapel dosimeter for those toys in Sonora; remembering also Sandy's ecstasy as she'd pressed them to her breast, six years before. Now he understood her remark about a tea party.

He found a moldy paper tablet and pencils of the old type, a curling polaroid—of himself in profile, for God's sake, aged fifteen!—and then, near a hollow filled with small-caliber ammunition, a finless canister the diameter of a cantaloupe. His heart leaped in recognition; Sandy had correctly identified it.

His footing was treacherous, the little nuke rust-stained; and he could not unsnap the small ribbon chute. A frayed cable-end trailed a meter long from an electrical pop-disconnect, and Quantrill wondered if there could possibly be any live power cells inside. Would it be damaged by brief immersion in water? He would have to chance it.

He pulled on the polymer line near the pool's surface, felt it taut, made three quick tugs, heard another shout. Now Lufo knew their goal was very near.

Quantrill folded the nylon ribbon chute into a bundle, thrust it within his body harness, cradled the heavy canister in his arms as he lowered himself into the water and took deep breaths to suffuse his tissues with oxygen. With the current and the heavy canister he would not need to attach his safety line, or so he imagined; and so he made his catastrophic error. He sank down to the lip of stone, saw the drowned tunnel in the light of the flashlamp, and started back. Headfirst.

Without encumbrances he would have had both hands free, might have slowed his progress, might have noticed the stone nubs like stubby fingers that his free harness ring engaged when he rolled sideways halfway down the tunnel. The ring was at his left side but in twisting to free himself he only managed to wrench his harness so that he could not reach the ring. The current was cold, cold, and too swift, and in his struggles he felt the ribbon chute slipping from his harness.

He fought, then. And lost the flashlamp, watched it laze away from him tumbling, flooding his world with hard light and bitter cold black as he clapsed twenty kilos of nuclear weapon to him against the pitiless pull of the current on the now-billowing ribbon chute.

He did not panic, not yet, not when he knew there was a hope that whatever held him might give, or that he might be able to unsnap the harness. But he could not do it while hugging that canister, no matter how incalculable its importance. When he tried to draw his knees up to capture and hold the canister so that he might free his hands, he underestimated the pull of the current. And then the canister slithered away, perhaps to be seen by the others or perhaps not, and now Quantrill was tearing away his fingernails as he fought to find harness disconnects; then to rip away the harness webbing; and when both failed, finally to find purchase for his feet so that he might somehow burst the bonds that held him. The last thing he knew was after he tried to breathe, after his disastrous coughing spasm, after his efforts to clamp his hands over his mouth and nose. That last thing was a paradoxical sense of tingling warmth, and of lassitude.

CHAPTER 67

Lufo knew, the instant he saw the swirling beacon of light come sliding from the tunnel, that Quantrill was in trouble. But Lufo was no aquatic mammal, and watched the flashlamp's progress on the clear bottom of the watercourse until it fell from their sight behind a stone undercrop downstream.

There was no need to say anything to Sandy who keened with worry, playing her own lamp upstream as she braced herself knee-deep in water. "It's the parachute," she squealed then, spying the ribbon pattern that nearly filled the channel, rotating slowly underwater as it approached. "Lufo, here he comes!"

Lufo splashed into the shallow verge of the pool, cursed as his lunge fell short, then grasped a nylon strip and scrambled to safety. Sandy held her lamp beam on the suspension lines, saw the canister slide into view; knew a hideous glacial paralysis when Ted Quantrill did not come with it.

Lufo hauled the chute out and pulled on the lines, hand over hand, until he saw the canister slide out of the water. He could not believe that their luck had held so long; that everything Sandy claimed was true. And then he remembered that their luck was not *all* holding.

"Lufo, oh Lufo, he's not signaling and he's not coming and *oh, God, Lufo*," she screamed. The echo ululated down pitch-black corridors and set

Lufo's teeth on edge. Bubbles frothed at the tunnel's exit. Quantrill's breath.

Lufo did not commit his insanity until he saw that Sandy was preparing to dive. Then he flung her back, took a deep breath, grasped the anchored safety line and dropped feet-first into the water without his lamp, fully clothed, the hand-line his only guide.

He found that his best pace was face-up, hauling himself blindly hand-over-hand in terrifying blackness along the ceiling of the drowned tunnel, groping ahead to be sure he did not knock his brains out against a protrusion. He could swear he had traversed half a hundred meters when his flailing boot kicked something fleshy, and then both questing feet told him of an inert human body just behind and below him, and for a fraction of a second after releasing that handline he felt stark terror. Lufo did not swim.

Quantrill hung limp in his harness, and by the time Lufo found the pinioned harness ring he was nearing panic himself and knew that Quantrill had drowned.

But his gringa, Sandy,—really never his but wait!, perhaps his after all now,—would never leave until they recovered the body. Lufo at last found the harness latches, stripped the inert form from the webbing in brute frenzy, then felt himself rolling backward in the current with Quantrill's body and found that he did, indeed know how to swim as the light of Sandy's lamp grew stronger.

He burst to the surface gasping, eyes wide; felt Quantrill brush his thigh, reached a hand back and caught one ankle. A moment later Sandy and Lufo pulled Ted Qauntrill's blood-streaked body from the water. As she grasped Quantrill under the arms to pull him further away, Lufo could only sit and gasp, "Sorry—he was—hung up. Too late."

But Sandy worked furiously over the body. "Two or three minutes aren't that long," she said, and hauled Quantrill's legs up a gypsum slope, rolling him onto his back. "Come help," she cried in frustration.

Together they placed Quantrill's body so that Sandy could press on his ribcage while Lufo held his head to one side. They could hear a muffled liquid slosh as Sandy applied sudden pressure, and then, so startling Lufo that he almost released Quantrill's head, an abrupt flow of water, at least half a liter of it, from the open mouth. But he was not breathing.

Sandy continued to force the ribcage bellows. Perhaps another cupful of water trickled out. "Now you," she panted, and gestured for Lufo to take her place.

Lufo's ministrations brought forth another trickle. Then, pulling Quantrill's chin forward, pinching his nostrils shut, Sandy Grange placed her mouth over his for the first time.

No response. She made Lufo stop, took another breath, force-exhaled again into Quantrill's throat. This time she heard a plopping burble, let more water trickle from the throat, exhaled again into his mouth. Finally she felt the stilled lungs inflate; let him exhale, force-fed him again. And again, and again. She could hear Lufo repeating the only prayer he remembered: Hail, Mary.

Presently the body coughed, gasped, coughed again, and Sandy fed life to her first love for another two minutes before she was sure his breathing was steady and strong. Then she wept.

Ten minutes later, Ted Quantrill lay wrapped in his dry clothes, shaking, while Sandy rubbed him down with her jacket. He was alert enough to refuse Lufo's offer of a fireman's carry. "I guess this is what mild shock is like," he said through chattering teeth.

Sandy wiped her nose and cheeks, sat back on her haunches in the reflection of fantastic shapes of amber and pink. "You'll be warmer if you can get your clothes on," she said, her tears of relief ebbing.

He managed, with help. But it was another hour before he regained enough strength to climb up from a cavern that an eleven-year-old girl had navigated, once upon a time.

CHAPTER 68

By microwave scrambler, Lufo contacted the Indy base with news of their success while Sandy robbed his 'cycle's first-aid kit to cover the various rents in Quantrill's hide. The afternoon sun was bright, the breeze soft, yet Quantrill shivered and grunted as Sandy's deft fingertips applied synthoderm and butterfly closures.

Lufo soon found himself patched directly to el jefe, old Jim Street. His companions listened shamelessly to his end of the conversation. At one point Lufo turned to Quantrill. "Think you can handle your 'cycle as far as the soddy today?"

Quantrill moved his arms and legs, judged the stiffness and the pain; made a face as eloquent as any sigh of resignation.

"I tol' you he's a tough little hombre, jefe. We'll

be there in three hours. Uh—can the chopper take us and both 'cycles?" Pause. "Well, I wouldn' worry about it. I can stay overnight and bring it—". Longer pause. Then with some reluctance: "Oh, I guess he could but I don' see why." After a moment he glanced at Quantrill, laughed, nodded. "You could always tie him up, jefe. And you might have to." Perhaps a minute of silence before, "Bueno, see you tonight then." Lufo flicked toggles and removed his headset.

Talking through mouthfuls of sandwich and jerky, Lufo passed his orders on. The Governor's tech crew were antsy to get their hands on the little nuke; several timetables depended on how soon they could inspect and, if necessary, repair it. A late-model surveillance chopper, one of the few stealth craft in Indy hands, would rendezvous at Sandy's place to pick up the canister, Lufo, and one hovercycle.

Quantrill ate slowly and little, heeding the queasiness in his belly. "So who gets tied up?"

"Ah. Nobody does. You go to Schreiner Ranch tomorrow and tell the safari manager who you are. He's one of us. Seems that a lot of Feds have been searching the area for a necklace that woman lost somewhere. Don' ask me why, but el jefe got word that the Lion of Zion will do almost anything to get his hands on it. And if it's numero uno to him, we'd like to get it first."

Sandy stopped chewing as she heard the word 'necklace', but kept her thoughts to herself.

Quantrill winced as he moved his arm. "I hope they don't want me ready for a firefight with Feds. I'm sore as a boil."

"No, compadre, jus' try and find that necklace. Between you and me, it's partly to keep you from underfoot while the penetration raid gets set. El jefe thinks you'd pester them silly tryin' to go along. And Lufo Albeniz thinks so, too," he added chuckling.

Soon they were retracing their path to Sandy's place, no real path at all but a series of landmarks. Quantrill carried their nuclear cargo, staying so far behind his companions that he sometimes lost sight of them, but always in microwave contact. They made the trip without incident and sooner than they had expected, yet a fast chopper was already parked near the soddy, a stub-winged, guppy-bellied insect with rotors idling. Both pilot and gunner cradled assault rifles, and Lufo waved his scruffy hat when he saw that the gunner was an old friend.

Quantrill helped load Lufo's 'cycle into the cargo bay, then jestingly thrust fingers into his ears as Lufo took the precious canister from his 'cycle pannier compartment. Lufo saw that his friend Espinel was far from amused; exchanged rapid TexMex banter with him; strapped the canister between inflated pallets in the chopper. Then Lufo spoke with the pilot and trotted back to his companions.

He said to Sandy, "Looks like I may not be out here again for a long time, chica. Maybe not ever." His big hands on her shoulders, the hint of a wry smile hanging like a cigarette at one corner of his mouth, he searched her face. Now, as he continued, his voice was deeply resonant. "But a man must do his duty."

She laid her hands on his forearms and stared quizzically at him, subtle shadings of emotion changing her face. "Lufo? Are you trying—" and then a sorrowful, "This is goodbye then?"

A manly frown, a nod. "It is not my wish. But I leave on a long mission tomorrow. Someday I may see you again, mi corazón." He hugged her to him; said gruffly to Quantrill, "You take care of her, compadre."

He ignored Quantrill's muttered, "Jee-zus, *Christ*."

Sandy pulled his head down to her with both hands in his straight black hair, kissed him soundly, then buried her face in her hands. "Go on, Lufo, before I beg to go with you."

The big latino draped an arm over Quantrill's shoulder, urged him to walk toward the chopper, now speaking quickly. "Tell Sandy to make her sister more careful. Espinel swears he saw her riding the devil not far from here. The pilot thinks he's nuts," he chuckled.

"Can do. But what the hell was that about a mission? You're not heading North with—"

A squeeze on his shoulder. "Clearing the air, I hope. I've owed you ever since they put that chingada critic in your head, compadre. After today, I feel like maybe I've repaid you."

"And then some," Quantrill replied. "I think maybe you're into *me* for a favor. All you'll ever have to do is ask."

At Sandy's cry of "Lufo," both men looked back. Sandy, lavishly appealing in her damp buckskins, ran to the latino under the idling chopper blades, her long hair now flying free. Lufo caught her to him, lifted her as they kissed. The chopper crew and Quantrill all saw her flex one calf as she kissed the broad-shouldered Lufo hungrily, stepped back, smiled a brave blue-eyed gringa smile as her lover vaulted into the cargo bay.

Then the pilot gestured and Quantrill pulled her away from the sudden downdraft as the chopper clawed for altitude. The two of them stood an arm's length apart, Quantrill with raised fist, Sandy waving vigorously as the chopper veered to the

Southeast. She waved until Lufo was beyond lip-reading distance.

With musical good humor, then, she said, "I *think* I've just been kissed off, Ted. How was I?"

Churlishly: "I may barf. You two looked like the worst holoplay I ever saw."

"Probably. But it was what he wanted, don't you think?"

Quantrill squinted at the dwindling insect. "I guess. You sure gave the crew something to remember. Lufo too."

"Remember, yes. Return? I doubt it. Lufo always liked the beau geste, some grand romantic pose, even without an audience. Not that I'm complaining," she complained.

He could not help grinning at her, and she backhanded his arm, gently, and together they hid his hovercycle before the breeze turned chill and drove them inside. Quantrill had time, now, to satisfy his curiosity about the soddy, the unique mix of ancient and modern trappings she had accumulated, her singular willingness to live this way; everything about her.

Sandy Grange, unused to this kind of attention, wondered for a time if it was genuine. Women almost never came to the soddy. Men were either anxious to get on with some pressing business, or clearly interested in learning what Sandy looked like without her clothes. Lufo had spoken of Ted's deadliness as if he were very much older than—what, twenty-one? Twenty-two? Yet he seemed willing, even anxious, to resume their old friendship as if he were some affectionate cousin.

She was mixing pancake batter with mesquite-bean flour when he asked about the social life around Rocksprings. "Not much of it; some weekend hoedowns. You could take me to one and find out," she purred, and then beamed an innocent smile. "Unless you have a lady who'd object."

He paused for too long and said, "She died," too quickly, running the words together. Sandy changed the subject, aware that the lady would not be one of his favorite topics.

Presently a long peculiar whistle sounded outside. Sandy said, "Oh lord—Ted, don't get up. I mean it," and hurried out for her whistled reply.

He wanted to peek through the window, to see what sort of apparition Lufo's friend had seen. But his joints and muscles protested, and Sandy's warning had a no-nonsense ring to it, and he stayed stretched out where he was. When Sandy returned with Childe ten minutes later she found him snoring, and did not choose to wake him until much later.

CHAPTER 69

Midway through the next morning, the Fourth of October, Quantrill began to appreciate what it meant to be free. True, he ached all over with abrasions and bruises; but he did not leave for the Schreiner ranch because he damned well chose not to. He snooped around in Sandy's smokehouse, fed her Rhode Island reds their cracked corn, and helped Childe hang bundles of vegetables for winter use. The beets and turnips were small but plentiful, the carrots and onions large and plentiful.

By lunchtime, he knew that Childe could speak when she chose.

Having dispatched a plateful of cornbread and blackeyed peas, Childe gnawed a blonde braid and watched her elders dally at their plates. She soon lost interest in their recountings of the years since Sonora. If Sandy accepted Ted so easily,—almost as a member of the family—then he must be Good, as Good as Mr. Gold. Besides, he paid her enough attention to flick her braids and to give her a nickname: 'sis'. But Ted elevated his brows in comic surprise as Childe said, "Wanta play."

'You're not finished with the onions," Sandy objected. But Ted interceded; he could finish the job if sis had pressing business.

Sandy relented, and Childe shyly smiled her thanks to Ted before sprinting away with an extra hunk of cornbread.

"Huh! She *can* talk," he murmured.

"You've made a friend, you sly dog."

He watched the slender waif speed into the scrub, heard a piercing whistle as he said, "And a little dynamo. I don't see how she'll keep that pace up on cornbread."

The cornbread, said Sandy obliquely, was in the nature of a bribe.

After long reflective silence, Ted forced a direct assault on the topic. Regardless of Lufo's admonition, he said, he saw no reason why Sandy needed him as a protector. "You've got a better one out there," he nodded toward the cedars. "Haven't you?"

"For some things, yes. But he can't tell me stories, or take me to a dance in town." The image of such a public pairing made her laugh aloud.

"Your laugh hasn't changed."

"And I'm beginning to understand why you said you hadn't laughed much since the war. But you're avoiding my request. Don't you dance?"

He did, he said, and quickly agreed to squire her. "Sandy, don't misread me. There's something about this," he waved his hand to encompass the soddy, "—this whole place that I like. You don't need much that you don't have except for friendly faces—and you may see more of mine than you'd like." She shook her head, started to reply. "Hold on, I'm not finished. Maybe you don't see any problem with me schlepping around here, and a— friendly tyrannosaur just over the hill. Bur if he isn't *my* friend, sooner or later he'll want me for a hood ornament." He read her dismay but pressed on. "Is it crazy to ask you to, uh, introduce us?"

Now her dismay became astonishment. Sandy had never dreamed that anyone might crave that particular introduction. Nor would it be without danger. Ba'al had learned to accept the presence of men at the soddy. It remained to be seen whether he would, in any sense of the word, befriend one. "I'm not sure he wouldn't charge you. You'd have to face him without a weapon. He can smell gun oil around a corner and he is very, very quick. And smart," she added in obvious worry. Yet her worry was tempered with relief, for Ted Quantrill was not demanding that she choose between them. Quite the reverse!

"Too bad you can't just ask him," he smiled.

It was his turn to register astonishment as Sandy said, "Childe can. They grunt and wag their heads and—all right, don't believe me! But Childe is the key. I'll talk it over with her and let you know." She arose to clear the table.

Quantrill filched a last hunk of her fluffy golden cornbread and resumed his job as onion-sorter, humming a merry tune despite his aches. Tomorrow he would be well enough to visit the Schreiner spread—but tomorrow was Saturday, and he might be recovered enough to swing a spirited girl on his arm, too. Relishing his freedom, he elected to escort Sandy into Rocksprings before recalling that the ranch was only an hour away by hovercycle. Why not make a quick business trip before the pleasure of Sandy's company? Surely she would be glad to see him discharge his obligation to the Governor, so that they could enjoy an uncomplicated Saturday night date. He did not want to complicate her life—and had no way to foresee that his trip would do precisely that.

CHAPTER 70

Quantrill found his round-trip longer than he bargained for. He used the excuse of job-hunting to meet the Schreiner safari manager, a grizzled professorial fellow named Jess Marrow whose degrees in veterinary medicine gave him enviable job security.

The unflappable Marrow conducted the interview while repairing a split horn on a sedated Texas longhorn bull of stupendous proportions. Why sure, there were Fed agents around; they stuck out a mile, said Marrow, applying cement to the horn. 'Course, they hadn't found that necklace the fat lady lost. For one thing, Marrow and others had given false directions to places where Eve Simpson had supposedly visited. For another, if she'd worn it the night that monster got into her cabin, the boar could have eaten it.

Did Quantrill know there was good evidence that she had let the boar into her cabin? Quantrill hadn't known and could hardly believe it, let alone understand it. Wouldn't a Russian boar charge the moment he saw a human? Not necessarily, Marrow said; you never knew what the brute might do unless you presented him with an oestrus female or a snake. A boar was very dependable then: all solicitude to a ready sow, pure hell on any snake.

Marrow bound the horn expertly with biodegradable tape, slapped the bull affectionately and eased off the tension from head bindings as he talked. As for the necklace, Marrow and two other Indy employees had gone high and nigh looking for it in the *right* places. With metal detectors? Sure, and r-f detectors too! A slow drawl, Marrow twinkled, didn't have to mean a slow brain.

Maybe Marrow could describe what the necklace looked like. Indeed he could, if the picture those young Search & Rescue fellas flashed was any guide. Marrow could describe it with a pencil, he said, and proved it with an exquisite sketch, his stubby fingers moving with surgical skill.

Quantrill studied the piece of polypaper, grubbing into his memory for the phrase Marrow had penciled: 'Ember of Venus'. Wasn't that a priceless jewel all by itself? Pretty near, Marrow admitted, but he suspected the decorations on its mounting meant that the thing was also a memory-storage gadget. Why else would the Feds put so much effort into its recovery? The bastards already had all the money in the country. And by the way, if Quantrill intended to go nosing around on the Schreiner spread, he'd best set up a cover activity. Marrow wouldn't mind having him as a helper for a spell; rumor had it that young Quantrill could tell many a fuzz-nutted yarn if he felt like it.

As Quantrill tucked the drawing away in a shirt
pocket, he asked Marrow his estimate of the chances
that the Ember of Venus would be found. Poor to
middlin', said the older man. If it ever turned up,
chances were the finder would try to sell it to a
rich Mex. Meanwhile, did Ted Quantrill need that
job?

Well, that depended on what the Governor
needed. Quantrill was no great shakes on a horse,
and said so. Hell, said Marrow, they had enough
wranglers in Wild Country already, and Quantrill
was built more like a bull-rider anyhow. What the
Schreiner spread really needed was someone with
special abilities to counter the poachers and other
lawless types that made life cheaper than it should
be.

Quantrill wondered why they didn't have U. S.
Marshals for that.

Jess Marrow wondered, too.

Quantrill took his leave with a handshake from
the shrewd Marrow—and with the air of a preoccupied man. It was already midafternoon, and he
had a long ride ahead of him.

He arrived at the soddy with most of the kinks
shaken—vibrated, actually—from his muscles, and
earned himself another long speech from Childe.
"Go wash, Sandy's not ready," was the full extent
of it.

He twitched her braid and called her 'sis', wash-
ing at the gravity-flow spigot from the big plastic
tank that nestled in earth near the soddy's roof.
Then he noticed the sweat and caliche stains on
his clothes, removed shirt and trousers, applied
homemade soap to them in hopes of making himself halfway respectable in Rocksprings. One thing
about Goretex clothing: it didn't take long to dry.

He was swinging the trousers to dry them, en-
during the chill on his bare shanks, when he heard

Sandy's call. Custom was a harsh taskmaster, he thought as he pulled the wet trousers on; Sandy had seen him nearly naked, breathed life into his body—yet custom dictated that he wear those goddam trousers no matter how they chilled his arse.

"Well,—you tried," Sandy giggled as he approached, his wet hair plastered to his forehead. "Surprise." And she drew a flesh-tinted bundle from behind her. Childe burst from behind the door then, shrilling, "S'prise, s'prise," like a Comanche, hovering near as he accepted his new shirt.

It was a lovely supple thing of softest deerskin, a pullover with long sleeves that puffed gently near the wrists. Its collar, its breast pocket with scalloped flap, the cut of it across the shoulders, all had the flavor of prairie tailoring but its slender fringes said 'mountain man'. "Didn't have time for the beadwork," she said shyly.

He turned it about, speechless, wondering how she could have magicked such a garment on a day's notice. Then he was wrestling into it, clasping the velcrolok wristlets, running his hands along the velvety sleeves. "And just my size," he marveled when his tongue came unglued.

"When you rub a man down you more or less take his measurements," she said airily. "High time those snooty girls in Rocksprings envied me a little."

Quantrill hugged her, winked at Childe, then hurried back to retrieve the shirt he had left near the soap. The folded polypaper lay where he had left it. He brought both articles into the soddy, tossing the sketch onto Sandy's wooden table.

Supper was catch-as-catch-can. Quantrill dipped into his toilet articles to shave and assault his unruly hair, talking with Sandy about his job offer at the Schreiner ranch. As though it were of no importance, Sandy asked if the missing necklace had been found.

"Nope. Probably just as well, too." Prodded to say what he meant by that, he addressed his cowlick with his comb and replied, "Too many people would kill for it, Sandy. Rumor says it's got a memory module with some kind of secrets the Feds want kept—but I have my own ideas about it. Matter of fact, there's a sketch of the thing on your table."

She moved to the table. Her fingers trembled but, peering into her broken mirror, Quantrill did not notice. She unfolded the polypaper, studied the sketch for a breathless moment, let the chill pass through her body before she asked, "What's your idea?"

"Oh—a crazy one, probably. I met a fellow up North who'd worked on something for the fu—the bloody Feds. According to the Canadians, it was a gadget that could synthesize stuff—rare metals, even gold. This guy was the boss of the lab, and somehow he got friendly with Eve Simpson. And believe me, he wanted out of his job badly enough that he'd agree to anything." He turned around "Will I pass inspection?"

"You're a wow, and don't change the subject. What about this gadget?"

"Oh. Well, it could make you an aspirin out of thin air, or enough gold to buy a Senator. So this guy gives a necklace to Simpson—but apparently she already owned this huge jewel, a kind of opal to end all opals. All he gave her was the *setting*, you see. And it's supposed to have a solid-state device of some kind in it. Now then: what if the gadget he gave her *included plans for that synthesizer*?"

Her voice was muted: "You tell me."

"No synthesizers anymore. Blooey. The Feds must have the plans for it, but they'd do anything to keep them secret. So maybe, I thought, that necklace has plans for a synthesizer."

Sandy folded the sketch; set it on a high shelf where Childe would not see it. She remembered the odor of very old eggs which Childe had somehow coaxed from the amulet. Teasingly she said, "I've got a wilder idea than that. What if the necklace had a *real* synthesizer built into it?"

Ted Quantrill frowned, cocked his head at her, then grinned. "Nah. Where d'you get those crazy ideas?"

And then he took her to the dance.

CHAPTER 71

Sandy's journal, 5 Oct. '02

My first real take-out date! What if I did have to coax Ted into it? Must be near 1 A.M. as my dance instructor snores softly in his mummybag & wanton creature that I am, I yearn to slip myself in with him. Intuition says I must not; it does not tell me why.

I felt a guilty thrill when Jerome Garner, the swaggering bravo who will one day run Garner ranch, jostled us on the dance floor. I know it was deliberate & his sidelong gaze made my dress transparent. His request for apology was really a challenge. Somehow Ted's open smile & his cordial, 'Why sure, hoss, I

*beg your pardon,' conveyed to us all that he per-
ceived no threat worth his notice.*

*Childish of me to mutter into Ted's ear (while
standing on his toes!) that he was free to do some
jostling of his own for all I cared. He implied much
about his recent life by replying that at last he was
free not to. If that shamed me, why am I not scandalized by easy allegiances to first one man, then another?*

*Perhaps because Ted is not just any man. Too,
there is a difference between being in love & being in
sex. Lufo, good luck to him, has taught that to me
more surely than all the books I have ever read.
Perhaps after all I shall find in Ted a kissing cousin
of sorts. I am not dismayed by the prospect. Am I?*

*Childe brings a disturbing report. Men are his ene-
mies though he kills only if, as Childe puts it,
'madded'. How to be certain Ted will not 'mad' him?
Mystery!*

*No mystery about that necklace. Sipping the mus-
cular punch of the Rocksprings grange ladies, Ted
confided that a synthesizer may be a Pandora's box
that no one, and no government, should unlock. So
what am I to do? One decision, at least, which I can
defer. But Childe will not wear it again!*

*Fingertips raw from sewing, but what an effect
that deerskin has below those green eyes. Rocksprings
girls would have swallowed him like a gingerbread
man . . .*

CHAPTER 72

By Monday, the synthoderm had done its work so well that Quantrill scarcely felt his abrasions. He used the microwave scrambler link on his 'cycle to contact Indy Base and, for an anxious few minutes, felt cast adrift when three successive listeners failed to identify him.

To the fourth, a suspicious knave with a New England accent, he said, "Just pass the word to Lufo or Ethridge that I'd like to know if our, ah, little canister from Sonora was of any use. And ask the Governor if he'd like me to accept a job at Schreiner ranch."

After too many minutes the knave was back, no longer suspicious but not very helpful either. Ethridge was in briefing but sent word that the canister would make a fine suppository for someone named Control. Neither Lufo Albeniz nor the Governor were available. If the Gov wanted Quantrill at Schreiner's spread, seemed like plain yankee horse sense to get on a payroll. And don't bother Indy Base again for a few days; they were busier than a one-armed man in a bull-milking contest.

By mutual consent, Quantrill and Sandy passed up lunch, forearm deep in a lime-and-'dobe mess with which they plastered crannies between the upper logs of the soddy walls. When the blue northers swept down from Canada, she warned, the

wind would chew up his spine with icicle teeth.
With Mex heating oil so expensive and mesquite
so damnably plentiful, the provident settler built
ricks of mesquite firewood near the North side of a
dwelling and hoped part of that windbreak remained for spring barbecues.

Child came frisking into the clearing near dark.
Quantrill knew better than to ask her about her
playmate; if and when they were ready, he would
know. He knew on Wednesday.

He had worn through a pair of work gloves cutting mesquite and stacking it on Tuesday. Wednesday morning, he paused with a tender biscuit
halfway to his mouth. "It just occurred to me," he
said in puzzlement, "that you don't have any vehicle big enough to pull all those damn' mesquite
trunks into the clearing. How'd they get here?"

Childe exchanged glances with Sandy who smiled,
"Don't believe the old saying, 'pigs is pigs'. sometimes pigs are trucks!"

He took a bite, thinking of the heavy red-hearted
tree trunks, some as thick as Childe's body. "Good
God," he said.

"You ought to be glad he can use those tusks
for peaceable chores," Sandy replied. "By the way,
do you mind if Childe takes that shirt you're
wearing? You can wear the new one instead."

To Quantrill's puzzled glance, Childe piped, "He
wants your smell." The earnest little face said that
the request was no small matter.

He exchanged shirts slowly, almost reluctantly,
muttering about the unbelievable hocus-pocus a
man had to undergo, just to get on good terms
with a hog.

Sandy: "Quit complaining; your smell is your
personnel file. If you'd rather not meet him today,
I can—"

"No, the sooner the better." He handed the shirt to Childe who performed her usual limber disappearance. "I want to know where I stand with Ba'al before I leave—and that might be any day now."

"But you'll only be in the next county."

That depended, he said. "If something goes wrong with the Indy plans, I might, um, have to disappear into Mexico for awhile." He did not add that Mexico would be only his conduit back to Eureka for a singleton mission on his own. It was all very well for Jim Street to talk of bloodless surgery against a secret police system; but if Ethridge failed, Quantrill would wield a deadly scalpel until they caught him.

"You don't fool me, mister," Sandy said. "You're just looking for an excuse to get out of cutting firewood."

To disprove that charge, Quantrill spent his next hours among the gnarled mesquite. But he worked slowly. He was not going to tire himself when he might need all his energy later.

Late in the morning he heard a familiar whistle. He turned, surveying the scrub, and then laid the saw aside as he saw Childe above the brushtops seventy meters away. She towered over the shrubs, his shirt slung over her thin shoulder, and with one hand she gripped the neck bristles of the demonic Ba'al. For one stunned moment Quantrill considered calling the whole goddam thing off.

Ba'al stood quietly, his enormous bristly shoulders aimed at the soddy, head turned in Quantrill's direction. Downwind, of course; oh yes, Ba'al knew where Quantrill stood. The long muzzle lifted, the tip of the snout flexing as it tasted manscent, the flywhisk tail switching impatiently. Childe whistled again, a subtly different tune. Quantrill estimated the great beast's weight at a full five hundred kilos, most of it forward of the sloping hindquarters. Childe actually sat astride his neck, feet hooked under his chin.

As Sandy strode outside, Quantrill saw the vast bulk suddenly trotting toward her, grunting, Childe leaning forward in effortless unconcern as she waved. Quantrill watched the movements of her huge steed with wariness, noting how suddenly those little hooves could accelerate such a massive bulk. Little? Well, only when compared with Ba'al himself. Quantrill was more concerned with the great head, as big as a horse's, and the twin scimitars that flanked the snout.

From long practice, Quantrill assessed the strengths of the boar, and wondered where weaknesses might lie. Such an opponent could accelerate like a big cat; would probably lower its head to bring those tusks into position for goring—and eviscerating. For all its thickness, that grizzly neck could twist sharply, directing the ivory tusks in any direction. The hooves would be murderous, and the brute was anything but stupid.

Perhaps Ba'al had no weaknesses. And perhaps, Quantrill thought, he would be wise to stop thinking of Ba'al as an opponent.

Sandy slipped an arm behind the boar's pricked ears; spoke with Childe as she scratched the sloping forehead; then looked around her. Childe pointed toward Quantrill who had not moved from his position, and Sandy trudged across the clearing.

Voice unsteady but determined: "I don't think he'll be as grouchy if you're holding my hand. If he lowers his head, you be ready to run for the soddy," she said, and then, "Are you sure you want to go through with this?"

He gripped her hand. "Yep," he lied, and together they strolled toward the watchful beast.

Childe continued to scratch and cajole the boar as the others neared him. At a low peremptory squeal from the great muzzle, Childe put up a restraining hand. Quantrill stopped, one foot planted for retreat, while Childe grabbed the dark gray neck ruff. Quantrill saw indecision in Sandy's face but only intense concentration in Childe's expression. As though cautioning a playmate in some serious game the little girl said, "Don't move, now." With short mincing steps, Ba'al began to circle the object of his scrutiny.

"Better move away," Quantrill said softly to Sandy.

"I don't know," she quavered.

"If you don't know, *then move away*," he gritted.

He did not turn his head but kept his legs flexed, listening to the steady thud of hooves, the snorts and snufflings behind him as Sandy backed off. He resisted the urge to giggle wildly, hearing Sandy's soothing, repeated, "soooo, pig." The small of his back itched like fury. He did not scratch.

When the huge boar completed his circuit, he stood almost near enough for Quantrill to touch, ears twitching fore and aft, eyes roving up and down. Then a peculiar ripple of shoulder muscles; Childe responded by shinnying down from her perch. The tiny girl and the great beast exchanged grunts and subtle headwags. "Just you and him," she said, nodding to Quantrill, stepping aside.

Quantrill showed both hands, spreading his arms slowly, then stood erect. This displeased the boar who snorted and reared, forequarters rising so that the forward hooves pawed higher than a man's waist.

Quantrill stepped back in a defensive stance,

and too quickly. Ba'al dropped instantly to all-
fours, his vast head lowering. The next moves se-
quenced almost too quickly for Sandy and Childe
to follow.

As Quantrill sprang backward, Ba'al rushed forward to close the gap—but without lowering his
head. Quantrill did not wait to see if this was a
true charge, but skipped aside in a double leap
like a sidelong fencer's *balestra* ending with a shoulder roll, the total maneuver covering ten meters.
He danced to his feet ready for a sprint to the
soddy; judged it hopeless; prepared to dodge again.

Ba'al just stood quietly, grunting, flicking that
ridiculous tail, studying the man. Childe clapped
her hands in glee. "You funned him," she explained.

"Great," Quantrill said, spitting dust, searching
for a fist-sized stone but, to his good fortune, finding
none. "He's scaring the shit out of me," he added,
and straightened up.

Again the boar reared, a faint squeal issuing
from his muzzle. "You're too high," Childe called—
and then Quantrill realized that the boar was inter-
preting his erect posture as a dominance ploy.
Flexing his knees again, Quantrill waited, now sharing the same eye-level with Ba'al, neither dominat-
ing nor submitting. The forequarters danced, the
great head lashing side-to-side. A demonstration; a
show of the boar's virtuosity with natural weapons.

Quantrill found himself grinning. He couldn't
match that demonstration if he wanted to. Instead
he went down on one knee, held his hands forward.
In his mouth there was not enough spit to float a
paramecium.

Then, each hoof placed with silent precision,
Ba'al stepped forward; snuffled the open palms;
placed his snout between Quantrill's hands. The
reddish little eyes were wary, and level with his
own. The musky scent, he told himself, wasn't all

that bad. He wondered if Ba'al was thinking the same thing.

Childe was cheering. "Scratch under his chin," Sandy called, and Quantrill did it. A soft repetitious grunting said that he was, at last, doing something right. A moment later, Childe and Sandy crowded close to scratch the boar's thick hide, laughing in relief.

In the next few minutes Quantrill learned that a Russian boar could be charmed by a belly-scratch, and that Childe was adept at searching out ticks within the secondary fur under Ba'al's coarse bristles. In all, Quantrill counted twenty-three scars, some of them obviously bulletholes in a hide tough as kevlar. From time to time he caught the eye of the indolent boar and knew that the animal did not wholly trust him; might never trust any man. Quantrill felt no disappointment. He felt exactly the same about Ba'al.

When Childe rode away to play that afternoon, Quantrill strode into the soddy and stretched himself out on his mummybag, exhausted. To Sandy he admitted that every fiber in his body buzzed with fatigue. "How could I relax," he sighed. "This is the only time in my life I've ever felt—well, —like I might be second-rate."

CHAPTER 73

A dying sun peeked beneath the overcast, a brief burst of pink and saffron against the bellies of bruise-tinted clouds that hinted of rain before morning. Quantrill tightened the tarp over his hovercycle, glad that he would not have to traverse fifty klicks of mud on a wheeled vehicle the next day. He hurried back to the soddy at Sandy's whistle: already he knew the bright three-note tune of 'come and get it'.

After dinner, the first wind-driven drops pattered against the window as Sandy shopped for a favored holo channel. The FBN channel was showing a rerun, and Sandy almost switched before the glowing legend crawled across the top of the screen in high relief: TECH DIFFICULTIES FORCE CANCELLATION OF FBN SPECIAL, 'THE QUANTRILL REPLY', SCHEDULED FOR THIS TIME.

Sandy turned to Quantrill who sat frowning with a handful of popcorn halfway to his mouth. "You? On a Fed channel?"

Shrug: "Not unless it's a countercharge against me. I made a dumb threat right after I—well, never mind. It was plain stupid. Anyhow, I'm not the only Quantrill in the world."

"That's debatable," she smiled, and tried the clear Mex channel which was nearing the end of its newscast.

A silver-haired gentleman sat alone while be-

362

hind him a crudely animated logo showed a silhouette running endlessly toward a green and yellow banner with a central star-flecked blue orb. ". . . But the Brazilian embassy would not comment on the rumor that Salter's defection is connected with the sharp seismic jolt which struck Utah's Cottonwood Canyon area earlier today. Now for the weather—"

But Ted Quantrill was on his feet, grinning. "Cottonwood Canyon? Seismic, hell; *Ethridge got through*!" He stood with arms spread, staring up as if to focus on something far above the low ceiling. "Hear that, Sanger? Now you can sleep." He turned, the light fading from his eyes, only half-aware of the startled looks from Sandy and Childe. Lowering his arms he said more softly to himself, "We can all sleep."

While searching for another newscast, Sandy bestowed a searching smile on him but murmured only, "What—on—earth?"

He chuckled, breathing deeply as he watched the screen. "I guess we missed the best part, but we can watch again at eleven. Now, if you'll turn that thing off awhile, I'd like to tell you about a girl named Marbrye Sanger."

CHAPTER 74

Long before he had finished, Sandy knew that Sanger was the woman of whom Quantrill had only said, "She died," with quick incisiveness to block further inquiry. Ted Quantrill was no yarn-spinner, certainy not with a lump in his throat, and Sandy was forced to interpolate often. Intuition told her that she must not ask questions or make comments, that this account was Quantrill's memorial service for his closest friend. In his memory, Sanger had lain in state until her killers were accounted for. Now perhaps he could allow time to bury her.

When he completed his tale, Sandy was weeping quietly. "I'm sorry," he said with a touch on her arm. "I've got no right to make you feel this way."

"You told me some very important things, Ted— one thing that you probably don't realize." She wiped her cheeks and went on, managing a smile for him. "And it makes me very happy. You demanded justice for Marbrye Sanger, but you didn't demand it by your own hand."

He thought of his plans, now fading, for a bloody surgical strike in case Ethridge failed. "The thought crossed my mind," he growled.

"But you place justice over revenge. If you can feel that way after all those devils did to you, then they failed in the most important thing. They didn't rob you of all decent human values."

Muscles knotted at his jaw. He hesitated for a long moment and then forced himself to say it. "I killed people, Sandy. Not all of them were guilty of any real crime. I don't want to mislead you about that. I was very good at it."

She responded with a serious nod, and then surprised him as her grin broke through. "I saw how good you must be, today. When you've known Ba'al awhile, you learn to read his expressions. I don't think he's ever seen a human move as fast and as far as you did in avoiding him today. He respects that."

"Respect from the devil; I love it," he said wryly.

"Well, we're two of a kind. Hey, you know what? I'm hungry."

Sandy tucked Childe into bed and brewed strong bitter coffee to go with the coarse pecan pralines she kept on a Childe-proof shelf. In retrieving the candy she displaced the sketch which fluttered down, Quantrill catching it in midair, studying it in the firelight as they waited for the eleven o'clock news.

She might never have a better excuse for asking: "If you ever do find that necklace, what will you do with it?"

Without hesitation: "Hand it over to Jim Street. I can't think of anybody better-equipped to make decisions about a thing that could permanently alter the way people live."

"Maybe you're right," she said, doubting it. Nibbling and sipping, they wrangled over the uses to which a synthesizer might be put—if every home could have one. Medicines, fuels, gold—if any precious metal could be amassed in endless quantity, what would that do to a gold-based economy? If heroin were free, what then?

"Now you see why I'd drop the damn' thing in

the Gov's lap," Quantrill said, licking the last traces of praline from his hand.

"Instead of burying it somewhere," she said almost hopefully.

"Not with a million bucks' worth of Venus opal I wouldn't—hey, watch that coffee . . ."

Sandy blamed the coffee spill for her agitation. The prospect of great wealth had never been real to her. In some ways she equated wealth with evil—and whatever else it might do, it would change her life irrevocably. More than ever, now, she resolved to wait for the time when her wisdom might be equal to the problem. "Uh, it's almost time for the news," she said, and switched on the holo trying not to imagine a new expensive set two meters in width. Only later would she imagine a ranch of her own, ten kilometers in width.

FBN news led off with a brisk, business-as-usual list of topics: "A deranged Search & Rescue official is charged with treason; President Young is under his physician's care with a mild stomach ailment; and Zion is briefly shocked by a small earthquake. All this and more—"

"Horseshit," Quantrill snapped. "Try the CBS Deadline News."

Sandy complied in time to hear CBS anchorman Hal Kraft say, "—From several independent sources that the tremor was characteristic of an underground nuclear test, with a seismic signature all its own. While Search & Rescue squads report no radiation leakage to the surface, CBS has received one report that a Utah State Police unit monitored significant radiation near the mouth of Cottonwood Canyon an hour after the shock. Government sources confirm that the genealogical vaults have sustained some damage, but continue to insist that the public has no cause for alarm."

Kraft's image was a small inset to a scene obviously filmed earlier in the day. Numerous hovervans and media vehicles flanked a highway barricade with Utah State Police vehicles behind. The highway leading into steep mountains was clear of traffic, and Quantrill saw the black bulk of a sprint chopper patrolling airspace over the canyon.

"At this hour, Cottonwood Canyon still remains under a complete news blockade. And therefore under a pall of mystery," Kraft editorialized acidly.

"Meanwhile, the Brazilian embassy in Salt Lake City has released a statement concerning Lon Salter, who earlier today fled to the embassy to avoid prosecution for what one government source termed 'high crimes and misdemeanors'. Here's more, from Connie Bergson at the embassy."

Flick. A slender wench in a smart trenchcoat stared into the camera, a high steel fence behind her and a low stone building floodlit in the background. "Brazil has rejected a sharply-worded demand from the State Department for the return of Lon Salter, Director of the Federal Search & Rescue Administration, who is reportedly somewhere in the embassy behind me at this moment.

"At approximately two P.M. today, roughly an hour after the seismic shock Southeast of here, a Loring aircraft with S & R markings was seen to land inside the Brazilian compound. A man fitting Salter's description fled into the building before the aircraft lifted. In reply to the American demand, Brazil's chargé d' affairs stated that Mr. Salter fled for his life after a vidphone conversation with President Blanton Young.

"According to the Brazilian report, Mr. Salter contacted the President to report an S & R team's verification that the Cottonwood Canyon tremor was nuclear in origin. At that point, the President became incoherent with rage and threatened Salter's

life while battering the vidphone screen with his
bare hands.

"The Brazilians say their responsibility is clear
in the face of conflicting reports about the nature
of the tremor, as well as varying reports on President Young's state of health. At least for the present,
Lon Salter is safe on what amounts to foreign soil
here in Salt Lake City. Now back to you, Hal."

Chortling, softly clapping his hands, Ted Quantrill
applauded the Indy penetration raid. "Notice that
S & R both confirms and denies a nuke under that
mountain," he said to Sandy. "Now that their
central computer is trashed, they don't know what
the hell they're doing. No coordination. I'm only
sorry that sonofabitch Salter got free."

"I wouldn't call him free," Sandy replied. "He
might be cooped up inside that building for the
rest of his life."

Quantrill brightened. "You've just made my
day," he laughed.

They fell silent then, trying to follow the tangled
trail of disinformation on the condition of Blanton
Young. He had a touch of ptomaine; no, he had
collapsed from overwork, poor man; on the other
hand, rumors of recent weeks repeatedly claimed
the Lion of Zion was starting to hold court with
the bats in his belfry. Another network had first
promised an interview with Young but later claimed
technical difficulties.

After reciting brief statements by two government spokesmen—both authoritative in opposite
opinions—anchorman Kraft leaned forward on his
elbows. "We at CBS Deadline News," he said in
ill-concealed irritation, "are often torn between
the need for all the facts, and the need to inform
Streamlined America of fast-breaking events as they
happen. The opinion of a high government official
is news. The opinion of a holovision journalist

must be clearly stated as only commentary. Well,"
he paused and donated a wry smile off-camera,
"the staff of CBS Deadline News is of the uniform
opinion that a commentary is in order, tonight.

"We share the opinion that, for some time now,
certain officials within the federal goverment have
manipulated the news far beyond what we might
call the limits of expectation. We do not place Mr.
Salter of Search & Rescue beyond suspicion—but
I wish to stress that this is *not* an accusation.
Slander and libel laws in recent years have returned almost to the point of, 'the greater the
truth, the greater the libel', and this too may be
worthy of re-examination—in our opinion.

"We also hold the opinion that Streamlined America tonight is shaken at the top by a shock, probably nuclear, that by great good fortune has not
resulted in widespread loss of life. We believe that
just below the top, our American system stands
undamaged and intact, capable of dealing fairly
with its troubles both domestic and foreign. We do
not—I repeat, do *not*, have evidence of any kind
leading us to suspect some military coup. On the
contrary, Mr. Salter might possibly strip the rumors away from, let us say, an alleged paramilitary
organization which may have operated as a death
squad throughout Streamlined America for some
years and which may, as of this afternoon, be adrift
and leaderless.

"If such a death squad exists tonight, then I and
Deadline News may be a dead line tomorrow."
Bleak grin: "Stay tuned. If ever an American death
squad *did* exist: who held its reins? This is a question that journalists in several media have been
asking.

"Speaking for myself alone, I would like to ask
Mr. Boren Mills, the chief executive officer of IEE
and of its wholly-owned network. But for the past

several days Mr. Mills has not been available for
comment. Unsubstantiated rumor suggests that Mr.
Mills has, in journalist's terms, 'pulled a Vesco'—
has left the country for some climate more to his
liking.

"It may be pure hubris to think that Boren Mills
would be watching us, a rival network, tonight. But
just in case, Mr. Mills: surely you are aware of the
reports concerning falsification of news by electronic animation. The late Eve Simpson left messages to be forwarded to various media, including
CBS, in the event of her death. At this hour there
is no question of her revelations becoming a news
item. The only question is whether you will come
forward to separate fact from fancy, or will remain silent when that story breaks during the next
few days. I can promise you this much: interviews
with the Reverend Ora McCarty by both CBS and
UBC suggest that you, Mr. Mills, could enlighten
us all.

"Let me repeat that my comments of the past
two minutes *were* commentary, for which I accept
total responsibility. If my decision has caused a
blurring of commentary and news, I apologize."
Then, grimly determined, Kraft added as if to
twenty million judges: "But somebody had to say
it." A sigh, an obvious attempt to regain his usual
imperturbable image: "In other news tonight, an
industrial barge has foundered near the Port of
Eureka. For an on-the-scene report, we take you to
Avery Bond in Arcata, California . . ."

And near Rocksprings, Ted Quantrill was laughing like a schoolboy.

Sandy's journal, 9 Oct. '02
*I must scribble carefully to avoid waking Ted, warm
against my side here on the couch. What, I wonder,
is he smiling about? I would prefer to think he dreams*

of me, but suspect he trysts with a spectre called Sanger.

I should be furious that we did not make love tonight—but in a sense of course, we did. We exchanged more genuine affection through speech & a few unhurried kisses than I knew in my frantic too-brief couplings with Lufo. Ted knew perfectly well I wanted him tonight, & for a time I feared the smell of Lufo, so to speak, was still too strong in his nostrils. Ted set me straight with a confession that astonished me: from the first time we ever met, he has viewed me as a surrogate for his long-deceased small sister!

How plain could I make it? "I don't want to be your sister," I bleated.

His exact words were, "Then we're agreed. Just give me a little time to disown you."

But how long is a little? Hard to believe that such a fine-tuned animal could have problems in his, um, fuel-injection system. (Bite your tongue, Sandy—or your pen.) I have much to learn about men, this one in particular.—How long before he can bury this Sanger creature beneath layers of fresh experience? Burial of a person is an event, but burying an allegiance is a process.

Well? Would I want Ted Quantrill less complex? To keep his loves and hates neatly, conveniently separate in little boxes?

I hate Marbrye Sanger, & envy her.

CHAPTER 75

The little man with the angry pink scalp shifted in his couch, reaching under harness webbing to palpate his anus. Five-gee acceleration had very nearly driven the tube of flawless emeralds up to his navel—but where else could he have hidden them?

Every square centimeter of his scalp itched from too many dousings in depilatory. Within a week he could let his hair start to grow again. If it *would* grow back. His face, the backs of his hands, his throat; all stung, though he had scrubbed furiously to remove the wrinkle-producing gunk. He wondered when he could indulge in the luxury of a hot shower. The vast ogive colonies of New Israel, orbiting somewhere ahead of his shuttle craft, might someday be manmade worldlets of milk and honey, but Boren Mills carried no illusions into space with him. The Ellfive structures were still incomplete and the Israelis could not afford many luxuries in their space colonies, even for an administrator of Mill's ability.

He stared glumly at the 'overhead' holoscreen, no longer overhead as long as the shuttle was in zero-gee, and decided in favor of sleep. He had watched Hal Kraft's veiled challenge on CBS Deadline News until dull anger gave way to relief. If he'd waited another day to vesco the hell out of there, he might now be lying dead at the hands of some vengeful S & R rover. With CenCom atomized under Cottonwood Canyon, those electronic animation routines would have to be reconstructed before FBN could hope to fake reality again.

He wondered which straw had snapped the back of Blanton Young's creaky self-image; wondered too if the Lion of Zion would ever recover enough to tar the image of Mills. One day, perhaps after he carved himself a firm niche in New Israel's administration with hard work and faceted emeralds, Boren Mills might dabble again in the fortunes of Streamlined America . . .

CHAPTER 76

Ted Quantrill snugged the wrists of his polymer slicker against a sprinkle of cold rain and warmed up his hovercycle before riding it to the soddy. No problem with dust on a morning such as this!

Sandy and Childe met him at the door. "Hot coffee and pralines," Childe explained, offering him the insulated canisters. He accepted them gravely, then returned her shy hug with surprise and gratitude. The blonde braids trailed as she whisked from sight into the soddy.

For a moment, he only traded smiles with Sandy. Then she murmured, "You're not going to repeat Lufo's farewell address, I hope."

Mock indignation: "After all these uh, blissful days and nights together? No possible way," he said. He bore blisters from those days, and no sexual memories from those nights, and teased her without complaint. "If this guy Marrow doesn't need me, maybe you could use a hired hand."

"If you're sure you can pull your weight," she grinned back, then stepped forward to the hoverfan skirt. She placed both hands on his shoulders, her smile now a trifle askew. "Do I have to tell you how welcome you are here?"

"It helps," he said. She kissed him gently, first on the mouth and then on the flattened bridge of his nose. "That helps a lot," he said. "Crazy as it sounds, I like it out here. Weather permitting, I'll take you to another dance as soon as I get a handle on this job."

One hand lingering on his shoulder, fingering the slicker: "You really think you'll like being a veterinarian's assistant?"

"I like animals; even big ones," he nodded, then looked into her face and lied: "And I'll be learning a new trade."

"Thank God! I couldn't stand thinking of you hanging around the Governor with Lufo waiting for more combat work."

This, he told himself, was not the time to tell her the truth about the job at Schreiner's spread; that dealing with poachers and banditti was very likely to mean combat when other methods failed. "Not me," he lied again, and reached for the handlebars.

Sandy stood back, blew a light kiss, and then remembered why old Jim Street had urged Ted to go to Schreiner's. "I hope you find that necklace," she lied, looking him in the eyes.

He smiled, nodded, gunned the diesel and waved without looking back. He could see her waving in the rearview until he passed from sight.

A hard kernel of self-disgust jounced in his head. He should've told her that his only marketable skill was single combat. One day, he thought, she'll learn the truth. And then?

She watched Quantrill top out on a distant ridge, pulled her collar close against the growing Wild Country drizzle, and wondered how big a spread she could buy if she sold the Ember of Venus. Big enough to need a foreman, for sure. Especially one with some veterinary skills and with eyes the color of spring grass.

And then he would learn that she'd had the damned necklace all the time. *One day*, she thought, *I'll have to tell him. And then?*